Men in Straw Hats

Michael Moy

First published in Australia by:
Alpha Orion Press
P.O. Box 207
Ashgrove QLD 4060
Australia
www.meninstrawhats.com.au

National Library of Australia
Cataloguing-in-Publishing Data

Moy, Michael, 1949– .
Men in straw hats: the story of Vincent, his curator and the drug baron.

ISBN 0 9581066 0 6.

1. Traveling exhibitions – Fiction. 2. Narcotics dealers – Fiction.
3. Fathers and sons – Fiction. 4. Air travel – Colombia – Fiction.

A823.4

Cover design by Peter Fenoglio, Brisbane
Typeset in 11.5/15.5pt Goudy by Post Pre-press Group, Brisbane
Printed and bound by Griffin Press, Netley, South Australia

1

There are strains of bacteria which have become immune to antibiotics: mutants, which, when given the chance, multiply and destroy. According to the same law of nature, there are classes of criminal which have become immune to the law: survivors, who, when given their chance, gain strength and thrive. Such was the case in Colombia.

'Our girl has caught a dreadful cold, señor,' the Dutchman said into his phone, his eyes tracking the plane he had come to Schiphol to farewell as it groaned towards the high cloud to the west.

'A pity,' came the voice from Colombia. 'The change in climate will do her good.' Both men snorted at the irony in the loosely scripted statements. 'Will she be on time?'

'She is Dutch, my friend,' the Dutchman replied, allowing his corpulent body to fall back into the Mercedes soft leather. 'She will not be late.'

'Good, amigo. We will talk again soon.'

A seasoned observer of protocol, the Dutchman waited for his superior in crime to sever the connection before switching off his end, then, thrusting back his ruddy head, he drew a deep breath, held it, and exhaled a long unhealthy groan. 'Cigar,' he barked in the direction of his bodyguard once they were underway.

The young man seated in front turned and while handing the required Havana across witnessed something he had never before seen in his two years in the job. His employer, Willem Imthorn, the grim king of western Europe's drug trade, was smiling.

Imthorn had good reason to smile. Phase one of his most creative and profitable operation in three decades of creative and profitable operations had been executed flawlessly. Now, he would watch with pleasure as his brainchild moved on to the public arena. The plan, handwritten on two sheets of paper, had already earned him five million dollars, money that came with the Colombian's unfeigned gratitude and admiration. And more would follow whether the plan succeeded or failed. It was all so easy, the Dutch trader mused as he expelled a cone of blue smoke towards the window. A once in a lifetime chance.

An ocean away, Carlos Vega, the pope of the resurrected Medellín drug cartel, returned to the meeting interrupted by Imthorn's call.

'My apologies, compadres,' he said and reached for coffee.

The six laboratory bosses seated at Vega's table, men with gold chains, flashy watches and toil hardened hands, knew nothing of Willem Imthorn's audacious plan to free Vega's errant son from his Dutch jailers, or of Vega's imminent departure from his own dangerous life. None needed to know. Any one of them, if made the right offer by the wrong people, would willingly become a Judas.

'Andrés?'

'One hundred and forty keys ready, Don Carlos,' the grey faced one to Vega's right replied. 'Another twenty tomorrow, if you need it.'

'Perhaps,' Vega replied after taking a sip of coffee. 'And heroin?' The shipment, seven hundred kilograms of cocaine and three hundred of heroin, although not included in Imthorn's plan, would be well worth the effort. The icing on the cake.

'There has been a problem, Don Carlos. My thirty kilos will be ready on Monday, guaranteed.'

'No, Andrés!' Vega brought his cup hard onto its saucer, splashing coffee.

'The growers, they were two days late,' Andrés murmured, his chemically induced complexion growing more sickly by the second.

'You will meet your quota,' Vega interrupted. 'On time, Andrés. Tomorrow.'

'Yes, Don Carlos,' Andrés replied with a forced smile. 'We will work all night.'

2

VINCENT, VINCENT, L.A. LOVES YOU! PLEASE
DON'T GOGH! The fluorescent words training their
way across the gas station's animated sign brought an
expression of mild amusement to Christina Jansen's face.
True, she thought as her taxi continued along Wilshire
Boulevard, LA had indeed loved Vincent. Attendance at
the three month long exhibition had far exceeded expectation producing a small but unanticipated profit for the
participants. But now it was over. Three hours ago, the
gallery closed its doors to the public and tomorrow, despite
the plea, Vincent's precious works would leave for Rio de
Janeiro.

The taxi came to a halt in front of the floodlit Los
Angeles County Museum of Art. Four large yellow ban-
ners ballooned in the gentle breeze proclaiming the
exhibition's title: "Vincent van Gogh at LACMA". In the
middle of each banner, a likeness of the bearded artist
looked to the distance and in small print at the bottom

was the description: "works of the genius on loan from the Vincent van Gogh Foundation, Amsterdam".

She walked across the museum's deserted central courtyard to the Hammer Building, smiling at the guard behind the thick glass of the entrance doorway as she flashed him her security pass. The lock released with a buzz.

'Good evenin', ma'am,' said the ex-marine, tipping his cap, and, after allowing himself a good look at her evening dress, 'Very handsome, ma'am, you look very handsome.' He glanced to confirm that the door had locked itself behind her.

'Thank you,' she said and passed her purse across. 'Is Nelson here yet?'

'Yes ma'am, he arrived 'bout an hour ago.'

She removed a silver bracelet, passed it beside the metal detector and stepped through.

'It's gonna be awful sad here next week, ma'am. Folks sure enjoyed havin' them pictures visit.' He checked her purse for anything that could be used to deface a painting. Scissors, knives, marking pens, lipstick. His orders were inflexible, no one was to be exempted. Not even the governor and his party who were due to arrive two hours from now. The Dutch had been very specific about the security requirements, and who could blame them. The combined value of the visiting paintings was put at over two billion dollars.

'Thanks, ma'am,' he said, handing back the purse. 'You be sure to enjoy your party tonight, ma'am.'

5

'I will,' she replied with a smile. The past month had been one of the worst, if not the worst, of her life. 'I've been looking forward to it.' Three weeks ago the tragic death of a cousin from a drug overdose had taken her back to Amsterdam, where, the day after the funeral, her fiancé of two years, told her it was over, he was moving in with a colleague from work. Grief, rejection, more grief. Enough nights of crying alone, she thought, pick yourself up, time to move on.

'Christina!' Nelson Schoute, her colleague in charge of security, a man twice decorated in a prior life as a police inspector, and, lately, a willing shoulder to cry on, spotted her enter the gallery. 'You look stunning, my dear.' He kissed her on both cheeks. 'Come this way, I have someone for you to meet.'

As she moved across the gallery, her arm draped over his, she systematically scanned the walls, checking the paintings for interference and savouring them too, in the evening's celebratory ambience. Despite the constant exposure, she never tired of seeing them nor of sharing her love of them. Occasionally, she would stand and watch the faces of visitors entering the exhibition. It was always easy to tell Vincent's admirers from the checklist tourists. The former's expressions were of exhilaration or even mesmerisation as they beheld a dimension lacking in the copies hanging on their living room walls or printed on their kitchen calendars. The originals were alive. For the true admirer, being in the same room as a van Gogh was a powerful spiritual experience.

She counted the usual five security guards on duty in the gallery. Two were stationed watching the caterers as they put the final touches to tables set up in the middle. Tonight was the only time during the visit that food had been allowed inside the gallery. The director of the Vincent van Gogh Foundation, Albert Voss, who had travelled from Amsterdam to attend the function, had given his approval, saying that the calibre of invitee was such that virtually no risk was involved. Nevertheless, Nelson had directed that the caterers not serve red wine and that they cut any food that needed cutting beforehand to dispense with the need for knives on the tables.

The man they were approaching turned from "Fishing Boats on the Beach at Saintes-Maries-de-la-Mer".

'Captain Jan Bekker,' Nelson announced. 'Our tour curator, Doctor Christina Jansen.'

'Nelson and I have discussed tomorrow's arrangements,' the senior KLM pilot remarked after pleasantries were exchanged. 'We'll look after Vincent, and everyone travelling with him.'

'Excellent!' Nelson said clasping his hands together to mark the end of business. 'Tomorrow will be a busy day, so tonight Jan must relax and enjoy himself, as must you, my dear. Why don't you tell him something about the paintings while I get some champagne?'

'You timed it well,' Christina said, gesturing to the elaborately presented fare as she led Bekker to the solemn, heavy-featured face nearby. 'When does your crew arrive?'

7

'Ten in the morning, they passenger with the aircraft from Vancouver.'

The face of the linen clad peasant woman gazed out at them, her downcast lips and strong nose reflecting Vincent's light, her dark eyes revealing years of silent suffering.

'Vincent painted her early in 1885, in Nuenen,' Christina said, meeting the peasant woman's eyes. 'He insisted on painting her as she normally appeared, rough, wearing dusty clothes not her Sunday best. She's a study for a later work, "The Potato Eaters".' She looked to Bekker. 'You've visited the museum in Amsterdam?'

'Many times, and I've seen other van Goghs all around the world.'

'Then perhaps I'm boring you,' she responded.

'No danger of that,' He pivoted and paused, soaking up the scene. 'You must be very clever, Christina, to have this job so young.'

'I worked hard,' she replied with a small smile, 'for a long time.' The ambition driven years of study and sacrifice were still very clear in her memory. At just thirty-three years old, Christina Jansen was already two years into the job of her dreams.

Nelson returned and passed out the champagne. 'A toast. To our wonderful achievements in the City of Angels.'

'And to a smooth transfer to Rio,' Christina added as the three glasses touched.

She continued chatting with Bekker and Nelson until

the guests started to arrive. By the time the Governor of California appeared at nine o'clock the party was well and truly under way. The two hundred or so well connected guests were in their element. Gallery benefactors and officials, politicians and movie stars ate the good food and drank the good wine in an atmosphere that would not be recreated again in Los Angeles in their lifetimes. Christina was grateful that she had no official duty during the evening. It was her time off to say goodbye to the dozens of people with whom she had come into contact over the period of the exhibition and to rub shoulders with the Californian elite. She found it very pleasant, despite the superficiality of many of those present. Very few knew anything of Vincent other than the ear cutting episode and his lack of financial success. None knew the Vincent she knew. A man who died by his own hand eighty years before her birth, who lived an afterlife through his work, who inspired her life and career, and whose soul she held close. Over the past two months she had often speculated how Vincent might react to his temporary adoption as LA's patron saint. And of tonight's function? She had imagined him appearing in a rage at the door wanting his paintings back. The security people would call the police. Another mental case on the loose! Just as well for him, she thought. Ten minutes with the Hollywood set would be enough to bring on an attack of his illness. No, Vincent wasn't one for adulation. She had read the original letter to his brother after a French art critic wrote an enthusiastic review of his work. Vincent asked that the critic not write about him again: "Making pictures distracts me, but if I hear them spoken of, it pains me more than he knows."

The speeches were short. The Governor thanked the Vincent van Gogh Foundation and the various sponsors for making the historic exhibition possible. The Mayor did likewise. The Netherlands Ambassador to the United States congratulated everyone involved. And Albert Voss wrapped it up.

The window of opportunity for the exhibition opened three years ago when a decision was made to extend the Van Gogh Museum, which houses the foundation's paintings, to display more of Vincent's work. After considerable lobbying by museums around the world, the foundation directors agreed to allow two sets of twenty paintings to go on tours while the museum was closed for the construction work. The other set, presently in Tokyo, would move to Sydney in four days time.

At midnight, Christina and Nelson left the gallery together. They were the last to leave. The security net closed behind them and the paintings of Vincent van Gogh went to sleep in Los Angeles for the last time.

3

At two o'clock in the morning Carlos Vega's demons were keeping him from sleep. Drumming his fingers on a small framed photograph, he sat on the balcony of his home, his mind roaming through the details of the coming day's operation as well as the victories and regrets of the past.

The pivotal event happened fifteen years ago when he was a small fish in the cartel's expanding pond, buying merchandise for the big man himself, Pablo Escobar. He would never forget the look of disdain on Escobar's face when the vitamin B test showed positive, the mocking words cutting like razors: "You have been taken for a fool, my friend. A stupid fool."

The laboratory boss who supplied the cut merchandise died painfully, kneecapped and force fed the offending powder, enough cocaine, in fact, for his autopsy report to be of international medical interest. That murder, Vega's first, was his biggest regret. While the Mafia holds the family sacred, the drug cartels see it as the weak point, the Achilles heel. Those aligned with the laboratory boss took only four days to exact retribution. The vision of his wife's burnt and twisted body woke him some nights still. They didn't get his son. Tried once, not twice. Hired assassins from Bogotá saw to that with just six bullets, their efforts producing an unexpected consequence. Twenty-four hours after the shootings, Vega was invited by Pablo Escobar himself to fill the shoes of one of the three victims, a particularly ugly individual who, it had been discovered, was friendly with one too many people in Cali.

Safe years followed in which Vega rose to become Escobar's most trusted lieutenant. They ended with Escobar's surrender, a mistake. Even as the government helicopter approached, Vega had tried to persuade Escobar to change his mind. "The prison walls are my best protection, compadre," the man had said. "You look after things outside."

Medellín prospered during Escobar's days in his luxurious prison. It faltered when he escaped, fell when he died. Cali filled the space, temporarily. Two years later, Vega had watched the Cali chiefs lined up on television, a big win for the police. Records were seized incriminating three thousand citizens, from judges to journalists. That night he gathered the laboratory bosses together and set plans in motion.

Now Medellín was well and truly back, and he was king. Power, wealth and a beautiful new wife. There had been one close call, a car bomb. Two guards died. Vega got out of it with shrapnel wounds and a ringing in his ears which had never gone away. Lucky, he knew it. But luck runs out, so do nerves. They did for Escobar, they would for him. Now was the time to escape it all. But first, there was Juan.

He snapped out of the daze and looked again at the four year old image of his son, beaming with pride, standing beside a single-engine Cessna. The picture was taken the day the then nineteen year old qualified for his pilot's licence. Eighteen months later, Juan was the only survivor when a Queen Air he was copiloting ditched in the Caribbean. He should not have been on the mission: a high speed, low altitude, night water drop east of Jamaica. Vega had forbidden him to fly outside Colombia. Headstrong youth had disobeyed.

Saved from drowning by a section of the buoyant but incriminating cargo, Juan was rescued at dawn by a Venezuelan fishing vessel. A Royal Netherlands Navy frigate arrived later and took him to its home port on Curaçao where he was hospitalised for two days before being transferred to the local prison.

Vega had acted immediately. Threat laden investigations revealed that Juan had bribed his way into the right-hand seat on the ill fated flight. Those mostly at fault, the senior pilot and cargomaster, were saved from Vega's retribution by the sea. Not so lucky was a member of the ground crew who had accepted money from Juan. He died the death of a traitor.

A mission to rescue Juan was mounted two weeks later. Five ex-commandos were dispatched to Curaçao. Weapons, including a rocket to blow a hole in the prison wall, were dropped offshore. A combined sea and air escape route was set. A phone call to the police from a suspicious motel owner destroyed it all. One of Vega's men was killed in a shoot out within sight of the prison. Three got off the island. The fifth was captured and the purpose of the failed mission revealed. Juan was transferred to a maximum security penitentiary in the Netherlands the next day. His much publicised trial two months later delivered a fifteen year sentence.

Vega had put the fiasco of Curaçao well and truly behind him. Willem Imthorn's plan was far more refined. It necessitated great respect for detail. It also called for polished talents not available in Colombia. He would be using an American pilot, an experienced airline captain who had been involved with the cartel for two years. And there were the two brilliant and well placed computer programmers recruited by Imthorn. They had already done their jobs and collected substantial fees, Imthorn's only significant expense. There were other costs, routine costs involved in all cartel flights. Vega owned air traffic control at three airports in Colombia. Certain controllers had accumulated small fortunes working for him. The loyalty of all cartel employees was governed by the inescapable fact that, once part of the operation, there were only two ways out: retirement by mutual consent and a pledge of silence or, more commonly, inside a coffin.

The smell of perfume preceded the voice. 'What is worrying you, Carlos?' Vega's wife of three years knew his answer would not be the truth.

'Margarita, you should be asleep.' He gestured for her to sit with him. 'The coffee is keeping me awake.'

'It's Juan?' she said when she saw the photograph on his lap. 'You are worried about Juan.'

'You must not try to read my mind, Margarita, one day it might bite you like this.' He pulled her to him and sank his teeth playfully into her neck.

She laughed like a child, then kissed him hard on the lips. 'I will take your dangerous mind off your secret problems.' Her voice was seductive, her young body irresistible. He took her to their bed for what he knew would be the last time.

4

By Dutch standards, the Los Angeles winter sun was absurdly warm, Christina Jansen mused as she strode across LACMA's central courtyard towards the Hammer Building entrance. Behind her was a morning of phone calls and packing, ahead lay an afternoon readying Vincent's paintings for the move to Rio.

'Mr Schoute's waiting for you in CS,' the door guard informed her and made arrangements for her access to part of the complex where few were allowed. Central Station, the nerve centre for LACMA's security system was housed in a reinforced concrete vault below the museum. Its array of monitors, alarms and computers was staffed by two operators, twenty-four hours per day, every day of the year.

An operator watched Christina approach along an isolation corridor and triggered the door release when she reached it.

'Welcome to Fort Knox, my dear.' Nelson was leaning

back in a chair, enjoying a coffee. He introduced her to the operators, one of whom offered coffee.

'Thanks. Cream, no sugar.' She turned to Nelson. 'Any problems?'

'Everything's fine,' Nelson responded and checked his watch. 'Packing starts in . . . seventeen minutes. We can relax for a while.'

Nelson had just finished a letter to the LACMA Board praising the security staff and stating that the few worrying incidents in the gallery during the exhibition had been foiled with the same degree of professionalism he would have expected in the museum in Amsterdam.

The most alarming incident had occurred in the third week of the exhibition. A visitor who refused to check his coat and bag pushed his way past an attendant and ran into the gallery waving a knife at the guards on door duty as he passed them. The guards followed and overpowered him using a combination of pepper spray and brute force. The police arrived two minutes after a central station operator raised the alarm and took the man into custody. He was carrying an aerosol can of red paint in his bag which he admitted intending to spray on "Self-portrait with a Straw Hat", the painting that seemed to attract strongest emotions in the less mentally stable in Amsterdam as well.

The paintings were protected by electronic movement sensors attached to the frames, pressure sensitive cordons, and laser beams running parallel to the walls. If a cordon was stretched, or a beam broken, or a painting touched, a siren would startle the offender, alert the guards in the gallery and trigger a signal in central station. One would go off every now and then, usually because a child had accidentally bumped a cordon.

The system had helped prevent a number of crazies, as they were known locally, from damaging the paintings. One drugged-out woman had attempted to mark "Sunflowers" with a felt-tipped pen she had concealed in her boot. People close by had grabbed her when she set off the alarm.

Another woman had stepped over the cordon and spat on "Self-portrait with a Straw Hat" before anyone got to her. She was questioned by police, but not charged.

A man had to be forcibly removed after yelling obscene abuse at visitors in the gallery. He shouted claims that the paintings were fakes, that the real ones were in a safe in the Swiss Alps and that everyone who paid to see the exhibition had been duped.

Another man had managed to stay in the museum after it closed by hiding in a rest room crouched on top of a toilet pedestal. He was in the right place for his bladder's spontaneous reaction when Pablo, the museum's German shepherd, came at him under the door during a closing check.

LACMA's central station was an impressive example of the technology now employed by most of the world's leading museums. Nowadays, there were few major incidents at such institutions. The theft in the nineties of Edvard Munch's "The Scream" from the National Art Museum in

Oslo, was one notable exception. The burglary, involving two people, set off an alarm and was filmed by the museum's surveillance cameras. One of the burglars climbed a ladder held in place by the other, broke a window, got inside, cut the wire holding the painting and got out, all in fifty seconds. The thieves left a note: "Thanks for the poor security". "The Scream" was recovered three months later, undamaged except for a small dent.

Five minutes before two o'clock, Christina and Nelson entered the temporary exhibit gallery. The director and curator of the Los Angeles County Museum of Art, both of whom were required to witness the packing, were already there. Also present were four armed guards, two museum employees who would assist with the packing and a photographer who would record the condition of each painting before it was packed. At two o'clock, the building was sealed. From then, nobody would be permitted to enter or leave until the paintings were aboard the armoured truck that would take them to the airport.

Three trolleys, each stacked with metal cases, were wheeled into the middle of the gallery. There were twenty custom made cases altogether, one for each painting. Each case, labelled on all sides with the initial letters of the work it was designed to hold, was locked with two latches controlled by a single four digit combination lock. Christina and Nelson were the only people in Los Angeles who had the combinations, arithmetic manipulations involving the year of painting and another number.

At two thirty, the packing began. Christina and the Los Angeles curator inspected each painting for damage before it was photographed and placed in its padded container. Once a container was locked, two seals were clamped over metal loops through the latches. One bore the imprint of the Los Angeles County Museum of Art, the other that of the Van Gogh Museum.

At five fifty, ten minutes ahead of schedule, the last work, "A Pair of Shoes", was locked in its case.

5

'Carlos, the men are ready,' Vega's lieutenant, Pedro Gómez, announced from the entrance to the candle lit courtyard where Vega and his wife had been dining alone.

Margarita grasped her husband's arm across the table. 'Carlos, promise me you will be careful.' She had sensed danger for some time, for him and also herself.

'Of course, my love,' he said and rose to embrace her. Vega had told Margarita nothing of Imthorn's plan, a secretiveness motivated by caution, not mistrust. This way, she could be honest with the police who were sure to come calling; there could be no unintentional slip-ups during questioning.

The usual three-unit convoy with a complement of eight guards was waiting outside. Vega's car, a Mercedes, was fitted with bulletproof glass and side panels as well as plates underneath capable of absorbing the shock of a land mine.

'Take El Palo onto La Playa,' Vega told his driver who

relayed the instruction to the lead car. The choice between several possible routes was always made just before departure, a precaution to reduce the risk of ambush. The Mercedes, with its accompanying Ford sedans, moved down the long tree lined driveway, through the heavy iron gates guarding the entrance to the property, then on towards the lights of Medellín below.

The convoy travelled at a steady speed with very little distance separating the vehicles. No matter what the conditions, there could never be enough room to allow another vehicle to squeeze in. And there was a standard procedure if the lead car was stopped for any reason: the Mercedes and the tail vehicle would immediately divert to an alternate route. The drivers were expert at avoidance procedures, they were always on the lookout for a set-up. Their lives were on the line too.

After an incident free forty-five minute journey, the convoy arrived at its destination, the basement carpark of a fifteen storey apartment building on Avenue Bolívar, three kilometres southwest of central Medellín.

An advance party had already secured the carpark to ensure Vega's move in would be as efficient and inconspicuous as possible. One man held a broom in front of the television camera which monitored the area around the elevators. Another held one of the two elevators with a control key. He had already taped a piece of paper over the lens of the television camera inside. A third was in the lobby holding the second elevator and a forth was blocking stairway access to the carpark. The convoy came to a halt close to the elevators and within a matter of seconds Vega, Pedro and three of the guards were on their way to the fifteenth floor.

The recently completed up-market building, financed with laundered drug money, was almost completely occupied. Five of Vega's men, none of whom were known to the Colombian authorities, had been installed in the two apartments which occupied the entire top floor: one in one and four in the other. Two of them were presently occupying the building manager, keeping him from monitoring the security system.

The elevator doors opened to reveal two guards, both armed with submachine guns, stationed in the hallway. Pedro directed Vega through a large wooden door to the left and followed him inside. Although Vega had never seen the apartment before, he knew it from the plans and the photographs his men had taken for him. There were four bedrooms. He went to his first, to the left of the entrance doorway. It was furnished with a double bed, a set of drawers with a mirror, a telephone, a small radio and a television set. The combined living and dining area was furnished with leather couches, a teak dining setting and matching coffee tables. The view from the room was partially obscured by a thick cover of plants on the balcony. The other bedrooms were clustered at the far end of the apartment, past the living area. The largest was the only one with any furniture: a single bed, a wicker chair, a bedside table with no drawers and a small television. Vega examined this room and its en suite far more carefully than his own. The windows were tinted and locked with keyed locks. Tall plants on the balcony obscured the view. The telephone socket had been removed from the wall, and a deadlock installed on the door. It suited Vega's requirements admirably.

The next bedroom was a metre and a half shorter than the plans showed but still large enough to be convincing. Vega ran his eyes around the edges of the false wall and tapped it in several places with his knuckles. It was perfect, undetectable. The cartel carpenter who built it and the matching one in the apartment across the hall had been taken on a holiday to Peru the day he finished the job. He would not be permitted to return for another two weeks.

The end wall inside the built-in wardrobe swung open with a squeak when Vega pushed it with his shoulder. He examined the work. There were three sturdy latches to secure the entrance panel from the inside. The false wall was padded with fibreglass bats, soundproofing. Two sets of headphones hanging on the wall were connected to a hidden microphone in the living area. Satisfied, he went on to a cursory inspection of the kitchen before going with Pedro to the apartment across the hall. The guards' apartment was, in all aspects, including the third bedroom compartment, the mirror image of Vega's.

One of the attractive features of such a high rent building in crime ridden Medellín was the security. There were television cameras all around the outside of the building as well as in the lobby, both elevators and the carpark. Pedro had engaged a cartel related electrician, now in Peru enjoying his compulsory holiday, to tap into the security system. The video signals from the various cameras in and around the building fed into four television sets: a large one in the living area and three smaller ones with headphones on a trolley, presently in the living area but also operable inside the third bedroom compartment. Each set had a picture-in-picture facility whereby a small box superimposed upon the regular picture displayed switching views from the various cameras. The main set had a recorder attached to it as did one of the sets on the trolley. Another set of headphones on the trolley was connected to the building's intercom system. If unwelcome visitors threatened, the trolley would be moved to the compartment and the box on the main set made to vanish. There would be absolutely no sign of the sophisticated surveillance system. The apartment would look quite innocent.

An ample supply of cash was on hand in both apartments in case, for whatever reason, silence had to be bought. That is, if it was for sale. If it wasn't, there were the weapons. The armory, the secret compartment in the guards' apartment, contained ten Heckler and Koch MP5K submachine guns, four Galil assault rifles, one Minimi light machine gun, a crate of Chilean MK-2 grenades, assorted ammunition and several canisters of tear gas. These armaments were in addition to the weapons the guards normally carried. The compartment also contained a small photo-copy machine, a laptop computer and printer and a set of headphones connected to a microphone in the living area.

The inspection complete, Vega joined Pedro and his men for coffee. He was confident the apartments would pass any cursory inspection by the authorities. There was nothing suspicious at all. At nine o'clock, he returned to his apartment. He did not expect to sleep.

At Medellín's José María Córdoba airport, all was in place. The small jet was fuelled and ready to go, its pilot asleep in the aisle, his two alarm clocks set for three and five min-utes past three in the morning. Two of Vega's men sat in a car not far from the plane. The off-duty air traffic con-troller who would be assisting with the operation had already visited them to collect half the five thousand American dollars he had negotiated for his services. Since the airport would be closed when the jet took off, he was needed to turn on the runway lights. He would also be needed for the early morning landing.

6

On schedule, at a quarter to seven, the convoy transporting the Vincent van Gogh paintings exited the LACMA complex onto Wilshire Boulevard. Christina and Nelson sat with the paintings inside the first of two armoured trucks. The second, a backup, was empty.

The routine to the airport was the same as that used for visiting heads of state. It involved eight members of a special police security unit travelling in three vehicles and ten motorcycle units whose job it was to facilitate passage of the convoy by blocking intersections and freeway entrances en route. Once the convoy passed a blocked entrance, the motorcycle officer would speed on, pass the convoy and repeat the procedure. The route was west to Santa Monica Boulevard and then south on Interstate 405 to Los Angeles International Airport, a distance of eighteen miles.

The convoy entered the airport through a side gate just south of an isolated KLM Boeing 767, the smaller of two aircraft types in the Dutch airline's fleet capable of flying to Rio non-stop.

The first officer greeted Nelson and Christina as they emerged from the truck and confirmed that their baggage and several packages of incidental museum material had already been stowed in the cargo hold. She also confirmed that seven members of the Netherlands Army Corps were on board.

The trolleys carrying the paintings were wheeled via ramps onto a catering truck platform which, with Christina, Nelson and the first officer on board, was raised to the level of the service door. The soldiers, a security contingent provided at no charge by the Netherlands government, rolled the trolleys onto the aircraft and went about strapping them to the floor. The front five rows of seats on the starboard side had been removed for that purpose and were stored in the cargo hold below.

The lieutenant briefed Nelson on the security arrangements. Two soldiers at a time would sit with the paintings and be relieved every two hours. Armed with batons only, their firearms were locked in a steel case behind the second bulkhead. Upon arrival in Rio, he and his men would change into civilian clothes and continue with the aircraft to Miami and then to Amsterdam. They had the worst part of the transfer, having to spend a total of thirty-five hours in the air over three days.

Seeing the trolleys secure, Christina went to the cockpit. 'Good evening, Jan.'

'Christina!' Bekker looked up from a computer display unit. 'Welcome aboard.' He removed a newspaper from the jump seat and invited her to sit. 'We're on schedule, take off at seven forty-five.'

'Any bad weather on the way?'

'There's some over Central America, but we'll be well above it. Rio looks clear.'

'Good, and you know to keep the cabin temperature at twenty-two Celsius?'

'Yes, ma'am. I can't do anything about the humidity though, the air gets pretty dry.'

'That's okay,' Christina replied as the first officer entered the cockpit. 'The cases are sealed.'

'Walk around complete, cargo secure,' the first officer reported as she took her seat.

'Let's go,' Bekker said and gave a thumbs up signal to a member of the ground crew outside.

Christina returned to the cabin and sat across the aisle from the paintings. The two turbo fan engines wound up to a constant drone and the aircraft began a sluggish movement. At exactly seven forty-five, the big jet turned onto the runway and, after a short roll, took to the air.

Christina watched the painting cases during take off and was pleased with the low level of vibration. The dampening protection for the priceless works was simple: each painting was suspended in sponge inside its container and each container was separated from its neighbour by a sheet of bubble wrap. In laboratory tests and dummy runs on commercial aircraft, this arrangement had proven the most satisfactory.

Jan Bekker's muffled voice came on once they'd gained altitude: 'This is the captain. We're on the outskirts of Los Angeles heading southwest towards Mexico. Our ETA in Rio is 11:30 a.m., local time. It's 12:58 a.m. there now, if you would like to set your watches. That's 12:58 a.m. Please let the flight attendants know if you need anything. I hope you enjoy the flight.'

After a hot supper and a little conversation, the small group of passengers dispersed. The off-duty soldiers took seats towards the back of the cabin to watch movies and play video games. Christina made a bed for herself across four seats and settled down with the airline magazine. Nelson took a slow walk around the cabin. The atmosphere: darkened, spots of light, rows of empty seats, the hum; it reminded him of Haywood Floyd's journey to the moon aboard the Pan-Am shuttle in the film "2001: A Space Odyssey". It was eerie.

Three hours into the flight, the only people in the cabin still awake were the two soldiers on duty. Flight KL-4021, as it was designated, was now just south of Mexico City. Its flight path and all radio communications were being monitored in Colombia. It was not to be a smooth flight at all.

7

Fifteen minutes past midnight, but not here. That was the time back in Los Angeles. In Rio, add five hours . . . five fifteen. Still over six hours to go. Nelson Schoute felt disoriented in time and space. As far as he was concerned overnight plane travel was something human beings were simply not meant to do. Straightening his shirt, he walked the short distance to the cockpit and pressed the intercom. 'Nelson here, would you like some company?'

'Sure, come in,' Bekker responded and released the door.

'I never sleep well on planes,' Nelson said as he settled into the jump seat. 'So, where are we?'

'Over Lake Nicaragua,' the first officer answered, 'just about to enter Costa Rican air space.'

Nelson peered out the side window to stars and a dark landmass below. 'Must be close to South America?'

'We are.' The first officer held the chart for him to see, tracing the track they were following with her finger. 'From here we head down to Panama, out over this little bit of the Pacific, and on across Colombia to Brazil.'

'I thought we'd be farther east.' Nelson's mental image of the relative positions of North and South America was, like most people's, hazy. 'I didn't expect to see the Pacific again tonight.'

'The great circle route,' Bekker announced. 'Straight over the curve of the earth.' He moved his hand in an arc to depict it. 'Shortest distance between any two points on the planet.'

'The scenic route too,' the first officer added. 'The Andes at sunrise, the Amazon after that.'

'I hope there's film in my camera,' Nelson said, pleased there was something on the horizon to break the boredom.

'First time over the Andes for me,' Bekker said after listening to a brief exchange on the radio.

'I thought you would have been everywhere by now,' Nelson responded.

'The Himalayas and Rockies many times, but not the Andes. But I've been to Rio before, in case you're worried. I know where the airport is, I've just never flown there from LA. Only from Amsterdam, across the pond.' Bekker gestured with a higher arc than before.

'As long as you can find the runway,' Nelson said with a chuckle.

'We don't need to. This ship will find it itself, and land too. It hardly needs us at all.'

32

'It must get pretty boring up here sometimes,' Nelson said, after a short silence.

'It does,' Bekker replied. 'But our passengers like it that way, so does the company.'

'I agree, the less excitement the better,' Nelson said and peered out the window again.

'Okay to visit the WC?' the first officer asked Bekker.

'Sure. You can check our passengers and cargo while you're back there.'

The first officer stowed the chart and turned off the light. 'It's quite a view from here,' she said to Nelson. 'Not much atmosphere to block the stars.' The view was magnificent: console switches and dim cathode ray tubes framing the black sky with its ancient constellations. Another scene from science fiction.

'Care to take the right-hand seat for a while?' Bekker asked Nelson as the first officer left. 'You can see out better.'

'Love to, I just hope I don't bump anything.'

'Don't worry, you'll be okay,' Bekker said and, after checking the time, excused himself to make a position report.

Nelson took a good look at his ergonomically designed high tech surroundings. The pilot on the way over had explained the functions of the various controls and screens but Nelson remembered little of it now. 'This thing's a flying computer,' he said when Bekker's radio report was complete.

'Three computers,' Bekker replied. 'They check each other all the time.'

The first officer returned. 'Everyone's asleep, except the soldiers on guard. The cargo's secure . . . and very tempting.' She lay her hand on Nelson's shoulder. 'Would you miss just one of those paintings? My apartment could use a little decorating.'

'I'm afraid so,' Nelson replied with a polite smile and vacated the seat. He'd been asked the question thousands of times before. 'You'll have to be satisfied with a copy, just like the rest of us.' He noticed that she had put on a fresh coat of lipstick. Pilots wearing lipstick, he was getting old. He returned to his seat in search of sleep.

Eighty minutes later, with only the pilots and two soldiers awake, the 767 entered Carlos Vega's web. 'TCAS warning,' the first officer reported out of the hum, gaining Bekker's immediate attention. The 767's traffic collision avoidance system had detected an aircraft entering its enveloping buffer zone. 'Above, twenty-five hundred, descending.'

'Military?' Bekker wondered aloud and reached for the radio.

'Could be,' the first officer replied just as flickering console lights signalled a more ominous problem. The instrument panels faded off. Both sensed the decrease in speed and sudden silence.

'Flame out in both engines, take action,' Bekker ordered anxiously, instinctively dropping the nose to maintain air speed. The basic instruments on his side glowed back on, their energy provided by the ram air turbine, a fan-like device which dropped automatically from the plane's belly when the engines wound down. 'He can't see us,' Bekker murmured as he searched above for lights.

'Igniters to flight, switches to cut-off,' the first officer reported and lifted the fuel switch. 'Run.' Both engines remained dead. She started the APU, the auxiliary power unit, a small jet engine in the tail normally used to provide AC power on the ground. All the instruments came back to life, the navigation lights returned.

'Memory items complete,' she said. The engines were still dead; the descent rate, two thousand feet per minute.

'Both engine flame out checklist, my RT,' Bekker commanded and reached for the radio to transmit a mayday call. They'd dropped seventeen hundred feet already. The first officer pulled the quick reference handbook and began a systematic search for the next procedure.

Then, strobe lights to the left. 'Good morning KLM.'

Bekker and the first officer looked in disbelief towards a small jet levelling out on their port side. Bekker raised the microphone to his open mouth.

'Check my starboard wing.' The accent was American, southern. 'Don't touch your radio.'

The illuminated rocket under the small jet's wing persuaded Bekker to cooperate. The horrible truth had dawned: they were being hijacked.

'Trust me, Captain,' the voice said as Bekker returned

the microphone to its cradle. Both engines whined back to life. 'That's better, eh?' the voice said.

Bekker lifted the nose, the small jet matched him. 'Don't worry, this isn't another September 11. You're quite safe. I'll have you on the ground in fifteen minutes and on your way soon after that. Just follow my directions and nobody will be hurt. Now Captain, adjust your descent rate to three thousand feet per minute.'

Bekker complied and then called Nelson, Christina and the lieutenant to the cockpit. 'To avoid confusion,' he said after relating what had happened, 'as long as we're in the aircraft, I'm the person responsible. I'm in charge, okay?' They all knew the protocol; the issue of command had come up in their training for the transfer. But no one, neither here nor back in Amsterdam, had foreseen a possibility as wild as this.

'Is there a way to contact the air force wherever we are?' Nelson asked.

'Not without him knowing,' Bekker answered. 'I'm going to follow his directions, as long as they're sane.'

'I'd like to unlock our weapons,' the lieutenant said.

'Not until we land,' Bekker responded. 'And let's hope we don't need them.'

The American pilot's voice broke in again at nineteen thousand feet altitude: 'Captain, we'll be doing a left turn soon. At eleven thousand feet you'll see runway lights come on ahead. The runway is high, elevation seven thousand plus two eight feet and there's plenty of length, three five hundred metres. I'll be with you all the way so don't try anything funny. Friends of mine will greet you on the ground. I repeat, nobody need be hurt. You know what we're after, if you just let us have the pictures, you can be on your way. Now, if you understand my directions, turn off your navigation lights.'

Bekker turned off the lights.

'Good KLM, you can leave them off and no landing lights until you're just above the deck.' The small jet moved farther away and extinguished its navigation lights.

At fourteen thousand feet the American ordered the left turn and at eleven thousand feet, the runway lights came on directly ahead. Bekker instructed everyone to return to their seats and prepare for landing.

The small jet stayed off the 767's port side all the way to seven thousand five hundred feet and then powered ahead.

Bekker called on the landing lights just out from the runway and guided the aircraft to a smooth touchdown. 'Take the first right exit, then a right onto the taxiway,' the American ordered. 'When you stop, shut down the engines and get ready to open the forward service door. Have your passengers stay in their seats. I'll talk to you again at take off.' The runway lights blinked off. The small jet was invisible in the still dark sky.

A catering truck and two sedans appeared ahead, parked across the taxiway. There were ten or so men. One had a machine gun trained on the cockpit, another signalled for Bekker to cut the landing lights.

'Brake on. One, two, off.' Bekker switched off both engines. 'Stay here and listen to the radio,' he said to the first officer and went back to the cabin.

The lieutenant had spaced his men around the forward cabin, their weapons under their seats. 'We'll shoot only if they shoot first, Captain,' he announced.

'Yes, no heroics,' Bekker responded so they all heard him.

Bekker peered through a window as the truck moved into position below. There was a knock from outside when its platform reached the level of the service door.

Bekker had the door half open when a gun barrel appeared pointing at his head. 'Back, señor,' its black owner demanded. Bekker backed off and counted as seven other men entered the cabin. One, carrying a small tool-box, went straight to the cockpit.

'Hands behind heads, everybody!' the leader, the one who'd threatened Bekker, shouted.

They all wore straw hats and bandannas hid their faces, almost as though they had stepped out of a cowboy movie. The difference was the submachine guns they were carrying. 'We don't want to shoot anybody, so be good.' The leader waved his gun at Christina who was standing with the paintings, and Bekker and Nelson near the door. 'Sit,' he demanded, gesturing to the front row of seats. The two men complied. Christina stayed put.

'Soldier boys, up, up, up,' was the leader's next order. 'Hands behind heads.' One by one the soldiers were searched then moved to the bulkhead and forced to kneel on the seats, facing backwards. Their guns and batons were collected and loaded onto the truck.

That done, two men shouldered their weapons and moved to the painting trolleys.

'No!' Christina grabbed vainly for an arm about to slice the strapping. 'Stop!'

The leader pulled her away. 'Doctor Jansen, you must come with me.'

Nelson jumped to his feet. 'You're not taking her!'

'Leave me alone!' Christina grabbed the second trolley as it passed her on the way to the door.

The leader released Christina to another man. 'Stay in your seat, señor,' he said and pushed Nelson down with the barrel of his gun. 'You can report that we took Doctor Jansen to look after the paintings.' He spoke softly, keeping the gun at Nelson's chest. 'She will be well cared for. Our mission will not succeed if anyone is hurt, understand?'

'What are you after?' Nelson asked with hate filled eyes.

'Be patient, señor,' the leader said and returned his attention to Christina. 'Do you have a bag, Doctor Jansen?'

She gestured to an overhead locker. 'You're making a very big mistake.' He retrieved her bag.

Two men then gathered the remaining bags from the overhead lockers and under the seats and emptied them onto the floor. Six phones were tossed onto the truck.

'Put her on the truck,' the leader ordered next.

'Let me go!' she demanded as two men forced her struggling to the door.

'You'll be rescued, Christina,' Nelson shouted from his seat as the truck platform began an immediate descent. 'Our government won't tolerate this.' The men in straw hats ignored the outburst.

The man with the toolbox emerged from the cockpit. 'Done.' He held up three headset microphones and a handset for the leader to see.

'Time for you to go, señor,' the leader said to Bekker and ushered him to the cockpit. 'Start the engines and go to the runway. Be quick.'

'As quick as is safe,' Bekker responded and commenced the weight and fuel calculations. With over one-third of the fuel already burned, they were well under the limit for this runway length at this altitude.

The checks done, Bekker started the engines and steered the jet to the runway threshold.

'Wait here,' the leader said and returned to his three remaining companions in the cabin. 'Go, amigos.'

One of them hooked a rope onto the service door hinge and used it to slide to the ground. His two companions followed. The leader then backed up to the door, keeping his gun pointed at the hostages as he did so. He grabbed the rope. 'You have done well, amigos. After I have gone, count to twenty, then close the door.' With that, he vanished.

Nelson and the lieutenant rushed to the cockpit. 'Where are we?' Nelson asked.

'Medellín,' Bekker said. 'We've got the latitude and longitude here.' He pointed to a display on the console. 'You write them down, for the record.' He handed a pen and pad to Nelson. Then to the first officer, 'Pull the circuit breaker on the cockpit voice recorder, we'll save what we've got.' The recorder operated on a loop, storing the last thirty minutes of conversation. The terminal building, two misty kilometres away, was just coming to life. José María Córdoba Airport would open in an hour.

The American pilot's voice returned: 'KLM, you're clear for take off. Leave your navigation lights off.' The runway lights blinked back on.

Nelson belted himself into the jump seat and listened as the pilots went through their final checklist.

They took to the air at three minutes past seven on Bekker's watch, three minutes past five local time. The small jet pulled in on their port side at nine thousand feet. 'Captain, set your course to zero eight five degrees. Climb to flight level two three zero. Maintain Mach point seven.'

Bekker set the course as requested. The dawn light improved quickly giving all aboard the 767 a good view of the enemy. The pilots agreed that it was a Dassault Falcon 50, a popular French-made business jet. The registration number on the starboard side of the white fuselage, the only side they had seen, was painted over.

'How the hell did he shut down our engines?' Nelson asked when things settled down.

'Some kind of interference with the flight management system,' Bekker said with a shrug.

'They got all the microphones?' Nelson inquired to be sure.

'I'm afraid so,' Bekker answered.

'Drilled into this one.' The first officer fingered a rough hole in the console.

The Falcon pilot remained silent as they rose towards the massive Andean cordillera silhouetted against a deep blue and violet dawn. Over the ice and snow covered peaks, the Falcon altered course to ten degrees magnetic which kept them over the mountains all the way to the Caribbean. There he made another course change to the west. As the light improved, Nelson took several photographs of the Falcon to assist in the investigation he knew would follow.

Ninety minutes after take off, the American broke his silence: 'KLM, I'll be leaving you soon. I want you to reset your course to Maiquetía beacon, that's Caracas, identifier mike india quebec. You should get there in just over an hour, if you hurry.' He laughed. 'I say again, reset to Maiquetía, mike india quebec and climb to flight level four one zero, four one zero, that will keep you out of everyone's way. A friend of mine will notify Venezuelan air traffic control so they can clear the way for you. If you try to go anywhere else, they might not see you coming. And we don't want to spoil this beautiful morning with a mid-air collision, do we?'

Bekker entered the identifier code into the console keypad and, as the aircraft responded, the American pilot made a final transmission, gloating: 'Goodbye, Captain, it's been a pleasure doing business with you.'

With that, the Falcon dropped out of sight. It would continue north, dump the dummy rocket in a stretch of empty sea and arrive in Jamaica forty minutes before the 767 reached Caracas. There, it would get a quick paint job, an innocent registration and an alibi. The pilot would vanish.

The sun was still below the mountains when the rental truck carrying the paintings and Christina Jansen arrived at the apartment building on Avenue Bolívar. It was ten minutes to six o'clock. The 767 was over northern Colombia. During the drive from the airport, the metal containers, photographs of which were sure to be featured on television and in the newspapers over the next few days, had been placed inside large cardboard boxes.

The normal precautions were taken with the television cameras and carpark access and a control key ensured that the two elevator journeys to deliver Christina and the paintings to the fifteenth floor were not interrupted. The operation took four minutes. There were no witnesses.

43

8

Christina Jansen, sick with worry for herself and those on the 767, hunched her shoulders together to avoid physical contact with her captors. The cardboard boxes took up most of the elevator floor space leaving too little room for her and the two straw-hatted men. Theories accounting for the hijacking whirled in her head: If it was a straight theft, the plane and all on board were disposable once the paintings were off. But would anyone in their right mind add murder to theft if it wasn't necessary? Probably not. If it was some kind of ransom scheme, murders would make success less likely. But were these people necessarily logical? If it was a theft, why bother taking her too? Maybe to help authenticate the paintings to a buyer. If it was for ransom, what was at stake? Colombia? Drugs? How did it all fit?

The leader, seemingly of African ancestry, spoke to her for the first time since the airport: 'Señorita Jansen, we are safe now.' He touched his hand to his chest. 'My name is

Rafael, my friend is Josef.' The other man, short and brown, mestizo she guessed, European-Indian blood, smiled heavy gold inlays. She remained silent, terrified.

'The apartment we are going to will be your home for a while,' Rafael said. 'It is very nice.'

The elevator doors opened to cigarette smoke and four men who went about unloading the paintings as soon as they were past. After removing his hat, Rafael opened the large wooden door on the left and led Christina inside.

Her immediate impression was one of spaciousness. Then she saw the figure standing with his back to the window. The imposing mountains, dark against the brilliant dawn sky, seemed hopelessly far away. She knew she was looking at the man responsible for her capture. Mid to late forties, more neatly dressed than his underlings but with the same basic articles: blue jeans, a short-sleeved shirt and an ugly revolver on his hip. 'Good morning, Doctor Jansen.' He walked towards her, his dark eyes on her face. 'I am Carlos Vega. It is I who am in charge of this operation.' A crooked smile. Rage welled within her. 'My apologies for the inconvenience it has caused you.' He held out his hand, withdrawing it when she did not respond. The smile faded but did not disappear.

'Whatever you're doing, Mr Vega, it won't work. These painting are red hot. Whoever you plan on selling them to will have to lock them up, forever.'

Vega turned from her and walked the few paces to the beige leather couch in the middle of the room. 'Doctor

Jansen,' he said, leaning on the back of the couch and folding his arms, 'I have no intention of selling the paintings. My aim is to see them returned to your country as soon as possible.'

'So it's ransom. What are you after?'

'That's better, Doctor.' He raised himself from the couch. 'Your government has my son in one of its prisons. I want him with me, it's that simple.'

Her gaze drifted from Vega as her mind made the links. 'The plane crash near Curaçao,' she murmured, then, vaguely recalling a television image of the young Colombian under police escort. 'The cocaine baron's son . . .' Her eyes darted to his. 'Your son.'

'My son,' Vega replied, 'Juan.'

The men began bringing the second load of boxes into the room stacking them along the wall next to the first. Vega moved to the one nearest him, took a hinged knife from his pocket and went about slicing the tape.

'What about the people on the plane?' Christina demanded from behind. 'What's happening to them?'

'Nothing,' he said, glancing back to her. 'They'll soon be safe in Caracas.'

Josef interrupted to report that all the paintings were now in the room.

'Good,' Vega said, lifting the metal case out of the box. He examined it from every angle. The letters ASCT, in bright green, were stencilled on all six surfaces. He rolled the combination tumblers and then took some glasses from his pocket to read the seals: 'Van Gogh Museum and . . . LACMA. Of course, the Los Angeles County Museum of Art. Nice work.' She winced as he tapped the top of the case with the handle of his knife. 'We will open it later, after you have rested.'

An argument to come, she thought. She had no intention of opening any of the cases. 'So where do I fit into this, Mr Vega?'

'Christina . . . I hope you don't mind if I call you by your Christian name.' She made no response. He smiled briefly and continued. 'No harm must come to these paintings. Damage to them would damage my cause, that must not happen.' He walked towards her folding his knife as he did so. 'As you can imagine, the care of such valuable art is beyond my area of expertise as well as that of my men. That is why you are here. You will be responsible for looking after them and, when it is required, confirming to the Dutch government that they are unharmed. You will be well cared for.' He lay his hand on her shoulder. 'You have nothing to fear.'

She twisted away from him and moved to the painting case now half bathed in the rays of the just risen sun. 'This should not be in the sun.' She moved it into shade. 'And please don't tap any of the cases again. Heat and vibration are very bad for the paintings.'

'See Christina, you are already proving your value. And please, you must call me Carlos.'

Another man came into the room. He was about the

same age as Vega, shorter, with a greying moustache. 'Pedro!' Vega waved him over. 'This is our guest, Doctor Jansen. Christina, I would like you to meet my right-hand man, Pedro Gómez.'

Pedro bowed his head and smiled. 'Buenos dìas, Señorita Jansen.'

She looked to him, nodded, but said nothing.

Vega spoke again. 'We will take care of the paintings now. I have a special space for them in the room next to yours.' He turned to Pedro. 'Have the men take the packages into the third bedroom and remove the cardboard. Allow Doctor Jansen to supervise their storage. As far as the paintings are concerned, whatever she requests is to be done.'

'I'd like to look at the room first,' she asked.

'Certainly, señorita,' Vega said, happy to accommodate such a simple request. 'Pedro will show you.'

Pedro took her along the hallway to the third bedroom, opened the secret compartment and handed her a flashlight. She didn't like what she saw. Her concern was a lack of temperature control. The compartment was isolated from the air conditioning system and the end was an outside wall, which, although probably thick concrete, would still partially transmit outside temperature variations. What she did like about the compartment was the measure of protection it offered against mishandling by Vega's guards. After a little thought she proposed a solution which Pedro happily embraced. The cardboard from the outside of the cases would be put up against the wall to provide additional insulation and the door leading into the compartment from the closet and the closet itself would be left open so there would be some exchange of conditioned air.

That settled, she looked around the room, partly out of concern for the safety of the paintings but also in her own self-interest. The more she knew about the apartment, the better. There was always a chance her captors had overlooked something that would enable her to signal outside.

There was no furniture. A sliding glass door led to a balcony on, what Pedro described as, the south side of the building. She examined it. It was secured with a lock, not just a latch. The curtains were lined with a rubbery material. She asked that they be left closed, for insulation.

Her next request was for a thermometer to monitor the temperature in the compartment. Pedro promised to get one.

Then, under her direction, Rafael, Josef and two other men carried the boxes down to the room. They cut off the cardboard, taped it against the compartment's outer wall and, under her supervision, stacked the cases.

Pedro then took her to her room. She noticed the deadlock on the door as she entered, it was the type that took a key on either side. Simply furnished and prison like, were her immediate impressions. Her bag was on the bed. Tinted windows, locks on everything. It faced south too.

Pedro slid open the closet door to reveal some clothes hanging inside and a small cardboard box on the floor.

'Señorita Jansen, if these or the things in the box do not fit, or if there is anything else you need, the wife of one of the men will go shopping for you this afternoon.' He closed the closet. 'You must be very tired. Carlos would like you to rest.' She would have no say in the matter. 'Lunch will be at noon.' He went to leave.

She looked at her watch, set to Rio time. 'Wait, what time is it now?'

He referred to his Rolex, a counterfeit. 'A quarter to seven.' Pedro, like many of his contemporaries in the business, was still ruled by the poverty of his past. The fake Rolex told time just as well as the real thing, and for a small fraction of the price. When it stopped working, he would buy another. He turned as he closed the door, 'Hasta luego, señorita.' She heard the lock.

She checked her bag. Her phone, wallet, passport and a small flashlight were missing. She hung the suit she had packed for her arrival in Rio and took the few toiletries she had into the en suite. She checked the box in the closet: a sweater, socks and a selection of underwear of various sizes, mostly too small.

She sat on the bed and turned on the television using the remote control. "Bananas in Pyjamas" glowed on, in Spanish. She pictured her far away nephew and niece watching the same perpetually cheerful characters, in Dutch.

She was able to understand some of what B1 and B2 were saying. An advantage of being Dutch, she mused.

Since her native tongue was spoken by few people outside the Netherlands, she, like many of her fellow citizens, was fluent in more than one foreign language. She had learned English, German and French at school. The little Spanish she knew had been picked up during two holidays in Spain.

Switching channels, she heard English. Cable News Network was broadcasting a story about an upcoming space shuttle mission. She watched, despite the heaviness of her eyes, hoping to hear something about the hijacking. There was nothing. A shower was the next priority. She assembled the change of underwear she had carried with her, a pair of jeans and a T-shirt from the closet, and started to undress. Then, realising her privacy could be invaded without notice, she went into the en suite and closed the door.

The shower washed away the grime of travel and tamed her tiredness. Her captors had left only one towel and there was no hair drier. Some other items for her list. She dried her hair as best she could. The sloppy stitching on the jeans labelled "Levi Strauss and Co." gave them away as counterfeit. They were too big around the hips and not long enough for her Dutch bones. The medium size T-shirt did nothing to raise the standard, the cotton was cheap and thin.

She checked the television. Still nothing about the hijacking. She lay on the bed and was overtaken by much needed sleep.

She woke disoriented. That first thought: had it been a dream? She lifted her head. No. She was in Medellín, a prisoner. The muffled voice from the television spoke of a G8 summit in Vladivostok. She closed her eyes and allowed the recent hurts to torment her, to kick her when she's down. Her betrayal by Henning. He'd been back in Amsterdam less than a month after spending two weeks with her in LA. A few disagreements but no great problems, no warnings, nothing she'd picked up anyway. He was to come to Rio in March. She'd done the right thing, been the faithful girlfriend when he was away in Surinam last year. False love. Bastard! The day after Marieke's funeral. Great timing. Bastard! Her mother always said bad things come in threes. Number three, prisoner in Colombia. What a mess.

The words coming from the television snapped her out of her melancholy daze. She sprang from the bed. The face of Vincent van Gogh and the outline of a plane filled a rectangle over the anchor's right shoulder.

The chief electronic engineer from Boeing came on the screen, live from Seattle. 'We suspect tampering with the aircraft's flight management system but we won't know for sure until our team checks the airplane's computers.' Relief. The plane was okay. Vega hadn't lied.

Next, the distraught director of the National Museum of Fine Art in Rio de Janeiro. She stood in the sunshine in front of a banner advertising the exhibition due to open in four days and expressed feelings of disbelief and devastation about what had happened and the hope that the paintings would soon be recovered.

Nelson's face appeared next. 'Good for you, Nelson,' she cried. A lump came to her throat, tears to her eyes. There were no tissues either. It didn't matter. She savoured the salt of her tears.

The interviewer suggested the possibility that somebody on board the 767 may have been involved in the hijacking.

'Impossible,' Nelson replied. 'The selection process for everyone, everyone except me and Doctor Jansen, was random. The hijacking was very professional. There could have been no reliance on chance.'

Christina knew the details. The Vincent van Gogh Foundation had, in fact, demanded that recruitment have an element of chance. The selection of the pilots and flight attendants possessed it because of the amount of schedule shuffling involved. And the soldiers were selected by lot just two days before departure.

The anchor thanked Nelson and went on to recap what had happened starting from when the paintings left the Los Angeles County Museum of Art. He finished by saying that further developments would be reported as soon as they came to light.

Christina watched a couple of the ensuing stories with little interest before closing her eyes again, Marieke coming to her out of the jumble. Pretty girl, lots of promise. The trouble started when she was fifteen, according to her mother. Fell in with the wrong crowd, arguments at home, at school. Left school then left home. So young, the vulnerable soul at the end of Vega's chain. They'd skated together when the canals froze, before the awful change. So sweet. Tried to help. Not enough. Could have done more. Why?

A knock on the door invaded her sleep. She sat up. The door was being unlocked. 'Sorry if I woke you, Doctor Jansen,' Pedro said from outside. 'Please come, Carlos would like to see you.'

She brushed her hair, still damp at the back, and washed her face. The rest had rejuvenated her.

Vega was sitting on the couch reading a newspaper when she entered the living area. The painting container he had examined before was now on the dining table, a pair of wire cutters beside it. The seals were gone. Pedro was sitting next to the case fiddling with a camera, a cigarette hanging from his mouth.

'Christina!' Vega got up from the couch. 'Did you sleep?'

'Yes,' she answered without looking at him.

'Good. If there are any things you require, make a list and . . .'

'He already told me,' she interrupted.

'Yes,' Vega replied, allowing her the point of disrespect, certain he could demand better behaviour and get it any time he chose. 'Pedro is very efficient. Order anything you like . . . perfume, make-up, alcohol. Anything.' He was at the table now, his hand on the case. 'There is a task that must be performed. I would like you to take the painting out of its case, you will be photographed with it as proof that we are the legitimate . . .' he paused and grinned, '. . .

54

for want of a better word, party. I'm sure you have access to the combination.'

Yes, of course, proof that he was the real perpetrator. She hadn't considered that. He was going to need a photograph and, one way or another, he was going to get it. With her cooperation there would be no damage. Then this painting could go in the compartment with the others. She would open it. Not yet though. 'Before I do, get Pedro and that man,' she said, pointing to a guard near the door, 'to put out their cigarettes. Smoke is very bad for the paint.'

Pedro immediately squashed his cigarette into an ashtray and, in Spanish, commanded the guard to do likewise.

'I'll wait for the air to clear, say ten minutes.'

Vega nodded. 'Okay.'

She went back to her room and watched television for more news on the hijacking. There was none. After the agreed time, she returned to the living area with the LACMA exhibition guide she had used when packing the paintings. It contained the combination information for everyone to see but only her to know. After a quick look at the page devoted to the painting she rolled the combination to 5154, opened the case and locked the hinges in position. Then, after spinning the tumblers off the combination, she carefully removed "Agostina Segatori in the Café du Tambourin": Vincent's image of a round faced woman with melancholy eyes sitting alone with her drink at a small table painted to resemble a tamborine; an empty chair opposite; a bright red hat flaring from her head.

Vega directed her to stand against the bare wall and hold the painting so the top of the frame was level with her shoulders. He examined the image. 'This is worth many millions of dollars, Pedro.'

Christina backed off as Vega pointed to the canvas. 'Don't touch it!'

'Relax, señorita, I won't touch the paint.' Then something in the painting caught his eye. 'Look at this, Christina, the woman is smoking. She was smoking when van Gogh painted this.' He laughed. 'You should have been there to stop her, smoke is very bad for the paint.' Pedro laughed along with Vega and moved into position to take the photograph.

She lowered the painting. 'You're not using a flash, are you?'

'Si,' Pedro replied, and looked to his boss for guidance.

'There's enough light,' she said. 'You don't need a flash.'

'Okay, no flash,' Vega said, an amused look on his face.

Pedro switched off the flash and lined up the picture.

'Don't look so miserable, Christina,' Vega said from beside his man. 'You look as unhappy as the woman in the picture.'

'Perhaps it wasn't a good day for her either,' she answered as the camera delivered the developing photograph with a whirr.

'Wait,' Vega ordered as she moved to return the painting to its case. 'I would like you to hang it.' He gestured to a hook on the wall.

'Why?'

'So I can enjoy the spoils of my victory.'

'Not a good idea.' She took the last steps to the case. 'There's a very good picture in the guide, you can look at that.'

'I would prefer to look at the original, please put it on the hook.' His tone was polite but determined.

'It would be much safer back in the case, you know that, Carlos.' She was sufficiently desperate to use the first name of the last person in the world with whom she wished to be familiar.

'Señorita, this wall is as good as the one in the Van Gogh Museum, is it not? The sun doesn't shine on it, no harm will come to the woman in the red hat.'

'You made me responsible for the safety of the paintings, that was my understanding.' She placed the painting in the case.

'Christina, hang it. It will go back in the case tomorrow. Then you can display another from the collection. It will be very civilised, we will have our own private gallery for as many days as we can. I want you to teach me all about your Vincent van Gogh.'

Christina was suddenly distracted as the guard who had been smoking before lit a fresh cigarette. She walked over, took it from his lips and extinguished it in a cup of coffee. The menacing-looking Colombian stood with his mouth agape. Vega, then Pedro, laughed.

'See what I mean,' she said. 'You have no understanding

57

of what's involved here. The painting must stay locked in its case.' She could not let Vega win.

'Christina, Oscar does not understand English.' Vega put his hand on the man's shoulder while he explained, in Spanish, the reason for not smoking. Then he turned to Pedro. 'Pedro, from now, nobody will smoke in this apartment. The consequences of breaking that rule will be significant. Please make that clear to the men.'

Vega did not need to say more. A significant consequence could mean a demotion to the far less comfortable and more dangerous debt collection cell within the cartel. The guards liked their jobs. They got to sit around, drink coffee and watch television for a good part of the day. Only on rare occasions did they have to deal with a problem. Most of them had done time in debt collection, none would wish to return to it.

'Señorita, there will be no more smoking, I give you my word.'

'I don't believe you.' Christina persisted, stalling what she sensed was inevitable.

'This is your last chance, señorita,' he replied, his voice suddenly harsh. 'Either hang it now or I will get Oscar to hang it, and Oscar is a very clumsy man.' He paused. 'Your last chance, señorita, or we do it my way.'

She could read his eyes. It was time to give in. It would be the lesser of two evils. She carried the container across the room and placed it on the floor under the hook.

'That's better.' Vega sat back and watched.

The painting had two eyelets a short distance down each side of the frame. It was set up for two wall hooks, not wire. Pedro apologised for not having any spare hooks and, as a temporary measure, produced some electrical wire. Christina strung it between the eyelets, secured it, and then tested the hook. It was strong enough. She hung the painting. Magnificent, despite the surroundings.

She turned to Vega. 'Nobody is to touch the surface. Or breathe on the painting. There can be no cooking in here either. Or insect sprays or air fresheners. Understand?'

'Your advice will be taken, señorita,' Vega replied.

She looked around the room. 'I would like to put something in front of the painting, a cordon.'

At her direction, Pedro and surprisingly to her, Vega too, carried chairs from the dining area. She arranged four in a semicircle in front of the painting more than an arm's length from it. Then, to Pedro, as she patted the wall to the left of the painting, 'I would like you to put a sign here, in Spanish, saying do not touch, in large letters.' She stood back. 'Also, a no smoking sign just inside the front door.' Out of respect for the artist and the civilised people of the world, she was determined to do her best to minimise the chance of damage in this hazardous environment.

'So, you want to know about the painting?' she said to Vega. 'Okay, I'll tell you.' She stood between him and the work. 'The subject of a woman sitting alone in a cafe is a traditional one. Notice the short, slashing brushstrokes that make the hat so vivid, and the Japanese prints on the wall behind.'

'Who is she?' Vega interrupted, staring into the work. 'Why do her eyes look so sad?'

'She's an Italian, Agostina Segatori, the owner of the cafe, in Paris. Possibly Vincent's mistress at the time.'

'She doesn't look very happy for a woman in love.'

Pedro remembered the Polaroid photograph in his pocket. He glanced at it before handing it to Vega who examined it closely. 'Very clear.' He gave it to Christina. 'A Dutch woman in Colombia holding a picture of an Italian woman in Paris, that's the title we shall use.' He laughed. 'Pedro may win an award.'

'Very amusing,' she said, registering the intelligence behind the witticism. She was not dealing with a stupid man, that was a positive. He has a plan, he should follow it through, with no injury to her or the paintings. Engage him, don't annoy him, that would be her strategy.

'My contact in Holland informs me that you are not married and have no children,' Vega said, 'but I do not know if you have parents who are alive.'

'I do,' she replied and returned the photograph to him. 'Both alive.'

'They will be relieved to see you are unharmed,' he said.

'They will.' She looked at him as he examined the polaroid further, intrigued by his concern. Family man, master criminal. Altruism and evil wrapped in one.

Vega put the photograph in his shirt pocket and

returned his attention to the painting. 'What were you saying, about the prints on the wall?'

'Are you really interested?' she asked. The situation was surreal, as if she were taking a VIP around the Amsterdam gallery, a visiting prince or politician.

'Very interested,' Vega replied. 'We Colombians have a strong culture . . . art, poetry, music. The Tayrona, the Muisca, then the Spanish, many cultures. Sometimes Europeans think they have a monopoly on art and literature. You, señorita, should know better.'

'I do know,' she said. 'At university I did some study of South American art, pre-Colombian. And I was looking forward to visiting the museums in Brazil, until this morning.'

'One day you will visit them, señorita,' Vega said and returned his attention to Agostina Segatori.

'Vincent had the prints displayed for sale,' she continued after a short silence. 'Later, he had his own paintings on the walls, but they vanished after an argument with La Segatori. It seems they were sold as waste canvas.'

'What a crime,' Vega replied with a huff.

'And, there's a bonus with this work,' she said, looking to him. 'It's two paintings in one. You have more van Goghs than you think.'

'I'm sorry, señorita, I don't understand.'

'Vincent painted La Segatori over the top of another work, another woman. She is visible with X-rays. He was probably short of money . . . couldn't afford a new canvas.'

'Unbelievable.' Vega examined the canvas for clues but visible light revealed none. 'For want of a pittance. A tragedy, Christina.' After gazing at it for a while longer, he turned to her. 'Now I must attend to some business. Please excuse me.'

The imperfect gentleman, she thought.

'Thank you for your cooperation and for your explanation about La Segatori.' He turned to Pedro. 'Please arrange for Doctor Jansen's lunch to be served in her room.' And then, to her, 'Tonight, you shall join me for dinner.'

'Thanks, but I don't think I'll be hungry.' Dinner for two seemed a little too cosy. She didn't want cosy, he may get wrong ideas.

'But I will be, Christina. I will be hungry for your passion.'

'Don't even think it.' Talk to me, yes. Touch me, no. That was how it was going to be.

He laughed at her reaction. 'I will be hungry for your passion about the work of your Vincent van Gogh.' He left.

Pedro ushered her back to her room and waited while she wrote out her shopping list: some toiletries, her size of underwear, a hair drier, a thermometer, some proper picture wire and hooks. The list complete, Pedro left, locking the door behind him.

At noon, Josef delivered her lunch which consisted of tomato soup, a chicken salad, fresh bread, apple juice and a small cup of black coffee. She ate while watching the latest news about the hijacking. There were pictures of the 767 parked at the airport in Caracas; the crew and soldiers walking into a room; a small jet similar to the one involved in the hijacking; and photographs of several of the stolen paintings. Then, Albert Voss, the director of the Vincent van Gogh Foundation, appeared with an announcement that the foundation was offering one million United States dollars for information leading to the solution of the crime. Great news, Christina thought. Somebody must have seen something or, even better, perhaps with that kind of money on offer, someone would betray Vega.

Vega was in the other apartment moving the operation to the next stage. The photograph of Christina with the painting was attached to the top of a printed page and the whole thing photocopied using the machine in the third bedroom compartment. Vega read the letter a last time.

To: The Prime Minister
The Hague, Netherlands

Sir

The photograph in this fax verifies our legitimacy.

I am responsible for the hijack of KL-4021 and the theft of twenty paintings belonging to the Vincent van Gogh Foundation. I have detained Doctor Christina Jansen to care for the paintings during our negotiations. Allow me to assure you that no harm will come to her or the paintings.

You are detaining my son, Juan Vega, in Bijlmer

Prison. My proposition is that the paintings and Doctor Jansen be returned to you once Juan has been returned to me at a place and time which I will nominate.

Juan has served two years of his sentence. He has paid a considerable debt for his small crime. He has not killed anyone. He is not a danger to society. I am sure you will agree that his release is a small price to pay for the return of your country's treasures.

I will watch for your response on CNN television.

Carlos Vega

Vega signed the bottom of the message, placed it in a large envelope and handed it to Rafael. The fourteen-digit fax number of the Office of the Prime Minister, The Hague, furnished by Willem Imthorn, was written on the outside. Rafael was instructed to send the fax at seven o'clock that night, one o'clock on Tuesday morning in the Netherlands.

9

Nelson Schoute peered out the window of the Avianca Boeing 737 as it descended over the massive Andean Cordillera Oriental towards Colombia's capital, Bogotá. It was four thirty in the afternoon, the day of the hijacking. His mind had detached itself from the traumatic events of the early morning; they swirled around him but did not touch. He would try to keep it that way, at least for now. The subconscious refusal to dwell on the experience enabled him to address his priority: helping to find Christina and the twenty van Goghs.

As the aircraft taxied to the terminal, he re-read the English translation of a press release prepared by the Venezuelan police media relations department earlier in the day. He had been too tired on his first reading to absorb it properly, but now, after a good nap on the plane, he felt refreshed. It was headed: "HIJACKING OF KLM BOEING 767 KL-4021 OVER COLOMBIA, KIDNAPPING OF CURATOR AND THEFT OF TWENTY VAN GOGH

PAINTINGS." He read carefully. "Maiquetía air traffic control was notified anonymously by phone at 08:10h, local time (12:10 GMT), that a KLM Boeing 767 designated as flight KL-4021, able to receive but not send radio signals, was on approach from the northwest with an ETA of 08:40h. At 08:15h a controller picked up an unidentified aircraft on radar which he subsequently identified as KL-4021 by having the pilot relay a code on the secondary surveillance radar, a piece of equipment carried on such aircraft to facilitate identification. The controller then guided the pilot to a direct approach while other traffic was kept away.

"Meanwhile, an administrative officer at Maiquetía contacted the airline's dispatch section at Schiphol, Netherlands, and obtained passenger and cargo manifest details. Maiquetía's fire units were placed on full alert.

"The 767 touched down without incident at 08:46h and was escorted to a parking position away from the main terminal. A team consisting of two airport police officers, a customs and immigration inspector and an airport representative went on board to investigate the nature of the aircraft's problem. They were informed by the commander, Captain Jan Bekker, that his aircraft had been hijacked and forced to land in Medellín where one of the passengers, Doctor Christina Jansen, an assistant curator at the Van Gogh Museum in Amsterdam, was kidnapped, and the cargo, consisting of twenty paintings by Vincent van Gogh, was stolen. (See attached report prepared by witness Nelson Schoute for details of the hijacking itself.)

"A team of detectives proceeded to the airport and took statements from the thirteen witnesses while officers in headquarters notified the jurisdictions of Colombia and the Netherlands as well as those in which the Falcon 50 jet used in the hijacking was most likely to have landed, namely: Haiti, the Dominican Republic, Jamaica, Puerto Rico, Cuba, Mexico, Belize, Guatemala, El Salvador, Honduras, Nicaragua, Panama, Costa Rica, the Cayman Islands, Venezuela and the Netherlands Antilles."

The release listed the names, ages and occupations of all on board the 767 when it arrived in Venezuela as well as a description of Christina Jansen and the titles of the twenty stolen paintings.

It continued: "A police forensic team took fingerprints from the surfaces of the aircraft identified by witnesses as having been touched by the men who boarded the plane. Copies of these have been forwarded to the Colombian National Police in Bogotá.

"A detailed report of the incident has been distributed worldwide via the International Criminal Police Organisation (Interpol) network.

"At the time of preparation of this statement, eleven Falcon 50 aircraft had been located in seven of the jurisdictions but none appear to have been in the vicinity of the incident this morning. The search for the Falcon and its pilot will continue."

Nelson's reading was interrupted by a flight attendant leaning over his seat. 'Mr Schoute,' she whispered. 'If you come with me, I'll get you off the plane first.' The courtesy was a consequence of his newly acquired status as liaison officer between the justice systems of Colombia and the Netherlands. Albert Voss, the director of the Vincent van Gogh Foundation, had suggested the appointment to the Dutch Minister of Justice within minutes of being informed of the hijacking and the minister had instantly agreed. Voss had also gained the Foundation's permission to offer a million dollar reward for information leading to a solution to the case.

Nelson heard his name being called as he exited the skybridge. 'Señor Schoute, Mr Schoute.' The young Colombian detective held a Dutch Ministry of Justice fax with a photograph of Nelson, an outline of his experience with the Dutch police, and various personal details including the languages he spoke: Dutch, German, French and English.

After collecting Nelson's baggage, the detective led the way out of the busy terminal to a waiting unmarked car. Once inside, he spoke his first words about the case: 'We think we know who's behind the hijacking.'

'Who?' Nelson asked, halting the seatbelt part way across his body.

'Carlos Vega, head of the Medellín cartel.' He turned the ignition.

'Carlos Vega,' Nelson murmured. 'His son is in Bijlmer.' He felt his hands go clammy. 'Of course!'

'We expect to hear from him soon.' The detective edged

68

his way into the chaotic assembly of horn-tooting vehicles. 'Have you been to Bogotá before, Nelson?' the detective asked as soon as he'd merged with the slow moving flow.

'No, but this is my second visit to Colombia,' he replied dryly, his mind still assimilating what he had just been told. 'The first was before dawn this morning.'

'Yes, señor, it was not a good introduction to my country.'

'It wasn't,' Nelson said towards the window.

'Colonel Martínez has booked you into the Nueva Granada Hotel, it is very good. And there is one thing I must warn you of, Bogotá is one of the highest cities in the world, we are on a plateau two thousand six hundred metres . . .' He swerved to miss a dilapidated Volkswagen Beetle that lurched out of a parking space in front of him, then, unperturbed, he continued the advice, '. . . above sea level. The air is very thin and many visitors suffer from altitude sickness, you must be careful for the first few days.'

'Good advice for a Dutchman,' Nelson replied, and, taking in the oblique landscape, 'Those mountains are huge.'

'They are, señor. I believe that your country has no mountains, most of it is below the level of the sea.'

'Two-fifths, anyway,' Nelson commented to be precise.

'That would be strange for me to see, señor,' the detective said with a mild chuckle. 'At present your body is used to Los Angeles at the level of the sea, so you must be careful. The advice from the doctors is that if you feel dizzy, just rest for a while. The feeling will pass. And it would not be good to drink alcohol today.'

'Okay, I won't run up any stairs to get to a bar.' The facetiousness was unintentional, Christina's predicament was playing on his mind.

'Si, señor.'

'Aeropuerto de El Dorado,' Nelson read the sign aloud as they crossed the airport perimeter. This was all impossible, he thought, far-fetched. He felt tiredness creeping up on him again. 'El Dorado, land of gold, right?'

'True, señor. I was told you didn't speak any Spanish.'

'I know about ten words, El Dorado just happens to be two of them.'

'Si,' the detective nodded with a smile and then changed to the faster moving lane on his left. 'But now the gold is not the metal, it is cocaine and heroin. Those two products account for the largest part of my country's economy.'

'So I've heard.' The traffic slowed again to a smoggy crawl.

'Central Bogotá, señor,' the detective said, pointing out a cluster of modern glass buildings piercing the brown sky ahead. Nelson took in his surroundings as they crept along. To the east, a colourless mixture of industrial buildings and slum dwellings was flanked by the spectacular lush green mountain peaks intercepting the last rays of the setting sun. To the west, more of the same with more distant mountains just visible through the smog. 'Bogotá is bigger than I imagined,' he said after a while, suppressing a yawn.

'Yes, seven million people live here, señor. It has grown very quickly and there have been many problems. The drugs are the latest. You must be careful in the streets at night, there are some areas where you must not go as a visitor, you would be robbed, maybe even murdered.'

'That's true in Amsterdam too, and Los Angeles,' Nelson replied blandly.

'Not as true as here, señor,' the detective responded, tragically certain that the murder rate in Bogotá far exceeded that in either of the cities Nelson had mentioned. 'There are many, many murders. Kidnappings too.'

'I see,' Nelson said, taking the point. 'I expected to be in Rio this afternoon, not here. All I know about Colombia is the problems I read about in the newspaper. The corruption, drugs.'

'They are the big forces in this country, the drugs cause much of the corruption.'

'When I was at school, your country was known for coffee, not cocaine. What went wrong?'

'The climate is the problem, the political climate as well as the rain and sunshine.' They passed a badly dented abandoned Renault, broken glass and plastic. 'The drug problem started in the sixties . . . with marijuana and just a little cocaine. North American criminals came down with plenty of money to invest . . . and the contacts back home to guarantee the market for their product.' They were moving quickly again. 'Their clients were the people who supplied the hippie generation.' He glanced to Nelson. 'Your generation perhaps, señor?'

71

'Not mine,' Nelson answered, flattered by the young man's low call. 'I missed that nonsense, just.'

'Just, señor?' the detective replied with a chuckle and pulled a packet of cigarettes from his pocket. 'You were lucky, or maybe unlucky.' He offered Nelson a cigarette.

'No thanks,' Nelson responded with a wave of his hand. 'Gave up years ago.' He wound down his window, photo-chemical smog rather than cigarette smoke.

The detective went on after lighting up. 'The hemp was grown in the hills, with peasant labour. The workers, they had no choice, there were no other jobs. Cheap labour, good climate, the crops thrived. The owners cut out land-ing strips so planes could pick up the product.'

'And the politicians and police were bribed to stay away?' Nelson added.

'Yes, there was much bribery,' the detective replied. 'Some army officers got their cuts too.'

'Very cosy,' Nelson commented, considering the brazen-ness of it all.

'The owners made a lot of money, but they weren't satis-fied. They started mixing other plants with the marijuana, some even mixed in horse manure.'

'Incredible!' Nelson huffed.

'They were stupid. The buyers didn't take long to work out what was going on. They got back at the producers by paying in counterfeit money. The whole business fell apart. By then, many people were dependent on crime to survive, so they turned their efforts to another drug, cocaine.'

'A bigger problem than the marijuana?' Nelson said.

'Much bigger.'

'And the suspect, Vega, he's the top man in the cocaine business in Colombia?'

'In the world, señor. He has a lot of money and much better resources than we do. And people are scared of him, so they don't come forward with information.'

The brief equatorial twilight had faded by the time they arrived at the heavily fortified police headquarters in central Bogotá. It was five thirty. The air had thickened and become grim.

After parking the car, the detective escorted Nelson upstairs and through security to his commander, Colonel Luis Martínez, chief of the Anti-Narcotics Branch of the Colombian National Police.

'Buenas tardes, Señor Schoute. Good afternoon, Nelson,' Martínez said, extending his hand. The Colombian policeman wore an immaculately presented green uniform: coat and tie, brass buttons and braid. Nelson guessed his age at early forties. 'Can I offer you a cup of my country's coffee?' Martínez gestured to a pot in the corner of the office.

'That would be wonderful,' Nelson replied. 'I need something to keep me awake.'

'It has been a long day for you, I know. With very little sleep last night, I imagine.' Martínez filled a small cup with the word "Visita" taped to it. 'I won't keep you long, you know we have a suspect?'

'Yes, Carlos Vega.'

'Vega is one of few people in Colombia with the resources to conduct such an operation.' Martínez handed Nelson his coffee. 'And I'm sure you are aware of his motive.'

'My government has his son in jail.'

'Precisely. We're still waiting to hear from him. Today I sent two of my men to Medellín to visit his house.'

'You know where he lives?' Nelson responded in amazement.

'He's not there now, of course,' Martínez replied in a detached tone. 'It may seem strange to you, Nelson, but the Medellín police have never been able to implicate Señor Vega in any crime. He's big, bigger than ten Al Capones, and he lives without fear of us.'

'But the FBI got Capone for tax evasion and sent him to Alcatraz,' Nelson said, instantly realising that his comment could be interpreted as a criticism. 'You know what I mean, can't they get him on some technicality?' he added, hoping to neutralise his faux pas.

'Señor, the corruption in Colombia is much worse than it was in Chicago in the nineteen twenties.' Martínez had not taken offence. 'Even if we arrest him, even if we got him for fifty murders, it would be almost impossible to convict him. A jury would be bribed and threatened and no judge would live to pass sentence.'

'So that's what you're up against?' Nelson said. He was a long way from the Netherlands.

'Vega is up to his ears in corruption. Bogotá air traffic control is an illustration. This morning, they did nothing when your plane failed to pass the way points listed on the flight plan. They should have reported you missing. I've had men out there all day, it's a mess. All kinds of excuses about equipment failing. We don't know who to blame, they could all be on Vega's payroll. We'll probably never get to the bottom of it.'

'They must have picked up the Falcon's radio transmissions,' Nelson added and took a first sip of the strong black. It was good.

'Maybe, but there is nothing on their tapes. We contacted Varig, Saeta and American, they had planes in the area, none heard anything. The experts think the Falcon pilot was using some kind of low power transmitter, maybe with a directional antenna, not the normal radio.'

'Vega thought of everything,' Nelson said. 'Did your men find anything at his house?'

'His wife, Margarita. She was very polite, even served them iced tea. Says she hasn't seen her husband since last night and claims to know nothing about the hijacking or where he is now.'

'Do you believe her?' Nelson felt comfortable falling back into the role of detective.

'It would have been risky for Vega to tell her, he knows we'll be watching her like a hawk watches its prey.' Martínez pulled open a desk drawer. 'Our reports to Interpol on Vega.' He handed Nelson a worn manila folder opening it first to show a five year old photograph of the man. 'They're in Spanish and English, everything else we have is just in Spanish. You can read them in the morning.'

'I'll look at them now, if that's okay?' Nelson was anxious to learn as much as possible about the man who had Christina at his mercy.

'Certainly.' Martínez showed Nelson to a desk that had been cleared for his use. The reports outlined Vega's rise from relative obscurity to his present position at the top of the Medellín cartel. Besides the drug dealing across four continents, he was also suspected of involvement in the murders of judges, politicians, police, other criminals and seemingly innocent people. Although nothing could be pinned directly on him, almost every crime listed in the reports had, in one way or another, protected his interests or led to the expansion of his empire. Nelson's experience in the Dutch police had not prepared him to deal with such a person.

One hundred and fifty kilometres to the northwest, Vega's man, Rafael, turned off busy Carrera Balboa into the deserted carpark of Iglesia de San Francisco, his headlights landing squarely on a stark white statue of the Virgin Mary. It was two minutes to seven. He quickly threaded Vega's ransom demand into the battery-powered fax machine on the seat next to him, entered the number printed on the envelope into the attached phone and sent the fax on its way. He turned the phone off the instant the transmission was complete, blessed himself and left.

One of five fax machines in the communications room of the Office of the Prime Minister in The Hague whirred to life. It was exactly one o'clock in the morning. The single staff member monitoring communication from Dutch embassies and other governments in the two-thirds of the world that was awake picked up the phone the instant she saw Christina Jansen's photograph.

The Prime Minister's principal secretary answered on the second ring. After hearing the origin and contents of the fax, he asked that copies be sent to his home as well as to the residences of the Prime Minister and the Minister of Justice. Then, almost as an afterthought, he asked that she clearly print the originating fax number at the bottom of her copy and fax the page to police headquarters in Bogotá for the attention of Nelson Schoute. In strict protocol terms, that task was the responsibility of the Minister of Justice, but he knew her well enough to take the initiative. Those wheels in motion, he woke the Prime Minister.

'It's Christina for sure,' Nelson said to Martínez of the photograph in Vega's fax. 'It's genuine.'

Martínez called out the originating number to an officer at a computer terminal before handing the sheet to Nelson to read.

'Belongs to Señor José Montenegro,' the officer at the

computer reported a short time later. 'He bought it last December, here in Bogotá. Hasn't been used before tonight.'

'Give Señor Montenegro the full treatment,' Martínez ordered and returned to his desk.

'Can you trace a mobile phone?' Nelson asked as he sat down across from Martínez.

'We can find which antenna is being used instantly, the exact location takes a little time. But Vega won't fall into that trap, he'll move, change phones. He knows how we got Escobar . . . stayed still too long talking to his son.'

'I see,' Nelson said, the image of Pablo Escobar's body on a roof flashing across his mind. He hadn't remembered the story leading to the inglorious end.

'And you and I already know what we'll find at Señor Montenegro's home.'

'No Señor Montenegro,' Nelson replied and lay the fax on the desk. 'So, now we wait for the Prime Minister's response.' Nelson checked his watch and did the arithmetic. 'It's one fifteen in the morning in The Hague so nothing will happen for at least seven or eight hours.' Dizziness overtook him as he got up too quickly. 'Woo!' he said, easing himself back into the chair.

'It's the altitude,' Martínez said and poured a glass of water. 'You must do things slowly for a few days, until your body adjusts.' He passed the glass across the desk.

'Good advice,' Nelson replied after drinking the water. The light headedness was fading quickly.

'Do you have any idea how your government will react?' Martínez asked once he was sure Nelson was okay.

'The Dutch stand has always been strongly against dealing with terrorists,' Nelson replied. 'But this is peculiar. Nobody is being threatened with physical violence, nothing is going to be destroyed. That is, according to Vega.' He looked to Martínez. 'For whatever that's worth.'

'Not much, señor,' Martínez quipped and poured more water for Nelson.

'Vega's men on the plane were very careful not to hurt anyone. They told us why. Maybe my government will be willing to come to a compromise, perhaps to extradite Juan Vega to Colombia.'

'There's no extradition treaty between our countries,' Martínez said. 'But if something could be arranged, and his son was moved to a jail here, it would give Vega the opportunity to break him out. That would be possible for him to do.'

'It would get him what he wants,' Nelson remarked.

'It would, but I think Vega will want more, he's holding some very good cards.' He opened the Interpol file still on his desk. 'Something interesting happened tonight, Nelson.' He tapped Vega's photograph. 'Tonight, Señor Vega admitted to committing a crime. Finally, we have something to charge him with.' Then, tossing the file onto the desk, 'If we ever find him, that is, and then get a judge willing to hear the case.'

'I'm glad there's a bright side to all this,' Nelson said.

'There's not though,' Martínez responded quickly. 'All it means is that Vega must vanish.'

'Sorry Luis, I'm still a bit slow.'

'Vega will have to leave, but not yet. At the moment he's safest where he has power, that's here.'

'You've got people at the borders watching out for him, I presume? Just in case.'

'At the ports, airports and borders. But don't forget, Vega owns people in those places.'

'A slippery snake,' Nelson commented.

'I'm sure Señor Vega has a nice hacienda in the mountains of Paraguay or Bolivia or somewhere like that, just waiting for him.'

'Out of your jurisdiction, Luis, out of your hair.'

'True, but the drug barons are like weeds. One gets cut out and another pops up to take his place.'

Nelson already felt a degree of admiration for the Colombian policeman. He had a tough and dangerous job to do and seemed to be doing it.

An hour later Nelson was in his hotel room preparing for bed. Searching his bag for a toothbrush, he came upon a family photograph, a recent one, the second grandchild on his knee. He knew that his wife, who he'd phoned this morning from Venezuela, would be worried sick for him and Christina. He would call her again in the morning. Had things gone according to plan, she and their youngest daughter were to visit him in Rio in three weeks time. Vega had sure ruined that.

At nine o'clock CNN broadcast a brief report updating the Van Gogh Hijack story, as it was now known. It included pictures of the 767 still on the tarmac in Caracas and an interview with Jan Bekker outlining the popular hypothesis that the flight management system had been subjected to some kind of interference. There was no mention of Vega's fax to the Dutch Prime Minister.

Nelson turned off the television and found much needed sleep.

His phone rang at four twenty. The Dutch Minister of Justice had just come out of a meeting with the Prime Minister, the director of the Vincent van Gogh Foundation and the head of the Special Branch of the Dutch police. She spoke quickly: 'Of course, no decision on the demand was reached, Mr Schoute. The Prime Minister needs to consult with Cabinet and some of the other European leaders. The policy is not to deal with terrorists. Countries that do, get targeted again. It's a path we cannot go down, Mr Schoute. We need more time to assess the situation. Vega expects to wait a while anyway.'

'You plan on stalling him, Minister, is that what you're saying?'

'More or less, Mr Schoute. That will give the Colombian police some time at least to track him down. We won't push our luck though. The Prime Minister will make an announcement at three o'clock this afternoon stating that the contents of the fax will be considered and that an answer will be forthcoming. He will stress that the people of the Netherlands wish no harm to come to either the paintings or Doctor Jansen.' She paused for an instant. 'Do you have any thoughts on what I've said, Mr Schoute?'

'Minister, only that Vega is not threatening violence, that may affect your decision.'

'Yes, we're aware of that, it will be considered. We're viewing his demand as an opening statement. We expect there will be room for negotiation, there always is.'

The conversation ended with the Minister informing Nelson that an envoy was on his way to Bogotá with letters to the President from the Queen and Prime Minister requesting cooperation at the highest level. She instructed Nelson to accompany him on his visit to the Colombian head of state.

Four hours later, Nelson was back in Martínez's office. Now it was the Colombian who looked tired. After hearing Nelson's summary of the conversation with the Minister of Justice, Martínez outlined the overnight events in Medellín, his despondent tone betraying the results: 'Before dawn this morning, we executed eight simultaneous raids on the homes of various acquaintances of Vega. The men I sent up there yesterday went on one of them. Unfortunately, they discovered nothing of either the paintings or Doctor Jansen.' He tossed his pen onto the desk. 'At this stage, I'm afraid, we have very little to go on.'

At five minutes before nine, Martínez turned on his television in anticipation of the announcement by the Dutch Prime Minister. He expected that Carlos Vega would also be watching.

10

Carlos Vega didn't finish his breakfast. That was unusual. He sat with Pedro and two of the guards at the dining table in the second apartment. The television, tuned to CNN, was showing highlights of a football match in Italy while the superimposed box switched between the building's carpark and lobby cameras. Vega was not at all interested in the play. That too was unusual. The inactivity in the smaller picture was, at least, reassuring. Vega had thought up the design for the surveillance system himself and was pleased with the result. The guards liked it too. It allowed them to combine work and recreation. As long as the security picture was never neglected and one of the two sets in the apartment with an attached video recorder was tuned to CNN, they were able to watch whatever they liked.

Soon after nine o'clock, the Van Gogh Hijack logo appeared on the screen. The female anchor paraphrased the text of Vega's ransom note while a picture of it was shown and gradually enlarged until the blurred image of Christina Jansen holding "Agostina Segatori in the Café du Tambourin" filled the screen. A five year old photograph of Vega, unclear because of the degree of magnification, then appeared as she detailed his background using the title "Cocaine and heroin baron" to describe him.

She then crossed to The Hague where the Dutch Prime Minister, Pieter de Groot, a robust-looking man in his sixties, appeared standing behind a lectern. He read a prepared statement. It was exactly what Vega had expected: a meaningless address, a ploy to pacify him and gain time in the hope that he would be found. He knew that stalling would be part of the Dutch government's game. He also knew that he could hurry negotiations along any time he chose to do so. But for now, he would wait. A slow start to the process suited him, there were still details to finalise.

'I spoke with Her Majesty earlier today,' the Prime Minister said, folding the statement. 'She expressed her concern over the safety of Doctor Jansen and the paintings and asked to be kept up to date on progress in the case.' He walked off without answering any questions.

'We have their attention,' Vega said, clasping his hands together as he moved from the set. 'But, Prime Minister, do not stall too long.'

Fifteen minutes later, Vega was five kilometres from the building in the back of a Ford van, the escort vehicles in place ahead and behind. As Rafael drove, Vega, using a succession of six separate phones, spoke with the cartel members who had visited his house on Saturday. The calls were to ensure that the merchandise they were to supply was ready and also to show that "the Pope", as he was called by them, was still in control. In the course of the brief coded conversations, he was told of the early morning police raids, which, because of tip-offs from within the police force itself, had caused no significant damage.

Without exception, the six cartel members admired the audacity of Vega's actions and had a certain sympathy for his cause. It was only natural for a father to do everything in his power to rescue his son. They all knew Juan as a very determined young man, a young man whose blood gave him the unique ability to defy Carlos Vega and live. Juan's plane crash in the Caribbean had cost each of them over four hundred thousand dollars in lost profit. None had ever complained. Over the years, Vega's pipeline had successfully landed over ninety-eight percent of their product on the streets of North America and Europe and made them all very wealthy in the process. For now, Vega would not be betrayed. None of them wished to disturb a system that worked so well and, certainly, none of them wished to die the death of a traitor.

Christina had been busy since breakfast writing an account of the events to date pausing only to watch the reports on CNN. She was thankful that whoever searched her bag on Monday had left the writing materials she'd packed to use on the plane. She hoped that one day soon she would see the diary used as evidence at her captor's trial; or, considering the worst outcome, if she didn't survive and it was later found by the authorities, both they and her loved ones would gain some insight into what had happened. She wrote in Dutch on both sides of the paper in small print.

'Doctor Jansen,' Pedro called from outside, unlocking but not opening the door, 'Carlos wishes to see you.' Responding that she would be right down, she went about secreting the pages under a corner of the carpet she'd pried loose for that purpose. That done, she left for the living area, taking her breakfast tray with her: the fewer reasons anyone had to enter her room, the better.

'Buenos dìas, Christina,' Vega said from the couch. 'Did you sleep well?'

'Quite well.' She put the tray down and went across to inspect the painting.

'And was your breakfast satisfactory?'

'Very nice, thanks.' As far as she could tell, the painting had not been touched. Vega's men had got the message.

'I shall pass on the compliment.' The meals were prepared by one of the men who had been hired on the basis of his ability to cook as well as kill. As compensation for his efforts in the kitchen, he was rarely asked to do guard duty. 'Your Prime Minister was on television,' Vega said and directed her to sit next to him on the couch.

'I saw him.' She shifted a large floral cushion from the corner so she could sit at the very end, farthest from him.

'He's stalling.'

'Does that surprise you?' She, too, had seen de Groot's statement as a ploy.

'It suits me, for now,' Vega replied with a shrug. 'Anyway, señorita, that is not why I asked to see you.' He leaned in her direction, his arm hanging over the back of the couch. 'You have had some time to become used to your surroundings. By now, you will realise that escape is impossible.'

'I know,' she replied, 'I'm trapped, like an animal in a very comfortable cage.'

'Don't think that, señorita. You are here as a curator, the paintings are my bargaining chips, not you.'

'Then why is my advice ignored? I wanted the paintings in their cases, not on the wall.'

'Christina, that topic is dead, forget it.' Then, leaning closer, 'I have a proposition.'

'Go on,' she responded apprehensively, pulling the cushion closer to her body.

'I would like you to feel free within the apartment, to join me out here, to read on the couch, or watch television. At times, you may even like to visit the other apartment.'

'Good.' His concessions had caught her by surprise. 'I detest being locked in that room.' The more she saw, the more she heard, the greater her chance of finding a weakness in the system that might allow her to get a message out.

'The provisos are that you do nothing to jeopardise my

plans, and you must not cause trouble with my men. If any of them cause you trouble, tell me and I will fix it.'

'Sounds fair,' she replied. 'And you know I have no intention of trying to escape, not while you have the paintings?'

'Very sensible,' he said, massaging his unshaven chin. 'Of course, at night and when I am conducting business, you will be locked in your room.' Then, pointing to the wall mounted phone, 'By the way, the phone and intercom go through the security system across the hall.'

'I'm not surprised.' She had always assumed there was a block on those obvious temptations.

'It's agreed then.' He extended his hand. She accepted it, hugging the cushion with the other. 'I would like you to join me for lunch at one o'clock. If between now and then you could select another painting, we will have something pleasant to talk about while we eat.'

'Can I visit the other apartment now?' She was determined not to waste any time. 'I could do with a change of scenery.'

'You may,' he replied, pleased to see her seemingly appeased. 'It will be good for my men too, they are unused to women of culture.' He took her across the hallway and handed guardianship to Pedro.

The decor in the second apartment was radically different from that in Vega's: cluttered with the stink of cigarette smoke, were Christina's immediate impressions. The three couches were occupied by guards recharging their machismo from an Arnold Schwarzennegger video. They glanced away from the mayhem just long enough to greet her. The coffee tables and dining table were littered with assorted breakfast plates, coffee cups and overfull ashtrays. 'This place could use a good clean,' she said to Pedro.

'Si, señorita, there are too many men living in here. And their mothers did not teach them how to clean.' He repeated the last part in Spanish loud enough for the men to hear. They responded with jeers. Each was fully aware of the mess but none was willing to be the first to do anything about it. Cleaning was a woman's job.

Before showing Christina to the table, Pedro explained the main components of the security system. 'The system is to warn of an attack, but, as you see, it also . . .'

'Prevents me from escaping, which I'm not going to do anyway,' she interrupted. Then at Pedro's invitation, she took a seat at the table.

'One thing, Doctor Jansen,' Pedro said as he shifted the plates and cups from in front of her, 'Carlos hears a sound in his head, from a bomb, all the time. Sometimes, with the pressure, it makes him impatient, he loses his temper. I have seen it many times. Be careful how you speak to him, I would not like any harm to come to you.' She recoiled when he placed his hand on her shoulder, an automatic response that caught Pedro by surprise. Although he seemed a very gentle man and had been kind to her, she knew he had to have another side, an ugly side. As Vega's right hand man, he must have killed, many times.

Pedro mumbled that he would get some coffee and moved quickly and awkwardly towards the kitchen. His embarrassed reaction intrigued her, she still had some power after all.

He returned with a tray containing two coffees, sugar and milk and asked her about her stay in Los Angeles, a city he had visited several times himself. To Christina, it was an unproductive topic and after a few banal reflections, she steered the conversation elsewhere. 'How did you get involved in this horrible drug business, Pedro?' she asked while adding milk to her cup. 'You don't seem the type.'

He laughed and opened up, just as she'd hoped. 'It happened many years ago when I was much, much younger. I had a business growing roses for export to the United States and Canada. It was a good business.' He paused and offered her a cigarette which she refused. He lit one for himself and continued after vigorously exhaling the first puff. 'One day, a man who I had not seen before came and offered to deliver my roses to the airport. It was Carlos. He said he would pay me one hundred American dollars. Of course, I knew he was going to smuggle and I knew it would be drugs. But since I would not be the one doing the smuggling, the danger to me was small. So I agreed. From that day on, Carlos came every day and picked up the roses, and paid me.'

'And put cocaine in with them on the way to the airport?' she tacked on, soliciting redundant material for her diary.

91

'It was a good way to smuggle the merchandise. Because they would perish, the roses were handled quickly when they arrived, and Carlos would put merchandise in only two or three boxes out of the shipment, so the chance of being caught was low.' He interrupted his smoking to take another sip of coffee. 'Other times, Carlos sent merchandise with fish.' He laughed. 'It was stuffed inside the fish.' He demonstrated by pushing air into his cupped hand.

'Clever,' she said, pretending to be impressed. She was onto the formula: reinforcement of bravado equals more information. 'But if people do that kind of thing for long enough, they're bound to get caught. How come Carlos wasn't caught?'

'His man in New York was, he went to jail. But nothing happened here. The police came and saw me. I told them I knew nothing and they went away.'

'Did Carlos pay them a bribe?'

'Bribes are part of life here, señorita, unavoidable.' He tapped the ash from his cigarette onto a saucer. 'The American customs started to look more carefully at flowers and fish. Other importers were caught, so Carlos made another plan.' Pedro's expression broadcast his genuine pride in Vega's adaptability. 'Every month I would visit my customers in the United States and carry merchandise with me. Carlos paid me three thousand dollars per trip.'

'And the cocaine, it was in a secret compartment in your suitcase?'

'Sometimes, señorita. There are people in Medellín who

are expert at hiding drugs in anything you give them. Radios, shaving cream containers, artificial legs, anything. They are called fabricators. The fabricator who worked for Carlos was the best. I saw her working once. She would cut out the lining of a suitcase with a scalpel, just like a surgeon.' He mimicked the delicate cutting procedure as he spoke. 'Then she would glue thin plastic bags of merchandise all around inside. When she put the lining back, . . .' He looked to Christina as if revealing a miracle. 'Señorita, you could not tell that the suitcase had been touched. With this woman there were never any signs of cuts or glue.'

'You were still lucky not to be caught.' She wished he had been caught, that they had all been caught. He wasn't telling the story of smuggling drugs, it was a story of death and despair.

'I was a charmed mule, señorita.' He held his hands to his head making mule-like ears. She laughed, thinking it a worthwhile investment. 'The demand was smaller in those days. Now Carlos does not bother with mules, now he sends merchandise across by the plane load, hundreds of kilograms at a time.'

'So you no longer take the risk, the pilot does.'

'I have taken enough risks for one lifetime, señorita. I have been stabbed and shot. Look.' He lifted his shirt and pointed out both scars.

'You should have stayed growing roses,' she replied, glancing at the ugly scars.

'Maybe, señorita. That is what my wife says.' He downed the last mouthful of coffee. 'I must leave now, I have a surprise I must get for you.'

'What surprise?' She prayed she hadn't been too friendly, sent the wrong signal. The prospect of an amorous advance from any of the men worried her.

'You will see at lunchtime,' he responded with a wry smile and extinguished his cigarette. On the way out he told one of the guards to take her back across the hall when she asked.

Ten minutes later, she was back in her bedroom adding the main points of her conversation with Pedro to her diary.

At noon, CNN broadcast an update on the hijack story. The anchor announced that a team of computer experts had found the source of the problem that caused the 767's engines to fail over Colombia. Boeing's chief electronic engineer appeared on the screen and, prompted by the anchor, gave a report.

'We discovered a virus in the flight management computers. It was triggered to act when the navigation system relayed the information that the aircraft was crossing a specific line of longitude, seventy-seven degrees west, just to the west of Medellín. The virus caused the flight management system to send a signal to the auto-throttle telling it to cut fuel to the engines.'

The anchor confirmed her understanding of the situation, at the same time simplifying it for the less attentive members of the audience: 'So when the plane crossed that line of longitude, the virus cut fuel to the engines?'

'Yes,' the engineer replied. 'The virus was in two of the three computers. If it had just been in one, that computer would have been overruled.'

'The computers take a kind of vote?'

'Right, two out of three wins.'

'How long were the engines shut down?' the anchor asked.

'The virus cut out eight nautical miles east of where it cut in. At the speed they were travelling, that would take . . . just over a minute. The altitude loss was about three thousand feet, so there was no real danger.'

'But the pilots didn't have the benefit of that information.'

'No, I imagine they were quite scared.'

'Wouldn't the aircraft have crossed that same line of longitude on the way from Amsterdam to Los Angeles on Sunday? And wouldn't that seem to indicate that the virus was planted in Los Angeles?'

'To answer the first part, yes. It did cross seventy-seven west, over northern Canada. But the virus was designed to work only if longitude and latitude were both decreasing when it crossed the line. In other words, it remained dormant until the plane crossed seventy-seven west while flying to the southeast. On the way out of course, the aircraft was going southwest when it crossed the line.'

'Ingenious,' the anchor remarked.

'Your point about Los Angeles. KLM has found the virus

in all its 767s, so it was probably put in the computers in Amsterdam during the last system update a couple of weeks ago.'

'And no other KLM planes followed that same route in the meantime?'

'No, this was a one-off charter. They don't normally fly southeast from the west coast of North America.'

'Someone went to a great deal of trouble to set this up,' the anchor commented before thanking and farewelling the engineer.

She then interviewed a spokesperson for KLM in Amsterdam who said that the 767 was now on its way back to Schiphol with only the pilots on board, adding that they would be flying it under manual control. She went on to say that the flight management systems on all the company's planes were being reprogrammed; most had already been done. When asked, she confirmed that the company was cooperating with the Dutch police in an effort to find the person responsible for planting the virus.

Christina was both impressed and disturbed by the findings revealed in the report. A man who had gone to such incredible measures to get his plan this far would not be easy to fool or trap. She hoped the Dutch government was not considering trying either.

At a quarter to one, she went into the third bedroom and found the large case marked TPE, the painting in the collection she admired most. No longer overly concerned about the safety of the paintings on display, she decided that a little self-indulgence would do no harm. This painting would probably have to come out sometime anyway, it might as well be today. She took it down to the living area along with the empty case from yesterday.

As she was returning "Agostina Segatori in the Café du Tambourin" to its case, Pedro came into the room carrying two chrome posts. Josef followed with a length of velvet rope. 'Señorita, your new barricade,' Pedro announced with an accompanying dramatic pose. 'It will be better than the chairs, more classy.' She watched as they and the duty guard removed the chairs that had acted as the temporary barricade and assembled the cordon. 'I got it from a compadre in the bank,' Pedro explained. 'Now his customers will not feel like sheep when they line up.'

'It's perfect,' she smiled. 'Thanks.'

Christina took out the new painting and had Pedro steady it while she attached a length of wire across its back. Meanwhile, at her direction, Josef installed the second wall hook fifty centimetres from the first and level with it.

'It reduces the lateral pressure on the frame,' she replied to a query from Pedro concerning the reason for two hooks. Once the picture was hung, Pedro and Josef set the cordon in place and left.

A short time later, Miguel, the guard who doubled as cook brought in a tray containing lunch. He greeted her politely in Spanish and went about arranging things on the table.

Vega appeared at one o'clock and dismissed the duty

guard. 'A more impressive picture than the one yesterday,' he said, strolling towards the new work.

'They found your computer virus,' she said. 'Very clever.'

'I saw the report, my programmers did a good job.'

'And if they hadn't?'

'Your plane had a little cold,' he replied, toying with the velvet rope. 'Nothing serious at all.' Then, turning his attention to the painting, 'A dark painting of ugly people. Is that your mood Christina? Why not some sunflowers, isn't that what van Gogh is famous for?'

'They were a small part of Vincent's work,' she said, moving to the metal post beside him.

'You see how ignorant I am of your hero,' Vega said with a laugh. 'You must continue to enlighten me.' He was finding it refreshing to be with someone willing to disagree with him. Christina's intelligence, attractiveness and, above all, her vulnerability added to the pleasure.

'This is one of Vincent's earlier works. The bright colours came later.'

'And the name of this dark painting?'

'"The Potato Eaters".'

He examined it in silence. She entered the painted scene: the small and dark peasant kitchen with its wooden beams and simple furniture; a single oil lamp illuminating the table and the solemn faces of the four peasants seated around it. On the right, an older heavy-featured woman in a dark dress and white bonnet pours from a pot into four small cups; her weathered-faced husband holds his cup towards her in expectation. A younger couple on the left reach with their forks for the chopped up boiled potato that is their meal; she looks, perhaps speaks, to him. In the foreground, a child stands facing sideways, her features not visible, the light reflecting off her neck and cheek and glowing around her form.

'These people are very poor,' Vega muttered, breaking her contemplation.

'Simple peasants, but honest.'

'Are you sure they were honest?' Vega said. 'The man could be a forger, the child a pickpocket. How would you know?'

'I don't. The family was known to Vincent, he admired them, so one would assume they were fairly honest.'

'There are not many saints in this world, that is my experience. The most honest person can be corrupted, I have seen it happen many times.'

'I don't accept that everyone is corruptible,' she answered. 'There are saints in this world.'

'And you are one of them?'

'No, but I am honest. I don't cheat people, I don't hurt them.'

'Everyone has a price, Christina, everyone. If I offered you a million dollars to take a small package of cocaine back to the Netherlands, would you do it?'

'You'd be losing money. You wouldn't make the offer.'

'But suppose I did?'

'No, I wouldn't do it,' she answered with conviction.

'Your price may be something else, something altruistic . . . an operation for a close relative, getting a friend out of trouble, a job at a museum.'

'You could find something for everyone if you looked deeply enough.' Vega was right, she knew it. She'd side-lined her scruples in the past to get what she wanted. Small failures but failures none the less. Taking a bicycle when hers was stolen to meet a boyfriend on time; embellishing her then scant résumé to get the first museum job. Minor things. The bicycle was returned, the résumé lies were white, no one was hurt. 'There would be a right time, a right set of circumstances for everyone, me included.'

'Which is exactly my point, señorita,' he said with a grin. 'None of us is totally black or totally white, we are all shades of grey.' He turned to meet her eyes. 'What is impor-tant to me now is survival, to leave this job, alive, and with my family. That is all I want to do.'

She hoped he meant what he said. If he exited quietly, it seemed probable that she would too. 'Too bad you got into this business in the first place.'

'Temptation, Christina. In Colombia there are many temptations, many opportunities.'

'There are legal opportunities too.'

'True,' Vega nodded. 'My father wanted me to run the family business, breeding race horses. I wanted to be a civil engineer. An honest profession, eh?'

'As honest as they come,' she replied.

'I went to university. One semester, I went to Miami . . .

with a kilo of Medellín cocaine strapped to my body.' He patted the small of his back as he said it.

'That's where it started?'

'The money I earned paid for parties, girls. I was hooked.'

'Too bad. You could have done something constructive for your country, instead of this.'

'You are naive, señorita, the product of a sheltered Dutch life. I did not start this drug business, it has a life of its own, the biggest business in Colombia. I merely jumped on board, for the ride.'

'Horse breeders and engineers don't need twenty bodyguards.'

'All wealthy people in Colombia need bodyguards, Christina. The poor do too, but they can't afford them.'

'This place is crazy,' she said, raking her fingers through her hair.

'You know nothing of South America, Christina. To survive here, one must have money and power. Colombia is not Holland, Colombia is not a welfare state.'

'I know from the newspapers that there's a lot of money here, rotten money, in just a few hands.'

'Yes, and people starve in the street, people are murdered on a whim, people disappear, their body parts are sold . . . kidneys, lungs . . . you can order them to measure.' He moved closer to her, face to face. 'I am, I am sure, the first big criminal you have met, up close, eye to eye.' She stayed put, returning his stare. 'Remember, no one is all bad,

Christina, not even me. No one is all good, not even you. I have given millions to charity, to hospitals, to schools, to the church. What have you done? Bad and good?' He turned and moved to the table. 'Come, our lunch will be cold.'

'Did I hear that correctly?' she asked sceptically as she unfolded her napkin. 'You give money to schools and charity?'

'Millions, señorita.' Vega, like Escobar before him, was not immune to the poverty he saw around him. 'There are parts of this city where I am a hero.'

'The Robin Hood of the Andes,' she said as he poured some wine.

'No one has called me that before,' he responded with a short laugh. 'Colombia is my country, señorita, it has suffered centuries of imperialism. It still does, American imperialism. I do what I can to help the poor.'

'And the poor protect you, they don't help the police.'

'The police rule their lives, señorita. If I donated nothing, they would not help the police.' He waved his fork in the direction of the painting. 'I would rather talk about your painting.'

'I really can't believe you're interested. This is just a game, isn't it?'

'No game, señorita. Please, I want to hear what you have to say.'

'Okay,' she said and sipped some wine. Pleasant, but one glass would be enough. 'Vincent painted it in 1885, in

Nuenen. It's a picture of peasants as they were . . . rough. He made no attempt to hide their coarseness.' She paused to remove a piece of crab from her salad and search for others. 'Would you tell the cook not to serve me crab again, or shrimp, or oysters? I have an allergy, I get very sick.' It was an allergy that had once almost cost her her life; an experience she was not anxious to repeat, especially in these circumstances. 'You'd have to take me to hospital.' She knew he wouldn't, or couldn't.

'I will tell Miguel myself, you must not get sick. Can you eat normal fish, like tuna?'

'Yes, just nothing that lives in a shell or crawls.'

'I understand,' Vega said as he scooped the pile of crab from her plate and dropped it into a small dish.

Satisfied she had got the last of it, she continued her explanation, 'Vincent believed that a peasant girl was more beautiful than a lady, that a peasant girl lost her charm when she changed her patchy work dress with its delicate hues of faded colour for her Sunday best for church. He loved the texture of the peasants, he wanted "The Potato Eaters" to smell of smoke and potato steam.'

'So this painting is a special one?' he asked, probing. Her fervour had betrayed her.

'One of the most important, some would argue, the most important. Vincent spent a couple of years preparing for it.'

He wiped his mouth with his napkin. 'Then, tell me Christina, why did you choose to take it out of the safety of its case?' He grinned like a cat should when it catches a

mouse. 'Why didn't you just put up one of the less important paintings and keep this one out of the danger you keep
telling me about? I wouldn't have known the difference.'
The cat playing with the mouse. 'Perhaps, Christina, you
are taking full advantage of this chance to indulge your
passion.' He refilled his glass waiting for the defence he was
sure would come.

'I have to do something to take my mind off all this.'
The excuse failed to convince even her. Vega was right, she
knew it, he had caught her out. She cursed herself for being
so stupid.

'I'm not complaining.' He laughed, raising his glass to
toast her. 'Salud! I'm impressed, I'm beginning to like you.'

She detested the way he had manipulated the conversation, she detested him. Her retaliation was instinctive,
ignited by the anger she felt towards herself. 'Well I could
never like you. You deal in death. It all looks very clean,
but you know and I know that, every day, people die to
make you rich!' She could hear her voice raised, but was
powerless to check it. 'They die in Colombia, they die in
America, they die in the Netherlands . . . my cousin died
from your drugs, just nineteen years old. How do you deal
with that, Carlos? How does it feel to be a murderer?'

His smile had dissolved. He spoke slowly, in a controlled
voice, all the time twisting the base of his glass against the
table. 'You think you know my business, you don't. My
business succeeds not because I'm a dangerous criminal, it
succeeds because of the illegality of cocaine in the United

States and other countries. The government of the United States keeps me in business, they are my partners.' He pushed the glass aside. 'I feed the decadence of that country and others and the governments, including yours, help me all the way. And the big banks too, addicted to the drug money spinning around the world. My cocaine provides a little harmless euphoria, a sense of wellbeing. It causes fewer deaths than alcohol or tobacco . . . or automobiles, yet, I am the villain. Not so, Christina. I would be out of business tomorrow if the politicians had the courage to legalise these drugs. Or even call the banks to account.'

'The euphoria business, sure! A wonderful rationalisation. Do you know how many lives, how many families, your little taste of euphoria has cost?'

'Christina, you should stick to discussing art, you are much better at that.' Then, leaning across, he grasped her arm. 'You are a very attractive and intelligent woman and you have the opportunity to do what no one else in Colombia would dare do, question me. But let me warn you now, do not push me too far. Señorita!' He stood and left the room.

Her eyes filled with tears. She had never felt so small, so helpless, in her life.

11

The fresh-faced Dutchman seated beside Nelson Schoute in the government Mercedes on its way to the Palacio de Nariño, unclenched his fists to let the air at his sweat covered palms. Simon Andriessen had never been more nervous nor more excited in his life. The thirty-seven year old Utrecht and Princeton educated bureaucrat had been chosen by his superiors in the foreign affairs ministry to act as emissary because of his fluency in Spanish, his academic qualifications in South American affairs, and his immediate availability. At his side he held his own leather briefcase containing the letters he was to hand to the Colombian President: one from Queen Beatrix, the other from Prime Minister de Groot. The task before him was intimidating but simple. It was also crucial: the life of a Dutch citizen and the survival of twenty of his country's most treasured works of art were at stake.

'The new Palacio de Justica,' Andriessen guessed upon catching a glimpse of the modern building on Plaza Bolívar.

'Nice work.' This was Andriessen's second visit to Colombia, the first had been as a student in the late eighties. 'I saw the old one, after the army blasted it to bits.'

'You know something I don't,' Nelson said, noticing the modern building on the northern end of the historic square for the first time. The topic of the old Palace of Justice had not come up in his two days in Bogotá.

'It was on television,' Andriessen said and proceeded with the recent history: 'In the eighties, guerillas backed by Pablo Escobar stormed the palace and took the Supreme Court hostage. Fourteen judges, I think. It was the day the Court was to make a ruling on extradition of drug criminals to the United States. Escobar didn't want that. A grave in Colombia rather than a prison cell in the United States was the way he saw it. Anyway, the Colombian army came in and ended the siege, they shelled the place. All the judges were killed along with the terrorists, some soldiers too. The building was destroyed.'

'Quite an overreaction,' Nelson murmured as they came to a stop behind crookedly parked police cars, flashing lights. Burning tyres blocked the other side of the road.

'Student demonstration,' Andriessen said. 'The government has just increased the tax on bank transactions.'

'You are well briefed,' Nelson said. The wind changed and blew the black smoke their way. 'That explains the long queues I saw outside the banks yesterday.' Helmeted police pushed three youths up against a wall and began searching them. 'Why are they the ones protesting?'

'They're always the ones,' Andriessen replied. 'Their parents are too afraid to protest. Colombia's a republic, Nelson, born from the blood of these people's ancestors. As for civil rights . . . well, they aren't quite what we have at home.' A fire truck appeared from a side street. 'And the police, I wonder what they think of this, their wages are dismal.'

'An open door for corruption,' Nelson commented as he watched a handcuffed student being bundled into a police van.

'Poorly educated, too,' Andriessen added. 'Makes it worse, same with the military. To be a policeman or a soldier is a very low job. The security guards outside the banks and businesses are much better off, better trained too.'

'It's a worry,' Nelson said. The fires were out, the pungent smell remained.

'Everyone back in The Hague is scared to death about this situation,' Andriessen continued a short time later. 'If the army finds Vega first, there's no telling what will happen.'

'I presume de Groot has made that concern clear to the President.' A policeman waved them on.

'He certainly has, I hope the man takes notice. According to our intelligence reports, he's relatively honest. His election campaign wasn't funded by the cartels, that's an improvement on at least one of his predecessors.'

The Mercedes veered from the main traffic flow and came to a stop at a military checkpoint at the side of the

Palacio de Nariño. After an identification check and a search of the car's trunk and engine compartment, they were allowed to proceed. It was ten minutes to two o'clock, they were on time.

An army captain, heavy with ribbons and medals, met the car at the palace door and escorted them inside, along a grand hallway decked with imposing South American art to a small ornately furnished waiting room. A middle-aged sergeant stood from a chair just inside the door and saluted. The captain returned the salute and, turning to the visitors, apologised for the security check they would have to undergo before meeting the President. He explained that it was a routine procedure to which all visitors, even members of Congress, were subjected. After receiving the go ahead from his superior, the sergeant, clearly chosen for the sensitive task because of his polite and cheerful manner, waved a metal detector over both visitor's bodies, frisked them and checked Andriessen's briefcase. That done, the captain took them back along the hallway towards a pair of elaborately carved wooden doors flanked by gold-trimmed Colombian flags. Two soldiers armed with submachine guns came to attention as they approached. The captain ushered the two visitors inside, past a secretary and several more guards and into another flag-flanked office.

The President, dwarfed by the large oak desk he was sitting behind, put down the papers he was perusing and came around the desk towards them. 'Buenas tardes,' he said, beaming a wide smile. He looked older than in his photographs widely displayed in the city and had a noticeable limp, the result of a wound sustained in an assassination attempt during his election campaign. He spoke in Spanish. 'Señor Andriessen, Señor Schoute, welcome to Colombia.' He extended his hand to Nelson first. 'I regret that your visits have been caused by such an unfortunate occurrence.'

'Thank you for seeing us, Your Excellency,' Andriessen replied nervously.

The President picked up a box of cigars from his desk and opened it towards them. 'Please señores, they are Colombia's best, take some with you if you don't smoke.' He grinned. 'Souvenirs of my fine country.' Relieved and relaxed by the politician's practiced warmth, Andriessen took three and pocketed them. Nelson followed suit. After inviting them to sit, the President returned to his side of the desk, took a puff of an already lit cigar and engaged Andriessen in some small talk about his flight from Amsterdam and his scheduled return before asking him his business.

'Your Excellency,' the younger Dutchman said after clearing his throat, 'My Queen and my Prime Minister are deeply worried over what has happened here in Colombia during the past thirty-six hours.' He handed the letters across the desk. 'These letters express their concern and their hope that the matter can be brought to a speedy and peaceful conclusion.' He knew exactly what the letters said; he'd translated the Dutch originals into Spanish himself. Both emphasised the concern felt by the people of the Netherlands and expressed the hope that the Colombian President would do his utmost to see the safe return of Doctor Jansen and the twenty van Goghs. The words "safe" and "unharmed" were used a total of seven times in the two letters. In its second last paragraph, the Prime Minister's letter introduced Nelson Schoute and requested that he be extended every courtesy.

The President returned his cigar to the ashtray, opened both letters with a gold blade and read them nodding and humming at, what Andriessen hoped were, the appropriate places.

'I agree completely,' he said, folding the one from the Prime Minister. 'Señor Andriessen, please tell Her Majesty and Prime Minister de Groot that I deeply regret what has happened, it has caused a great deal of embarrassment for my country. You can assure them that I will do all in my power to bring about the safe return of Doctor Jansen and the paintings. I have already issued an order that additional units of the army assist the police in the investigation.' He then directed his words to Nelson, waiting at the end of every sentence for Andriessen to finish the translation. 'Señor Schoute, I am pleased that you are with us. If there is anything I can do to assist, you should not go through the police chain of command, you must contact me directly. I promise I will do my best to help.' With that, he stood and limped back to them around his desk. 'I shall respond to these letters now, Señor Andriessen. If you would care to wait in the palace, it will not take long.'

'Thank you, Your Excellency,' Andriessen said, welcoming the earnest response.

'My aide will look after you,' the President said and gestured towards the officer standing near the door who immediately came to attention. 'And Señor Schoute,' he said touching Nelson on the elbow, 'as a man who works with art, you may find a tour of the palace particularly interesting. It contains many of Colombia's finest treasures.'

Two hours later, after the tour of the palace and two cups of coffee with the much decorated captain, they were taken back into the office where the President handed Andriessen the replies, written in English as well as Spanish. He also gave Nelson a card with his second most direct phone number printed on it.

Both men left the palace feeling optimistic. If the man they had just spoken with couldn't accelerate the investigation, nobody could. Andriessen was pleased: his journey from the Netherlands had been, in his estimation, a great success.

Later, over beer at Andriessen's hotel, Nelson outlined the progress to date along with his impressions of the Colombian police. The emissary took notes. Tonight, he would transmit a report of both meetings to his minister. Tomorrow morning, he would leave Bogotá for home.

Late in the afternoon, the American pilot who had flown the Falcon jet involved in the hijacking, was ushered into Vega's apartment. 'Amigo, welcome to my new home,'

Vega declared, grasping him by the shoulders before vigorously shaking his hand. 'You did a great job, thank you.'

'My pleasure, Carlos,' the pilot replied, wishing the show of emotion over. His eyes found the cordoned-off painting. 'I see you're exhibiting the loot. A real van Gogh, eh?'

'Very real,' Vega said, releasing the American's hand. 'Can I get you something to drink?' The skilled pilot was crucial to Willem Imthorn's plan. It was important that he be treated well, it was equally important that he be watched.

'Thanks, Scotch and water,' the pilot said, sauntering towards the painting.

Vega retrieved the Scotch and two glasses from a kitchen cupboard. 'How did things go in Jamaica?'

'Like clockwork. Your man had someone take the Falcon for a spin before the cops showed up, to get rid of the paint smell. They left happy, I'm told. The phoney flight plan did the trick. That little plane was taking off from Managua when the hijacking occurred. It's amazing what money will buy, eh Carlos?'

'Anything,' Vega replied, pouring the drinks. 'Money will buy anything.'

'And your man said for me to tell you that Gregory had twins, whatever that means.' He had no idea what the phrase meant and knew not to ask.

'Excellent,' Vega remarked. He now had the two shells for his illusion. He handed the pilot his glass. 'Salud!'

'Salud!' the pilot replied and swallowed a sizeable gulp.

'And you're sure the painters and air traffic people will

keep quiet?' Vega asked, not needing the pilot's confirmation.

'Positive. They know the deal, your man showed them the pictures of what happens to squealers.'

'Good,' Vega said and took a second sip. Informers were rare in the business and as a rule didn't live long enough to enjoy the fruits of their betrayal. Over the years, a series of photographs taken during and after various executions had proven very efficient promoters of loyalty amongst those who had dealings with the cartel. 'A picture of a dead informer is worth a thousand threats,' Vega quipped and turned his attention to Vincent's peasants. 'It is one of the most important of van Gogh's works.'

'Pretty drab. I thought he did bright paintings, like sunflowers and windmills.' He looked at it more closely. 'Who the hell are these pathetic-looking people anyway?'

'They are the potato eaters, amigo.'

'Is that so?' he said examining the older woman's weathered face. 'Looks like they could do with more protein and a little less starch.'

'Did you not visit the Van Gogh Museum when you were in Amsterdam?' Vega asked. The pilot had flown one of Vega's cash collection missions from the Netherlands a year ago, his only visit to that part of the world. He knew nothing of Willem Imthorn nor did he know any more of Imthorn's plan than he needed to know. It was best that way.

'Not a chance, Carlos. I skipped the art galleries, the red light district had all the culture I was after.'

'You're a wicked man,' Vega said with a deliberate cackle. 'I've heard of that red light district in Amsterdam, prostitutes in windows . . . take your pick.' He joined the pilot in a boisterous laugh.

'How much is this sheet of canvas worth?' the pilot asked after a short silence.

'Many, many millions of dollars.' Vega took another sip of Scotch eyeing the younger peasant husband as he did so. 'Incredible, isn't it, that a painting could be worth so much money?'

'Incredibly stupid, if you ask me,' the pilot said in scornful disbelief. 'You'd have to be crazy to pay that just to look at a bunch of people who need a bath. It's too dark and grimy.'

'According to Christina, van Gogh had a great admiration for peasants, he wanted the picture to have the look of poverty and the smell of potato.'

'Carlos, my friend, what's happening to you,' the pilot said, laying his hand on Vega's shoulder. 'All of a sudden you're an art expert. Are you sleeping with this broad?'

'No, compadre,' Vega replied, enjoying the accusation. 'I cannot upset the Dutch government more than I already have. Christina fills in part of her day by giving me an education in the art and life of Vincent van Gogh. She's very well informed, you will meet her later.'

'You never know, the little Dutch girl and Captain Jim may get along just fine. And she's not bad looking, judging by the newspaper picture.'

'She is quite attractive,' Vega replied, arching his eyebrows, 'but off limits.'

'I know, señor.' He drained the last of his drink. 'We're professionals right. Don't want to mix business with pleasure.' He placed his glass on the closest coffee table. 'Now Carlos, if you don't mind, I'm in urgent need of a pee and a shower. If you would direct me to my quarters, sir, I would be most appreciative.'

'In the apartment across the hall. It's crowded, so if you need a break anytime, come here.' Vega swallowed the rest of his drink. 'Of course, you must not leave this floor.'

'No problem,' the pilot replied and picked up his bag. 'It's a hell of a lot safer up here than it is in the streets.'

'Pedro will show you where everything is, and he'll tell you the procedure if we have unwelcome visitors.'

'Thanks for the drink, Carlos,' he said with a salute. 'Hasta pronto.' As he turned towards the door he caught sight of Christina coming down the hallway towards him. 'Well hello, hello,' he crooned, turning in his tracks. 'You must be Christina Jansen.' He dropped his bag and extended his arm towards her.

'Hello,' she murmured and walked past him into the living area. Whoever he was, he had to be some kind of criminal. Honest people didn't visit Carlos Vega. She had agreed to be tactful, not friendly.

Not easily put off, the pilot followed her back into the living area. 'Nice painting you have there, Doctor Jansen. I bet it's worth a few bucks.'

The comment annoyed her, she stopped and turned. 'You're an American.' She was always intrigued by how quickly Americans got to, what they called, the bottom line.

'Yes, ma'am, Jim Avery, at your service.' He bowed as he said it.

'Well, Mr Avery, the painting is priceless, it's irreplaceable, it does not have a value in dollars, it can't be bought, it can't be sold, it can just be . . . wait a minute. That voice. You're the pilot from the little jet, aren't you?'

'Yes ma'am. Sorry about yesterday morning, orders from the boss, you know.' He gestured towards Vega who was on the couch watching their exchange with obvious enjoyment.

'It was a horrible experience,' she said and walked on into the kitchen. 'I hope you go to jail for a very long time because of it.'

'Nice meeting you too, honey,' Avery replied, then rolling his eyes in Vega's direction, 'You caught a mean one there, Carlos.' He left for the other apartment.

After pouring herself some coffee from the vacuum flask that was now kept in the kitchen, Christina sat at the table and opened a two week old copy of "Newsweek" that had been left there.

Vega spoke to her over the top of today's "El Mundo". 'When you've finished your coffee, there are a couple of details that must be taken care of.'

'Such as?' She was relieved to see him calm. She had

117

expected unpleasant repercussions from the heated exchange at lunchtime.

'I need another photograph for your Prime Minister, to show him how well you're being looked after. And you have an appointment with a hairdresser.'

'A hairdresser?'

'We need to change your appearance a little,' he replied, returning his attention to the newspaper.

'What's a little?'

'A trim and a colour change, that's all,' he said without looking up.

'What colour?'

'Certainly not blonde, señorita. You will have black hair, like everyone else in South America.'

'Did anyone suggest a wig?'

'Too easy to pull off . . . at the wrong time.'

Pedro entered a short time later carrying the Polaroid camera he'd used on Monday. Vega handed the newspaper to Christina and directed her to stand against a blank wall holding the front page below her chin. She glanced at it first: a photograph of her, an enlargement of the one used on her identification badge at the museum, appeared next to Vega's under the headline "CARLOS VEGA RESPONSABLE POR LA PIRATERIA DEL AIRE VAN GOGH." Pedro took the picture, this time using the flash. Once he was sure it was developing itself properly, he gave it to Vega and left.

A few minutes later, he returned with a young woman, the hairdresser. He introduced her as the wife of one of the guards. No names were mentioned. She sat Christina in a chair in the kitchen and proceeded to shorten and reshape her mid-brown hair, remaining silent as she did so. Vega and Pedro watched, a deliberate ploy to intimidate the woman and prevent collaboration. There was always a danger using a guard's wife for such a task: If the marriage was not sound, there could be disastrous consequences. For that reason, only two wives would see the apartment, her and the woman who did the shopping. Both had children and both knew that betrayal would cost the life of a child.

Christina protested the instant the woman produced the Schwarzkopf package. She didn't want chemical fumes anywhere near the paintings. After a brief exchange, they moved across the hall to the master bedroom's en suite.

An hour later, Christina sat with Vega at the table in the second apartment, her transformation complete.

Rafael arrived with the second letter for the Dutch Prime Minister. Not anxious to be ridiculed in the international media for a typing error, Vega read it twice.

To: The Prime Minister
The Hague, Netherlands

Sir

I regret that I have not had a meaningful response to my earlier communication. I expected you to reach a quick decision on this matter. My demand is simple.

119

My son in exchange for the paintings and Doctor Jansen. There will be no tricks.

Doctor Jansen will sign this letter to indicate that she is safe and that the paintings are being well cared for. As you can see, she is in good health.

I expect a response within 24 hours.

Carlos Vega

There were no errors. He handed Christina a black pen and asked that she read and sign the page next to the second last paragraph. She did so. Vega then signed it at the bottom, attached the photograph with a paper clip and gave it to one of the guards to photocopy. The photocopy was given to Rafael with the instruction that it was to be sent at eight o'clock.

After seeing Rafael off, Vega gathered his men around him. 'Compadres, the past few days have been very demanding. You have all done well. My plans are coming together. Tonight we will relax a little, we will have a celebration.'

On that cue, Pedro unlocked a cupboard and pulled out two bottles of whiskey and another of rum. The glasses appeared, the music was switched on and the party began.

Christina's urge to leave immediately for her room was overcome by the pragmatic desire to gather intelligence. She accepted a drink from Avery who launched straight into a joke ridiculing Colombian pilots. She let the joke fall flat at his feet. She had as good a sense of humour as anyone, but for the cocky pilot, she would remain as cold as ice. Feeling the fool, Avery turned sincere and spoke apologetically: 'Look ma'am, I can tell you hate me, but for the record, I'm not like these guys. I'm not a killer, I'm just a pilot.'

'You may not go around shooting people but people die because of what you do.'

'People die all the time, Christina. They die from this too.' He stubbed a finger into his glass. 'I'm not as bad as you think, believe me.'

Vega joined them from behind. 'Are you two arguing?'

'Hey, there's no problem Carlos,' Avery said. 'We'll get along just fine once we get to know each other, won't we honey?'

'You must be joking,' she responded dryly.

'Señorita,' Vega said. 'My friend, Jim Avery . . . Captain Avery, is the best pilot in the whole of the Americas. He was the man for the job on Monday.' He clinked his glass to Avery's. 'You were brilliant, amigo.'

'Always happy to please,' Avery replied, returning the clink.

'And Christina,' Vega said, 'nobody was hurt, not even a scratch, nor were the paintings harmed, true?'

'True,' she answered seeing no alternative and tasted the rum.

Vega took another gulp of whiskey swirling it around in his mouth before swallowing. 'My business requires that I visit one of the plantations tomorrow, I would like you both to join me.'

'Tomorrow?' Christina responded, taken aback by the invitation, delighted. 'Sure.' It would be an opportunity to get a message out. 'Anything to get out of here for a while.'

'If the pretty lady goes, I go too,' Avery said, holding his glass towards her's. She ignored him.

'Good,' Vega said as Avery touched his glass to her's anyway. 'We must leave very early, at five o'clock.'

Vega had just discovered that one of the plantation owners under his control had been visited by a competitor from Cali who had tried to do business. He knew his disappearance would set the sharks circling but he hadn't expected them to move in for the kill so quickly. An appearance would quell any concerns that his interest had waned.

Christina looked around the room while the two men proceeded to engage each other in superficial conversation about an upcoming football match in Bogotá. She observed the cook mix a cream powder, she assumed to be cocaine, with tobacco from a Marlboro cigarette. He rolled the resulting mixture in a cigarette paper, then prepared another while he smoked it. She was surprised Vega allowed his men to take the drug, or drink for that matter. She spotted another guard sniffing cocaine. And then two others leering at her.

By the time she finished her drink, the macho atmosphere had reached, for her, an intimidating level. 'I'd like to go back to my room, Carlos. Would you please take me?'

'You are not enjoying yourself, señorita?' Vega asked.

'I'm not big on parties,' she responded, placing her glass on a nearby table, 'Please.'

'Pedro will take you.' He pointed across the smoke filled room to his lieutenant who was engaged in animated conversation with Josef. 'And ask him to give you an alarm clock.'

She took an indirect route to Pedro to avoid the two men still ogling her. Pedro escorted her to her room and, after finding an alarm clock, locked her inside.

She wasted no time in preparing for tomorrow. She retrieved a sheet of writing paper from her bag and, at the top, printed a heading promising a reward for anyone taking it to the police: "POR FAVOR LLEVE ESTO A LA POLICIA. RECOMPENSIR". She paused to consider the amount. One million dollars. What would that do? she wondered. Too much, too suspicious. The message could not appear connected to the hijacking, that may scare the finder off. "US$1000". That should propel a finder to immediate and rational action. She continued, in English.

"I am a hostage of a man whose name is that of a bright star. I come from a country that is the home of rembrandt. I am being held in the penthouse apartment of a fifteen storey building on a wide avenue. I can see a park across the road with a large statue of a man on a horse. There is a sign advertising a lottery on the corner opposite the horse. The city business district is not very far to the north or northeast." She went on to describe the number of guards and the security system. On the other side of the sheet, she drew a rough plan of the fifteenth floor including the compartment where the paintings were stored. She then folded it and stuffed it in the bra she would wear in the morning. All she needed now was a chance to leave it somewhere it could be found.

After preparing for bed she watched CNN to see if there was anything new on the Van Gogh Hijack story. There wasn't. Tonight, because of the drinking and drug taking going on in the other apartment, she felt more vulnerable than ever. She wondered who had access to her room key, what was to stop the men who leered at her from coming in? She got up and wedged the chair between the door knob and the floor. At least she would be awake and ready to fight if someone did intrude.

Across the hall, Vega, Avery, Pedro and Josef played poker around a coffee table while the other men conducted an arm wrestling competition on the dining table. At nine o'clock, the guard monitoring the television in the living area announced that the girls were on their way up. The men applauded their boss for his generosity. Tonight they would work and play in shifts.

Vega wanted his men to let off some steam, to enjoy themselves. The next few days would be more arduous than any so far. The prostitutes he had ordered were regulars and, as part of their business, made a point of not concerning themselves with his business. In this instance, as an added safeguard, at the end of the night, they would be taken on a ten day holiday. Upon their return, they would keep tonight a secret. None of them wished to be charged for not informing the police and none of them wished to die the death of an informer.

The colourfully and scantily dressed women burst into the apartment. There were five of them. A voluptuous brunette went straight to Vega and straddled his body. She kissed him and ran her fingers through his hair. He threw down his cards. Vega knew María well, he had shared her bed at least once a week for almost four years.

The other girls found their targets and went to work. The music was South American and the dancing was hot. The short mestizo woman with flaming red hair who found Avery, got things going by giving him a merengue lesson. Disappointed to find that his skill in the atmosphere didn't translate to the dance floor she soon reverted to the tried and true full frontal shuffle. The only one who made no attempt to join the foreplay was the freebasing cook who had gone into a zombie-like trance. His occasional use of the drug was ignored in the interests of maintaining harmony in the kitchen.

After a while, Vega and María left the party for his apartment. He guided her body to the van Gogh. 'What do you think of my painting, María? It is called "The Potato Eaters".'

She moved to take a closer look. 'Carlos, it is an ugly painting. It is so dark and the people look so miserable. Except for the young woman, she has a certain beauty.' She moved away and looked at it from a distance. 'Where did you get it?' She knew. It was impossible to live in Colombia and not know.

'From Europe, my dear, do you like it?'

'No Carlos, it has no colour, I like a painting with colour.' She turned from it and pressed her body against his. 'Anyway, my love, I did not come here to see your painting.' She unbuttoned his shirt and ran the tip of her tongue over his hair-matted chest. Vega smiled to himself, relishing the thought of the uninhibited passion ahead.

12

Vega's ransom demand was the only item on the agenda for the emergency meeting of the Dutch Cabinet on Wednesday morning. All fourteen ministers were present along with the director of the Vincent van Gogh Foundation and the chief inspector of the Special Branch of the Dutch police. The mood in the unpretentious second-floor room of the Binnenhof, the parliamentary complex, was sombre. Each minister had been provided with a folder containing a profile of the Colombian drug baron, copies of his two faxes, two reports from Nelson Schoute, a report from Simon Andriessen including copies of the letters he delivered to the President of Colombia as well as the President's response, and an inventory of the stolen paintings.

The Prime Minister lay down the notes he had been perusing as the clock outside struck ten. 'Ladies and gentlemen,' he began, looking around the table over the top of his reading glasses. 'We have ahead of us some very important deliberations, the outcome of which will affect the safety of the assistant curator of the Van Gogh Museum, Christina Jansen, and the twenty paintings of the great Dutch artist stolen so boldly two days ago.' He removed the glasses, folded the arms and placed them beside his watch. 'The issues are not simple. We must consider the crimes that have been committed by, or at the behest of, Mr Carlos Vega. Firstly, the hijacking of KLM flight 4021. Secondly, the illegal detention of Doctor Christina Jansen, a citizen of the Netherlands. And thirdly, the theft of the twenty paintings belonging to the Vincent van Gogh Foundation.

'The safety of Doctor Jansen is of great concern to us all. So too is the safety of our national treasures. Against these concerns is the fact that compliance with Vega's demands would set a precedent for further acts of this kind.' He turned to the minister seated to his right. 'I believe you have some comments, Lydia?'

'Thank you, Prime Minister.' The Minister of Justice, one of five women in the Dutch Cabinet, had been involved in the drama from the beginning. 'I share the Prime Minister's concern that if we give into Vega's demands, we will be tempting similar terrorist activity here in Europe and in other parts of the world. On the other hand, we cannot refuse to negotiate with him, that would be irresponsible. I believe we should proceed with negotiations, but slowly. We should stall him as long as possible in the hope that the authorities in Colombia can find his hiding place.'

The Minister of Home Affairs, a seasoned member

known for his forthrightness, lifted his hand to speak. The Prime Minister gave him the nod. 'Corruption is rife in Colombia. It has the worst kidnapping record in the world. Their murder rate is ten times that in the United States, for goodness sake. I believe the Minister is dreaming if she thinks we can rely on the Colombian authorities to solve the problem for us.'

'I will address that point now,' the Minister of Justice responded while looking for the appropriate page in her folder. 'Referring to the second report from Nelson Schoute, security chief from the Van Gogh Museum, now liaison officer with the Colombian authorities.' She withdrew it and continued, sometimes reading highlighted sections from the report, 'Mr Schoute acknowledges that drug related corruption is a major problem in both the police and military in many parts of Colombia. Apparently, these corrupt elements have shielded Vega and his associates from justice for a number of years. But this time, Vega may not get the protection to which he has become accustomed. His contacts within the police and military know he is about to leave Colombia so their loyalty to him is, in all probability, diminishing. Since Vega won't be paying them in the future, they'll be looking for a new deal. The present situation gives the crooked elements inside the police and military a golden opportunity to do something to counter the constant criticism levelled at them, at little or no cost. As soon as this situation has been resolved, they will find their level with the new cartel structure and be left alone for a while.' She turned to the chair. 'In summary, Prime Minister, Mr Schoute is reservedly optimistic that the Colombian authorities will win this one.'

'Thank you, Minister.' The Prime Minister turned his attention to the member sitting opposite the Minister of Justice. 'Minister, perhaps you would like to summarise the report from your representative, I believe it concerns the same matter.'

The Minister of Foreign Affairs, a handsome man in his early fifties, removed his reading glasses and cleared his throat before speaking. 'Certainly, Prime Minister. I received a report from our emissary, Simon Andriessen, earlier today. Mr Andriessen, along with Mr Schoute, visited the President of Colombia yesterday and presented him with official requests for assistance from Queen Beatrix and you, Prime Minister. The President gave Mr Andriessen his assurance that he would put his full weight behind the investigation. He has already put some army units at the disposal of the police to help with searches, surveillance and such activities.

'In support of what the Minister of Justice said, if Vega is found, and there is a peaceful end to the situation, the President will gain in international and national stature. And this man needs to gain in stature, especially with his own citizens. Things haven't been going too well for him lately.' He continued over the subdued laughter spreading around the table. 'He isn't making false promises of support, I'm sure he means what he says.'

The Minister of Welfare, Health and Culture, an ambitious junior member of Cabinet, spoke next. 'Of course the best result for us, and the international community, would be for Vega to be found, but we can't be sure that will happen. So, while I agree we should proceed with negotiations, I hope we can be flexible in our thinking. In my view, we should not be too eager to jeopardise the safety of the curator and the paintings just to keep one drug smuggler imprisoned here in Holland.'

'Minister,' the Prime Minister responded sharply. 'As I thought I made clear in my opening statement, this isn't simply a case of one prisoner against a life and twenty paintings. Giving in to terrorism only encourages terrorism. This government has always stood firmly on that principle.' The reprimand over, he turned back to the meeting. 'Now, I for one, would like to hear what Chief Inspector Vermeer has to say.' The Prime Minister turned to the policeman sitting with Albert Voss away from the table. 'Chief Inspector, if you would please help us here.'

Every head in the room turned to the man whose reputation in the investigation of matters of terrorism and extortion was world renowned. Without exception, the ministers expected his analysis to be the most insightful and his advice, the most constructive. Kees Vermeer had risen to national prominence in 1983 when he headed a special operations network set up to solve the most sophisticated kidnapping ever carried out in the Netherlands. In November of that year, Alfred Heineken, the head of the

131

Heineken beer company, and his chauffeur, Ab Doderer, were kidnapped at gunpoint and an enormous ransom was demanded from the Heineken family for their release. The government of the day, not anxious to allow the injection of such a large sum of money into the criminal network of Europe where it would be used to finance more crime, was determined that the police would win and a massive operation was mounted to foil the kidnappers. Thanks in a large part to the organisation imposed by Vermeer, Heineken and his chauffeur were rescued unharmed, the kidnappers were brought to justice, and most of the ransom money that had been used as bait was recovered. That victory virtually eliminated the incidence of kidnapping in Holland and the techniques used by the Dutch police in the investigation had since been adopted by forces all over the world.

Vermeer, a slightly built man in his early sixties with steely blue eyes, moved to the table. 'Ladies and gentlemen, Carlos Vega is a man used to winning. He controls high ranking officials in the Colombian justice system and army. In many ways, he is more powerful than the government in Colombia, and he is well protected.

'In this instance, as you are all aware, his bargaining ability rests with the twenty paintings in his possession and his hostage, Doctor Jansen. If you string him along too long, he will be forced to somehow apply pressure to speed you up. I doubt that he will harm Doctor Jansen, except as a last resort. Her presence there seems incidental. In my

132

opinion, his most likely response would be to damage or perhaps destroy the paintings, one at a time. You must be prepared for that if you stall.' Several faces turned to gauge the reaction of the director of the Vincent van Gogh Foundation. None was evident.

Vermeer continued. 'The simplest solution would be for the Colombian police to find him quickly. I don't think that will happen. The hijacking operation to gain possession of the paintings was extraordinarily well planned. Carlos Vega is no fool. You can be sure he is well hidden, and the people who know where he is won't talk, they value their lives too much.' He looked to the chair. 'That's all I have to say, Prime Minister, unless there are questions.'

'Thank you, Kees. A few questions, if you don't mind.' The Prime Minister's tone telegraphed his deep respect for the policeman. 'How do you think Vega wishes us to handle this? What would be the ideal outcome for him?'

'Although he hasn't yet described what he wants in detail, Prime Minister, it's not difficult to make an informed prediction. Presumably, at the end of all this, he aims to be living in seclusion in another country with his son and perhaps his wife. In the process to achieve that end, he won't leave anything to trust or chance. He would probably plan on revealing the location of some of the paintings once his son is out in the open ready to be exchanged. That would have to happen in a place where the son can be made to vanish afterwards. A large city perhaps. Bogotá, Mexico

City, Miami . . . who knows. Of course, Vega would probably plan on using an intermediary at the exchange points. He would want to be at his new hiding place or somewhere close to it. He would promise to release the other paintings after his son is safe. He'd expect you to trust him on that.'

'We would have no choice, would we?' the Prime Minister said. 'What about the curator?'

'Ideally, he would want to keep her as long as possible. But that would be out of the question.' Vermeer paused to remind himself that he was giving advice, not setting policy. 'In my opinion, Prime Minister, that would be unwise, and unnecessary. He'd still have enough paintings to protect his interests.'

'Finally, Kees, what action would you advise at this stage?' de Groot asked.

'My suggestion, Prime Minister, is that you try to appease him. Keep communicating, work in the direction he wants, try to negotiate some kind of compromise. The transfer of his son to a Colombian jail was mentioned in one of Nelson Schoute's reports. I think it's a good offer. Not the first you should make though. Vega probably won't accept it, but there's always a chance he will . . . especially if he's starting to feel pressure from the police and army. He knows he could have his son broken out of jail and with him in Paraguay or Chile or wherever within a month.'

Next, the Prime Minister solicited the opinion of the director of the Vincent van Gogh Foundation. Albert Voss had hardly slept since receiving Nelson Schoute's phone call from Caracas two days ago. He was worried sick and it showed. He gave a concise statement saying that, while he had every confidence Cabinet would act wisely, he hoped they would not stall to the point Vermeer warned of, where Vega might take action against Doctor Jansen or the paintings.

The director and the inspector were then asked to leave the room. As always, the final deliberations leading to a decision would be conducted in private.

The discussion was shorter than the Prime Minister had expected. A final position involving the transfer of Juan Vega to a Colombian jail after Christina Jansen and fifteen paintings nominated by the Vincent van Gogh Foundation were in Dutch hands, was agreed upon. A less conciliatory opening position was also accepted in order to buy some time for the Colombian authorities. It was exactly what Vermeer had recommended.

De Groot was content with the decision from both a moral and political standpoint. If Vega did accept the final offer, the Dutch government would come out of the incident looking pretty good. The Netherlands would have both the paintings and hostage back and Juan Vega would still be in jail. It would also be good for the Colombian government. They would be seen as good international citizens assisting the Dutch. Later, when the inevitable happened and Juan Vega was broken out of jail, it would not reflect badly on the Dutch government at all, it would be the fault of the Colombians. The only catch was that

Vega might reject the final offer. For de Groot, that was a very uncomfortable thought. His government could go no further.

Carlos Vega was awake and preparing for the journey to the plantation when Josef knocked on his door. It was five o'clock in the morning. María and the other women had been escorted out of the apartments earlier and were now on the way to their Peruvian holiday in a cartel aircraft.

Christina was awake too, anxious for the day to start. She had slept well despite her concern that someone may try to enter her room during the night. No one had.

After a light breakfast in the second apartment, Vega, Christina, Avery and two guards rode the elevator down to the carpark and climbed aboard the Ford van which Josef had backed up to the elevators. The usual precautions were taken in the various aspects of their departure.

An hour later, the convoy arrived at a small airstrip on the outskirts of the city and came to a stop beside a well used Cessna. 'She's a beauty!' Avery raved when he saw it. 'A 206, my first job was flying a 206.'

'The Bolivian special, my pilots call it.' Vega had been using the single-engine station wagon of the air for years to transport cocoa paste from Bolivia and sometimes chemicals from Venezuela. Its reliability and ability to carry heavy loads made it perfect for that kind of work and for today's outing too. The guards, their straw hats a reminder to Christina of the hijacking, loaded a box of grenades, two

Minimi machine guns and ammunition on board. Josef gave Vega a submachine gun and ammunition to supplement the revolver he always carried on his hip. Defensive weapons, all of them, just in case. Although Vega hadn't told the plantation owner of the impending visit, there was always the possibility of a leak from inside his organisation: a guard, the pilot, a wife, someone. And if the owner was already involved with Cali, a leak could lead to an ambush. The precautions were prudent. In the drug business, those who did not take them tended to be buried at a young age.

The small plane took to the air just as dawn was breaking and flew east towards the mountains. Despite some mild turbulence, Vega and Josef fell asleep. It had been a heavy night for both of them. In the front, Avery and the pilot talked constantly about flying, using a hybrid of English and Spanish to do so. The stink of alcohol overindulgence on the guard seated next to Christina made the journey, for her, a long and unpleasant one.

They arrived two thousand feet over the plantation an hour after leaving Medellín and circled, grenades and machine guns at the ready. After convincing himself there were no more cars than seemed reasonable and that the workers were spread over a large area, Vega gave the okay to signal their identity. With that, Josef dropped a large yellow handkerchief with a coin tied in the corner out the window, this week's code for friend, and watched as it fell. Vega gave the order to land as soon as it hit the ground.

The Cessna came to a bumpy rest halfway up the sloped grass landing strip. Vega's men jumped out and set up the machine guns at the sides of the strip while the pilot turned the plane around and prepared for a quick escape. After a tense delay lasting a few minutes, an ancient station wagon came up the hill towards them, its sole occupant, a middle-aged man wearing a baseball cap, waved at them through the window. Josef signalled for him to stop when he was about twenty metres from the plane, had him get out of the vehicle and searched him for weapons. Finding none, he walked the man to Vega.

'José!' Vega shouted through the open door and signalled for the pilot to cut the engine.

The man moved reverently towards Vega. 'Buenos dìas, Don Carlos.' The visit by the powerful cartel chief was a monumental event for the peasant landowner. 'It is a great honour that you have come to visit my home.'

Vega, donning a straw hat as he got out, greeted José warmly before introducing Avery and Christina as friends. Their names were not mentioned and the plantation owner didn't ask, the protocol of the drug trade was well understood even in these remote hills. The group, except for the pilot who would stay with the plane to guard against tampering, boarded the station wagon for the short drive to the main house. Vega's men in the back seat kept their guns at the ready.

José's wife, Gabriela, beaming at having her otherwise routine day interrupted by such a proud event, ushered the group to a table on the verandah where she had started to lay out coffee and cakes.

After questioning José about the rainfall and the crops, Vega brought up the reason for his presence. 'Amigo, my visit today is to demonstrate how much I value our relationship and to show that I am still here to do business with my friends.'

'Thank you, Don Carlos,' José replied meekly. 'I am honoured to be your friend.'

'José, someone from Cali has visited you?'

'Yes, Don Carlos. A man came yesterday, a man who knew Andrés. He told me you had fled Colombia, he offered to buy all my product. I said no. I did not believe you would leave, Don Carlos. So I phoned Andrés. He said you were in Medellín and that you had placed a large order. Of course, I believed Andrés.'

'Andrés told me of your phone call, that is why I came. He suspects one of his men is taking money from Cali. A spy. It is a problem that will be fixed.' Vega clasped the plantation owner's hands across the table. 'José, you must tell the other growers of my visit. Tell them that Carlos Vega is still in charge. And José, if this man makes any threats to you, tell Andrés immediately, I will take care of him. I want no harm to come to my loyal friend, José Rodríguez.' He spoke as if bestowing a blessing, validating his title, "the Pope", to all around.

'Thank you, Don Carlos,' José said, his large smile revealing several spaces once occupied by teeth.

The conversation then reverted to small talk. Gabriela, who had said little so far, spoke to Christina using a combination of Spanish and pantomime. She asked if she was married, if she had children.

Christina replied with a shake of her head. In the current situation, husband and children were concepts from a different world.

Josef, who had tuned into the awkward exchange between the two women, translated Gabriela's response for Christina: 'You should have children, señorita. When you are old they will look after you. I have three sons and a daughter. My girl and one boy are in Bogotá, the other boys work here, they are good children.' She ran a finger along Christina's arm. 'Your skin is so fine, señorita. You are very pretty. When you go back to your home, you should find a good husband, like José, and have children, before you get too old.' Josef laughed.

'I'll try my best,' Christina responded with a smile.

After coffee, Vega accepted the customary invitation for a tour around the plantation. They went behind the house first where two workers were adding kerosene to drums of leaves immersed in a sodium bicarbonate solution, the second step in the cocaine extraction process.

'Oro verde,' José repeated again and again, grinning all the time. 'Green gold,' Vega told Christina who answered that she had worked it out for herself.

They followed José to a coca field. 'This is the first crop of the year,' Vega explained. 'If the weather is good, there will be three more.' He whispered something to José causing him to exclaim 'Nunca!' and laugh.

'I asked José if he would like to grow coffee instead,' Vega explained and stopped to gather a few small leaves from a plant. He handed some to Christina. 'It is an ancient crop in South America. The Incas sucked on these leaves for relief from hunger and tiredness, and the cold in the mountains. Try one, like this.' He put a leaf in his mouth and chewed.

Intrigued by the Inca connection, Christina did what Vega suggested. Her mouth tingled and numbed. 'Funny feeling,' she said and spat out the pulp, 'like going to the dentist.'

'They made a tea with it, too,' Vega said before spitting. 'Did you ever try drugs, Christina, back in Holland?'

'Alcohol,' she responded, glancing sideways at him as they walked on, 'a number of times.'

'So have I,' Vega said with a small laugh. 'But like the wise bartender who does not drink, I do not use hard drugs.'

'I guessed that.' She had not seen anyone in his organisation, other than Miguel and another guard, use the products upon which his empire was based. Nicotine and alcohol seemed to be as far as their drug taking went.

He stopped to examine more leaves. 'Did you not smoke marijuana? I know it is sold in coffee shops in Amsterdam.'

'Once,' she answered. 'But not in a coffee house, at a party. Didn't do much for me.'

'You had a cousin who went further.' The leaves were free

of blight and insect damage. 'You mentioned her yesterday, at lunch.'

'I did,' she replied hesitantly as they moved on. It was a lunch and a topic she would just as soon forget.

'You tried to stop her taking the drugs?'

'Of course,' she replied, irritated by the intrusion into that part of her life. The thought that she could have done more had haunted Christina ever since Marieke's death. Marieke had been difficult to help. Marieke had returned her attempts at help with deception and theft and, for two months before her death, no one in the family knew where she was. 'This business, your business, killed her.'

'Do you think so, Christina?' Vega said looking ahead to a field of a different crop.

'And right now there could be someone else dying from the cocaine grown right here.'

'Possibly, and they are dying from cigarettes and food poisoning too.'

'You must know the death you cause,' Christina said as they came to a gate being held open by one of José's men, a box of bottled water under his arm.

'Free will.' Vega took two bottles from the box. 'I do not force anyone to take drugs.' He unscrewed the lids and handed a bottle to her. 'Therefore, I do not accept responsibility for the occasional death.'

'You make it possible for people to get the drugs,' she said as he took a drink.

'And a whiskey distiller makes it possible for someone

who drinks too much to kill innocent people on the road.'

'Well, maybe we should ban whisky.' Now she knew she was losing the argument.

'They tried that once in the US,' he countered with a grin. 'It didn't work.' He followed José through the gate. 'Wait here, señorita, I must inspect José's flowers.'

She crossed the rough track they had come along and sat on the grass in the shade. As much as she hated to think it, she suspected Vega was partially right. Perhaps hard drugs should be legalised, their distribution controlled. Anyone who wants them can get them now . . . in Amsterdam, Los Angeles, in prisons, anywhere. Users are a minority, victims of sorts, not evil people. Would legal heroin have helped Marieke? Perhaps. Human nature. She took a drink. Flawed human nature.

In the field on the other side of the fence, José slit the swollen seed capsule of one of the plants and handed it to Vega.

'I'll be shipping one hundred loaves next week,' the plantation owner said as Vega wiped off the milky fluid oozing from the cut and rubbed it between his fingers. Dried, the resulting opium gum would be shipped to a laboratory in Medellín and turned into the purest heroin in the world.

'Excellent,' Vega said before throwing the pod towards some birds on the fence. The cartel's trade in heroin had grown twentyfold in just five years and now accounted for one in every four dollars of income.

It was after nine o'clock by the time they got back to the plane.

'Did you enjoy meeting my friends, Christina?' Vega turned around and asked after take off.

'Nice people, but they should have stuck with coffee.'

'With coffee, they were poor,' Vega replied. 'The merchants made the money, not the growers, not in these hills.'

'That made it easy for you,' she said, grasping the back of his seat against some turbulence, 'to come in and make your money off their work.'

'At least I pay a fair price,' Vega replied. The ride was getting rougher. 'In that sense I am more honest than the coffee merchants.'

They landed on the airstrip near Medellín shortly after ten thirty. The guards met the plane with their usual efficiency and, within minutes, the convoy was on its way.

As they approached the outskirts of the city, Vega announced another surprise visit. 'Josef, contact the lead driver, tell him to drive to Andrés'.'

The convoy drove around the outskirts of the city for half an hour before arriving at their destination, a village surrounded by thick forest. The advance car came to a stop to the side of an alley between two derelict buildings while Vega's van and the other car drove down it to a courtyard. The advance car then reversed into the alley, blocking it.

The guards from the rear car took positions around the

van before Vega got out. Christina followed, the noxious fumes almost overpowering her. She held her breath and followed Vega into the shade of the laboratory: a tin shed with half the walls missing. Avery followed her. Out of the sunlight and with a large fan drawing fresh air from the alley, the fumes were not as bad. A short man with grey hair and skin to match appeared and embraced Vega. 'Buenos dìas, Don Carlos. It is good to see you, I have been concerned for your safety.'

'Buenos dìas, Andrés. As you can see, I am quite safe.' Vega introduced Avery and Christina, once again, not mentioning their names. Christina could hear as well as see the effort behind each breath taken by Vega's grey acquaintance, the result of long term exposure to the fumes, she assumed.

Vega went inside with Andrés, leaving Christina alone with Avery and one of the guards.

'So this is where they make the finished product?' she asked.

'Yep! This is where they make the snow, the good stuff. I'll show you.' He walked her a short distance inside the shed, the guard followed. 'The coca paste from the hills is dissolved in acetone.' He pointed to some large drums in the middle of the shed. 'Then acid is added to form the cocaine hydrochloride crystals. They're filtered out and put in the sun or under the heat lamps over there to dry.' He pointed to some product covered sheets under a bank of heat lamps. 'It ain't that complicated.' The smell forced them back outside. 'The fumes are a killer,' he said, wiping his eyes with the back of his hand. 'You saw the owner, they made his skin go like that. You can imagine what his lungs look like.'

'Terrible. And heroin is made here too?' she asked, blinking repeatedly in an effort to get the burning out of her eyes.

'Not today. Can't smell any acetic anhydride, just acetone. When one of these places goes up, there aren't too many survivors.'

'And how often does that happen?' She looked around for somewhere to leave her note. Vega's guards were stationed in the alley. There were three houses around the courtyard near where they were standing. Not surprisingly, all had their windows closed, not that they were possibilities anyway. The occupants, if there were any, would have to be connected with the operation.

'A couple of months ago, I flew over one that had just blown up. Carlos wanted some pictures. There wasn't much to photograph, just a few charred bodies, some burnt trees and bent tin sheets.'

Christina came to the dismal realisation that the note would be returning with her to the apartment. Vega had everything worked out too well. Her next challenge would be to engineer some way of getting onto the apartment's balcony; then she could drop it over the edge.

'To tell you the truth,' Avery continued, 'I'll be glad as hell when we're back in that van and out of here.'

'Me too.' She looked for Vega. He was on the other side of the shed examining some product in a plastic zip-lock bag. He seemed annoyed.

'That's one thing I won't do for Carlos, fly chemicals. He can get his Colombian cowboys to do that.'

'Don't they get the chemicals locally?'

'Nope, they're not made here. The stuff that's filling our lungs at the moment was made in the States or Europe and then smuggled here through Florida or Venezuela.'

'Why smuggle chemicals, they're not illegal? Can't they just buy them from an importer?'

'The Colombian government monitors chemical imports . . . part of its campaign against drugs. All that means is a longer line-up of bureaucrats waiting to collect bribes. So what Carlos and his friends do is fly the stuff in on the drug planes' return journeys. It saves a lot of messing about.' He shook his head. 'Honey, if you ask me, those planes are bombs waiting to explode.'

'Cual hombre?' Vega's demand came above the laboratory noise. He tossed the plastic bag to the ground and pulled his gun. 'Cual hombre, Andrés?' Vega repeated waving his gun in the direction of a group of workers.

Vega's men had the plant covered, weapons to their shoulders, safety catches off.

'Get her behind the van,' Josef shouted to Avery.

Andrés instructed his men to stay calm as he led Vega to a man emptying a can of acetone into one of the drums. The man's right hand was missing, the metal pincers which took its place making the task difficult. Avery hurriedly led Christina behind the van.

'Cerdo!' Vega pulled the can away from the man and, holding a gun to his chest, emptied his pockets. A handkerchief, coins, a roll of US bills, a notebook. The man stood terrified as Vega explored the pages of the book.

'Esto esta en Cali, este numero tambien.' Vega pointed to the entries with his gun. 'Cali!'

The man cried that he knew no one in Cali.

'Eres un traidor, compadre.' Vega pocketed the notebook, picked up the acetone and shoved the man into the open. Andrés followed meekly behind.

The man fell to his knees, joining his left hand and the pincers in a begging gesture. He swore that he knew no one in Cali, he begged for mercy for his wife, his children.

'Traidor.' Vega kicked the man to the ground and thrust the can in Andrés' direction. 'Viertanlo con acetona.'

The man started to get up. 'Madre de Dios, piedad, Don Carlos.' Vega shot his left knee. He screamed and fell.

'Stop!' Christina shouted as she came from behind the van. 'Carlos! Please stop!'

'Back! Get her back!' Vega shouted.

She continued her pleas as Avery pulled her back behind the van.

'Andrés,' Vega shouted. 'Pour.'

His hands shaking, the laboratory owner emptied the acetone over his man's prone body and withdrew.

'Cerdo!' Vega shouted as the man tried to get up again

and fired a round into the ground near his head. 'Cerdo!' The man was just whimpering now, praying, his face in the dirt, his left hand still holding the pincers. Vega shouted for Andrés to set fire to the man.

Fumbling through his pockets, Andrés produced a lighter and, after two failed attempts to ignite it, dropped it to the ground. Cursing the laboratory owner, Vega picked it up, lit it and moved the flame towards the man's bloodied trousers. He paused just before making contact, his mind drawn to Christina's muffled pleas. Until now he had done nothing ugly in front of her. Until now she had nothing particularly unpleasant about him to tell the world. That is how it must remain. He released the lighter valve and stood. 'Fix his leg and send him to Cali,' Vega said as he returned the lighter to Andrés. 'He can tell Señor Díaz that I am still in business.'

'Si, Don Carlos,' Andrés replied exhaling a long breath, 'Si.'

Vega boarded the van ahead of Josef and looked to Christina who was crying into the seat. 'Enough, señorita, the man will live.' As the convoy got underway, he closed his eyes and prayed for the ringing in his head to subside.

13

The massive peaks of the Andean Cordillera Central towered above the lone Sikorsky H-76 Eagle helicopter as it twisted its way through a high mountain pass. The spectacular scenery was lost on an increasingly airsick Nelson Schoute as he sat inside the noisy machine wishing the journey to Medellín over as soon as possible.

'Take deep breaths,' Martínez shouted, observing the lack of colour in his companion's face. 'Slowly, just relax.'

'I'll be going back by road,' Nelson replied humourlessly, his voice quivering with the vibration.

'That wastes half a day,' Martínez replied. 'The road winds all over the mountains,' he added, snaking his hand for effect. 'No compadre, in Colombia, this is the best way to get around.'

In the belief that his presence would help minimise deceit, Martínez was on his way to take control of the command centre his underling in Medellín had set up yesterday. He also wanted to meet Vega's wife.

The Colombian policeman was delighted to have the untethered support of the army. Their support could well make the difference between foiling Vega and not. Lines of communication and cooperation had existed between the two forces for some time. The army's ongoing battles with guerilla groups in the mountains often brought them into contact with marijuana, coca and poppy growers. In such cases they were required to make arrests and destroy crops. But Martínez knew that didn't always happen. The money offered by drug criminals for the poorly paid army officers to ignore what they found was often too tempting to refuse.

To Nelson's great relief, the helicopter steadied its course. They were out of the pass and the sprawling semi-industrial city of two million, providing cover for Vega, his hostage and booty, lay before them.

A team of police snipers covered their landing on the grey roof of police headquarters just before two o'clock. The sun was intense at this hour. The shadows, short. The air was less smoggy than Bogotá's.

'I could get used to having the army at my disposal,' Martínez said light heartedly as they walked away from the noise. 'Our President had better be careful.'

Nelson paused to take a few breaths and regain inner ear equilibrium before following his companion down a flight of stairs to a waiting elevator.

The two men spent the rest of the afternoon in meetings with senior officers in the command centre going over what had already been done. Vega's house had been under increased surveillance since Monday morning. His wife had left only once since then, to go shopping for clothes with a female friend. As far as the surveillance teams could tell, none of her phone conversations had been with her husband or anyone acting on his behalf.

The police chief reported that, as a result of investigations related to the case, his officers had discovered and closed down four cocaine laboratories. Martínez saw the pronouncement as meaningless, but did not make the point. Experience told him that by now the laboratories would be back in operation or in the process of setting up somewhere else. There were forces at work within the Medellín police which he knew he had no hope of controlling. Not that he was tempted to try. Others who had tried had paid for their dedication with their lives or, even worse, had their wives or children slaughtered as a warning.

14

Pieter de Groot stood by his office window high in the centuries old Het Torentje, a small tower in the parliamentary complex, gazing out at the rain blurred lights, waiting for his secretary to set up the phone call to South America. A storm had moved in off the North Sea bringing heavy rain and strong winds to the whole of western Europe. Dismal weather to match the mood in Holland.

Since their spheres of influence did not overlap, the Dutch Prime Minister had never before had occasion to speak with the Colombian President. He hoped the retired general's English would be good enough to facilitate an efficient and unambiguous conversation. If it wasn't, a Spanish interpreter waited by another phone on the other side of his desk, ready to help.

The President came on the line, his clearly limited ability to exchange simple pleasantries in English prompting Pieter de Groot to introduce the interpreter into the conversation

153

straight away. She translated the Prime Minister's Dutch as he spoke away from the mouthpiece.

After each expressed regret over the events that presently linked their countries, de Groot outlined the decision of his Cabinet concerning the initial and final offers and requested the President's cooperation with the proposed transfer of Juan Vega to Colombia. Because of the absence of an extradition treaty between the two countries, a special case would have to be made. De Groot didn't expect a problem. The Colombian government's opposition to extradition had always been to stop the transfer of drug criminals out of Columbia, not into it. The President agreed without hesitation. He said he would have an official request drawn up immediately and couriered to The Hague. De Groot followed up with a suggestion that in order to give the first offer some much needed integrity, it be made by both of them, simultaneously. After consenting to that, the President made a proposal of his own: that Juan Vega be offered a reduced sentence in Colombia, an enticement which, he argued, would increase the credibility of both offers. De Groot welcomed the proposal despite its irrelevance. The length of Juan Vega's imprisonment in Colombia would be a function of Carlos Vega's will and little else.

They went on to discuss how the initial offer would be presented on television. Although it was an obvious ploy to buy time, which both knew would not be taken seriously, the statements had to be consistent. A contradiction would not only bring ridicule on both of them, it would also damage Vega's confidence in de Groot's ability to negotiate.

That set, the Colombian President restated his country's embarrassment over the matter and expressed his eagerness to do everything within his power to bring the situation to a satisfactory end.

The conversation concluded twenty-five minutes after it had started.

Emotionally drained, Christina Jansen had slept an uneasy sleep for most of the afternoon, the cries of the man with one hand were playing inside her head.

'Dinner will be ready soon, señorita,' Pedro said after knocking on her door. 'And Carlos would like a new painting.'

She must get a message out, somehow. She would have to humour Vega, hope for another journey. She washed her face and went to the third bedroom to make her selection.

Vega was watching CNN when she entered with the painting. The deadline he had imposed on the Dutch was about an hour away.

She lay the case on the kitchen bench, rolled the combination and cut the seals with the wire cutters that were now stored there. 'You wanted something brighter,' she said, opening the latches. She showed him "The Harvest": A bird's eye view of yellow and green fields in bright summer light; scattered earthen-toned farm buildings dot the banded patchwork; simply painted workers, blending in, not dominating their surroundings; in the distance, the untamed hills of Crau. An ocean of colour beneath a clear blue sky.

'More to my taste than the potato people,' Vega said from the couch. 'Señorita, I'm sorry you were present this morning, at the laboratory. My temper, it sometimes over-rules my good sense. I should have dealt with the problem more quietly.'

'Will we be going on another trip?' she asked, deciding it wisest not to share her thoughts on the laboratory incident.

'Our next trip will be when we leave here,' Vega said, heartened by what seemed the ready acceptance of his apology.

'And when will that be?'

'In time, señorita.' He returned his attention to the tele-vision as she carried the painting to the wall. 'Will your Prime Minister meet my deadline?'

'Probably, we Dutch have an aversion to missing deadlines.'

'So I've noticed,' Vega said, thinking of Willem Imthorn.

She took down "The Potato Eaters", retrieving the wire from it before returning it to its case. After attaching the wire to the back of the new painting, she hung it. The scat-tered room lights and intersecting shadows did not do it full justice. The colours were weaker than in the predomi-nantly natural light of the museum in Amsterdam.

Avery appeared with a bottle of wine. 'Dinner is ready.' He stood aside to allow Miguel and Josef, both carrying trays, to pass him.

'Excellent,' Vega said as he got up from the couch. 'The journey has given me an appetite.' He gestured for Christina to precede him to the table. 'Jim will be joining us. He needs a lesson in art even more than I do.' He winked at Avery. 'True, compadre?'

'He'll want to know how much this one is worth,' Christina remarked before the pilot had a chance to answer Vega. 'That's about the limit of your interest in art, isn't it, Jim?'

'Ma'am, you are so cruel,' Avery said, cradling a hand over his heart. 'You already told me, it's priceless.'

'I'm amazed,' she said, taking her seat. 'You've learned something after all.'

After pouring the wine, Vega proposed a toast: 'Señorita and señor, to our next journey together.'

'Happy trails,' Avery added, the words conjuring up an image of Roy Rogers in no one else. Christina said nothing but did touch her glass to theirs. She presumed Vega was talking about the journey that would lead to the exchange for his son.

'Now, Christina, tell us of this new painting,' Vega said, breaking a dinner roll with his thumbs.

'Yes, ma'am, I'm putty in your hands,' Avery added, with a hint of sarcasm.

'You are so keen,' she responded dryly and took a sip of

the chablis. It was as if nothing had happened this morning. How often, she wondered, how often has Vega sat down to a meal after torturing, even murdering someone? Nice food, pleasant conversation, blood on his hands. 'Vincent painted "The Harvest" in the summer of 1888 during his stay in Arles, in southern France, not far from the Mediterranean. He moved there the winter before to escape the high cost of living and cold weather of Paris. He enjoyed being able to paint outdoors. He loved the light around Arles, he said it was different, that the colours were more vivid than those in Holland or Paris.'

'It's a pretty scene all right,' Avery said, twisting around for another look at the work. 'You'd never guess he was mad.'

'Vincent wasn't mad,' Christina responded. His arrogant ignorance annoyed her. 'That's a popular view, but it's an oversimplification.'

'The guy cut off his ear, didn't he?' Avery replied. 'I'd call that mad.'

'The lobe, only the lobe.' She pulled on her left earlobe to clarify the point. 'Anyway, that was one incident in a thirty-seven year life. It's astounding how many people know nothing of one of the great geniuses of the nineteenth century other than the ear cutting. And most of the time they get that wrong.'

'That's me, honey,' Avery said, unashamed of his primitive outlook. 'Never have been that interested in art, or artists.'

'So tell us, Christina,' Vega interrupted, 'if he wasn't crazy, what made van Gogh cut himself?'

'It happened in Arles, a few months after he painted "Harvest".' She took another sip of wine. 'Exactly what happened isn't clear. Vincent never commented on the incident in his letters. Gauguin said something, but not until fifteen years later.' She looked to Avery. 'Paul Gauguin, a French artist.'

'I've heard of him,' Avery said, proud of the quantum of knowledge.

'I'm impressed,' she said. She wasn't. She turned back to Vega. 'Gauguin had been staying with Vincent for a couple of months. He was a brutish man, quite unlike Vincent. Their relationship was intense and electric, they argued, often heatedly. According to Gauguin, he, Gauguin that is, left the house after arguing with Vincent, it was night. Vincent came after him with a knife, threatening him. Then Vincent cut his ear. No one knows if that's true, Gauguin could have made it up. There are theories that present other possibilities. It may have been an accident, Vincent may have had a seizure while shaving. We know he shaved his beard off around that time.'

'How do you know?' Vega asked.

'It vanished from the self-portraits.'

'Of course,' Vega nodded. 'The pictures are a record.'

'Another theory is that it was self-mutilation, while hallucinating. There were bull fights in Arles. Vincent had seen how a matador gives the vanquished bull's ear to a female spectator. That could have been playing around in his mind. There's a biblical theory too, involving Peter cutting the servants ear in the Garden of Gethsemane.' She picked up her cutlery to eat. 'All that's known for sure is that, later that night, Vincent wrapped the lobe in paper and gave it to a prostitute in a brothel he and Gauguin had visited.'

'Sounds perfectly normal to me,' Avery interjected. 'Shaving, perhaps. Hallucinating, maybe. But giving an earlobe to a hooker does sound distinctly odd, maybe crazy. Wouldn't you say so, Carlos?'

'I'm not sure.' Vega, who was at the table to absorb culture not repel it, paused to think. 'As Christina said, the ear cutting has been blown out of proportion. Vincent did it once, for whatever reason. He didn't chop off other bits and pieces, did he? One's life, one's sanity, should not be judged by a single episode.'

'An insightful analysis,' Christina remarked, not particularly surprised that he'd come up with it. She'd never doubted Vega's intelligence. Her compliment, however, had shocked them both.

Vega smiled, welcoming the tribute. 'Thank you, Christina.'

'Well, I don't know what to make of you two,' Avery said, hauling the conversation back to earth. 'Back where I come from, people don't go around cutting off bits of their bodies and giving them to hookers.'

She paused to take some fish, the man with one hand

suddenly invading her consciousness, a reminder of where she was, who she was with. 'Vincent did have a health problem,' she continued, putting the fish down. 'An undiagnosed illness. A recent theory is that he suffered from acute intermittent porphyria, AIP for short, a genetic condition. The symptoms vary from abdominal pain to seizures. In his case, it was made worse by too little food, too much alcohol and tobacco and frequent exposure to chemicals.'

'How do they know that?' Avery asked, hoping he was onto a flaw in her analysis. 'Did someone dig up his bones and do DNA tests?'

'The evidence comes from things he said in letters to his brother. Many of the letters were kept. We have about eight hundred of them in the museum.'

'What do the letters say?' Vega asked, breaking more bread.

'Vincent wrote very openly and with good detail. He spoke of his drinking and smoking, his fits of anguish and depression, his insomnia. He described how he would suddenly be overcome by hallucinations of sight and sound.'

'The illness causes hallucinations?' Vega asked.

'Not exactly. His illness probably made him more sensitive to the alcohol and other chemicals. They may have caused him to hallucinate, to behave irrationally.'

'What were these hallucinogens, Christina?' Avery asked and nudged Vega, 'Anything the boys in Medellín should get involved in?'

161

Christina ignored Avery, Avery deserved to be ignored. She sipped more wine. 'One of the worst chemicals was in a drink called absinthe,' she said, looking to Vega. 'It was popular in Arles. Absinthe was over sixty percent alcohol, it also contained a material called wormwood which we now know is toxic. It can induce hallucinations and seizures in healthy people. If Vincent did suffer from AIP, the absinthe would have had an even more pronounced effect on him. The ear cutting incident may have happened after an afternoon on absinthe.' She accepted wine from Vega stopping him at half a glass. 'Unknowingly, Vincent did just about everything he could to make his problem worse. As well as the alcohol, nicotine and caffeine, he took camphor as a treatment for insomnia. At one stage, he even tried to drink the turpentine he used with his paints.'

'He was the one who licked his paintbrush,' Avery announced, assuming he was correct. 'I've heard that before.' Then, leaning toward Vega, 'Can you imagine that, compadre. When the guy was creating that priceless masterpiece over there, he was getting high on paint?'

'That can't be proved,' Christina said. 'What we do know is that, when Vincent painted outside scenes like "Harvest", he sat in the sun all day, he didn't have lunch and he drank alcohol in a cafe at night. Such behaviour was bound to cause problems.'

'Fascinating,' Vega commented, sliding his knife and fork together on his empty plate. 'It's amazing that he was able to accomplish anything at all.'

'He didn't paint while hallucinating,' Christina said, picking up her fork again. 'For the most part, he was quite clear headed. He was an intelligent, talented and hard working man. Vincent was a genius in spite of his sickness, not as a result of it.'

Pedro rushed in. 'Carlos, the Prime Minister is on.' He turned up the volume on Vega's set. 'Josef is taping it.' It was just before eight o'clock.

The Dutch Prime Minister was reading from a prepared statement: '. . . to transfer Juan Vega to a Colombian institution. The transfer is conditional upon the safe return of Doctor Jansen and nineteen of the Vincent van Gogh paintings, these paintings to be nominated by us. The transfer would occur after the paintings and Doctor Jansen are back in the Netherlands.'

The Colombian President appeared next, his statement voiced over in English. He said he had requested the transfer of Juan Vega to Colombia and that Prime Minister de Groot had given his word to make the move as soon as his government's demands were met. He then added the cosmetic inducement that, under Colombian law, Juan Vega would be eligible for release sooner than he would be in the Netherlands. He could be free in four years.

After a recap of recent events in the story, the anchor turned to a report on an election in Ireland.

'How does that sound?' Christina asked, fully aware of its complete lack of appeal.

'Not good enough, señorita,' Vega replied. 'I think Juan and I would both end up in jail, forever. They will come up with something better.' He shared the remainder of the wine between himself and Avery. 'Anyway, I'm enjoying my education in art too much to cut it short.'

'You can buy books, you know,' Christina remarked.

'A good teacher is always better,' Vega said with a smile. Then, after a short pause, 'A week, Christina, you will be home in a week.'

When Miguel arrived with coffee, Vega directed him to take it to the balcony. 'We will have our coffee under the stars tonight.' He turned off the balcony light before leading them outside.

Christina cursed herself for not having the note, it was under the carpet in her room. Vega had let his guard down and she wasn't prepared. Thinking quickly, she asked if she could go to her room to get a sweater.

Vega responded by retrieving his jacket from the couch inside. 'The age of chivalry is alive in Medellín,' he said as he draped it over her shoulders.

She cursed again in silence and vowed that from now on she would carry the message all the time.

They took their seats at the plastic table where the coffee had been set. Christina sat back and enjoyed the cool air, keeping her frustration to herself. The traffic below made freedom seem so close.

The host offered cigars. Avery accepted. Vega searched his pockets for a lighter. 'One rule about the balcony, señorita,' Vega said, 'you must not go near the edge.' He told Avery to watch her while he went back inside.

'Your situation has hope, Christina,' Avery whispered as soon as Vega was gone. 'I can't say any more now, but we'll talk soon.'

She stared at him, agog. 'What do you mean?'

'You'll find out, just trust me, okay. And don't drop the disdain you show towards me, he'll notice if you do.'

Vega returned with the lighter.

15

Shortly after noon on Thursday, Luis Martínez and Nelson Schoute left Medellín police headquarters for Vega's house. Martínez had an appointment to see Margarita Vega at two o'clock.

'This was taken when she worked in a government laboratory in Bogotá,' Martínez said, pulling a photograph out of a file folder while waiting for a traffic light. 'Señora Vega has a degree in microbiology.'

'Pretty, and smart,' Nelson murmured, taking the photograph and file marked "VEGA/CARLOS/SEGUNDO ESPOSA" from Martínez. 'Too bad she didn't find an honest husband.'

'Margarita is no innocent,' Martínez replied as they came to a stop by an Indian woman in traditional dress selling apples from a basket, a baby slung on her back. Martínez shook his head, the woman moved on to the next car. 'Her family has been in the drug business for many years, it killed her father.'

'Murdered?' They continued past a man hawking sunglasses, seven or eight pairs wedged between the fingers of each hand.

'He had a laboratory. One day, it blew up.'

'A cocaine laboratory?' Nelson asked.

'Yes, Margarita was very young when it happened.'

'And Vega was somehow connected to the father?' Nelson thumbed his way through the rest of the file written entirely in Spanish.

'Margarita's brother worked for Vega, as a mule. Student . . . law, I think. The cartels like students. New blood, intelligent, and US Customs pays less attention to them. They did in the past, anyway. It's good money.' Martínez flicked a short siren burst to a smoke-belching truck slowing their way. 'But sometimes a condom bursts inside the mule's stomach.' The truck pulled to the side giving off a thicker cloud of smoke.

'End of life,' Nelson surmised.

'In seconds,' Martínez said with a click of his fingers. 'The Mexicans arrested him a year or so ago, but he was broken out of jail before his trial.'

'Vega?'

'Maybe. He was just a little fish.'

'Do you have anything on Margarita?'

'No, she seems to have played it pretty straight.'

'What are you going to ask her?' An old Chevy convertible passed them. Polished black and chrome. Three young men in sunglasses, red upholstery, quadraphonic

167

"La Bamba". Nelson thought of "West Side Story", with smog.

'My men asked all the questions on Monday. I want to frighten her a little, offer a compromise. She may be able to influence Vega. Who knows? And I want to size her up myself. One day, she may lead us to him.'

'You're pretty certain he'll send for her?'

'My men didn't get the impression she'd been abandoned.'

'She may not know yet.' They stopped at a red light, behind the convertible, the boys doing their macho best to get noticed by a young woman walking in front of them. The woman, dressed in a business suit, smiled and walked on.

'Perhaps,' Martínez said with a shrug. 'But the rumour is that Señor and Señora Vega are a happily married couple, hard as it is to imagine.'

'He's in love with her youth and beauty, she's in it for the money and power,' Nelson said dryly, looking back at the photograph. They were moving again. 'Vega can buy new youth and beauty wherever he ends up.'

'You're very cynical, my friend,' Martínez remarked with a half-hearted laugh, knowing full well his companion could be right.

'It wouldn't be the first time that kind of thing has happened, would it Luis?'

'I hope you're wrong. We need Vega to stay in love with his wife.'

They arrived at the fortress in the hills just before two

o'clock. After their identities were checked at the gate, a guard accompanied them up the long eucalypt lined driveway to the house.

A crisply dressed maid greeted them at the door and led them along a short hallway into a spacious sitting room. Martínez looked to a painting, one of several on the thick white walls: colourful bouquets hang from a pole resting on the shoulders of four proud young women walking in line; the third woman looks to the viewer; the others, intent on getting where they are going, look straight ahead. 'I know very little about art, Nelson,' Martínez whispered, 'but I like this one.'

'"Las Floristas",' came a woman's voice from behind. Margarita Vega, more attractive than her photograph had promised, greeted them, 'Buenas tardes, señores.'

Martínez bowed. 'Buenas tardes, Señora Vega.' He held out his identification. 'Usted habla Ingles, señora?'

'A little, señor.'

'Good, señora. I am Colonel Luis Martínez of the Colombian National Police and this is Señor Nelson Schoute of the Van Gogh Museum in Amsterdam.' He flashed a polite smile. 'Señor Schoute speaks many languages, but unfortunately for us, Spanish is not one of them.'

'It will be good to practise my English, Señor Schoute,' she said and, gesturing to the painting, 'It is one of two "Las Floristas" by Camilo Egas. A larger one hangs in the National Museum of Ecuador. Carlos went to Quito to buy this one himself.'

'It is beautiful, señora, very nice,' Martínez said, welcoming the chance to flatter.

She led them into a courtyard in the middle of the house. A maid was waiting with iced tea.

'Señor Schoute, I am sorry about what is happening.' Margarita spoke delicately as the maid poured the tea. 'I know in my heart that Carlos will not harm the paintings, or your colleague, Doctor Jansen.'

'I hope you're right, Señora Vega,' Nelson responded, resisting her considerable charm.

'Carlos misses his son badly, it has made him do this strange thing.' She lay her slender hand between herself and Martínez. Two silver bands, a single diamond, nails long and perfect. The woman had class. 'Colonel, I told your men all I know, I have not heard from my husband since their visit.'

Life with Carlos Vega had more than satisfied Margarita's ambitions. She wanted for nothing and was the envy of all her friends. But the cost of that satisfaction, the underside of the wealth and power, had been far more invasive than she had ever anticipated. She, like her husband, had her life threatened routinely, she was a virtual prisoner in their home, she could not shop or meet friends without taking extreme precautions, and now the police were monitoring her every move. As for the strength of the relationship with her husband, although she was sure of his love for her, she had never really fallen deeply in love with him. She felt comfortable in the marriage but there was no great passion, although she had done an admirable job pretending there was. Margarita was a pragmatist, she knew she had a good deal and was committed to it. Not that there was a choice. She'd known all along that leaving the marriage could never be an option, not even now: betrayal of Carlos Vega in any shape or form was a capital offence.

The only cause of friction in the three year marriage had been disagreement over children. She had argued against his desire for more saying that a fortress in Medellín was no place for babies. In fact, she felt no urge whatsoever to be a mother and was determined to avoid the status completely.

And now, as he had spoken of many times, Carlos was on the way to a new life, a life which, she was absolutely certain, included her. She would do nothing to assist the police.

'We did not come here to ask questions, señora,' Martínez said and took a slice of lemon from a dish in the middle. 'We came to make a request.' He squeezed the juice into his tea and slowly stirred it in. 'It would be easier on your husband if this did not go any further. If he surrenders now and returns the hostage and the paintings, I am told by my superiors that an arrangement can be made for special consideration.' The precedent for special consideration had been set in 1991 when the government of the day, desperate for a victory in the drug war, accepted Pablo Escobar's outrageous terms of surrender. Escobar gave up his dangerous life to be imprisoned with inmates of his choice in a facility designed by him, "The Cathedral", as it became known. The prison had its own bar, discotheque and Jacuzzi. Visitors were allowed any time. Women stayed overnight. Escobar's luxuriously furnished quarters included telephones, fax machines and computers, all the equipment necessary for him to continue managing his empire outside. The guards, whose meagre government salaries were supplemented by stipends from the inmates, turned a blind eye to the excesses. Escobar was as snug as a bug in a rug. He blew it all a few months later when he summoned four of his lieutenants to explain some financial irregularities. They arrived in the prison to their own executions. The government sent soldiers to apprehend Escobar and move him to a normal prison. Escobar simply paid some bribes and walked free. Martínez knew that such a deal would never be made again but a lesser one to end the crisis would certainly be considered. He had been told by his superiors that the President had said so himself. 'I would rather this end in a compromise than a gun fight, señora.'

Margarita nodded, her deep brown eyes glistening.

Martínez watched her over his glass as he sipped. He was satisfied with the progress so far, her discomfort was becoming more pronounced by the second. 'Otherwise, señora, when we locate Carlos, and we will, blood will be spilled. You do not want your husband to die the death of Pablo Escobar, do you?' Martínez hoped that the reference to the Medellín police's greatest victory would further help his cause. After two years on the run, the man who started his career as a tombstone robber and rose to dominate the largest crime syndicate in the world, who was adored by many of Medellín's poor because of his charitable works, who was elected to national political office, died barefoot on the roof of a town house, shot by the police. He had only one bodyguard with him at the time. Martínez had travelled to Medellín to see the body for himself, to be sure that Escobar was really dead. Events had come full circle since then: Carlos Vega, today's Escobar, was now approaching the end of his run. Martínez wanted him alive. 'In the past, I know the police have ignored your husband's activities. That cannot happen this time.' His voice firmed. 'That will not happen this time, señora. Your husband has committed a crime against the international community. This is bigger than Colombia. Our President must see the government win, no matter what it takes.' He could see a frightened look now, tears starting to flow. He leaned back and softened his tone. 'So, señora, when your husband contacts you, think about what I have said, try to talk some sense into him. A deal can be made, it may save his life.'

'Thank you for this advice, Colonel Martínez,' she sobbed. 'But I do not know when he will contact me.'

Martínez handed her his handkerchief.

'I do not want Carlos to be killed,' she said and wiped the tears away. 'I do not know what to do. If he calls me, he will not listen to any advice. He is a very stubborn man.'

'All I ask, señora, is that you try.' Martínez, his mission accomplished, took a last sip of tea. 'I am sorry to upset you, Señora Vega, but I felt I should tell you this myself.'

173

He stood and placed his card on the table in front of her. 'I may be contacted at that number day and night, señora. Thank you for seeing us.'

'Please forgive me for crying.' She reached to hand him his handkerchief.

He waved her off. 'We will leave you in peace, señora.'

'Thank you, Colonel. It has been very difficult for me these past few days.' She turned to Nelson and wiped more tears. 'Señor Schoute, I hope it will not be long before this is over.'

Martínez led the way to the door, turned and bowed. 'Buenas tardes, señora.' Nelson did likewise, only self-consciously.

'Buenas tardes, señores,' Vega's wife replied as the maid led them away. Margarita Vega regained her composure the instant they left. Forcing herself to cry on cue was a skill she had used to her advantage many times and Martínez had acted predictably. Men are so gullible, she thought and dropped the handkerchief to the floor.

'Señora Vega is either a very sweet lady or a very good actor, which do you think is true?' Martínez asked once he and Nelson were back inside the car.

'The second.'

'Me too.' He looked up at the house and turned the ignition. 'We will be watching you señora, we will be watching like hawks.'

It was late afternoon by the time they got back to police

headquarters in Medellín. There was another fax waiting, a copy of the third message from Vega to the Dutch Prime Minister. They read it together.

To: The Prime Minister
The Hague, Netherlands

Sir

You can do much better than the offer made last night. I am no fool, do not play games with me.

I will exchange ten of the paintings for my son. Such an exchange would happen at the earliest possible time in a location to be named by me immediately beforehand.

After Juan is in a safe place, I will reveal the location of Doctor Jansen and the other ten paintings. You would be free to collect her and them at that time.

I am willing to accept nothing less. Please respond by 9 a.m., Colombian time, tomorrow.

Doctor Jansen's signature on this page indicates that both she and the paintings are in excellent condition.

Carlos Vega

An attached note indicated that it had been sent from northern Medellín at 3 p.m.

16

At eight o'clock on Friday morning, an hour before the deadline he had imposed upon the Dutch Prime Minister, Carlos Vega returned to his apartment after having had breakfast across the hall. Christina was in front of the living area television, finishing her breakfast.

'Buenos dìas, señorita,' Vega said and gestured for the duty guard to leave.

'Good morning,' she replied without looking up. 'No announcement overnight?' She had slept soundly until 7:30.

'No.' Vega's attention was drawn briefly to television images of an avalanche in the French Alps. 'I'm not concerned, last time he waited until the last minute.' He wandered to the painting Christina had hung yesterday afternoon, Vincent's most recognisable work, "Sunflowers". 'Many people in Colombia have this picture.'

'There are millions of copies, all over the world,' she said, pouring herself some coffee from the flask that had come with her fruit and toast. 'Postcards, calendars, tea towels, refrigerator magnets. You name it.' She dropped the volume on the television, adjusted a pillow and sat back, facing his direction. 'There's one sunflower painting, in Japan, an insurance company paid about forty million dollars for it.' The coffee was cool and weak, undrinkable. She put it down. 'It's thought to be a fake. It isn't mentioned in any of Vincent's letters.' She was referring to a recent allegation by a British expert that a struggling artist by the name of Claude-Emile Schuffenecker who was hired in 1901 to do some restoration work on a real "Sunflowers" had, afterwards, manufactured one himself, the one presently in Japan.

'But this one is genuine?' Vega asked, peering into it.

'Of course,' she said, moving to the kitchen. 'We're a museum, we check things.' She picked up the vacuum flask. It had not been filled this morning. 'Empty,' she said, waving it. 'And mine's cold.'

Vega got on the phone and ordered a fresh brew.

'Thanks,' she said when he hung up. She moved towards the painting. 'This caused a lot of trouble when it was first exhibited, in Brussels.'

'Trouble, what kind?' Vega asked, only mildly interested, but happy to fill the time.

'One of the organisers arranged for Vincent's brother to send along some canvasses. Renoir, Cézanne and Toulouse-Lautrec had work there too.' Vega was beside her now, in front of the painting. 'The trouble started when one of the other exhibitors, Henry de Groux, a painter of religious scenes, refused to allow his work to be hung in the same room as this. De Groux denounced Vincent as an ignoramus and a charlatan.'

'A charlatan! I too have been called that, the word is the same in Spanish.'

Tempted to mock him, but resisting, she went on. 'Henri Toulouse-Lautrec, a friend of Vincent's, got angry. He challenged de Groux to a duel.'

'A hot blooded man,' Vega remarked, the hint at violence securing his interest.

Miguel entered carrying a cup of coffee. 'Café con leche para la señorita,' he said and placed it on the coffee table.

'Thank you,' Christina responded in Miguel's direction and turned back to Vega. 'The other artists defused the situation. De Groux left the exhibition the next day, with his paintings.'

'Better a live coward than a dead hero,' Vega quipped and moved to a couch.

'One of Vincent's paintings sold at that exhibition, "The Red Vineyard".'

'How much did he get?' He turned the television volume down further.

'Four hundred francs.' She did the conversion via Euros. 'About eighty US dollars. Back then, it was enough for Vincent to live on for a couple of months.'

'Now it would be worth millions,' Vega said and picked up today's newspaper. He'd already read the Van Gogh hijack update on page one.

'It would.' She moved back to her spot on the couch, opposite him. 'The news of the sale upset Vincent.'

'A curious man.'

'Vincent wasn't well at the time. It was his second experience of success that year. Earlier, an art critic with "Mercure de France" wrote the first article ever published about Vincent's art. It was very flattering. The critic raved about the work he'd seen in Theo's apartment and in Paris. It's in the guide.' She picked up the LACMA guide from the coffee table and found the appropriate page. 'Here. He described Vincent's work using phrases such as: "excess in strength, excess in nervousness, in violence of expression" ... "often brutal and sometimes ingeniously delicate" ... "an ebullient brain which irresistibly pours its lava into all the ravines of art, a terrible and maddened genius, often sublime, sometimes grotesque, almost always on the edge of the pathological."'

'What did Vincent think of that?' Vega asked, skimming the horse racing results.

'He was upset.' She closed the book and placed it back on the table. 'He didn't want the attention. He said his art was secondary to that of Gauguin and others and asked Theo to tell the critic not to write any more about his work. And when he found out about "The Red Vineyard" sale, he said he expected to be punished for the recognition, he said success was the worst thing that could happen to an artist.'

'He was afraid of success,' Vega announced conclusively,

putting down the paper. 'To me, success has always been something to seize, and I have done so. But to others, it is something to be avoided. They would rather be comfortably mediocre for their entire lives.'

'But Vincent wasn't mediocre,' she retorted, rendering his tangent irrelevant.

'He was afraid of something,' Vega said, and checked his watch, the deadline was just forty minutes away. 'I think it's time for a new painting.' He stood to leave. 'The portrait in the hat.'

'"Self-portrait with a Straw Hat",' she said for the sake of correctness. 'Why it?'

'I've seen it in your guide, it seems appropriate for my mood today.' With that, he left for the other apartment.

A guard entered a short time later, one of those who had worried her at the celebration on Tuesday night. He acknowledged her politely in Spanish and sat tamely in front of the television. Seeing him now, sober, she assumed the whiskey had been responsible for his behaviour that evening. As soon as she finished her coffee she went to the third bedroom and retrieved the painting Vega had requested.

Ten minutes later, it was on the wall. A bearded Vincent under a yellow straw hat looked out at her. His face, a tempest of brushstrokes: long and brownish-red for the beard, horizontal across the nose, angled at the cheeks, radiating from the eyes and curving to his forehead largely hidden under the yellow strokes that were the hat. The suggestion of motion in a subject at rest. He wears a simple shirt and yellow coat with red trim. A snow storm of blue and green feathered strokes fills the space behind.

She looked into Vincent's pained eyes, to his soul, she promised him she would prevail.

Rather than spend any time alone with the guard, she went to her room to watch television.

The deadline came and went. Finally, at eleven thirty, CNN crossed to the Netherlands, to Leiden University, where the Prime Minister was attending a ceremony. Vega watched from the second apartment as Pieter de Groot made what seemed to be an impromptu statement to a group of reporters huddled around him under a building's sheltered entrance. The darkness and drizzle of the Dutch winter evening was evident in the background. 'Mr Vega has refused the offer put forward on Wednesday by both me and the President of Colombia. Cabinet will be meeting this evening to formulate a new proposal.' De Groot misled the audience, there was no need for another Cabinet meeting just yet.

Then came some questions. 'Prime Minister, has Carlos Vega imposed a deadline on this?'

'An unrealistic one. Mr Vega must realise that my government has other obligations to fulfil. It was not possible to get Cabinet together in time to meet his deadline. We will have a new proposal later tonight, I will announce it then.'

'When was that deadline, Prime Minister?'

181

'I have no comment other than to say it was unrealistic. I must emphasise that my government wants to see this situation resolved as soon as possible. We do want to find a solution.'

'Prime Minister, if you do accept Vega's demands, are you afraid other such crimes will result?'

'It is definitely a concern. We would not want to see that happen. If I say more, our negotiations may be jeopardised. Thank you, ladies and gentlemen.' He vanished from the screen.

Vega, clearly agitated by what he had just heard, turned to Pedro and Josef who had also been watching. 'They're taking too long.' He went back across the hall.

Christina arrived in the living area a short time later.

'De Groot is damaging your reputation for punctuality,' Vega said, turning from the self-portrait, his anger evident in his voice.

'You heard what he said, it takes time to get his Cabinet together. You know he wants a solution.'

'Nonsense, he's stalling, he's buying time for the Colombian police.'

'He has other obligations, for goodness sake, he still has a country to run.'

'He's stalling,' Vega repeated, her transparent excuses annoying him further. 'He already knows what he can offer.' He turned back to the painting. 'This is magnificent,' he said after a few seconds. 'Perfect in fact.' The anger was gone from his voice. 'He has green eyes, just like yours.' He moved closer to Vincent's face. 'How old is he in this?'

'He did it in 1887, so . . . thirty-four.'

'A year older than you.' The information had come from her passport. 'How old was he when he died?'

'Four years older than me,' she said with a frown. 'If that means anything, which I can't see it does.'

'He was very young,' Vega said, amused by her response, 'that's all I meant.' He stepped backwards, keeping his eyes on the painting. 'Tell me about it, Christina.'

'Don't you want to wait until lunchtime?'

'I'll be busy at lunchtime.' He looked more closely at the work. 'His left ear looks okay, but we can't see the right one. Which one did he cut?'

'It's too early. He cut it in Arles, a year and a half after he did this.'

'Did he do any self-portraits after he cut his ear?'

'There's one shortly after, his ear is bandaged in it. He cut his left ear but in the painting it's the right one that has the bandage.'

'Why?'

'If you think about it, you'll work it out,' she said, sure he could.

'I'm too preoccupied to think.' He couldn't be bothered, the negotiations were too heavy on his mind. 'Tell me.'

'He used a mirror, he painted what he saw in the mirror.'

'His mirror image, of course. So right is left.' He moved closer, defying Vincent's unrelenting stare, enjoying the power he held over the Dutch artist's helpless soul. He had convinced himself that this was the most suitable painting for his purpose. But there was no hurry, he would stalk his prey a while longer. 'He looks very serious, very reverent, like a priest.'

'You're closer than you think.' She wondered where Vega was leading. 'He did study theology for a while, before he took up art. He even trained as an evangelist, but he got too involved in the problems of the poor. He gave away everything he had, even the clothes off his back. So the church leaders dismissed him for, what they said was, his own good.'

'The man was destined to be poor,' Vega said.

'He wasn't poor. His brother believed in his talent, he sent him a monthly allowance, about one hundred and fifty francs, enough for one person to survive on quite comfortably, more than a postman he knew made. But food came low on Vincent's list of priorities, he spent most of the allowance on painting supplies.'

'It was his choice then, art over everything. It's unfortunate he didn't get the rewards he deserved.'

'He didn't get financial rewards, nothing significant anyway. The popular myth is that he didn't sell anything.'

'You told me about one painting he sold, "The Vineyard".'

'"The Red Vineyard". That wasn't all. Early on, his father hired him to make some biblical maps and an uncle paid him to do some sketches of scenes in The Hague. He also sold some drawings in The Hague and Paris and one of his self-portraits was bought by a London dealer. And he bartered with pieces of his work, he paid bills with them.'

'I must go,' Vega said after a short silence. As he walked to the door, he turned and added what appeared to be an afterthought. 'Please return the cases to the room.' He gestured to the two cases near the painting. 'I have some business to conduct.' He left.

She did as he requested.

Pedro and Josef were waiting in the hallway when she came out of the third bedroom. Pedro told her that Vega had a visitor and that she should wait in her room. She argued, suspicious of what Vega was up to, but in the end had no choice but to comply. She heard the door being locked behind her.

At one o'clock it was unlocked. 'Lunch is ready, señorita,' Pedro announced, sounding meek through the door.

She walked down the hallway to the living area, Pedro behind her. She could sense there was something wrong.

She blanched when she saw it, stunned. It wasn't possible. 'No! Oh God no!' she screamed. She ran towards the mutilated painting, the rage welling inside her. 'No!' Pedro raced over and held her by the shoulders. She was shaking uncontrollably. She pushed him away. 'He's destroyed it! Oh! . . . God!' She collapsed on the floor in tears. Vincent's face had been cut out of the painting.

17

The Medellín Channel 3 news producer who took the call at eight minutes past two on Friday afternoon was sure it was not a hoax. Unlike seven previous callers claiming association with the van Gogh hijacking, this person hadn't gloated, made wild threats, or waited for a reaction from her. He had delivered the precisely worded message in a cold monotone and clicked off the instant it was finished. He had also provided an obscure detail about the hostage that would make verification easy.

The news director jumped on the phone to his contact in police headquarters as the tape was repositioned while the producer scrambled her team for the bus terminal.

Martínez was alerted and listened on another line as the message was played a second time: 'I represent Señor Carlos Vega. Doctor Jansen does not eat shrimp. I suggest you look inside locker number seventy-one, number seven one, at the bus terminal on Calle 78, it contains your biggest story this year.'

'Does Christina Jansen eat shrimp?' Martínez asked Nelson, now standing beside him.

'She's allergic to it, why?' The response propelled Martínez to immediate action. He related the gist of the message to Nelson in between issuing orders for the bus terminal to be evacuated and for a bomb disposal team to be sent to check out the lockers. Both were routine precautions, prudent in such a city.

Martínez and Nelson's arrival at the modern bus terminal ten minutes later was filmed by the Channel 3 television crew whose cooperation with the phone call had gained them the right to film whatever was going to be found.

The military bomb disposal team arrived with a sniffer dog and quickly declared the lockers safe. Martínez cautiously opened number seventy-one with a master key provided by the terminal manager.

The locker contained nothing but a large brown envelope. The television camera operator moved in for a better view as Martínez slid it to the edge of the locker and cut it open with a Swiss army knife provided by one of his men. He lifted the top side of the envelope and looked inside at what seemed, to him, a piece of yellow cardboard.

'It's a piece of one of the paintings,' Nelson said as Martínez began sliding it out. 'Let me do it, Luis.'

Without saying a word, Nelson edged the board out onto his left palm. This can't be true, he thought, as he looked down at Vincent's green eyes. The rectangle of painting, slightly smaller than his two hands, contained the whole face and part of the rim of the straw hat.

'Is it real?' Martínez asked.

'I'm afraid so,' Nelson murmured in reply.

Martínez examined the envelope. There was no writing on it, nothing inside. 'There could be something on the back,' he said of the face.

Nelson moved his hands to the edge of the yellow rectangle and raised it to look underneath. The camera operator sat on the floor and filmed up. The world would get to read the hand-printed message: "De Groot, you missed the deadline. My offer is not negotiable. Do not fool with me any longer. Vega"

Nelson edged the piece of painting back into the envelope and, barely controlling his rage, spoke to the camera: 'Carlos Vega is a savage. This mutilation is a crime against civilisation.' Martínez tugged at his sleeve. They left the terminal without further comment.

The television pictures of the sensational find were broadcast by Channel 3 in Medellín at three o'clock and sent via satellite to stations around the world.

The Dutch Prime Minister was in his office reviewing the statement he was due to deliver in less than an hour when an aide rushed in to tell him the news from Medellín.

Pieter de Groot's first thought was one of utter contempt for Carlos Vega. Vermeer's words rang in his head: ". . . his most likely response would be to damage or perhaps destroy the paintings, one at a time. You must be prepared for that if you stall." He had gambled and lost. From now on, there would be no stalling.

As arranged, he faced the media at precisely ten o'clock, the context enveloping his announcement had suddenly gone terribly sour.

'Ladies and gentlemen, Carlos Vega has sent a warning to me not to fool with him. I can assure everyone that neither my government nor I was fooling. I can act only after consulting Cabinet. It is unfortunate that the implementation of that democratic safeguard did not fit with Mr Vega's time frame.

'I'm sure the people of the Netherlands and the rest of the world will join with me in condemning the actions of Mr Vega in damaging Vincent's self-portrait. We were hoping that reason would prevail in the negotiations. Unfortunately, we were wrong. I will do my best to ensure that Mr Vega has no cause to mutilate any other paintings.

'After meeting with Cabinet and also discussing the matter with the President of Colombia, I am authorised to make the following proposal to Mr Vega.

'The governments of the Netherlands and Colombia have agreed to the transfer of Juan Vega to Colombia. The appropriate papers have already been signed in anticipation of the acceptance of this offer.

'According to this agreement, Juan Vega would be transported from the Netherlands under custody to a penitentiary in Colombia. The transfer would occur upon the safe return of Doctor Jansen and fifteen of the twenty paintings. Those paintings would be nominated by us. Once Juan Vega is safely in Colombia, we would expect the other paintings to be returned.

'This offer meets many of Mr Vega's demands and represents a considerable compromise on the part of my government. No further movement is possible on our part without jeopardising our commitment to international security.'

De Groot looked up from the text and spoke to the cameras. 'That is our final offer. I now wait upon word from Mr Vega and ask that he consider alternative ways of communicating. It is inappropriate and cumbersome to use international television broadcasts to proceed with this matter. Thank you.'

The message was broadcast live in the Netherlands and carried by CNN around the world along with a full report on the bus terminal discovery and a background story on "Self-portrait with a Straw Hat".

Vega watched the whole thing in the second apartment. While the speed of the Dutch Prime Minister's response had impressed him, the substance of the statement had not. He expected his disappointment to be short lived, however. With increasing pressure, the Dutch Prime Minister would soon see things his way. And it was timely that de Groot had suggested the use of an alternative method of communication. Although the present system had served them well, it was awkward and outlandish. Today, according to his plan, Willem Imthorn should have arranged the delivery of a phone to the Dutch Prime Minister's official residence.

Vega lingered over coffee with Pedro before returning to face his hostage.

Christina, raw and distraught, was waiting when he entered the apartment. She bolted towards him from the couch and caught him by surprise. He grabbed her flaying arms but was too slow to prevent her knee connecting with his groin. 'Dios! La puta!' he yelled as he stooped in pain.

She pounded his back with her fists, tears flowing down her face. 'You bastard! One day you'll pay for what you did.'

Vega's arm swung, numbing the side of her face and sending her flying hard against the back of a couch. 'Next time, I won't be so gentle.' There was madness in his eyes. He waved off the guard who had rushed over from the table. 'Think yourself lucky, señorita, it was either do something to the painting or do something to you.'

'Then why the hell didn't you do something to me?' she screamed, holding her hand over her numb and ringing ear. The guard stood back, ready to pounce if she attacked again. 'You could have cut off one of my fingers and sent it to them. That's what people like you normally do, isn't it?' She wiped more tears away. 'Why did you have to destroy the painting?'

'Enough!' He turned and moved away.

'I hate you! You're pathetic! You're the enemy of every civilised person in the world. You've got your immortality.'

'Enough!' he said again to no effect.

'A hundred years from now, the children of Colombia will learn of Señor Carlos Vega, the man who defaced the van Gogh. Your grandchildren will spit on your grave.'

Vega turned in rage. He went to strike her again but stopped. Instead, wrapping his hand around her throat he pushed her up against the back of the couch, immobilising her and forcing her to gasp for breath. 'It had to be done, understand? Your government was stalling, they want time to find me. I have everything at stake here, señorita, my life, my son, everything.' He released his grip but remained in front of her, preventing her from getting up. Christina caught her breath as Vega went on. 'I cannot take chances, I cannot let them stall.' He stepped back. 'They had to know I was serious.'

Christina raised herself, massaging her neck where he'd held her.

'Anyway, I used a very sharp blade. I'm sure the talented people at your museum can put the face back together.'

'How considerate. Did you use the knife you normally use to stab people? Did you wipe the blood off it first?'

'It's over, forget it.' He moved towards the door. 'Take that down and put another one up,' he ordered, pointing to the mutilated canvas. 'I'm sure de Groot has learned his lesson, I won't need to cut any more.'

'No other paintings, ever.'

'Don't be so difficult, Christina. I'll be back in an hour, if there isn't another painting, I'll put one up myself.' He left.

Christina retrieved the case belonging to "Self-portrait with a Straw Hat" and packed what was left of it. She had been a fool to believe that Vega appreciated Vincent's art. To him the paintings were weapons. If he needed to damage another one, he wouldn't hesitate. She got the wire cutters from the kitchen and twisted the hooks on the wall until they broke. Then, frustrated and depressed, she retreated to her room.

At six o'clock she heard movement through the wall. Then the sound of a hacksaw cutting metal. She covered her ears to block out the sound. It didn't work. The sawing stopped. She waited as long as she could bare before going down to the living area.

"The Courtesan" looked at her from the wall, the damaged case below it. Vega was sitting on a couch with Avery across from him on the other side of an almost empty bottle of Scotch. 'I hope you approve of my choice, señorita,' Vega said.

'Drink, honey?' Avery asked as she examined the new painting for damage. There was none.

'No,' she answered and checked out the wire and single hook supporting the painting. They were satisfactory, just.

Vega went on. 'Jim and I have been waiting for you to tell us about this Japanese woman.'

'Forget it,' she replied. 'The lectures are over, you'll have to read about it yourself.' She was repelled by the thought of allowing him back into her world.

'I already did.' He picked up the LACMA guide from the coffee table and waved it at her. 'I chose the painting from your book. I've read it from cover to cover, you know.' He put on his reading glasses and searched through the guide for the appropriate page as he walked towards her and the painting. 'Let me see . . . now. This was painted by Vincent in Paris in 1887. It's based on a Japanese print which appeared on the cover of "Paris Illustré" in 1886.' Vega looked over the top of his glasses to Christina. 'How about that, he copied it.'

'So?' she responded. 'It wasn't exactly easy to go to Japan in those days, was it?'

He smiled and went on. 'A woman wearing an elaborate kimono framed within a background of cranes, bamboo and water lilies.' He pointed to two frogs, one green, the other brown, at the bottom of the picture. 'They didn't mention the frogs.'

'You should write and complain.' It was her writing. The frog and crane were synonyms for the woman's occupation, high class prostitute. She was in no mood to share that with Vega.

'I should,' he replied and turned to Avery who was occupied refilling the glasses. 'It's quite a different van Gogh from the ones Christina has shown us so far, do you see that Jim?'

'It looks Asian to me,' Avery said, glancing up. 'Are you sure it's Vincent's?' He stood and moved towards them. 'Maybe the Van Gogh Foundation was taken for a ride.' He handed Vega his glass.

Christina ignored the comment and remained motionless beside the painting, her arms folded.

'Come on Christina, don't sulk,' Avery said, trying to get a reaction. 'Thanks to you, I was becoming interested in Vincent's paintings. Don't nip my art education in the bud.'

She shot him a sullen look and maintained her silence.

'Don't worry, Jim,' Vega said, holding up the guide, 'It's all in here.' He read: 'The Japonaiserie style developed in Paris in the 1860s, a decade after a previously isolated Japan was opened for trade with the West. Japanese ceramics, lacquers, textiles, fans, books, scroll prints and prints made their way to Europe. These exotic and previously unobtainable Japanese items were actively sought because of their technical excellence.'

He took a sip of the drink before continuing. 'Van Gogh admired the Japanese style. He experimented with it and eventually abandoned other methods in favour of its heightened colours and simplified form.

'In a letter to Theo from Arles . . .' He turned to Avery and explained, 'Theo was Vincent's brother, he supported Vincent while he painted,' then, back to reading from the book, 'Vincent wrote, "I foresee that other artists will want to see colour under a stronger sun and in a more Japanese clarity of light. From Arles onward you are bound to find beautiful contrasts of red and green, of blue and orange, of sulphur and lilac. There is another kind of colour than that of the North".' He closed the book and turned to face Christina. 'Is that true, what he says about the light? Would your beautiful Vincent van Gogh,' he parodied her Dutch pronunciation of van Gogh, 'be impressed with the strong light here in Medellín?'

She turned away, still silent.

'Come now, Christina,' Vega said, grasping her shoulder with his hand.

'Let go!' She pushed his hand away, she could smell the alcohol on him.

'I prefer your explanations, Christina, the guide seems so dry in comparison.' He walked behind her. 'Will you ever talk to me again?'

She was astonished by the way Vega was acting. Here was the most feared criminal in South America reading from an art guide and trying to sweet talk her out of a tantrum. Her logic took over, this was a situation she had to capitalise upon. There was no point brooding over what had happened, the stakes were too high. She consoled herself with the thought that, in the end, Vega would pay for his crimes. She vowed to be there to watch when it happened.

'I'm going crazy in here,' she said, sounding and acting restless. This was her chance to see Avery, alone. 'I need some fresh air, can I go out on the balcony?'

'Okay.' Vega reached for the keys in his pocket. 'But I'll come with you.'

'For goodness sake, can't I go by myself? It's dark, who's going to see me?'

'I'm afraid you can't, señorita.'

'What do you think I'm going to do, jump over the edge, or throw down a message? Look!' She pulled the front pockets out of her jeans, they were empty. 'The back ones are empty too. Look!' She turned and slapped both back pockets. The sound was that of cloth against flesh. 'I just need to get out of here for a while, away from you. I need to cool down. I won't try anything. You promised not to damage any more paintings, I'll promise not to do anything out there, just sit, okay?'

'Very well, but with Jim.' He tossed the keys to Avery. 'Leave the light off and don't let her near the edge.'

'Sure, Carlos,' the American replied. 'I could use some fresh air myself. Come with me, honey.' He took his drink with him.

'Don't call me honey, okay!'

'Whatever you say, ma'am,' he responded, holding his hands in surrender. He picked up the LACMA guide on the way out. 'I might have a read of this myself.'

'Honey, that performance deserves an Oscar,' Avery said after sliding the door closed.

'The other night, what did you mean when you said you were on my side?' They took seats at the table, facing away from the apartment.

'I'm not sure it's such a good idea to tell you. Your temperament's a little hot for my liking, you could blow the whole thing.'

'I won't, promise. Please tell me.'

'Okay,' Avery replied, 'but move, so you can watch him.'

She moved the chair out from the table and stretched her legs next to his chair. 'He's reading the newspaper, looks settled.'

'Okay, keep your eye on him and listen.' He spoke softly. 'After the hijacking on Monday, I flew to Jamaica, dropped the plane off and went on to Miami that afternoon. When I arrived at the airport on Tuesday to come here, I was picked up by the DEA.'

'The DEA?'

'US Drug Enforcement Administration, they've got people crawling all over central and South America trying very hard to kill the drug trade at its source.' He offered her the drink. 'Without a great deal of success, I might add.'

She declined the offer. 'What's the deal with the DEA?'

'They waved this warrant for my arrest on charges of drug smuggling in front of me, said they could put me away for twenty years. Then, like the nice guys they are, they made me an offer. The more I did to help them bust Vega, the more pleasant my life would be afterwards. The witness protection program, heard of that?'

'Yes,' she replied. 'On television.'

'It has levels. I want the top, five star . . . new identity, nice house, nice town, and I get to keep my money.'

'So you're on my side?' she said after a short silence.

'Honey, I'm mostly on my own side, but sure, this could help you too. You're the only person in Colombia who knows what I just told you. At least I hope you are, otherwise I could be a dead man.'

She glanced to see Vega still reading the paper. 'Won't the DEA tell the Colombian police?'

'Hell, I hope not, then I'd be dead for sure. There are plenty of rotten apples in that box. The Dutch don't know either. Neither do the DEA people here. There's a few of those cowboys who aren't exactly kosher. Only the two guys in Miami and their boss in Washington know about me. Nobody else needs to know, just yet. Which makes me wonder why I told you.'

'I'm glad you did,' she said. 'Is there anything I can do to help?'

'Yes, don't try anything like this again. Carlos is a suspicious son of a bitch. If I need to talk to you, I'll set it up, not you, understand?'

'Okay, sorry, I didn't mean to put you in danger.'

'Forget it, just don't do it again. And while I'm giving orders, watch your mouth with Vega, he's got noises in his head, tinnitus. Bad. You've seen him turn nasty. That won't help us at all.'

'Okay, I know about the tinnitus.'

'Good, now I'm going to move over there.' He pointed to another chair near the door. 'The less we're seen talking, the safer I'll feel.'

'I have a note I wrote, saying where I am. I was going to drop it over the side, or have you drop it.'

'Forget it, don't. If it gets into the wrong hands, you could end up dead, so could I. Play it Vega's way and everyone will end up happy. Except him, of course.' He glanced around towards Vega to see that he was still reading. Then, back to her, 'Where is this note?'

'In my bra?'

'Now?' His eyes widened as they dropped to her chest.

'Yes.'

'What a gal. Well honey, I want you to give it to me right now, and don't write another one, understand?'

'Okay, I'll play it your way.' She reached under her shirt, retrieved the note and, after checking that Vega wasn't watching, gave it to him. He tore it in two without looking at it. 'That's yours,' he said, giving a piece to her. 'Bon appétit.' He stuffed part of his piece into his mouth and chewed.

'Bon appétit,' she replied, and did likewise.

He washed the paper down with a mouthful of Scotch and offered it to her to do likewise. She did, coughing afterwards.

Vega looked up, he had heard the cough. 'You have a nap, honey, or pretend to have one,' Avery said and moved to the chair near the door. He opened the guide but was too nervous to read the words.

Vega appeared at the door about twenty minutes later and asked them to come back inside. He handed Christina the fourth message to the Dutch Prime Minister and a pen.

To: The Prime Minister
The Hague, Netherlands

Sir

I am unwilling to accept anything less than what was outlined in my proposal of Thursday. I will hand over ten paintings of your choice and then you will give me my son. After that is done, you will get Christina Jansen and the other paintings.

I suggest that you publish the list of paintings you want first in the Colombian newspapers as soon as possible.

A phone will be delivered to your residence. Carry it with you day and night. I will use it to contact you from now on.

Doctor Jansen's signature on this page indicates that all the paintings, except for the self-portrait, are in good condition and that she is being well cared for.

Carlos Vega

'Well cared for, am I?' she said, accepting the pen from Vega. 'Was the hit on the head part of your hospitality?'

'You started that,' he responded. 'Anyway, it's a small detail, there's no need to bother your Prime Minister with it. Do you agree?'

She signed the letter without further comment.

Fifteen minutes later, Rafael parked his car on a deserted street and sent the fax on its way.

18

Pieter de Groot opened the Saturday morning emergency Cabinet meeting on the stroke of nine. Once again, Kees Vermeer and Albert Voss were present. The phone, which had arrived by courier at de Groot's residence yesterday, rested on the table in front of him, ready to receive Vega's call; it was connected to a battery-powered recording device supplied by the police.

Vega's vandalism of Vincent's self-portrait had stunned and angered the Dutch nation. Overnight, the home phones and office fax machines of every single member of parliament had been busy with calls for action and results. Almost invariably, the calls had included the qualification that no further harm come to the paintings or Christina Jansen. Pieter de Groot felt himself in an almost impossible position, as did each of his Cabinet colleagues. They had to examine alternatives.

Drained but intense, de Groot commenced his opening statement: 'Ladies and gentlemen, no doubt each of you is as appalled as I am over the recent action of Carlos Vega in damaging Vincent's self-portrait. Nevertheless, I, for one, still believe that, considering what we knew at the time, our decision to stall was the proper one. Unfortunately, our gamble has not paid off. According to Nelson Schoute, the Colombian authorities are no closer to finding Carlos Vega.

'In his latest message,' he said, opening the file folder in front of him. 'Carlos Vega says he is unwilling to bend.' He raised the offending piece of correspondence from the file. 'But he must!' He threw down the fax. 'We have what he wants and he has what we want, he must compromise.

'To summarise the present situation, there are three points of difference. Firstly, Vega wants his son freed, not moved to a Colombian jail. Secondly, he wants to keep Christina Jansen until after the transfer. And, thirdly, he wants to keep ten paintings, when we say five.' His eyes swept around the table as he spoke, telegraphing his grave mood to each of the fifteen individuals before him. 'Of course, we can't allow Vega to keep Doctor Jansen, that would be stupid. And we cannot openly agree to hand him his son, we would have every government in the world on our back if we did.' Then, flicking the phone with his fingernails, contemptuous of the man it represented, 'He is liable to phone at any time demanding our decision.' He sat back in his chair and took off his glasses. 'Are there any comments before I call on Chief Inspector Vermeer?'

The Minister of Justice got in first. 'Prime Minister, your

comment about not being seen to move on the first point, are you hinting that we do move on it?'

'It's an option worth discussing,' the Prime Minister replied. It was an option he and the Minister of Justice had already considered and agreed upon. Now it was just a matter of convincing their colleagues. 'I'm suggesting we make the clandestine offer to give Vega his son if he hands over Christina Jansen first. Of course, this can only be considered in the context of our zealous determination to apprehend Vega and his son afterwards.'

'I agree, Prime Minister,' the Minister of Justice confirmed. 'Under the circumstances, it sounds a sensible proposition. A risk worth taking, for the sake of Doctor Jansen and the paintings.' Then, looking around the room for indications of support, 'And I'm sure we could keep it to ourselves.'

'We'd have to,' the Prime Minister replied. 'For one thing, our neighbours would crucify us if it got out.' De Groot was not particularly worried about a leak. Such an act on so sensitive an issue would be certain political suicide for whoever did it. 'They would take us for either liars or fools depending upon whether they thought losing the prisoner was a deal or a bungle. They may even think we're both. But if it works, and we end up with father and son in prison, we would be heroes.'

After allowing a few comments from various ministers, all of which supported the idea, de Groot turned to Vermeer. 'Chief Inspector, time has proven you correct in your assessment of the situation, we are all very interested in what you have to say now.'

Vermeer stepped to the end of the table. 'Prime Minister, Ministers, as you are already aware, Carlos Vega is a man unused to compromise. If you refuse to move on the release of his son, he will apply more pressure and, although you may get your way in the end, the price of the delay would be damage to other paintings and increased danger to the hostage. Of course, he can't keep on damaging the paintings, he needs them. And he won't kill the hostage, he needs her.' Then, spidering his fingers on the dark polished oak, he went on in a reassuringly intimate tone, 'I can only give you my view, the view of a simple policeman. I think the proposal just discussed should be considered very seriously. It will speed things along and minimise the damage . . . and pain. If you recall the Heineken case, we cooperated with the kidnappers in order to achieve our goal, we paid the ransom money.'

'And got most of it back, I seem to remember,' the Prime Minister added to ensure the point was not overlooked. 'You ended up heroes.'

'Yes, Prime Minister, we did. We won in the end and the rate of kidnapping in the Netherlands dropped afterwards. But that case was simpler, the kidnappers were just after money, the international repercussions were less onerous.'

'Yes, Chief Inspector,' de Groot said and, not wishing to involve Vermeer in that aspect of the discussion, solicited clarification, 'In summary, Kees, am I correct in saying that you believe there's a good chance Vega will move on the hostage and the number of paintings if we offer to give him his son?'

'Yes, Prime Minister, your concession is greater than his. You would be taking a big risk giving him what he wants. Any reasonable person would see that and give you something in return. Unfortunately though, Vega is not a reasonable person. He won't jump at it, but if you stand your ground, he must eventually see it as his only way.'

'Which it is, Chief Inspector,' de Groot said. 'It's inconceivable that we would free his son without getting Doctor Jansen.'

'Yes, I agree. What I'm saying, Prime Minister, is that you must be prepared for a tough fight.'

After fielding a few questions from various ministers Vermeer returned to his seat. The Prime Minister then called on the director of the Vincent van Gogh Foundation. It came as no surprise to anyone that Albert Voss supported the option now on the table. The international implications were least relevant for him.

The short discussion which followed the departure of the two visitors resulted in a unanimous endorsement of the Prime Minister's proposal.

'Carlos Vega has joined the ranks of the world's art vandals,' the CNN reporter announced. 'His weapon, a blade.' Christina was in her room watching television, avoiding

Vega. 'A hammer was used by the vandal who did this to Michelangelo's "Pietà" in Saint Peter's Cathedral, Rome.' A still picture of the defaced sculpture was followed by video images of how it appears now. 'Skilled restorers took many months to repair the damage.' Images of the relevant works as they appear now followed. 'Varnish saved Picasso's "Guernica" in New York's Museum of Modern Art when a vandal sprayed it with red paint. Rembrandt's "Night-watch", the centrepiece of Amsterdam's Rijksmuseum, was slashed by a knife wielding tourist. Two years later, somebody used a syringe to spray sulfuric acid on the same artist's "Jacob's Blessing" in a museum in Germany. In 1978, in separate incidents only three weeks apart, two of the Vincent van Gogh Foundation's paintings were slashed with knives: "La Berceuse" and "Self-portrait in Grey Hat". The self-portrait was cut from corner to corner by a Dutch artist released from a mental institution a short time beforehand.' The reporter appeared next, standing outside the LA County Museum of Art. 'Art lovers the world over live in the hope that Carlos Vega will do no further damage to the paintings in his possession.' A story about elections to the British House of Lords followed.

At eleven o'clock, Pedro knocked on the door. 'Señorita, please come down, Carlos wants you to hang another picture.'

Christina prepared herself for the encounter as she walked along the hall. Stay calm, she told herself, co-operate. It won't be easy, but it is best for the paintings.

'Buenos dìas, señorita,' Vega said when she entered. He seemed in a good mood.

'Hello,' she replied, glancing across at him as she walked over to inspect "The Courtesan". It was unharmed.

'I have chosen a new painting,' Vega said, strolling over to an unopened case on the floor near the Japonaiserie. He tapped it on the side with his shoe. 'You would prefer to open this one yourself?'

'I would.' She looked for the initials on the case: WR. 'I can do it without the hacksaw.'

'Your way is the way I would prefer, señorita,' he responded. 'That's what I have said all along.'

After removing the wire, she packed "The Courtesan" into its latchless case and turned her attention to the one Vega had brought down. She opened the guide at the appropriate page, did the arithmetic and rolled the combination to 9116. Vega stood nearby and watched.

'The combinations come from the dates under the pictures, don't they?' he said.

'What makes you think that?'

'Don't roll the numbers,' he ordered as she was about to, 'I'm in the mood for a challenge.'

'You won't work it out,' she replied, and left the tumblers in place. She knew that if he set his mind to it, he would work it out. Perhaps it would be best if he did, she considered, that way he wouldn't need to destroy any more of the cases with a hacksaw.

Christina stretched the wire across the back of

"Wheatfield with a Reaper" and, with Vega's help, hung it on the two new hooks that had appeared on the wall since yesterday. She stepped back and looked: A distant figure reaping a field of swirling golden wheat under a bright yellow sun. Uncomplicated, open and bright.

She went to the kitchen and poured herself some coffee leaving Vega to examine the painting alone.

'Aren't you going to tell me about this one?' he asked when she sat on the couch behind him.

'I always do,' she replied blandly and, staying put, went straight into her patter. 'Vincent's "Wheatfield with a Reaper" was painted in Saint-Rémy in the summer of 1889, a year before his death. It displays his dominant theme of a peasant working with nature to extract an honest and good life.' The emotion that had been a feature of her previous lessons was gone. 'You may remember that from "The Potato Eaters".'

'I do,' Vega replied, a little perturbed by her gloominess. 'Please go on, Christina, but a little more cheerfully.'

'More easily said than done,' she said.

'The world has not ended, señorita. Vincent's portrait will be repaired, like new, you will see.'

'Sure,' she said and continued. '"Wheatfield with a Reaper" is the kind of nature Vincent loved to paint. Nature that is inhabited and cultivated, not wilderness. There is a link with another painting, "The Sower", which he painted the preceding autumn.'

'Whatsoever a man soweth, that shall he also reap,' Vega

recited. 'The nuns taught me that when I was a child. It's a philosophy I have found quite profitable.'

'I'm sure you have,' she said and reached for a magazine, hoping he was satisfied.

'With such a name, there must be an element of religion in this painting?'

'There is.'

'It's quite unlike the paintings we have in our churches, what religion does it represent?'

'Vincent's religion,' she said, and gave up on the magazine. 'By the time he painted this he was very cynical about religions but still had faith in a god, he adopted the view that religions come and go but God endures.'

'Was it a case of sour grapes? They wouldn't let him be a priest so he didn't believe in their god, is that what happened?'

'Maybe,' she said, thinking that he must have very little to do, or was he sizing this one up for destruction too? More pressure on the Dutch government. She had to find out and, if that was the case, try to dissuade him. She moved to the painting, near him, to better gauge his intentions. 'Vincent wasn't impressed with the humanity shown to the poor by some clergymen he knew, that's for sure. And there was something else that influenced the way he thought, and acted. Early in his artistic career he fell in love with his recently widowed cousin, Kee. Kee was visiting his family for a vacation, to get over her loss. Kee's husband had been a clergyman and her father was one too. Unfortunately,

Kee didn't love Vincent . . . but Vincent wouldn't accept that and kept pressuring her. It was all too much for Kee and she fled with her young son back to her parent's house in Amsterdam.' Vega stood quietly, his arms behind his back, listening intently, amused by the insight into the man behind the work before him. 'After she didn't reply to his letters, Vincent went to Amsterdam to see her. When Kee saw him coming she went out the back door leaving her parents to tell him that a meeting wasn't possible. Vincent responded by thrusting his hand into the flame of a lamp and demanding to see Kee for just so long as he could bear the pain. Apparently he fainted. Anyway, that was the end of that romance.'

'Jim should be hearing this,' Vega said with a laugh. 'Another crazy episode.'

'I think I've had enough of Jim Avery on that topic,' Christina remarked and went on. 'The rejection was a painful memory for Vincent for the rest of his life. It changed him, he looked for someone to accept his love, someone in such a poor state that she wouldn't reject him. He found Sien, an alcoholic prostitute, she was pregnant at the time.'

'Quite a change in taste, from saint to sinner,' Vega said, and laughed again. 'My men start with women who are already sinners, it saves them time.' He turned from the painting and moved to leave. 'You are the only saint in their lives, Christina.'

'What are you going to do if de Groot doesn't accept your offer?' She wanted an answer before he left.

'I will change his mind.'

'How are you going to do that?' She followed him to the door.

'You will see, señorita.' He turned, waved and was gone.

'You're not going to damage this painting are you?' she shouted and went to go through the door behind him.

The incoming guard blocked her way and told her to go back. She went to the painting and stood staring into it, embracing her body, trying to quell the anxiety that was overwhelming her. Why had Vega chosen this one? What did he have in mind? Was he going to cut out the reaper like he cut out Vincent's face? She knew the promise he made last night was meaningless, she'd known it then. She cursed herself for not throwing the note off the balcony.

An hour later, Pedro came from across the hall. 'Put your shoes on señorita, you are going out.' She quizzed him for details but got nothing.

While she got ready, two of the guards packed "Wheatfield with a Reaper" and took it downstairs.

A few minutes later, with Vega, Christina and Rafael in the back and Josef behind the wheel, the Ford van left the building accompanied by the usual two car escort. Christina's hands were cuffed behind her and her seatbelt was pulled tight.

Fifteen minutes later, they turned off Carrera Balboa into the deserted carpark of Iglesia de San Francisco. The escort cars took up positions on either side.

Vega took a phone from a box on the floor and punched in a fourteen digit number.

Willem Imthorn answered on the second ring.

'Did you send the phone?' Vega asked after anonymous greetings were exchanged.

'It was delivered yesterday, as planned,' the Dutchman replied.

'Any problems at our destination?'

'None at all,' came the response. 'Everything looks good. How is the visitor?'

'Homesick, but well,' Vega replied, glancing at her.

'Quite a celebrity, your visitor, thanks to us. I very much hope we meet one day.' Christina could hear Imthorn's laugh coming from the earpiece.

'Goodbye, amigo,' Vega said and turned the phone off before handing it to Rafael. He then proceeded to remove the painting case from under the seat.

'Why's that here?' Christina demanded, 'What are you doing?' She strained helplessly against the seatbelt as Vega removed the painting and propped it on the seat next to his. 'Leave it!' she shouted.

'Cover her mouth,' Vega ordered Rafael and retrieved another phone from the box. 'And take care of her quickly if there's a problem.' He entered the number of the phone Imthorn had sent the Dutch Prime Minister.

'De Groot.' Christina could hear the Prime Minister's voice.

'Prime Minister, good evening,' Vega said calmly.

'What do you want Mr Vega?' the Prime Minister's distaste for the Colombian came with his words through space.

'I have with me Doctor Jansen and the painting "Wheatfield with a Reaper". I will allow her to confirm that.' He held the phone towards her while Rafael raised his hand from her mouth just far enough for her to speak. 'Yes, it's tr . . .'

'Wait please, Prime Minister,' Vega said and put the phone down.

'Mr Vega, I have an offer,' de Groot's voice announced vainly from the seat.

Christina began to struggle against Rafael and the seatbelt as soon as she caught sight of the cigarette lighter. Her eyes pleaded with Vega not to do what she could see he was about to do. She kicked violently, desperately, shaking the van until Josef locked his body around her legs. Now completely immobilised, she watched in horror as Vega brought the lighter to the reaper in the wheatfield and flicked it on. She bit for Rafael's finger. The reaper bubbled. Rafael cursed her. She managed only a shriek in the short time it took him to bring his other hand hard against her face. He cursed her again, waving his bitten hand.

'What's happening Vega?' de Groot demanded.

The odour of the burnt paint diffused throughout the van. The reaper was gone, forever. An ugly oval of black now scarred the swirling wheat.

'What's happening? Answer me!' de Groot demanded again.

Vega patted the canvas with the butt of his revolver to halt the smouldering.

'What's happening? Answer me!' de Groot shouted. 'What's going on? Christina?'

'Tell him, Christina,' Vega said and held the phone in her direction.

She was crying, terrified, breaking. 'He's burnt a hole in the painting! He's burnt the reaper!' To hell with Avery's plan, she thought. 'Een nieuw . . .' Rafael slammed a cupped hand over her face forcing her head into the back of the seat. She struggled for breath as Vega continued.

'My proposal is not negotiable, Prime Minister. I will phone again very soon. Next time I will burn a hole in Doctor Jansen.'

Vega switched off the phone immediately to starve any equipment the police had in place to track his whereabouts. 'Let her go,' he said to Rafael and moved close to her. 'Something new, you said.' His ears were ringing wildly. 'What was the first word?' He struck her on the side of the head with the back of the phone. 'Tell me!'

'Een,' she shouted, 'in, it means in.'

'Bitch!' He hit her again, harder and told Josef to drive off. Christina regained consciousness quickly but remained silent, more frightened than she had ever been. Vega checked her head. There was a lump where he had hit her but no blood. He felt a tinge of remorse, as did Rafael. It did not last long for either of them.

The convoy returned to the building carpark and waited

for fifteen minutes before emerging and driving south. By then, Christina was fully alert, wishing both Vega and Rafael dead.

They came to rest in a football field carpark hidden from the road by billboards. Josef sat at Christina's feet and held her legs while Rafael put some duct tape over her mouth, she was not going to get another chance to disclose their whereabouts. Vega selected another phone and entered the Netherlands' number.

The answer was instant. 'Vega?'

'Prime Minister, have you reconsidered my offer?'

'Mr Vega, I have a counter offer, you must hear me out.'

'What is it?'

'I had it before but you didn't give me a chance to speak. Please listen, nobody need be hurt. Is Doctor Jansen all right?'

'Yes, hurry.'

'I want to hear her for myself,' de Groot demanded.

'Not now, you will hear her soon.'

'Okay, but I do want to hear her,' de Groot replied after hesitating briefly. 'The problem we have is that we can't be seen to set your son free.' He spoke quickly. 'There is no way. It would create a precedent for other acts such as yours. So what I'm proposing is this: you give us Christina Jansen with fifteen paintings, then we deliver Juan, we say to a Colombian prison but we give him to you. We say the transfer was bungled, he escaped. Then you give us the remaining five paintings. Everything is arranged on this phone, no CNN, no involvement with the Colombian government.'

'You plan to deceive my President?' Vega laughed. 'Very sensible, Prime Minister. I have a feeling that under more favourable circumstances we could be friends.'

'I doubt that, Mr Vega,' de Groot replied. 'That is definitely the best offer I can make.'

'You deserve to be congratulated, but it's still not good enough. I meant what I said, I'm not willing to modify my offer. I'm not interested in any problems you have with the media or anyone else.'

'You expect too much,' de Groot answered in frustration. 'I'm taking a big risk with my offer and you refuse to move. You're being unrealistic, Mr Vega.'

'We are very close, Prime Minister, perhaps I can convince you to make that final concession.'

'You won't, no matter what you do.'

'Perhaps if I hold my cigarette lighter to the pretty face of Doctor Jansen you will change your mind.'

'I would advise against doing that, Mr Vega,' de Groot said, his anxiety evident in his voice. 'It will accomplish nothing, just strengthen my government's resolve.'

On Vega's signal, Rafael grabbed Christina by her hair and pushed her head forward and to the side. Vega moved beside her and ignited the flame below her face.

'Prime Minister, the lighter flame is thirty centimetres from the unblemished right cheek of Christina Jansen. I will now move it to twenty.'

Christina could feel the heat on her skin, she could hear her heart racing.

'Do you want a deal, Mr Vega, yes or no?' de Groot shouted. 'If you harm her, I will withdraw my offer. Do you hear me?'

'But you want your paintings, don't you?' The calm was gone from his voice. Christina tried helplessly to propel herself higher. 'Fifteen centimetres.'

'And you want your son, yes or no, Mr Vega? Deal or no deal?'

'Ten centimetres.' Christina squirmed, moaning through her nose as discomfort turned to pain. Her face muscles strained against the tape, forcing it to give. Rafael clamped his hand over her mouth and nose.

'Yes or no, Mr Vega?'

'Eight centimetres.' Her skin was burning, she couldn't breathe. Suddenly, her latent strength burst free. She lurched back forcing Rafael to lose his grip and smashing Josef's head against the seat in front. The tape tore off her upper lip taking skin with it. She screamed, 'Gebouw . . .', Dutch for building, and was silenced again.

'For the last time, Mr Vega,' de Groot shouted, 'yes or no?'

Vega hurled the lighter to the floor. 'I agree! You will hear from me.' He terminated the call.

19

Pieter de Groot lay the phone on his desk and slumped forward, burying his face in trembling hands. The Minister of Justice, Kees Vermeer and Albert Voss sat opposite him at his desk. They had been summoned after the first call from Vega and had listened in anguish to the second through a small speaker attached to the recording device.

'Well done, Pieter,' the Minister of Justice whispered.

De Groot looked up. 'Do you think so, Lydia?' He took a slow breath and exhaled. 'That was awful. The girl, she has courage. God knows what giving us the clues cost her.' The showdown with Carlos Vega had unsettled the veteran politician more than anything he could remember. 'That man is grotesque.' He looked to Vermeer. 'Kees, tell me what you're thinking.'

'You stood up to Vega and won, Prime Minister. That's what you had to do. And I agree, Christina Jansen has courage.' Vermeer's years of dealing with the grimy side of life made him the most able to offer an objective point of view.

'Courage at a price,' the Minister of Justice added.

'She's still alive,' Vermeer said. 'And the deal increases her chance of survival enormously.'

'That's the way to look at it I suppose.' De Groot reached for a carafe of water. 'Better to be injured than killed. Oops!' Some of the water flowed over the edge of the glass he was filling. 'Look, I'm still shaking.' He held up his trembling hands.

'Can I get you something stronger, Pieter?' the Minister of Justice asked as Voss helped de Groot mop up the spillage with tissues.

'Good idea, Lydia.' He looked to the others. 'I think we could all use a drink.'

The Minister of Justice went to the liquor cabinet and poured each person their choice and a gin and tonic for herself.

'Should Nelson Schoute hear this, Prime Minister?' Vermeer asked as he removed the cassette tape from the recording machine and inserted a blank.

'Too risky over the phone,' de Groot said, 'The media could end up with a copy. I think it's best if we keep the deal to ourselves. Schoute doesn't need to know, not yet, anyway. Just play him the parts where Christina gives the clues, out of courtesy. Nothing else would be of any help to him, would it?'

'No, Prime Minister,' Vermeer replied and slid the cassette into his coat pocket. 'I'll do as you say.'

'To our deal with the devil,' de Groot said, holding up his glass.

'And justice to the devil in the end.' the Minister of Justice added. They drank.

'The devil still has to stand by the deal,' Vermeer said, compelled to check the optimism. 'There's always a chance he'll want to make changes as things progress.'

'I hope you're wrong, Kees,' de Groot said, sounding exhausted. 'But what worries me is, so far, you've got everything right.'

'I hope I'm wrong this time Prime Minister,' the policeman replied.

Albert Voss, considering himself to be the most peripheral member of the group, waited for a lull in the conversation before speaking. 'Prime Minister, I must congratulate you on the way you handled Vega. I don't know how you kept your resolve under that pressure.'

'Thanks, Albert.' De Groot raised his glass to the director. 'I hope these black days for your foundation end very soon.'

After a few minutes of relaxed conversation, de Groot got back on the job. He announced that he would phone Christina Jansen's parents himself and break the news of her injury before the story was released to the press. Voss, who had been keeping Christina's parents informed from the beginning, provided their numbers.

'Has the Foundation prepared the list of paintings?' de Groot asked the museum director.

'I have it with me, Prime Minister.' He withdrew an envelope from his coat pocket. It contained a single sheet of paper with two lists titled "First delivery" and "Second delivery" respectively.

De Groot put on his reading glasses and perused the sheet. 'What was the basis for choosing the five in the second list, the ones Vega keeps?'

'It wasn't easy, Prime Minister. We placed the paintings in order of importance and drew a line. We considered whether there were others like them, where each fell in Vincent's development, that kind of thing.'

'Difficult, I'm sure,' de Groot commented, looking up from the list. 'I see that "Wheatfield with a Reaper" is on the first list.'

'We hope to fix it, Prime Minister,' Voss replied. 'A very important work.'

'And "The Bedroom" too, even though it isn't unique. I've seen another one in Paris.'

'At the Musée d'Orsay, Prime Minister, and there is a third at the Art Institute of Chicago. But the Foundation felt it belonged on the first list . . . it's hard to imagine the museum without it.'

'Without any of them, Albert. And of course, what's left of "Self-portrait with a Straw Hat" is on the second.'

'Yes, Prime Minister,' Voss replied and remembered the photograph in his pocket. 'A photo of the section Vega cut out, it arrived from Colombia this afternoon.'

De Groot held the photograph to the light.

'Not as bad as we expected,' Voss explained. 'Vega must have used a sharp blade. The restorers tell me the cut should be barely visible when it's repaired, presuming of course we get the rest of it back.'

'We'll do our best to make sure you do, Albert.' He looked to the Minister of Justice. 'Lydia, you had better get Juan Vega ready to move at short notice.'

'Already done, Pieter.'

Seeing that the visitors had finished their drinks, de Groot stood to end the meeting. 'Gentlemen, thank you for your help. I'll be calling a press conference for eight o'clock to give our story to the media.' The Minister of Justice saw them to the door.

'Let me know when you're ready,' Kees Vermeer said to Nelson Schoute from the other side of the Atlantic. The Dutch policeman had just revealed the official government version of the phone conversations between de Groot and Vega to the liaison officer. Martínez signalled that he was ready to record and put on a set of headphones. 'Okay Kees, go ahead,' Nelson said into the mouthpiece. He knew Vermeer from his days in the police force.

'Okay, here it is.' Vermeer's calm monotone was replaced by the Dutch Prime Minister's shout: 'What's happening? Answer me! What's going on? Christina?' Then Vega, controlled, 'Tell him, Christina.' Christina, frantic, 'He's burnt a hole in the painting! He's burnt the reaper!' then shouting, 'Een nieuw . . .' A bump. Vega again, 'My proposal is not negotiable, Prime Minister. I will phone again very soon. Next time I will burn a hole in Doctor Jansen.' A click.

'That's all on the first call,' Vermeer announced. Nelson's complexion had become pale. Vermeer's description prior to the tape hadn't prepared him for the hysteria that accompanied the sound.

'Here's the relevant part of the second one,' Vermeer said and played it.

'A maniac,' Nelson said breathlessly when it was over, his hatred for Christina's torturer consuming him. 'God, I hope we get him!'

'So do I,' Vermeer replied. 'You got the new building. She's a brave girl.'

'She sure is. That clue's better than anything we have so far, Kees. Why didn't you play us the whole tape?'

'The Prime Minister didn't like the idea, sorry about that.'

'Why on earth not?'

'He's concerned about it getting into the wrong hands. Don't worry, I've heard it all, there's nothing else to help you.'

'Okay, seems strange though,' Nelson said. 'A few days ago he was sending copies of Vega's fax to anyone and everyone. Politicians, eh?'

'Don't be too hard on de Groot,' Vermeer said, a little amused to hear himself defending a man he had voted against in two general elections. 'He did well.'

'He did,' Nelson replied. 'I'm surprised Vega settled for the transfer.'

'Did Colonel Martínez get a location on the calls?' Vermeer asked, avoiding comment on what Nelson had just said.

'We got rough locations on both of them but not quickly enough to act.'

Pleasantries were exchanged and the conversation ended. After switching off the recorder, Martínez sat down opposite Nelson. 'That was pretty tough on you, Nelson.'

'That man's torturing her and all I can do is listen to it happen. I feel so damn helpless.'

'Be patient, my friend, you may get to see Vega in handcuffs yet.'

'I hope so. There can't be too many new buildings in Medellín, can there?' Nelson asked.

'Depends what she meant by new, and building for that matter. I'm sure there'll be enough to keep us busy. Medellín's enjoying a boom, laundered drug money, much of it. We can pull the men out of the hills, that will help. I'll set things going. We'll start looking at places, say . . . under a year old . . . especially large apartments. Vega has bodyguards to accommodate. We'll check new businesses and warehouses too. There may be hundreds . . . but we have the resources.'

'If we find him, what happens then?'

'It depends,' Martínez said, leaning back in his chair. 'You've seen his house.'

'His fortress, you mean.'

'Exactly. Wherever he is now, I'm sure he's just as well protected. And with Christina and the paintings inside, it may be too risky to storm the place.'

'That's for sure,' Nelson said. 'We don't want a smaller version of what happened at your old Palace of Justice. De Groot would rather hand over ten Juan Vegas than have anything like that happen.'

'Don't worry, my President made your government's concerns very clear to the commanding officers.' Martínez paused to contemplate the situation. 'Whether we find his hiding place or not, our best chance to get Vega is when he moves to leave Colombia.'

'And that should be soon.'

'The initial building checks should give us a fairly small list of possibilities so we can watch them . . . and, hopefully, catch Vega when he's vulnerable.' Martínez had already requested that the army increase its surveillance at the airports and strengthen the checkpoints that were already in place on the road routes and railway out of Medellín. 'It's going to be very difficult for Señor Vega to get through our net.' Then, drumming his pen against his chin, 'I wonder how he plans to try?'

'I wish we knew,' Nelson said and stood to leave. 'I've got some phone calls to make, Luis. I'll be at my desk if you need me.'

Nelson made three calls. The first to his wife in Amsterdam to share his distress over Christina's trauma.

Then he phoned Christina's mother in Utrecht to offer his consolation and encouragement. He'd met her once at a dinner she'd attended with Christina: a handsome woman, intelligent, a bank manager in Nieuwegein. She'd never remarried. She was delighted to hear from Nelson and took comfort from the call. She also provided her ex-husband's number. Nelson made that call too. He'd never met Christina's father, an art teacher in Arnhem with a small reputation for his own work. The profound anxiety for a child in peril came across very clearly during both conversations. Nelson prayed it would be relieved soon.

At eight o'clock, the overcrowded press briefing room fell silent as the Dutch Prime Minister took his place behind the lectern.

'Ladies and gentlemen, I am pleased to announce that an agreement has been reached to resolve the situation in Medellín. Juan Vega will be transferred to Colombia to serve the remainder of his sentence in an institution there as soon as Doctor Jansen and fifteen of the paintings are returned to us. The Minister of Justice is making arrangements to prepare the prisoner for immediate travel.

'I am sorry to report that our determination to minimise the risk to Doctor Jansen's life has had an unfortunate consequence. In an effort to pressure us into agreeing to his unacceptable terms, Mr Vega has injured Doctor Jansen and damaged another painting. Doctor Jansen suffered a burn to her face from a cigarette lighter, on her right cheek,

I believe. And a hole was burned in the painting "Wheatfield with a Reaper" in the spot where the reaper is ... or was. Now that we have an agreement, I trust no further harm will come to either Doctor Jansen or the paintings.

'That's the end of my statement, ladies and gentlemen. A list of the paintings to be returned first will be distributed to you shortly. My government would appreciate it if the list was published in the Colombian papers, which I'm told, have representation here. That seems the best way for us to get it to Mr Vega. Now, questions?' He pointed to the first hand that shot up.

'Prime Minister, how bad is the burn to Christina Jansen's face and do you expect Vega to include a photograph of her in the next fax?'

'We don't know how bad the burn is. As for a photograph, I have no idea.' He pointed to another hand.

'Prime Minister, what was the unacceptable demand you mentioned in your statement?'

'That Doctor Jansen not be released until after Juan Vega's transfer. It would have exposed her to too great a danger, totally unacceptable.' He pointed to another reporter.

'Prime Minister, what guarantee do you have that the second set of paintings will be returned?'

'None, I'm afraid.' He shrugged his shoulders. 'How can we? We'll just have to hope Mr Vega keeps his word.' Another hand.

'Prime Minister, were you surprised Vega agreed to have his son extradited instead of freed?'

'Surprised is not the right word,' he answered, evasively. 'Negotiations were very intense.' He turned his attention to the other side of the room.

'Prime Minister, do you think Vega will try to break his son out of jail in Colombia, like he did on Curaçao?'

'As far as I know, Mr Vega has never been charged over the incident on Curaçao. All I can say is that once Juan Vega is in Colombia, his confinement will be a matter for the Colombians. One more question.'

'Prime Minister, have the efforts to apprehend Carlos Vega been altered in light of the agreement? Have they been increased? What's happening there?'

'Our liaison officer, Nelson Schoute, has reported that the Colombian authorities are doing their utmost to find Carlos Vega. And I can assure you, ladies and gentlemen, we will not rest until Carlos Vega is found and brought to justice, no matter how long it takes. Thank you.' He left the room.

It was late afternoon when Christina Jansen awoke. The painkiller Pedro had given her when she arrived back at the apartment had knocked her out. She went straight to the mirror in the en suite, her anger rising as she examined the raw and blistering flesh. She would demand that a doctor treat it. Vega must agree. There must be one he can trust, one he uses, a crooked one, any doctor would do. She didn't want a scar to remind her of this ordeal.

She went down to the living area to be met by the sight of Vega and Avery sitting on the couch drinking beer. The damaged "Wheatfield" was hanging back on the wall. 'Have you put this here to annoy me?' she said as she moved towards it.

'It's there as a reminder of what I am willing to do when people don't cooperate.' Vega's anger over her shouting the clues to de Groot was simmering just below the surface.

'I don't need reminding,' she said glaring across to him and pointing to her burned cheek, 'I've got this to remind me.' She examined the damage to "Wheatfield". The reaper's head and torso were gone. His legs and the arm wielding the sickle were okay except for some cracking and flattening, the result of being struck by Vega's revolver. Part of the picture above the burn had been discoloured by smoke. She felt beaten. No matter what miracles were performed on it back in Amsterdam, it would never be the same, it could never again be Vincent's reaper.

She turned to Avery, pointing again to her cheek. 'Did he tell you how this happened?'

Vega had not told him. 'Your Prime Minister mentioned it on television.' The act had angered Avery, but he was not about to criticise Vega for having done it, he was not a fool. 'How are you feeling now?' he asked, his tone disguising his true concern.

'How would you feel?' she responded sharply.

'Not too good, I guess.'

She turned to Vega who disregarded her by taking

another mouthful of beer. 'How can the Dutch government trust you? That's what I don't understand, your promises mean nothing.'

'Señorita, that's enough.' He put his beer down, got up and moved towards her. 'Let me look at your face.'

'Forget it,' she said, backing away. 'You're not coming near me, I want a doctor.'

'Why?'

'I don't want a scar to remind me of you every time I look in a mirror.'

'Sorry, Christina, my doctor is dead.' He laughed. 'He had a terminal tongue condition.'

'Then please get me another doctor.'

'There will be no doctor. Just keep your cheek clean, it will heal. And if you do end up with a little scar, I'm sure the best plastic surgeons in Holland will fight over the chance to fix it for you.' Vega had cursed himself for burning her cheek immediately after he'd done it. Now things would be more difficult later on. He should have thought before acting, should have burned her somewhere else. He returned to the couch.

'I've got a first aid kit, Carlos,' Avery said. 'If you like, I can patch her up.'

'You see, Christina,' Vega said, tilting his bottle towards her, 'Jim will be your doctor.'

'I want the real thing,' she said, giving it a final try. 'The Dutch government won't be too impressed if you refuse to get me proper medical help.'

'I didn't sign the Geneva agreement, señorita, you're not a prisoner of war. Jim will be your doctor. Take him or leave him, it's up to you.'

'Okay,' she said and turned to Avery. 'I guess you're better than nothing.' At least it would be an opportunity to see if he had devised a plan.

'Thanks for the vote of confidence, honey,' Avery said and drained the last of his beer.

'I told you not to call me that,' she snapped for the sake of appearance.

Avery got up and examined her burn. 'I'd like to wash it. You go to your room, I'll get my kit and come down.' He looked to Vega. 'Okay, Carlos?'

'Okay, but make sure Christina doesn't steal your scissors, I have a feeling she would like to bury them in my heart.' He opened another beer.

Avery turned on the television when he entered her room. 'In case the room's bugged,' he whispered. He looked at the burn again. 'Nasty.'

'Done by a nasty individual.'

'The man's got a real ugly side. There was no need for this.' While turning her head to get her cheek in a better light, he felt the lump on the side. 'My goodness, you have had a bad time.'

'You're telling me,' she murmured. 'I can't wait for Vega's day of judgement, I'll be there cheering.'

'I can understand how you feel.' He let go of her head and leaned back. 'The burn looks clean, I won't wash it.'

'I had a shower when I got back.' She turned to him. 'Do you have anything planned?'

'Not yet, I can't do anything until we leave this place. Too many eyes and ears keeping a check on me.'

'Any idea when that's happening?'

'No, Vega plays the game pretty close to his chest. But it should be soon. And he'll have to give me a bit of warning so I can catch up on some sleep and quit the drink.' He opened his kit and found a burn dressing. 'I'm no doctor, but I think you'll be okay. If it gets infected though, he'll have to get you some proper help, or send someone for antibiotics.'

'I'll keep it dry, that's the idea isn't it?'

'Yep!' Avery went into the en suite and washed his hands.

'What was so funny about Vega's doctor?' she asked when he returned.

'Doctor Cortez, he used to load up Vega's mules with the cocaine condoms. A couple of frequent fliers died on the plane when the latex burst in their intestines. A quick death, I'm told. So Vega took the doc off the payroll.' He paused while he opened the dressing. 'Cortez should have realised how lucky he was to be left alive. Most people go off the payroll in a coffin. But he figured he was smarter than Vega. That was his big mistake, he squealed on the boss. Picked the wrong policemen. Carlos had him executed, the death of an informer, I believe.'

'And what's the death of an informer?' she inquired, expecting to be appalled.

'Well honey, it's not pretty. They slit your throat from here to here.' He ran his finger from his chin to the top of his shirt. 'Then they pull your tongue out. They call it the Colombian necktie.'

'God!' she exclaimed, her face contorted. 'These people are barbarians.'

'Hey, Christina, don't knock it. The Colombian necktie is a great way to keep the troops loyal. You talk . . . slash, slash,' he gestured, 'you don't talk any more. If Vega finds out I've been talking to the DEA, I'll be wearing one too. It scares the hell out of me.' He smoothed the dressing around the burn. 'There, how does that feel?'

'Fine, thanks.' She smiled the little she could.

'See, I'm not such a bad guy.'

'Maybe not.'

Avery found a blister pack of painkillers in his kit and gave it to her. 'They're not as strong as the ones Pedro gave you.'

'His were deadly,' she said and put them on the bedside table. 'Knocked me out.'

'Not a good idea in the present situation.' He stood from the bed. 'We'd better go back.'

'Good luck, and be careful,' she whispered.

'Thanks. You be careful too.'

She walked ahead of Avery into the living area. The burnt painting had been replaced with "Almond Blossom". Vega stood admiring it.

'Did you hacksaw the case?' she asked.

'The combination, señorita,' Vega replied. 'I worked it out while you were asleep.'

A dull pain rekindled her resentment. 'The locks were never meant for people like you, anyway.'

'Be careful, señorita,' Vega responded, his eyes narrowing. 'I'm growing a little weary of your insults.'

'Look Carlos, the less I see of you the better it will be for both of us. I feel terrible, I'm going back to my room.'

'No, I've ordered something for you to eat.' She would have no choice in the matter. 'After all, señorita, you missed lunch.'

'Thanks, but I'm not hungry.' She started to walk away.

He strode after her and grabbed her by the arm. 'But I am, and I would like you to join me.' It was time to put her in her place. 'But first, tell me about this painting.'

'Read about it yourself.' She struggled to escape his grip.

'Christina, you don't understand. Now that I've hurt you once, it would be easy for me to hurt you again. And as long as I don't kill you, it won't make any difference to the deal I have with your Prime Minister.'

'Go ahead then, do whatever you want,' she shouted, the effort producing another painful twinge in her cheek. 'I'm not going to set you up with another painting just so you can get a bigger thrill when you destroy it.'

'I get no thrill from damaging the paintings. But business is business.' He let her go. 'Now, I will try again. Tell me about the painting, please.'

'Christina, tell him,' Avery called out. 'He means what he says. You don't want any more trouble today, do you?'

'If I were you, señorita, I would take Jim's advice. He knows me well.'

'All right.' She knew Avery was right. She walked to the painting and, folding her arms, recited into it. 'Vincent painted "Almond Blossom" in the Asylum St-Paul-de-Mausole at Saint-Rémy in the south of France in the year of his death, 1890.'

'Did you hear that, Jim?' Vega interrupted from behind her, 'An asylum.'

'And asylums are for crazy people,' Avery added in the interest of maintaining his role.

She moved to the side, away from Vega, before continuing. 'Vincent entered the asylum voluntarily. He was suffering attacks of anxiety and depression, they worried him. In the asylum he ate properly and drank far less. His health improved. He was given a room for painting and was eventually allowed to paint outside the institution as long as an attendant went with him.'

'It's a pretty picture,' Vega commented. 'What do you think, Jim?'

Avery looked to the painting. 'It's beautiful.' He didn't care for it at all.

'Continue, Christina,' Vega said.

'Vincent painted it to celebrate the birth of Theo's son. He considered the subject of almond blossoms against the clear blue sky appropriate for the infant Vincent.'

'Named after his uncle?'

'Yes.' She felt more pain but went on. The sooner this was over, the better. 'Unfortunately, young Vincent's father died a week before his first birthday, just six months after Vincent's death.'

'How tragic,' Vega said, insincerely.

'Theo's wife, Johanna, raised the child. She, like Theo, had faith in Vincent's work, she took it upon herself to promote it.'

'Lucky for us,' Vega said and stepped towards her, 'otherwise we may never have met.' He seized her by the shoulder and, glaring into her eyes, whispered, 'Nieuw gebouw, new building. Attempt to betray me again, señorita, or not show me proper respect, and you will feel real pain. Understand?'

She nodded, terrified.

'Good,' he said, and sauntered out of the apartment.

20

It was just after eight o'clock on Sunday morning when the police car pulled up outside the new building on Avenue Bolívar. It was the second on a list of six buildings the seasoned police sergeant and the young army corporal accompanying him had been assigned to visit before noon.

Neither thought anything of the television cameras they spotted on the roof as they walked towards the entrance. Conspicuous security was a big selling feature in the high end of the market in Medellín.

After a brief exchange over the intercom, the manager released the door lock and came to meet them in the lobby.

'Do you recognise either this man or the woman, señor?' the policeman asked, showing the manager the photographs of Carlos Vega and Christina Jansen. Vega was watching on a television in the second apartment, ready to go into hiding the moment they made a move to come upstairs.

'Yes, Sargento, I have seen them on television. The man

is Carlos Vega and the woman is from Amsterdam, she has been kidnapped by Vega.'

'Have you seen either of them here, señor?'

'No, Sargento,' the manager replied truthfully.

'Did anyone move in last Monday morning, they may have been carrying some large metal cases or boxes?'

'No,' he said, shaking his head. 'Nobody moved in last Monday.'

'Are you sure you saw everything that happened here last Monday morning?' The policeman searched the manager's face for a lie.

'Si, Sargento.'

'Does that camera record?' He pointed to the camera mounted on the ceiling. 'Do you have a recording from last Monday morning?'

'Si, the cameras do record, but only for twelve hours at a time. The tape from Monday morning has been erased, there was no reason to keep it. Nothing strange happened, Sargento.' He gave a short nervous laugh. 'If Señor Vega moved in here, Sargento, believe me, I would tell you.'

'Señor, I would like a list of all the people who have moved into this building in the past three months.'

'The building is new, Sargento, everybody in here has moved in over the last three months,' the manager replied.

'Then, I will take a list of all your tenants, señor,' the policeman responded with a forced smile.

'Si, Sargento, I have a copy I will give you.'

'We will look around the building, señor, and meet you

back here.' The sergeant summoned the elevator and he and the soldier rode it to the top floor.

They exited into an empty hallway and walked along it to the fire door barely glancing at the two large wooden doors as they passed them. The only detail either of them noticed was the lack of a handle on the stairwell side of the fire door, it had been sheared off. The policeman made a note to ask the manager about it. They walked down the stairwell to the fourteenth floor, inspected it and went on to repeat the procedure all the way down.

The manager was waiting when they arrived back in the lobby. 'The list of tenants, Sargento,' he said handing across the list and a sealed envelope containing, what he hoped was, enough money to ensure freedom from unnecessary intrusions in the future.

The policeman, without saying a word, unbuttoned the thigh pocket on his grey camouflage pants and slipped the envelope inside. At the end of the day, he would split this and the other offerings with the soldier, 60:40, as already agreed. 'Do any of the apartments have several male tenants or a large number of male visitors?' the policeman then asked, perusing the list.

'There are many male tenants, Sargento.'

'Are there any apartments that seem unusually crowded?'

'No, Sargento,' he lied. 'There is a clause in the leases that limits the number.'

Manuel Rojas had prayed every night that his suspicions were wrong and that it was not Carlos Vega on the fifteenth floor. He was a simple family man who happened to get a job in a good place at a bad time and now found himself lying to the police.

His brother-in-law, a small-time drug dealer, had helped him get the job a month before the building opened. Rojas had know all along that cartel money built the apartments, his brother-in-law had told him. There was nothing unusual about that. It was common knowledge that laundered drug money had financed many buildings in Colombia and other parts of the Americas.

'The handle is missing from the fire door on the top floor. Do you know that, señor?'

'Si, Sargento, it is a problem the builder must fix. It broke off. It should not happen with a new lock like that.' He lied again. One of the tenants on the fifteenth floor had paid him to leave it broken.

'I thought it might be to stop anyone walking up the stairs to that floor.'

'No, Sargento.' He shook his head. 'It's just a faulty lock. A new building has these problems.'

'It's against the fire regulations, señor, it must be fixed.' The policeman clamped the list inside his clipboard folder. 'I would like to see the carpark.'

They took the stairs to the two level carpark where, with the aid of a flashlight, the policeman peered inside each vehicle through their windows while the soldier made a list of licence numbers. There was nothing suspicious at all.

'One reason crime is so bad in this city,' the policeman

said to the manager as they walked to the elevator, 'is that many people see things and don't report them. That makes crime worse. Do you understand what I mean?'

'I understand, Sargento, but I am a good citizen.' He touched his hand to his chest. 'I would report any strange things happening.'

During the short trip back to the lobby the policeman gave the manager his card and asked that he call if anything aroused his suspicion.

Vega watched on the large television in the second apartment as the policeman and soldier walked back to their car. He had just emerged from hiding in the secret compartment across the hall. From what Josef had told him and the little he had seen himself, the policeman's visit seemed routine, nothing to worry about. He'd expected such a visit to result from Christina's outbursts in the van. Now he would check that the visitors left with no reason to be suspicious. He instructed Rafael to phone the manager and invite him to his apartment.

Rafael, under a false family name, was the registered tenant in Vega's apartment and had been ready to play that part had the visitors knocked on the door. The alarm had provided the only opportunity so far to test the thrice practised drill, and, as far as Vega could tell, all had gone well. Within two minutes of the visitors' arrival downstairs, Pedro and one of the guards had moved Christina, her possessions, the van Gogh and its cordon as well as themselves to the third bedroom compartment. Vega had waited for the visitors to enter the elevator before retreating to the compartment himself. None of the details had been forgotten. Even the picture hooks held a work by a local artist in place of the van Gogh.

There was a knock on the door. 'You know what to do,' Vega whispered to Rafael. 'Make sure Señor Rojas understands the rewards of ignorance, and the dangers of thinking.' With that he went back into the third bedroom compartment and listened to the living area conversation on the headphones.

'Good morning, Señor Rojas,' Rafael said. 'It is good to see you, please come in.' He showed the manager to a couch. 'I will get you a drink.'

'It is okay, Señor González, I am fine,' the manager said, wishing nothing but a short stay.

'But you must, Señor Rojas, I have not seen you for so long.' Rafael opened the refrigerator and removed two bottles of beer. 'I am very happy with my apartment, it is very comfortable.'

'That is good to hear, Señor González.'

'I see that a policeman and a soldier visited you, Señor Rojas. Is there a problem?' He opened both bottles and handed the manager his. 'Salud!'

'Salud!' Rojas took a swig. 'They were looking for Carlos Vega and the señorita from the museum in Amsterdam.'

'I see, señor. Carlos Vega has committed a terrible crime, I hope he is a long way from here.' Rafael laughed. 'A clever man like you would have seen him if he was living here, right Señor Rojas?'

'Yes, señor, I am sure he is not here, that's what I told the policeman.'

'What was the paper you gave him? What was in the envelope?'

The question startled the manager. 'How did you know that I gave him these things, señor?'

Rafael smiled. 'Someone saw you and told me, Señor Rojas.'

'Ah! I did not see them, Señor González,' he replied, certain that no one else was in the lobby at the time. 'It was a list of the people living here, and some money.'

'I understand, a list and a bribe, señor.' Rafael forced a laugh. The manager, thinking it wise to join in, did so. 'What information was on the list about me and my friends across the hall?'

'Only your names, señor, and the dates you moved in, a month ago.'

'What else did the policeman ask you?'

'Nothing, Señor González, except the door.'

'The door, señor?'

'The policeman noticed the handle was missing from the fire door.'

'Ah! A very observant man. Did he seem to be concerned about that?'

'No, señor, I told him it had been broken and would soon be fixed.'

'Good, amigo. Of course, I think it is best to leave it broken, I don't want noisy children coming up the stairs. You understand?'

'Si, señor, I understand.'

'And how is your family, Señor Rojas? Sometimes, when I look out the window, I see you walking with your wife and beautiful daughter.'

'They are fine, thank you for asking, Señor González.'

'How old is Teresa?'

'She is ten years old next month,' Rojas said, visibly disturbed by the references to his loved ones. 'How did you know her name, Señor González?'

'I take an interest in the people around me, Señor Rojas.' Rafael took another swig of beer before continuing. 'She seems to be a very healthy young girl. Does she like the Santa Isabel school? Is she a good student?'

'Si, señor.' Rojas felt the blood go from his head.

'You must be very proud of her.'

'She is a wonderful daughter,' Rojas said and, having lost the taste for the beer, put it down.

'It was good to talk to you again, Señor Rojas,' Rafael said, getting up from the couch. 'As you know, I value my privacy very much and you have been very helpful to me.'

As Rafael escorted the manager to the elevator, he handed him a small roll of money. 'To buy some gifts for your wife and your beautiful daughter.'

Rojas thanked him and waited what seemed an eternity for the elevator to arrive.

'I wish many years of good health for your family,' Rafael said as the doors closed.

Manuel Rojas breathed a sigh of relief as the elevator began its descent. He was in no doubt as to why he had been summoned to visit the man he knew as Rafael González, he also recognised the seemingly innocuous comments about the health of his family as a warning. González had even found out where Teresa went to school. He felt sick with fear. He had been warned before, when the apartments on the fifteenth floor were first rented to the secretive tenants. Now he was positive that Carlos Vega was hiding there, he would say nothing about it to anyone.

'Good, Rafael,' Vega said as he emerged from hiding into the living area. 'Señor Rojas will keep any suspicions he has to himself. Anyway, the poor man won't have to worry much longer, we leave tomorrow night.'

'The men will be happy, Carlos, they are tired of watching television and playing cards, they are asking for the women to come back.'

'I'm afraid that's not possible, compadre. Thanks to the señorita, the police will be watching this building day and night. Besides, the women are on a holiday. Tell the men that two days from now they can have all the women they want.' They laughed.

Vega sent Rafael across the hall to stand his men down and to fetch Jim Avery. Then he told Pedro to bring

Christina out. 'And tell her to bring the van Gogh, the painting on the wall is ugly.'

Avery arrived in the living area at the same time as Vega. 'Jim, you're leaving this afternoon, with Rafael. You'll be taking one of our King Airs to a destination three hours away. Rafael will tell you the location when you get to the airstrip.'

'And the cargo?' Avery inquired.

'No cargo.'

'Whatever you say, Carlos.'

'There's another plane waiting at the destination. Check it and be ready to leave on very short notice, okay?'

'Yes, sir, I read you loud and clear.'

'Rafael will have money and a phone. I'll contact him with more information later.'

Christina entered the room carrying "Almond Blossom" and proceeded to hang it.

'Where do we go after that?' Avery asked, loud enough for her to hear too.

'You'll find out later. Rafael doesn't know either.'

'No problem, Carlos.' He gestured towards Christina. 'I should check her face before I leave. You don't want a sick señorita when it's your turn to travel.'

'No, that would be awkward.'

'Honey, how's the face today?' Avery asked.

'Painful, worse than yesterday.' She exaggerated in case it was to her advantage to do so. Then, certain of what Avery's reaction would be, 'If you give me a dressing, I'll change it myself.'

'No, I want to check for infection.' He turned to Vega. 'If it's okay with you, I'll do it now?'

Vega nodded his approval.

Christina took a seat on the couch opposite Vega while Avery went to get his first aid kit. 'Will I be leaving soon?' she asked.

'Tomorrow night,' he replied and picked up the newspaper. 'With me.'

'We're flying out tomorrow night,' she said, elated by the prospect of an end to her ordeal.

'Not flying, there are too many police at the airports. We'll go by road.'

'What about the police on the roads?'

'It's kind of you to remind me of them, señorita, but we'll be invisible.'

'A magician, too.' She was relieved to see his angry mood of yesterday gone. 'How do you do that trick?'

'You ask too many questions. I think it's better that we talk about art. Where's the book?'

'Your men took it into the compartment.'

'Of course. I'd like you to hang the one of the fields and sky. You know the one I mean?'

'"Wheatfield under Thunderclouds".'

'There isn't much time left for us to enjoy the paintings together.'

'I'll put it up after he changes my dressing.' Having made an effort to cooperate, she felt in a better position to gather more intelligence. 'Will the paintings be going with us?'

249

'Yes.'

'All of them?'

'No more questions.' He turned his attention to the newspaper.

Avery returned a short time later and went with Christina to her room. Once again, he turned on the television.

After washing his hands he removed the dressing. 'Looks good, no sign of infection.'

'I'm going with him by road tomorrow night, with the paintings. He says we'll be invisible to the police. Sounds like we're going to be in a shipping container or something.'

'Either that or in with a bunch of horses.' Avery found a fresh dressing in his kit.

'I hope not,' she said with a roll of her eyes.

Avery went on in a whisper. 'Obviously we're going to meet up later, outside Colombia. My guess would be north, Venezuela or Panama. He said about three hours in a King Air, that's seven hundred miles, a long way by road.'

'Thrilling.'

'Rafael's coming with me, he'll have a phone. I'll try to use it to contact my friends in the DEA.' He applied the dressing and carefully smoothed the edges. 'There, you'll be fine.'

'I hope so.'

He pulled another dressing from the kit. 'Last one, take it.'

'Thanks.'

He snapped the kit closed. 'Better go back.'

'Good luck, Jim.' She touched his arm. 'Take care.'

'You too, honey,' he replied before giving her a kiss on the cheek. 'We're gonna need it.'

21

The police sergeant and soldier who had visited the fifteen storey apartment building on Avenue Bolívar reported back to the command centre just before noon, the sergeant richer by fifty thousand pesos, the soldier by two-thirds of that. The offerings they'd accepted were routine, part of the job, nothing large enough to interfere with how they did it. They and forty-one other teams, all with pockets fuller than before, had visited a total of over two hundred new buildings during the morning. The lists they worked from had been compiled with the help of various government inspection authorities. Each team rated their buildings on the basis of three criteria which had been identified by Martínez in consultation with other senior police officers: the level of security in and around the building; the level of suspicion generated by an interview with the building manager or owner; and the instinctive feelings of the team members conducting the visit. Each criteria was scored from one to ten and the resulting three numbers added. Martínez had resources to cover eight buildings and chose the top scoring assessments accordingly. The scores ranged from three for a recently constructed warehouse to twenty-eight for a two month old eighteen storey apartment complex. With a score of twenty-six, the building on Avenue Bolívar was third on the list.

Martínez scheduled a briefing session for the surveillance teams at three o'clock, an hour before the first shifts would take their positions. As an interim measure, he sent plain-clothed officers to each of the eight buildings to meet with the managers and commence the monitoring of the internal security systems.

After the frenzy that surrounded her awakening and concealment inside the secret compartment, Christina Jansen had spent the rest of the morning in her room catching up on her diary and watching television. She hoped that whoever was responsible for triggering the early morning alarm had found reason for suspicion and would return with reinforcements. She was happy with herself for successfully exploiting the opportunity the exercise had presented her. The guards who cleaned out her room had missed the US quarter she'd wedged, partially concealed, in the corner of the carpet above her diary. She presumed that any future police search would be less rushed and therefore more thorough.

The Van Gogh Hijack story was now getting less

prominence on CNN, pushed aside by other world events and the lack of new images. But it was a long way from being forgotten. This morning, in the absence of any further developments, the network had interviewed Albert Voss who described Vega's abuse of her and the burning of "Wheatfield with a Reaper" as "the deeds of a barbarian". More importantly to Christina, he also gave a reminder of the Vincent van Gogh Foundation's one million dollar reward.

As lunchtime approached, she made her way to the living area. Vincent's panoramic "Wheatfield under Thunderclouds" now hung on the wall: A gently undulating landscape of green and yellow fields; a wide sky, jumbled cumulus clouds, the deepest blue horizon; in the foreground, a thin cluster of red flowers, defiant beacons in the green and yellow and blue.

'Magnificent,' Vega said, strolling over to her and the painting. 'Such thick brushstrokes. And that cloud!' He pointed to a jumble of finger-wide strokes of white in the top left of the metre-wide canvas. 'So simple, a few tangled strokes of paint creates a cloud.'

'You're getting good at this, Carlos, perhaps you missed your calling.'

'Very amusing, señorita,' he replied with a thin smile and after considering the painting a while longer moved back to the couch. 'By the way, Jim will be joining us for lunch.'

'Wonderful! Another meal with Mr Culture himself. I can hardly wait.'

'You have been lucky to have me as your keeper,' Vega said, 'Think how dull this would be if you weren't able to talk about Vincent and his art.'

'I'll try to remember that,' she said as Avery entered the room. 'When I'm recovering from the trauma.' Josef and Miguel followed carrying the cold meat and salad meals.

At the table, Vega poured the wine and held his glass to Avery. 'To a successful journey, compadre. Salud!'

'Salud!' Avery clipped his glass against Vega's and held it towards Christina. 'Salud! Señorita.'

Unsure of the significance of the toast, she kept her glass planted.

Undaunted, Avery struck her glass with the base of his, causing a chime. 'To your safe return to Amsterdam.'

'I'll drink to that,' she said. 'Anytime.' She took a sip of the Chilean white.

'Nice,' Avery said after taking a mouthful of wine. 'Your drink allowance is way more realistic than the airlines', Carlos. That's one of the things I like about this job.'

'We have a beautiful woman and a magnificent painting, amigo.' Vega gestured to both with his glass. 'The wine makes it perfect.'

'Si, compadre.' The new painting caught Avery's eye as he lowered the wine from his mouth. 'That one, I like.'

'Where are those fields in the painting?' Vega asked Christina after giving her a chance to enjoy some of her food.

'Near Auvers, outside Paris.' She placed her cutlery on the plate. 'Vincent moved there after becoming bored with life in the asylum at Saint-Rémy.'

'Did he check into a madhouse in the new place?' Avery injected, deliberately inviting trouble.

'Not this again,' she said, sounding more exasperated than she was. 'Too bad you haven't got an imagination Jim, it would be nice if you thought up a new theme.'

'My apologies, honey,' Avery replied. 'I didn't mean to upset you. Please go on, and don't leave anything out.'

'I'll try not to,' she answered and continued, 'In May of 1890, two months before his death, Vincent left Saint-Rémy. He travelled by train to Paris where he visited Theo and met Theo's wife, Johanna, for the first time. He also got to see his nephew.

'Johanna later wrote that she was surprised when she first met Vincent. She expected a sick man but found, as she described: "a sturdy, broad-shouldered man, with a healthy colour, a smile on his face and a very resolute appearance." She said he looked healthier than Theo.

'At their house, Vincent was reunited with his work. Theo and Johanna had his paintings covering every space on the walls and others were piled under the beds.'

'Quite the collection,' Vega interrupted.

'Be worth billions now,' Avery said, looking up from his plate.

'It all boils down to money, doesn't it, Jim? I'm sure your idea of great art is a framed thousand dollar bill.'

'Christina, you're right.' Avery raised his hands in surrender. 'I won't say any more.'

She was secretly enjoying the charade, still not sure how much of Avery's part was an act. 'While he was in Paris, Vincent saw some of his old artist friends. He talked about staying to do a few paintings and also of going to Madagascar with Gauguin. But the noise of the city got to him and he decided to leave after only a few days.

'Theo and a friend arranged for him to go to Auvers. There was a doctor there, Paul Gachet, well known in the artistic community. Gachet agreed to keep an eye on Vincent, he even found him somewhere to stay, a room above a cafe.'

'Your book mentions that doctor,' Vega remarked. 'A strange man.'

'Gachet was an interesting character,' Christina responded. 'Vincent described him as being "rather eccentric". He was in his sixties, had thick red hair and believed in socialism and free love.'

'My kind of guy,' Avery remarked in support of Gachet's philosophy on lovemaking, not politics.

'He also promoted a strange society,' Christina continued, 'the Society for Mutual Autopsy. He tried to get his friends to join. The idea was that he would study their hearts and brains when they died.'

'And this doctor was looking after Vincent's health?' Avery scoffed.

'It seems strange, I know.' She paused for some water.

'Gachet prescribed work as the best therapy for Vincent's condition. That pleased Vincent. He painted almost one canvas a day while he was in Auvers. "Wheatfield under Thunderclouds" is one of those.' She looked towards it. 'It and "Wheatfield with Crows" are two of the last paintings he did.'

'This "Wheatfield with Crows", does it belong to your museum?' Vega asked.

'It's in the Foundation's collection, on the other tour. It should be in Sydney at the moment.' Then, cutting into a wedge of avocado, 'Maybe you two could hijack the plane over the outback.'

'Sorry, Christina,' Avery remarked with a grin, 'We'll pass on that. Carlos told me he wants some Picassos next.'

The men laughed.

'Very funny,' she said, a little amused by the comment herself. 'Have you heard enough?'

'No, please go on,' Vega said, 'Tell us the rest of the story, how Vincent's life ended.'

'On July the twenty-seventh, a Sunday, Vincent went into the wheatfield with his easel and a pistol he'd borrowed, seemingly on the pretext of using it to shoot crows. That afternoon, he shot himself in the chest.' She'd related the final episode of Vincent's life countless times, not once had she felt detached from it. 'The bullet missed his heart. Somehow he managed to get himself back to his room above the cafe. The owner became concerned when he didn't come for dinner and went upstairs to check. He found Vincent lying on the bed.'

'Had he been hitting the absinthe again?' Avery asked. 'Or was he having one of his fits, like when he cut his earlobe off?'

'Vincent reported that he was feeling quite lucid at the time. Gachet and another doctor decided against removing the bullet. That night Vincent lay awake smoking his pipe, apparently in little or no pain. Theo came from Paris the next day and the brothers spent that day and night talking. Just after one o'clock the next morning, Vincent died in Theo's arms. It was July twenty-ninth, harvest time in the fields of Auvers.'

'What caused him to do it?' Vega asked. 'What was depressing him?'

'Nobody knows for sure. It could have been his health . . . the pain, fear of another attack. People who saw him in the weeks before thought he was okay. He felt some pressure because of the changes in Theo's life. The infant Vincent had been quite ill some weeks before, and Theo wasn't getting along with his employer, he was thinking of leaving and setting up his own business. Vincent knew that such a move would make it difficult for Theo to support him as well as his own family.'

'Such a tragedy,' Vega mused, bringing his glass to his chin and holding it there.

'Vincent's friends came from Paris and decorated his room with flowers and his paintings before the funeral. He was buried in the churchyard at Auvers, surrounded by those same wheatfields.'

'Have you visited his grave?' Vega asked and took some wine.

'Several times. Theo is buried there too.'

'A sad story, Christina,' Avery remarked in an uncharacteristically humble manner. 'It makes you wonder what was going on in his head when he painted that, when he looked out on those fields.'

'Just as well you're leaving, Jim,' she said. 'After a few more sessions, who knows, you might become a devotee of Vincent's.'

'Anything's possible,' Avery said, smiling sideways at her. 'I'm already a devotee of Vincent's curator, it may be an easy next step.'

'Too bad his curator could never return the devotion.'

'Touché, honey.' Avery raised his glass to her.

Rafael entered carrying a small suitcase.

'Jim,' Vega interrupted. 'I'm afraid it's time for you to leave.'

'All good things come to a end.' Avery took a last sip of wine. 'Thanks for lunch, Carlos,' he said as he got up. 'And Christina, thanks for the inspiration, about your Vincent van Gogh.'

'You're inspired!' she said mockingly, 'And I thought I was wasting my time.'

'No need to be cruel, honey,' Avery said, holding his hand over his heart.

'Do you have everything you need?' Vega asked Rafael as he followed Avery from the table.

'Yes, Carlos.' The case Rafael had with him contained fifty thousand dollars in cash, a phone and false papers for both him and the American pilot.

'Good,' Vega said and grasped Avery's shoulder. 'If anyone asks, you've been hired by Rafael to take him to the destination. He's going to visit a chemical factory he owns there. On your way to the airport, memorise the details from the identification, okay? And leave your wallet and passport with Pedro.'

'Yes, sir,' Avery said. 'I'll just get my bag.' He turned to Christina. 'Adios, honey.'

'Bye,' she said, glancing up to catch his eye.

Vega walked with Avery to the door. 'Jim, no drinking when you get to the destination, and get plenty of rest. I want you to be fully alert for the next flight.'

'Don't worry, Carlos, I haven't gone to sleep at the stick yet.'

Vega spoke to Rafael in the hallway while Avery collected his bag. 'Don't lose sight of him and keep the phone with you all the time. Jim is not to use it, under any circumstances.'

In his two years of employment, the American had done nothing to legitimise Vega's distrust. He had performed all his assignments flawlessly, and regular investigations by Vega's contacts in the DEA had uncovered no evidence of any involvement with that organisation. Nevertheless, Vega was suspicious. It was not unknown for the DEA to recruit or coerce people already

261

involved in the drug business to turn informer, people just like Jim Avery.

Silence fell across the one hundred and fifty police officers assigned to the building surveillance teams as Martínez moved to the rostrum before them. 'Gentlemen,' he said, looking around the crowded briefing room. 'I spoke with our President a short time ago to bring him up to date on progress in the case. His Excellency expressed his admiration for what we have done so far and asked me to stress the importance of this undertaking to Colombia's international reputation. His Excellency is following the case very closely. Great rewards await the men who are involved in the arrest of Carlos Vega and the rescue of his hostage and the paintings.' Martínez was confident that the Presidential incentive was at least competitive with anything likely to be offered to his men by the other side. 'Great rewards, compadres.'

There would be eighteen men, three shifts of six, in each of the eight teams. At each site, two men would be stationed in each of two unmarked vehicles. Another man would be stationed inside to monitor the building's security system. And the sixth member, a communications specialist, would be tapped into the building's phone and intercom systems. In addition to the normal equipment and weaponry, each surveillance vehicle would have night vision binoculars, a parabolic microphone to pick up distant conversations and a video camera. All teams would have direct and immediate radio access to the command centre through the team leader stationed in one of the vehicles. The army had stationed three mobile squads at strategic locations ready to move at a moment's notice.

'Wherever Vega is hiding,' Martínez continued, 'he'll have a small army of well armed killers protecting him. And, almost certainly, he has the Dutch woman and the paintings with him. Because of these considerations, we have decided that if his hiding place is located, we will not storm it. The risk to the hostage, ourselves and the valuable paintings would be too great. Instead, we will wait until he is vulnerable. We will wait until he comes out. We will follow him and, with the help of the army, we will ambush him with such a show of force that he will have no option but to surrender.

'Your part in this operation is vital. You must be vigilant. You must try to find where he is and then see him when he moves.

'Vega is smart. It won't take him long to discover that you are watching, and he will be watching you, he will try to trick you.

'Each team's vehicles must park in positions that give clear views of the whole building including carpark entrances. Use the night vision equipment. Make note of what you see and tell the shift that replaces you. Videotape anyone entering or leaving the building. Radio all vehicle licence numbers to the command centre so they can be checked immediately.

'The people working inside the buildings must never be seen talking to the people in the surveillance vehicles. They must arrive and leave separately. We don't want Vega to know we have people inside.

'I have great faith in your abilities, compadres. I know we will find Vega, and when we do, it will be a very proud day for the police and army of our country.'

Their spirits suitably lifted, Martínez sent the men on their way.

Josef became suspicious of the two cars that pulled up outside the building just after four o'clock when nobody got out of either of them. He called Pedro to take a look on the televisions. One car was parked across the street from the front of the building, the other was on the side near the carpark entrance. Pedro immediately summoned his boss.

Upon seeing the situation for himself, Vega sent Miguel, who was unknown to the police, for a walk in the park to check out the cars. He returned ten minutes later and confirmed the suspicions.

'What's happening with the truck?' Vega asked Pedro after hearing Miguel's report.

'Rodrigo says it is ready to go.'

'Okay, we still leave tomorrow night. Between now and then, be careful with the phones. No calls out and use code on any coming in. And, Pedro, keep the men off the balcony.'

22

It was eight o'clock in the morning and the fumes from the traffic had already spread a grey haze over Avenue Bolívar. Inconspicuous in the Monday rush, a middle-aged woman got off a bus and made her way across the wide avenue towards the fifteen storey building facing the park. Rosa Portales was a reluctant courier, pressured into service by her husband. She had not asked him anything about the contents of the envelope she carried, nor did she have any interest in the true identity of its intended recipient. As with all matters relating to her husband's business, she preferred not to know. The only hint Rosa had of the importance of her task was the serious manner in which she had been coached to perform it.

'Si,' the voice from the speaker crackled in immediate response when she pressed the intercom button for apartment 1502.

'Señor Raúl has sent me about the maid's job,' she recited towards the console.

Pedro didn't recognise the face on the television screen but Rodrigo's code name was a good enough password to gain her admittance. He sent two men to the hallway and watched her on the screen.

The men in the hallway surprised Rosa from the sides as she stepped out of the elevator. After confirming that she was unarmed, one of them tapped on the door of apartment 1502. Pedro emerged. 'Buenos dìas.'

'Buenos dìas, señor,' she said, her voice trembling. 'My husband is Sergio Portales, I am Rosa. Rodrigo asked that I give this envelope to Don Pedro.'

Pedro signalled for the guards to give her some space. 'I am Pedro, señora. I know Sergio, he is a good man.' He accepted the envelope and sliced it open with a knife he took from his pocket. 'You must pardon the impatience of my bodyguards, señora. There have been threats against me, so I take precautions.'

'Si, señor,' she replied, praying her stay would be a short one.

Pedro removed two pieces of paper from the envelope and examined them. Neither was addressed but both were clearly meant for his boss. 'Señora, please wait here.' He knocked on the door of 1501 and entered.

Vega put down today's edition of "El Colombiano" and listened as Pedro explained the origin of the two messages.

'Why is Rodrigo taking such a chance?' Vega responded, agitated by what seemed an unnecessary risk. 'Where is the woman now?'

'In the hallway, Carlos. She is harmless.'

Vega read the larger of the two messages. 'It's from one of our friends in the police, an outline of the plan to apprehend us.' He read the main points aloud. 'There's a list of buildings under surveillance, this is one of them. Eight altogether. Phones are tapped, vehicle licence numbers are being checked, visitors are being photographed. There is a man inside each building monitoring the security system. He says the police and army won't storm the hiding place if they find it, they think it would be too risky for the hostage and the paintings. How sensible of them. They will attempt an ambush when we're on the move. Ha!' He folded the note and turned his attention to the other one. 'It's good to be informed, compadre.' He read the brief message. 'Rodrigo will take the truck to the rendezvous this afternoon.' With that, he stood and handed the notes to Pedro. 'Give Señora Portales some money, she has done well.'

'Si, Carlos,' Pedro replied as Vega moved towards the window.

'Tonight, amigo,' Vega said, gazing out at the city lights, 'we will be free of these jaguars that surround us.'

Intensely bored and frustrated after a week of captivity, Christina Jansen was watching television in her room. At ten o'clock, CNN broadcast several items under the Van Gogh Hijack banner. The first was a live report from Medellín. The young male reporter stood on a balcony with the city's skyline behind him and gave an account of the building searches that had been conducted yesterday. Christina tried to work out where he was, relative to her, but couldn't. As for what he said, she knew it and more already.

Next was a brief interview with the chief restorer at the Netherlands' largest art museum, the Rijksmuseum in Amsterdam. Christina knew the woman well. Her staff had a worldwide reputation for excellence in the field and had, on several occasions, done repair work for the Vincent van Gogh Foundation. Her explanation of the nature of the damage was accompanied by magnified images of the edges of the piece returned from Colombia. She expressed her confidence that the work could be restored close to its original state if the rest of it was returned in no worse condition than the face. In answer to the interviewer's question about the repair of "Wheatfield with a Reaper", she said she was unable to comment without seeing it.

The third part of the report was of most immediate interest to Christina. The topic was the Stockholm syndrome, described by the anchor as the seemingly bizarre affection that sometimes develops between captive and captor. He introduced a professor of psychiatry from Harvard medical school and asked him to explain the condition in more detail.

Clearly enthralled, the young academic spoke rapidly. 'The term was coined after a hostage incident in Stockholm in the early 1970s. An escaped convict walked into a bank with a submachine gun hidden under his coat and, after firing it at the ceiling, took control. He and another convict held several hostages inside the bank's vault for about a week and threatened to kill them if he and his companion weren't given a large sum of money and safe passage out of Sweden.

'The police and psychiatrists involved in negotiations became puzzled when they observed two women hostages becoming increasingly antagonistic towards everyone except their captors. The women seemed to have developed a sympathy for the convicts. Later, one of the women admitted that, driven by her determination to survive, she'd allowed the gunman to lie on the floor with her and caress her body. She also revealed that he'd asked to have intercourse with her but she'd refused. She said that if she'd allowed that to happen, she would have lost the little power she had left. On the other side, the gunman later admitted that he'd grown to like the women too much to kill them.'

'How did the incident end, Professor?' the anchor asked.

'Quite successfully . . . for the authorities, that is. The police drilled holes in the top of the vault, dropped in some tear gas and stormed inside. The case is considered a landmark in the investigation of the psychology of hostages and their captors.'

'What's the explanation for the behaviour the psychologists observed?'

'There are a couple of theories. One is that, under

duress, a primitive urge for survival can turn to affection. It may be that being a hostage is a bit like being an infant. The infant is dependent upon his or her parents for food and comfort, the hostage is dependent upon the captor for their survival. In that situation the hostage may naturally revert to the same tactics used to please their mother when they were young. The other theory is that it's too psychologically exhausting to sustain the terror and fear of being threatened and dehumanised for very long so the hostage makes the jump and identifies with their captor, but in order to keep their self esteem, they come to believe the captor is not a criminal at all, but someone who needs compassion and understanding.'

'And how do kidnappers normally react to this?' the anchor asked.

'It depends. Trained kidnappers, such as those working for political groups or the military in countries that do this type of thing, know about the syndrome and try to avoid it. They dehumanise their captives by doing things like putting hoods over their heads or referring to them by false names . . . or even numbers. And they avoid speaking with their hostages. A relationship makes torture or execution more difficult . . . that's what they, or the people giving them their orders, don't want.'

Christina squirmed at that cold analysis.

'Professor, if you could speak to Christina Jansen what advice would you give her?'

'It's my guess that Doctor Jansen's life is not in any great danger. I say that fully realising that she's had her face burned by Vega. This kidnapping is unique. It doesn't involve money in exchange for a life nor does it involve political reform of some kind in exchange for a life. Vega has put an absolutely extraordinary amount of effort into his plan, he really wants it to work. If Christina Jansen is killed, it simply won't, and he knows it. The deal the Dutch government has settled on is very good for her. I understand she'll be exchanged with some of the paintings before Vega's son is taken to Colombia. So, I think she's safe. Let's hope so anyway.'

'Nevertheless Professor, what advice would you give her?' Christina was pleased the anchor had gone back to the question the psychiatrist had rambled past. She wanted to hear his answer.

'I'd give her the same advice I give anyone who's in danger of becoming a hostage. Firstly, she should do her best to become a person in the eyes of anyone who may pose a threat to her . . . Vega, his bodyguards, anyone. She should talk about her family, her childhood, her aspirations, her interests . . . that kind of thing. She should avoid disagreement or criticism of any kind. There have been several instances of captives who have been marked for death literally talking their way out of it, just talking about the kinds of things I mentioned. Unfortunately, their survival has sometimes meant that another person, someone who hadn't built up the rapport, was killed in their place. The other point I should make is that hostages who survive the first three days of captivity generally survive the whole thing, and Christina Jansen has done that.'

Christina found it spooky, hearing her chance of living discussed so clinically. Become a person in Vega's eyes, the psychiatrist had said. She was doing that, it came naturally. And Vega was allowing it, encouraging it. There was no mask, no number. She'd lost her cool with him twice. She wouldn't again. She would leave the moral pronouncements to someone else.

The anchor then led into an old story on the United States' most publicised illustration of the Stockholm syndrome. Christina was too young to remember the Patty Hearst kidnapping but she had heard it referred to over the years. She watched the report with interest: 'On the night of February the fifth, 1974, Patty Hearst, the pretty, nineteen year old granddaughter of the American newspaper tycoon William Randolph Hearst was kidnapped from a San Francisco apartment she shared with her fiancé, Steven Weed. Weed was knocked out and Ms Hearst, who had been taking a shower at the time, was carried away naked. Her captors, a small radical group known as the Symbionese Liberation Army, offered to release her on the condition that a food distribution program be set up for San Francisco's poor.

'Patty was held captive in this one bedroom apartment on Golden Gate Avenue. There, she spent her time listening to music, watching television and discussing the revolution with her captors. It's been said that because of her privileged and sheltered upbringing, Patty had never before associated with people who held a strong commitment to any cause. That, some experts believe, led to the fascination she developed for her fanatical captors.

'The kidnappers communicated their demands by means of cassette tapes. On an early tape, Patty abused her father, Randolph Hearst, whom she referred to as a pig, for taking too long to pay the money to set up the food program. When food was finally distributed in what became ugly grabbing brawls, she accused him of organising it poorly and providing food of an inferior quality to that which she had enjoyed at her parents' home herself. She also told how she was learning to use a shotgun loaded with cyanide buckshot to protect herself in the event of an FBI raid.

'Thirteen weeks after the kidnapping, her father settled the ransom demand by paying four million dollars into a trust account dedicated to the provision of food for the poor. He also agreed to provide more money after his daughter was released.

'When the time finally came for her to be freed, Patty stunned her family and everyone else following the sensational case by announcing that she'd chosen to stay with the SLA to fight for, as she said, freedom of the oppressed.

'Then, a few days after Easter, Patty was identified as the woman wearing the black wig in this photograph taken during a hold up at San Francisco's Hibernia Bank. Shots were fired during the robbery wounding two passers-by.

The police put out a wanted poster on Ms Hearst describing her as armed and dangerous.

'In mid-May, a large contingent of police closed in on a house in Los Angeles thought to be the headquarters of the SLA. In the shooting and fire which followed, six members of the group, about half the total membership, were killed. But Patty wasn't found and remained at large until September the next year when she was finally captured by the FBI in San Francisco.

'Despite her plea that she had been brainwashed and was not responsible for her actions, a court found her guilty of armed robbery and sentenced her to seven years in jail. The verdict and sentence generated much debate across the country and, after serving twenty-two months of the sentence, Patty Hearst was pardoned by President Carter.'

Strange case, Christina thought. But a different kidnapping altogether. There was no chance of her ever sympathising with Vega as Hearst had with her captors. There was no high minded creed to seduce her. She dropped the volume on the television and lay on the bed to rest. Communicate with Vega, be friendly, you will live.

She emerged from her room at noon and packed away "Wheatfield under Thunderclouds". Today, for the last lunch in the apartment, as Vega had earlier requested, she would display two paintings. Maybe she would even compliment him on his choices. The two he had selected from the guide did belong together.

She hung "The Yellow House": a peaceful street scene in

the bright midday sun of Arles. A block of light coloured buildings beneath an ink-blue sky. The closest building, a duplex, fronts onto a town square. Its left is a shop. Its right is Vincent's home in Arles: A small two level yellow house with green windows and door and a red tiled roof. Behind the yellow house, a hotel, also yellow, with tall chimneys. Patrons relax at tables in the shade of its awning while other folk go about their business in the clay streets. In the distance, past the hotel, a steam train crossing an overpass smudges the sky with its smoke.

She propped the other painting against the wall to the right of the first. "The Bedroom": Vincent's bedroom upstairs in the yellow house. A small, neatly furnished room with a look of loneliness about it. The walls are pale lilac, the floor streaked and faded red, the window is the same green as outside. There are two chairs in the room, a table with a blue wash basin and toiletries. The sturdy wooden bed, the colour of fresh butter, has lime-yellow pillows and a scarlet cover. Above the table, a small mirror hangs, a flash of white in the brightly coloured work.

Vega arrived behind Josef and Miguel who carried the lunch trays. 'So our meal today will be twice as enjoyable,' Vega said upon seeing the paintings. He took a close look at them before ushering Christina to the table.

The food was accompanied by the customary bottle of white wine. Vega poured and then raised his glass towards her. 'Salud!'

She touched her glass against his.

'Now we have a problem, Christina, which painting first?'

'The one Vincent painted first,' she said, pleased to see him in a good mood. 'Which do you think it is?'

'The street scene?' he said after a moment of consideration.

'Good guess.' She smiled, as did he. 'Vincent painted "The Yellow House" in late 1888. The scene is in Arles in the south of France looking from the town square, Place Lamartine to be precise. The Rhône river is behind where he sat. Vincent rented the yellow house with the green shutters in the middle of the picture. It was in a poor state of repair and he took a couple of months to fix it up before he moved in. The house had four rooms which gave him space to work and the opportunity to invite artist friends to stay.'

'Gauguin?' Vega inquired offering hot sauce, suggesting she spoon a little onto her fish.

'Yes, Gauguin,' she replied, and did as Vega suggested. '"The Bedroom" was done in anticipation of Gauguin's arrival. Vincent described it as a painting to rest the brain, or the imagination. Of course, not everyone sees it like that. Some see tension in the way the room is depicted. It's crooked, the furniture seems to be falling, the pieces are mismatched. The room looks lonely but there are two chairs, one for a visitor.'

'It doesn't disturb me at all,' Vega commented and cut into his fish. 'Gauguin and Vincent argued, true?'

'They did,' Christina replied. The sauce, only mildly

hot, worked with the fish. 'But they got along for a good part of the time. They both accomplished a great deal of work during Gauguin's visit.'

'Is the house still there?'

'No, it was hit by a bomb during the second world war.'

'How unlucky,' Vega huffed, looking again to the works. 'I read in your book of another "Bedroom" painting,' he commented after a while.

'There are three. The first was damaged in shipping so Theo had Vincent do another. He did it from memory in Saint-Rémy, and he did a smaller version for his mother and sister.'

'Where are the others?' Vega asked.

'In Paris, at the Musée d'Orsay, and the Art Institute of Chicago.'

'Paris, Chicago and Medellín,' Vega said, and sipped some more wine. 'Are the other two the same as that?'

'More or less. Memory was involved, so there are a few differences. The pictures he has hanging on the walls, for instance. The colours vary too, the one he did in Saint-Rémy is brightest.'

Vega reached into his shirt pocket and retrieved a newspaper clipping. 'I have a task for you, after lunch.' He handed the clipping to her. 'You must separate the paintings on that list, they are the ones your government wants first.'

She examined the list, printed in English and Spanish, nodding as she read it. 'Okay.' She placed the clipping to the side. The time was right to gather more intelligence. 'Is it going to be hot or cold where we're going tonight? What should I wear?' The information might make a useful diary entry.

'My advice is to wear what you're wearing now, but pack for any kind of weather.'

'I don't have anything for cold weather, you know that.' She was wearing a pair of the counterfeit jeans and a T-shirt. They and another set like them, the clothes she wore on the plane, a light sweater, and the suit she'd packed for her arrival in Rio were all she had.

'If it is cold, señorita, I will give you my jacket,' Vega said with a smile. He had already ordered the appropriate clothing and footwear for the final destination.

'Where will the second set of paintings be stored?' she asked, giving up on the first line of questioning.

'Somewhere safe.'

'It has to be air conditioned. The temperature must stay constant at twenty-two Celsius, humidity at fifty percent.'

'They'll be stored properly, just like they are here,' he replied, then, reaching for the wine, 'Enough questions.' He topped up their glasses. 'Our lunch is near its end, señorita.' He raised his glass. 'To your future.'

'My future,' she said with a frown. 'Whatever it is, it has to be an improvement on my present.'

'True,' Vega replied with a soft laugh. 'May you live a long and healthy life.' He touched his glass to hers.

'So, where to now for you?' she asked after sipping the wine. 'Not that you'll tell me.'

'Unfortunately not,' Vega responded with a smile.

'Even if you do get past the police, you'll have to hide for the rest of your life.'

'I've become used to living an isolated life, Christina. Where I am going, people will not know me, and my money will allow me to do anything I please. I'll be free to read and fish, maybe I'll learn to paint.'

'Sounds a little too peaceful,' she said, placing her knife and fork on the plate. 'What about your wife?'

'Arrangements have been made for her to join me,' Vega said. 'Incidentally, Margarita had nothing to do with the hijacking.'

'I believe you.' She did. His statement seemed candid. 'Won't she mind being cut off from her family and friends?'

'Perhaps.'

'It seems quite a price for her to pay.'

'I can't force Margarita to join me, but she will. It may seem strange to you, but she loves me, despite my faults.'

'You're right, I do find that strange.'

'You see, Christina, Margarita is not the angel you are. Consequently, she is more tolerant of my imperfections.' He emptied his glass and got up from the table. 'You must excuse me. Pedro will help you organise the paintings this afternoon. I must make plans to escape the jaguars around us.'

23

Manuel Rojas got up from watching television wondering which of the pampered tenants was knocking on his door this time and what their complaint would be: air conditioning, parking, noise. The building manager cursed under his breath when he saw Josef's distorted face peering at him through the peephole and prayed he wasn't about to be invited to another audience with Rafael González on the fifteenth floor. After a moment of hesitation, he forced himself to twist the knob. 'Buenas noches, señor,' he smiled.

Josef stepped forward, deftly bringing a gun from under his coat and pushing its barrel into the building manager's throat. 'Take me to the policeman, Señor Rojas,' he whispered.

Another two of Vega's guards appeared from the side, entered the apartment and locked the door behind them.

Josef kept the gun at the manager's throat as he pushed him down the hallway. 'Don't try anything foolish, or María and Teresa will die.'

The manager's wife and daughter were sitting in the living area watching "The Simpsons", oblivious to what was happening behind them. The policeman sat nearby watching the program from a chair in front of four small television monitors mounted on the wall.

The two guards overpowered the policeman before he could react while Josef pushed the manager onto the couch next to his startled wife and daughter. 'Don't move!' he ordered, waving the gun at them. The family members embraced each other, the wife pleading for mercy for the child.

Josef moved behind the couch and took hold of the trembling ten year old's shirt. Then, fixing the policeman with maddened eyes, he lifted her up and brought his gun to her head.

'Leave her out of this!' the policeman shouted, struggling uselessly against the guards.

'Where are the police who are listening to the telephones, señor?'

'In the electrical room, off the lobby,' he answered without hesitation.

'When do you have to report to your supervisor?' Josef demanded, keeping his gun to the girl's head. She was crying now.

'Eight thirty.'

Josef glanced at his watch. It was five minutes past eight. 'Take care of them,' he ordered and dropped the girl back between her parents.

The guards pushed the policeman to the floor, handcuffed him to a short length of radiator pipe and covered his mouth with duct tape. That done, they ordered the Rojas family into the kitchen where they handcuffed Manuel's arms around the drain pipe under the sink and María's and Teresa's around his. Their mouths were then taped over.

Josef removed the videotape from the recorder mounted under the monitors and switched it, the monitors and the policeman's radio off. He then unplugged the telephone, ripped the handpiece off and threw both pieces out of reach. 'Get the elevator,' he ordered and moved to the Rojas family. 'My friend here,' he said, gesturing to the remaining guard, 'will stay with you until we have left the building. Don't do anything to upset him or he will kill you. After he goes, I want no one banging the walls, I want no noise at all. For an hour. If I hear you have disobeyed that instruction, Señor Rojas, your beautiful daughter, Teresa, will not have another birthday. Do you understand?'

The manager nodded, his eyes signalling absolute terror.

Josef moved to the policeman, grabbed his chin and twisted it around until he looked up the barrel of his gun. 'Is that clear to you too, señor?' The policeman nodded.

Josef and the guard rode to the fifteenth floor and reported the success of the first stage of the operation to Vega.

'Bravo, compadres,' Vega said and gave the order to move the paintings which had been piled in four stacks near the door. The ones to be delivered first had yellow string tied to their latches. Christina stood beside them with Pedro who she hardly recognised now that his moustache was gone and his hair combed back. 'Careful!' she shouted when the guards converged too enthusiastically on the paintings. They obeyed.

While the elevator was delivering its first load downstairs, Vega took Christina with him into the second apartment. Two guards, both of whom would stay in Medellín, remained monitoring the television sets. After confirming that they were to abandon the apartment as soon as his car left, Vega led Christina back to the elevator.

'Put this on,' he said as the elevator began its descent, handing her what appeared to be a small band-aid. 'It prevents travel sickness.' He pointed to a patch below his ear. 'I have one, see.'

She held her hair back and applied the patch below her left ear.

'You'll thank me for that later,' he said as the elevator doors opened to reveal a Chevrolet sedan, backed up, its motor running.

Pedro pushed Christina into the back seat in front of him. Vega got in on the other side and checked his watch. It was twenty-three minutes past eight. The operation, so far, had gone perfectly.

Two kilometres away, outside an apartment building on Avenue la Playa, Miguel had a lucky break. He would not need to buzz the building manager with his bogus story about having a document for him to sign, a complication he was happy to avoid. He followed a few steps behind the well dressed young woman laden down with groceries as she walked towards the front door.

The building he was about to enter was one of those listed by Vega's police informant as being under surveillance. He stood back as the woman entered a four digit code into the keypad beside the door. As the latch released, he made a great show of opening the door for her.

She watched him as he entered the lobby behind her, clearly suspicious of how he had gained access but saying nothing. He checked his watch, he had six minutes.

He helped her carry the groceries into the elevator and waited for her to press her floor. She pressed seven, he pressed nine. 'Beautiful weather, isn't it?' he said and, in an effort to appear legitimate, took some keys from his pocket. She exited in silence.

Miguel didn't think the woman was suspicious enough to contact the building manager. Not that it would matter if she did. The manager would soon be very busy.

He pressed the button for the upper level of the carpark and waited impatiently as the elevator took him to the ninth floor and then down.

As he hurried through the carpark towards the large metal door, he removed a phone from his pocket, turned it on and pressed a memory button. 'Go,' was all he said and turned it off.

Thirty seconds later he stomped on the rubber sensor which triggered the door opening mechanism. A small rental van followed by a green Renault were on their way down the ramp.

Once the vehicles were inside, Miguel ran to the stair-well and up to the second floor where he removed a small bottle of gasoline from his pocket, unscrewed the lid and inserted a wick. Checking first that the hallway was empty, he lit it and walked quickly to the first fire alarm station. He tossed the bottle in front of him and pulled the lever. Startled by the immediate loud clanging, he turned and ran to the stairs.

Ignoring the shouting behind him, he ran across the carpark towards the waiting Renault which got under way as soon as he was inside, the van right on its tail. He picked up the submachine gun from the floor and sprayed the tyres of the closest surveillance vehicle as they sped past it. The two men inside ducked below the windows. The men in the second vehicle ran into the darkness when they saw what was happening, enabling Miguel to empty the rest of the magazine into their car unhindered by any concern that he may hit someone.

His part in the first stage of tonight's operation com-plete, Miguel fell back in the seat and pictured the stunned policemen trying to stop the other vehicles pouring out of the building's carpark. They would be looking for some of Carlos Vega's men, half expecting to find them, surely a frightening proposition for even the bravest of men.

The vehicles pulled into a nearby side street and glided to a halt behind the changeover car. Once inside it, Miguel and his two accomplices removed the false moustaches and caps they had worn since leaving the building on Avenue Bolívar and drove off.

Back on Avenue la Playa, they were treated to an array of police cars, army vehicles, fire trucks and even a helicopter speeding past or over them in the opposite direction. Miguel congratulated himself. He was confident that he had created more than enough confusion to ensure Vega's quiet escape.

Vega and his companions heard the distant sirens as they waited in the carpark. Four cars had already left, each carrying four paintings. Two of them would be waiting close by, ready to escort Vega's Chevrolet to the destination.

At eight thirty-two, Vega gave the command to leave. He and Pedro crouched on the floor pulling Christina down with them. Josef drove past the surveillance vehicle near the carpark exit but turned left to avoid passing the second. He reported that one of the policemen wrote something down, presumably their licence number. It was not a concern to Vega. The car had been bought at a bankruptcy auction a few weeks before the hijacking by the girlfriend of one of his guards. Like all vehicles used in the operation, it could only indirectly be traced to Vega, and that would take time.

Once Vega's car disappeared off the television screens, the remaining guards abandoned the fifteenth floor apartment. On the way down, they stopped to collect the man inside the manager's suite who repeated Josef's threat to the policeman and the Rojas family before leaving.

They drove out of the carpark at eight thirty-six. The surveillance police took their licence number but didn't interrupt the frantic communication between the command centre and the police who had converged on the area around the building on Avenue la Playa. And they were too preoccupied listening to the radio communications to notice that the man on surveillance duty inside the building was late with his report.

24

'The green Renault involved in the shooting came from the Bolívar building,' the voice on Luis Martinez's radio announced. 'Left there at 19:15 hours.' Martínez was in the lobby of the building on Avenue la Playa being briefed by the surveillance team leader.

'Dios!' Martínez cursed, his fears about the La Playa incident suddenly realised. He spoke rapidly into the radio as he and Nelson Schoute hurried outside. 'Command, this is Martínez, La Playa is a decoy. Move operation to Bolívar. I repeat, move to Bolívar, immediately. Officers at Bolívar stop anyone leaving the building.'

As Martínez's and three accompanying police cars sped under siren towards the Avenue Bolívar building, the second-in-command issued orders over the radio redirecting the police and military units to their pre-assigned stations around it. 'Command,' Martínez injected when the channel was clear, 'Give me descriptions, licence numbers, times of departures of vehicles leaving Bolívar since twenty-fifteen hours.'

Within seconds, a woman's voice came over listing the information he had specified.

'Vega's in one of those Fords or the Chevy,' Martínez responded when he heard the sequence of departures around the time of the La Playa shooting. 'Repeat the information on the last three, then give us the others. I want every available unit looking for those cars, let the media know too.' Martínez glanced at his watch. It was twenty-five minutes since the incident at La Playa. 'Damn it Nelson, we were so close!' He slammed his left palm on the steering wheel. 'Someone told Vega we were watching La Playa.'

'That's no great surprise, is it Luis?' Nelson responded.

'Damn it!' Martínez hit the steering wheel again.

'There are still the checkpoints,' Nelson said as they charged on through a red light.

'He won't find them so easy.'

Martínez's second-in-command came back on the radio. 'Colonel, the sergeant at La Playa has a video image of the man who started the fire. We'll get copies. There's no clear image of the drivers.'

'Okay, send the picture to all checkpoints as soon as you get it.'

'Yes, sir.'

'Is forensic on the way to Bolívar?'

'Yes, Colonel, they won't be far behind you.'

'Was anyone hurt in the La Playa fire?' Martínez hadn't had a chance to find out when he was there.

'No, sir, it was pretty small. A tenant put it out.'

'Okay, let me know when you hear anything about those cars.'

They pulled up outside the building that had been Vega's hiding place for the past eight days. An army helicopter was circling, a voice booming from its public address system ordering everyone to stay locked inside their apartments, warning that anyone appearing on a balcony or attempting to leave the building would be shot.

A surveillance officer was waiting at the front door. 'Colonel, the officer in the manager's suite isn't answering his radio.'

'Where is it?' Martínez asked.

'First door on the left,' the officer replied pointing to the appropriate hallway.

The army commander who'd been at La Playa rushed into the lobby. 'Colonel.' He saluted Martínez. 'I've sent one section to search the carpark, another is covering the outside of the building.' He gestured to a dozen or so soldiers just outside the door. 'These men are ready to secure the hide-out.' There was a sudden loud sound of metal being smashed. 'My men getting into the carpark, Colonel,' the lieutenant explained.

Martínez loved working with the military. There were always so many of them and they had all the right gear. He saw that two of the soldiers were carrying a battering ram. 'Have them and another two follow me,' he ordered and hurried down to the manager's suite with two of his own men.

When his pounding on the door got no response, Martínez ordered the soldiers to bust it open.

'They left at 8:30,' the policeman said as soon as the tape was removed from his mouth. 'Rojas must know where they were.'

Martínez went to the Rojas family whose mouths had just been liberated by his men. 'Where was Vega staying?'

'The top floor, señor,' Manuel Rojas cried. 'But I didn't know . . .'

'How many of them were there?' Martínez interrupted to hurry the process along. He would question the manager later.

'Four in one and one in the other,' the manager replied, certain there were more but not wanting to say so.

'What apartment numbers?'

'They had both apartments on the fifteenth floor. You must believe me, señor,' the manager pleaded. 'I've never seen Carlos Vega or the Dutch woman in my life.' His wife and daughter backed him up with pleas of their own.

'We'll worry about that later,' Martínez responded. 'Is there a master key?'

'Yes, in the drawer, at the end.' He pointed with his head. 'There's a blue tag on it.'

One of the soldiers found the key.

'Stay here with them,' Martínez ordered his men. 'I'll send someone to cut the handcuffs.' He took the soldiers with him back to the lobby and told the lieutenant what he'd discovered. 'Be careful, there may still be someone inside. And tell your men to avoid touching anything, forensic is on the way.'

'Any possibility of booby traps, Colonel?' the soldier asked.

'I doubt it, Lieutenant,' Martínez answered. 'Vega's been careful not to kill anyone, I don't think he'll start now. But take whatever precautions you normally would.'

The lieutenant called the helicopter pilot on his radio and requested a reconnaissance of the top floor. That done, he ordered one of his men to give Martínez a radio. 'Colonel, I'll let you know when we've secured it.'

As the soldiers ran up the stairs, the helicopter circled the building illuminating the inside of the fifteenth floor apartments with its intense spotlight while a crew member broadcast an order for anyone inside to come out in the open with their hands up. The soldier manning the machine gun matched his aim to the beam watching for movement of any kind, ready to shoot if shot at or threatened first.

'No sign of life on the top floor,' the helicopter pilot announced over the radio. 'No one on the roof either. I'll keep circling.'

The missing handle on the fifteenth floor fire door was a minor obstacle for the soldiers. One of them smashed the cover off with a hatchet and used his bayonet to twist the exposed mechanism and retract the striker. It took only a few seconds.

The battering ram was used to open the door to 1502 after the master key failed to work. Five soldiers rushed inside while the remaining men repeated the procedure on the other side of the hall.

'Floor fifteen empty and secure, Colonel,' the lieutenant radioed less than a minute later.

Martínez dislodged the chair which had been jammed in the elevator door to prevent its use and rode up with Nelson and four of his men.

Upon their arrival on the top floor, a corporal directed them to his commander in apartment 1502. The televisions were still on, the pictures switching between the building's various cameras. 'Very clever,' Martínez commented after watching them for a few seconds.

'Vega had eyes everywhere,' the lieutenant remarked.

'I wish I had one-tenth his budget,' Martínez said dryly, and walked to the kitchen. It was a mess. 'Seems too many plates for so few men, or maybe they didn't like washing up.'

After a quick tour through the bedrooms they went with the lieutenant across the hallway to the other apartment. 'This is more Vega's style,' Martínez commented as they walked into the luxuriously appointed living area.

'Look at this, Luis,' Nelson said upon sighting the cordon and hooks. 'Vega had his own little gallery.'

'An art connoisseur,' Martínez huffed.

'Saboteur, is more the truth,' Nelson replied.

They went to the main bedroom. The bed was unmade. Martínez slid open the cupboard with a pen and looked inside. It was empty.

Then on to the second bedroom. 'The hostage's room,' Martínez said when he saw the deadlock on the door. The bed was unmade. The cupboard was open and empty except for a cardboard box. There was a book on the floor. The bathroom towel was still damp. Nothing particularly helpful at all.

Then Nelson caught sight of the coin sticking out between the carpet and the wall and, on closer observation, saw that the carpet wasn't quite flush in the corner.

'There may be something underneath,' Martínez said and lifted it, uncovering the small pile of paper.

'Notes,' Nelson exclaimed, observing the date on the top page. 'Good for you, Christina.'

'Smart girl.' Martínez flipped through the pages. There were five sheets altogether. 'Dutch, I presume,' he said, handing them to Nelson.

'It's lucky you have me here,' Nelson replied and commenced scanning the sheets. 'Here's a licence number. Visited a cocaine laboratory. She has a description of the surroundings. And here, the last page, it's today.' He checked his watch. 'About three hours ago.' He translated the last entry. 'Leaving here tonight. Don't know where. Jim already there. Vega says to take clothing for any kind of weather. A joke? Trying to confuse me? The paintings are ready. First fifteen have yellow string on latches. 6 p.m., Monday.'

'Where's there?' Martínez asked. 'Does she say?'

'Here,' Nelson said after searching for a few seconds. 'Jim

leaves tomorrow, to Venezuela or Panama? Three hours flying. Seven hundred miles.'

'Jim who?'

Nelson looked back over the pages for an answer.

Christina had been careful to give no hint of her collaboration with Avery or of his deal with the DEA. She had been well aware that no matter who found the diary, such revelations could spell Jim Avery's death.

'This is him,' Nelson said. 'Jim Avery. Not a Colombian, obviously. Could be the American pilot who did the hijacking.'

Martínez spoke into his radio again. 'Command, I have a name for you. Jim Avery, alpha victor echo romeo yankee. See what you can find on him. Check with immigration. He may be a visitor, possibly a pilot, get any information you can.'

The five member forensic team arrived a few seconds later and went about their work while Nelson sat at the dining table with Martínez and continued his analysis of the diary.

'Nobody to smoke in apartment,' Nelson read. 'Pedro got cordon from bank to keep men away from paintings. Lunch with Vega. Displayed "Potato Eaters". Here, descriptions of his men and the vehicles.'

Martínez contacted the command centre again and gave the names and descriptions of Vega's men along with the descriptions of the vehicles, translating from English into Spanish as Nelson read them. He did the same with

Christina's description of the area around the cocaine laboratory she had visited. 'Draw a map based on that and send it to all stations in and around Medellín. Someone may be able to identify it. With a little pressure, the owner may give us something useful.'

A member of the forensic team interrupted with the news that he had discovered a hidden compartment. They followed him to the third bedroom.

Martínez tapped the false wall. 'Fooled me.'

Nelson followed Martínez inside the compartment and, in the darkness, stood on something. He bent down to find out what it was. 'A thermometer, I broke it. This is where he kept the paintings. The temperature has to be regulated.'

Martínez's radio came back to life. 'I have something for you, Colonel. One James B Avery arrived in Bogotá last Tuesday. He carried a United States passport and you were right about his occupation, he's an airline pilot. This is his fourteenth visit to Colombia in the past two years.'

'As a crew member or a visitor?'

'All tourist visits. And the hotel he named on his entry card doesn't have him registered. According to their records, he has never stayed there. That's all we have for now.'

'Okay, get in contact with the head of the DEA station in Bogotá and ask him to get a picture of Avery from the US passport office. He can organise that type of thing faster than we can through Interpol.'

Martínez signed off and told Nelson what had been said.

'So, Jim Avery,' Nelson responded. 'The voice from the little jet. I'd like to see him locked up with Vega.'

'You will,' Martínez replied, sounding optimistic for a change. 'If we find where Avery has flown, we'll find Vega.'

'Panama or Venezuela, according to the diary.'

'Right, but beware of decoys,' Martínez said. 'We've had one too many already today. If it was Vega who told her, it may not be true.'

'She may have overheard it. What are the other possibilities?'

'I wouldn't rule out Ecuador. He can get there by road. Then into Peru, he's bound to have friends there. He can't drive over the Andes to Brazil, so that way's blocked. And let's not forget the Pacific and Caribbean ports.'

'I'd go north,' Nelson said. 'Convenient for making the exchange with my government.'

'My intuition tells me Panama and Venezuela too.'

Nelson borrowed Martínez's phone and punched in the number the Dutch Prime Minister's private secretary had given him yesterday. According to her, it offered the fastest access to the Prime Minister, no matter where he was. It was the number of the phone Willem Imthorn had sent.

'De Groot,' came the answer after the third ring.

'It's Nelson Schoute in Colombia, Prime Minister. Sorry to wake you.'

'Nelson, I thought it would be Vega,' de Groot said sluggishly. 'What's happening?'

'Vega has left his hiding place, sir. That's where I am now. He's on the move with Christina and the paintings. We think he's travelling by road. We expect him to try to enter Venezuela, Panama or Ecuador within the next day or so. What we need, sir, is the highest level of cooperation from the governments of those three countries.'

'I understand, you want half their armies at the border crossings, right?' De Groot sounded alert now.

'More or less, Prime Minister.'

'Save me the arithmetic, what time is it there?'

'Nine thirty at night, Prime Minister.'

'I'll have my office put me in touch with those presidents. Panama, Venezuela and, what was the other one?'

'Ecuador, sir.'

'Sorry, it's taking me a while to wake up.' It was 3:30 a.m. in The Hague. 'I'll look after it right away. You want them to act immediately, correct?'

'Yes, thank you, sir.'

After asking a few questions about the evening's events, de Groot finished by wishing Nelson and Martínez good luck.

'Now it's your turn, Luis,' Nelson said, and handed the phone back. He found the card the Colombian President had given him the day he visited the palace with Simon Andriessen. 'He told me to phone him if we needed help. We do, and you speak Spanish.'

Martínez didn't hesitate. An aide answered immediately. After giving his own and Nelson's name and a brief explanation, he was put through to the President. The conversation was short. The President agreed to make the appropriate calls immediately.

'Your neighbours can't ignore two such high level requests for assistance, can they Luis?'

'Certainly not,' Martínez answered, then, holding up the phone, 'Anyone else you want to call?'

'No,' Nelson replied with a wink, 'We'll let your Pope sleep.'

25

No news is good news, Willem Imthorn thought as the 2 a.m. bulletin went to the weather. After muting the set he found another remote control and turned up the volume on Bach's "Brandenburg Concerto Number 2". In the safety of his home, Imthorn was a creature of habit. Dinner alone at seven prepared to exacting specifications by his young male housekeeper and accompanied by a half-bottle of dry red wine. Then television: the "NOS Journaal" and whatever American law or medical drama happens to be on. Jenever with a snack, usually liverwurst and cheese, at nine. Then bed, also alone, normally at 10:30, but later tonight. He looked again to the phone beside him and wished it to ring.

The fifty-seven year old native of Haarlem had made his first fortune trading in legitimate commodities, mostly foodstuffs and industrial chemicals shipped from and to the rest of the world through the great port of Rotterdam. As his contacts, knowledge, and hunger for power grew, he supplemented incoming cargoes with Indian hemp from Southeast Asia. During the eighties, he added Colombian cocaine and Thai heroin. Imthorn's business dealings with Medellín, both with Vega and Escobar before him, had created the bulk of his wealth, a wealth largely hidden in a slippery labyrinth of international companies and bank accounts. Imthorn delighted in the knowledge that, when everything was taken into account, he was just as well heeled as many of Europe's middle ranking royals. And there was the power, the power he had with even the powerful. Vega had trust in him, that was clear. And so he should. All through the lean years after Escobar's surrender, Imthorn had remained loyal to Medellín despite frequent advances from their rivals in Cali. The loyalty was not blind, Vega knew that as well as he. It was loyalty motivated by fear. Imthorn had known all along that no matter where he was, no matter how safe he felt, he was always within reach of the Medellín assassins.

The phone beeped.

'Señor, some good news,' a Colombian minion announced. 'Our baby arrived tonight, a boy.'

'Congratulations, to you and your wife,' Imthorn replied flatly. Phase three of the operation was under way, Vega was on the move. 'I am very happy for you.'

'Thank you, señor,' the voice came back. 'The birth was without a problem.'

'Wonderful,' Imthorn replied, pleased to hear the exit was clean. 'May the child bring you great happiness.'

The conversation over, Imthorn reached for the stone bottle of jenever by his side and topped up his glass. 'Señor Vega,' he toasted, holding his glass to the window, 'to your continued success.' He downed the liqueur, levered himself up, and shuffled his way to bed.

A few minutes before nine o'clock, Vega's convoy arrived at its destination, an old warehouse in an industrial area north of the city that had been leased a month earlier solely for the purpose of acting as tonight's rendezvous. Alerted to their imminent arrival by two rings on his phone, Rodrigo, Vega's lieutenant responsible for the second stage of the escape, rolled open the large steel door allowing the three vehicles to drive without stopping into the dimly-lit building.

They came to a halt beside a large tanker truck which dwarfed the assortment of vehicles occupying the rest of the floor space. The name "Maracaibo ChemTrans" was painted on the side of the tank in large green and yellow letters.

Vega was greeted by Miguel who recounted the highlights of his success in the building on Avenue La Playa. 'Bravo! Compadre,' Vega said, shaking the man's hand a second time. 'Bravo!' He turned to Christina as she got out of the car. 'Señorita, once we start, we won't stop for a long time. So use the toilet here.' He looked to Pedro. 'Take her, and make sure there's no way out.'

Pedro did as he was ordered. The only window in the

cramped toilet was protected from break-in by a metal grill. After checking the grill, he went outside and waited.

Rodrigo, wearing glasses and with much shorter hair than last time Vega had seen him, joined his boss and handed him a flashlight.

'What do you think, Don Carlos?'

'About you, amigo, or the truck?' Vega replied with a crooked grin.

Rodrigo laughed. 'I know I look very handsome, Carlos. I mean the truck.'

'Looks good from here, compadre. I would like to take a closer look.' He went around the truck, systematically examining the surface with the light. 'Perfect, no sign of welds.'

'Sergio is very proud of the work. You will like the inside too.'

'Did you check the guns in the cars?'

'Three in each car and two in the truck cabin, above false bottoms under the seats.'

'Good.' Vega knelt down and shone the flashlight underneath the tank. 'The air vents?' he asked, jiggling the beam between two metal disks set slightly below the tank surface.

'Si,' Rodrigo replied.

'Have you checked the seals?'

'They're tight, so is the entry hatch.'

'Excellent.' Vega got back up. 'A useful vehicle Rodrigo, it will pay for itself many times over.' At two hundred thousand dollars on top of the price of the truck, the fabrication had not been cheap. In Vega's experience, quality never was. 'Okay, load the paintings.'

Rodrigo climbed under the tank and twisted a lever releasing a large hatch. He helped two guards climb inside the tank and, from the hatchway, explained how they should stack and secure the paintings. Josef had the remaining guards gather the cases from the various cars.

The loading underway, Rodrigo took Vega up the ladder at the back to the top of the tank. He unfastened one of the inspection hatches and pulled out the dipstick. Vega shone the flashlight through the small hole and looked inside as best he could.

'It will deceive the customs inspectors,' Rodrigo announced confidently. 'You can smell the last cargo too. Sergio poured a can of benzene inside. But don't breathe too much, it is very bad for your health.'

'Sergio is a very talented man.' Vega slid the dipstick back. 'There's no smell in the compartment?'

'None at all,' Rodrigo replied, closing the hatch. 'I checked myself.'

The loading was complete by the time they got back down. Pedro was waiting by the side of the truck with Christina.

'Beautiful isn't she, señorita?' Vega said, slapping the tank with his hand.

'Whatever turns you on,' she replied without expression.

'It's our chariot to freedom, señorita,' Vega said and directed Pedro to help her climb inside the tank. She insisted on getting in by herself, and did.

Inside, she sat on one of several large pillows set on the curved floor and examined her claustrophobic surroundings. The lighting was dim but adequate, provided by small lamps high up on two cone shaped metal pillars at either end of the compartment. A faint whirr emanated from fans inside two air vents protruding from the floor. Except for the flat ceiling, the interior was oval in cross section and covered in thick grey padding. She checked the painting cases which had been strapped onto deep shelves at the front of the tank. They seemed secure. A similar set of shelves at the back were packed with boxes labelled as coffee. Cocaine, she presumed. She guessed that a speaker device mounted to the side of the front shelves was an intercom to the driver. Her and Vega's bags were on the floor next to a large water container, a vacuum flask and a styrofoam cooler which, she discovered, contained sandwiches, fruit, mosquito repellent and duct tape. She was in no doubt what the tape was for. After her efforts in the van on Saturday she'd expected to be gagged before leaving the apartment. Then there was what she assumed to be the toilet facilities: two ice cream buckets with lids, one pink, the other blue. Vega had thought of everything.

Outside, Vega and the guards emptied their bladders against the warehouse wall joking amongst themselves about the rudimentary toilet facilities in the very expensive truck. Rodrigo reminded the men of an earlier suggestion of his that Vega and his hostage wear diapers, like those worn by the astronauts who went to the moon. They laughed raucously. Morale was high. So far, everything had gone their way. 'We start our journey with laughter, compadres,' Vega said after doing up his fly. 'May it end that way too.'

With that, everyone moved into position. For the first part of the journey, Vega and Christina would travel inside the tank alone while Pedro would accompany Rodrigo, the driver, in the front of the truck. Three guards had been assigned to each of three fresh escort vehicles. The cars they had driven to the warehouse would be left behind along with all the guns they had carried. The only exception was Vega's revolver. He could never be without it.

Rodrigo closed the hatch behind Vega and waited to the side while his boss checked the release. Not willing to be a prisoner inside a metal tank under any circumstances, Vega had specified that the hatch must open from inside as well as outside. The hatch fell open.

His boss satisfied, Rodrigo shut the hatch, removed the telltale lever and took it inside the cabin with him.

Just before nine thirty, the truck, accompanied by two of the escort vehicles, rolled out onto the road. The men assigned to the third vehicle locked the warehouse and quickly caught up to take the rear position in the convoy.

'I hope you brought something to read,' Vega said, settling into a pillow opposite Christina.

'How long will we be in here?' she asked. On the basis of Avery's information, she had estimated twelve hours.

'Thirteen or fourteen hours. We have about a thousand kilometres to travel, we'll be in Maracaibo around noon.'

'And where's this Maracaibo?'

'Across the border, in Venezuela.'

'Venezuela,' she repeated. Avery had been right. She prayed that by now he had contacted the DEA. 'And where to then?'

'You will be one of the first to know.'

'Afraid I might tell someone?' she replied, gesturing to the walls around her.

'Old habits die hard. I am a cautious man.'

The ride in the back as the truck travelled along the well worn streets of the industrial area was rough. A few minutes in the swaying environment was enough for her to appreciate Vega's insistence on the motion sickness patch. She had been motion sick only once in her life, on a ship in the Mediterranean. It was an experience she had no desire to repeat, especially in the present circumstances.

The truck came to a sudden stop throwing both her and Vega towards the front shelves. 'Will you tell whoever's driving to take it easy, I'd like the paintings to survive this trip.'

Vega pressed the intercom button. 'Rodrigo, slow down until we get to the highway, the señorita is worried about the paintings.'

'Si, Carlos,' Rodrigo replied with a barely audible laugh.

Christina got up and checked the cases again. Although they were well secured, there was no external protection against shock and vibration. 'How far to the highway?' she asked.

'Just a few minutes.' He rubbed the patch on his neck. 'Now you see why we have these. This isn't the first time I've bumped around the streets of Medellín hiding in the back of a truck.' The truck turned a corner, throwing her towards Vega. 'Hold on to the shelves,' he said and eased her back to her side. 'Last time I did this was in a shipping container. It was very stuffy and hot. I vomited and had to live with the smell for hours.'

'Do you mind,' she said, contorting her face, remembering the Mediterranean. 'I don't want to get sick.'

'Sorry, señorita. If you do feel ill, there's fresh air coming in that vent near you, and your bucket.' He held up the pink one.

'Okay,' she said, a feeling of slight nausea causing her to question the effectiveness of the drug seeping into her bloodstream. 'What's in the ceiling?' she asked, trying to get her mind off the motion.

'The same as what's in this.' He slapped the hollow pillar next to him. 'And the tanks at either end. Air. We're returning to a chemical plant in Venezuela after delivering a load of benzene to a factory in Medellín.'

'That's the story, is it?' She took some deep breaths, wishing the nausea away. 'Benzene's a solvent, right?'

'And a raw material for making some type of plastic, I'm told. It's very toxic so the customs people don't stay around it too long.' He tapped the pillar again. 'And if they do look inside, everything looks normal.'

'Quite the magician,' she said. The nausea was retreating.

'The conical shape is the secret. Narrow at the top, wide at the bottom. Through the small port at the top, an inspector can't see the walls, just the bottom. And there's just a little benzene inside, for the smell.'

'You think of everything.'

'I try to.' He didn't go on to brag about the future use of the truck to import ether and acetone in its two authentic compartments and export large quantities of cocaine in the middle. He would leave that for the police to work out when they eventually interviewed her about her experience. By then, the truck would have a new identity and would be on the less prominent Colombia to Peru run.

The ride smoothed out a few minutes later when they got onto the northbound highway. Christina took a book from her bag and read while Vega lay back staring at the ceiling, his mind going over the details of the next stage of the operation. So far there had been no problems. He hoped it remained so.

Twenty kilometres out of the city, Rodrigo guided the truck around a wide bend in the highway to find a military roadblock ahead. He brought the truck to a slow halt while Pedro notified Vega. As ordered, none of the men from the lead vehicles had phoned back to warn them. Roadblocks could not be avoided. The plan was to go through them as inconspicuously as possible and that meant not using any method of communication that could be monitored.

Pedro informed Vega that the two forward cars were in separate lanes amongst the twenty or so vehicles lined up.

They had been travelling some distance in front of the truck to avoid drawing attention.

As they crept forward, Pedro spoke towards the small microphone hidden in the ceiling lining. 'I can see two APCs and a jeep with a machine gun. There are many soldiers.' Then a pause. 'It will be our lead car's turn soon.' To be secure from electronic detection, the intercom between the truck cabin and the tank compartment used wire not a radio signal. Vega flicked off the air vent fans and pulled the levers that retracted the hatches flush against the bottom of the tank. Then he took the duct tape out of the food box. 'Sorry, señorita.' He tore some off the roll and taped it diagonally across her mouth to avoid putting it over the skin that had been damaged on Saturday. He pressed the intercom button. 'Rodrigo, have the papers ready. I'll leave the intercom on.'

'Okay,' Rodrigo replied. 'There's only one vehicle in front of our lead car.'

All the guards had rehearsed stories to deliver and the baggage to support them. They were on their way to the seaside at Palomino on Colombia's Caribbean coast. It was a journey made by thousands of their fellow citizens every week.

'It's our lead vehicle's turn,' Pedro announced, sounding anxious. 'The soldier is looking at the registration papers.' A pause. 'He's shining a flashlight around inside. He seems to be checking everyone's identification.' A longer pause. 'Now he has the driver opening the trunk. He's having a good look . . . he's taking the bags out and lifting the mat.' Another pause. 'He's checking inside the bags.' Then finally, 'It's okay, he's finished. He's letting them go.'

There was a contingency plan in the event that, at some point in the journey, an inspector discovered the weapons under the seat or something else that could place the operation in jeopardy. The first part of it was fundamental to any criminal operation in Colombia: a substantial bribe would be discreetly offered for the party to ignore the discovery. All the men carried pre-folded money for that purpose. If the price was right, a poorly paid Colombian soldier may be willing to ignore the weapons under the seat. The money would be dropped on the floor, nothing would be said. The soldier could rationalise his acceptance. After all, he was looking for Carlos Vega, a woman and some paintings . . . not guns. Or he could reject the offer and cause trouble, a possibility that would, in less intimidating circumstances, result in the immediate implementation of the second option. Each of Vega's men carried a small knife in a scabbard attached to his leg which could be used to neutralise a troublesome party while the guns were pulled out from under the seats. In this case though, it was clear to all Vega's men that if a bribe had to be offered and was rejected, the game would be over. It would be a simple choice between surrender or death.

Pedro reported as the second car was inspected in the other lane. The soldier ordered the men out of the vehicle while he looked around inside. It was another anxious few minutes which ended with the soldier waving them on. As Vega had experienced a number of times before, the result of the search justified the fabricator's high fee.

'Two through, two to go,' Pedro said as the truck crept forward. 'There are a couple of cars in front of us. Rodrigo has our papers ready.'

Vega moved to Christina and put his gun to her shoulder. 'Just be quiet, señorita. Don't move, breathe gently.'

After a minute or two of silence, Pedro spoke again. 'Here we go.'

'Good evening, señor. Please turn off your engine.' The engine and the vibration died enabling them to better hear the voices. 'Your papers, please.'

'Certainly, Cabo. What is happening?' It was Rodrigo's voice.

'I'm checking for narcotics, señor. What's your cargo?'

'We're empty, on our way back to Maracaibo. We took benzene to Medellín.'

There was a pause while the corporal checked the papers. 'Your papers are in order, señor. I'd like to check the tanks. Would you come up to the top with me please.'

Vega listened beyond his quietly ringing ears, first to the soldier tapping along the length of the tank, then to the muffled sound of the footsteps on the ladder and then above them. He heard the inspection hatches being opened and closed. Then the steps down, followed shortly after by the sound of the diesel pre-heater. Christina stayed motionless, Vega's gun still on her arm.

Pedro came back on the intercom once they were under way. 'No problem, Carlos.'

'Well done, compadres,' Vega said. 'You have good nerves, Rodrigo.'

'They were ready for anything back there,' Rodrigo announced. 'Our guns would have been no match for them.'

Vega opened the air hatches and removed the tape from Christina's mouth. 'That was easy, eh señorita?'

'Sure,' she replied as she checked the skin above her lip for blood. There was none.

A few minutes later, Pedro reported that he could see the tail vehicle behind them. They'd all got through. Vega leaned back on the pillow and closed his eyes. The next big test of his magic would come in the morning, at the border crossing into Venezuela.

26

It was almost midnight when Luis Martínez and Nelson Schoute left Vega's abandoned hiding place. The forensic team's sweep of the apartments had revealed a total of seventeen different sets of fingerprints along with hair samples, a few pieces of clothing and receipts for food, clothes and assorted items including picture wire and hooks. The most significant find of the evening, Christina Jansen's diary, along with Nelson Schoute's hurried translation of its main points, had been taken back to headquarters earlier for photocopying and distribution.

During the evening, command centre staff had located and interviewed the registered owners of all but one of the vehicles seen leaving the Bolívar building around the time of the La Playa fire. They included the owner of the Chevrolet sedan in which Vega had escaped, a woman who claimed her boyfriend had given her the money to buy the vehicle three weeks ago. She swore she had not seen him or the car since.

Martínez had also conducted a short interview with a very frightened Manuel Rojas who admitted having harboured a suspicion that Vega was living on the fifteenth floor. The veteran policeman understood only too well the fear which prevented the building manager from coming forward. Several times in his career, he had seen for himself the mutilated bodies of wives and children of men who had acted against the cartel. Manuel Rojas would not be charged.

Martínez and Nelson, both exhausted from the evening's events, arrived back at the command centre to find a phone message from a presidential aide confirming that the President had made the three calls requested. The detective in charge went on to report that updates on the case had been sent via the Interpol network to police forces throughout the Americas and the Netherlands and directly to all border crossings out of Colombia and the checkpoints within Colombia itself.

'And the photograph of Avery?' Martínez then asked.

'Nothing yet, Colonel,' the detective replied. 'I'll follow it up with the DEA.' He handed Martínez a slip of paper. 'That car entered Vega's compound just before midnight, we haven't seen it before.'

Martínez perused the registration details of the black Mercedes seen entering Vega's compound at 11:52h. 'How many aboard?'

'Three, Colonel.'

'Vega wouldn't have taken all his bodyguards from the

apartment with him. They could be the ones he left behind, going home. What's the latest on Margarita Vega?'

'Hasn't left the house for two days.'

Martínez turned to Nelson, 'I'm going to Vega's house to talk to the new arrivals and anyone else I can find, care to come along?'

'Wouldn't miss it for the world,' Nelson replied. Sleep could wait.

By one o'clock in the morning, Vega's convoy was two hundred and fifty kilometres north of Medellín. Other than for short stops at a weighbridge and two police district checkpoints, their journey had not been interrupted since the military roadblock just outside Medellín. Christina had been drifting in and out of sleep since putting her book away at midnight. Vega, his mind preoccupied with the progress of the plan, had not slept at all.

'Carlos, Carlos.' Pedro's voice and the accompanying microphone tapping woke Christina.

Vega reached for the intercom button. 'Si.'

'We just passed the Monteria turn-off.'

Vega checked his watch. 'Ahead of time, good.'

Pedro came back on a few minutes later. 'We just passed Josef, he waved.'

Josef's wave had been the signal that he had contacted one of Vega's men still in Medellín and instructed him to act.

'It's time for us to wake Pieter de Groot,' Vega murmured and closed his eyes.

The call at eight minutes past seven on Tuesday morning interrupted the Dutch Prime Minister's breakfast-time conversation with his wife.

'De Groot,' he declared into the phone and looked to see that the cassette spools in the recording device were rotating as they should. He heard the click of a switch being pushed followed by Vega's now familiar voice.

'Good day, Prime Minister. I am ready for business. I have the paintings and Doctor Jansen with me. Please have my son flown to Bermuda immediately and wait for my next direction. I will say that again. Have Juan flown to Bermuda and wait for my next direction. Goodbye.' The line went dead.

De Groot hurriedly summarised the call for his wife before disappearing into his study with his coffee.

He phoned the Minister of Justice first. 'Lydia, Vega just called, it's time to move his son.' After giving her a brief account of his overnight calls to the neighbouring presidents, he phoned the Minister of Defence and instructed him to proceed with his part of the operation. The third call was to his counterpart in London to obtain permission for the Dutch aircraft to land in Bermuda and to request the assistance of the authorities in the British dependency. Both requests were agreed to without hesitation.

Meanwhile, the Minister of Justice phoned the warden

of Bijlmer, the prison where Juan Vega was being kept, and instructed him to act. She then phoned her state secretary, Otto Dolsch.

The sound of the bedroom door opening woke Margarita Vega's lover, the bodyguard who sometimes shared her bed when her husband, his employer, was absent. He reached across her naked body towards the gun hanging from the bed post.

Margarita, stirred from sleep by his movement, heard the thud from a pistol's silencer and screamed as his body collapsed with a grunt across her chest. A second thud caused him to twitch and become limp and heavy on her. She felt a stream of warm blood on her face. He was dead. She lunged for the gun.

'No!' the stranger barked and yanked her fingers from the handle.

'Please don't shoot,' she begged. 'I'll give you whatever you want.'

The stranger rolled the body off her. 'My apologies for interrupting your entertainment, señora.' He put the gun to her blood-smeared face. 'Now roll over and put your hands behind your back.'

'I've got money, jewels. What do you want? I'll get it for you,' she pleaded as she complied with his demand.

'I just want you, señora,' he said and laughed a vile laugh. 'That is all.'

'Is this how Carlos sends for me?' she asked, desperately

hoping it was true, that this man would kill others but keep her alive.

He fastened her wrists with a plastic strap. 'Your husband would be angry if he found you had been unfaithful, señora.' He tossed her over using more force than was necessary and sat down on the bed beside her. 'You're a very beautiful woman, Margarita.' He ran the silencer over her breast, down the length of her torso to the inside of her leg. 'I'm very jealous of Carlos.' Then, in the direction of the corpse, 'Not your lover though, he has run out of steam.' He laughed again and lifted her so she sat up. 'I will be your new lover.'

She smelled the stink of alcohol as he moved close to kiss her. 'Leave me alone, you pig!' She slammed her shoulder into his chest.

He grabbed a handful of hair and jerked her head around to face him. 'Don't make me angry, señora, or I will hurt you.' He moved to kiss her on the lips, pressing the gun to her groin as he did so. She didn't resist. 'That's better.'

'Why won't you tell me who you are? I'll pay,' she said, frantically trying to work out what this was all about.

'There'll be time for us to get to know each other later, now we must hurry.' He stood and pulled her to her feet. Then, wrapping a bathrobe around her, he forced her outside into the hallway where two other men were waiting.

The surveillance police stationed outside Vega's property informed the command centre as soon as they heard the helicopter coming along the valley towards them. They watched and videotaped it using their infrared equipment as it landed inside the compound and took on board three men carrying what appeared to be a live body. It left immediately, over the hills.

Martínez, on his way up the mountain, cursed when he heard the report. He knew he'd lost Margarita Vega.

27

Juan Vega didn't need to be told what was happening when his morning exercise was interrupted by a guard who hurried him to the shower block. Every day for almost a week now he'd woken expecting it to be his last in the cold and damp of the Netherlands.

Vega had followed the public negotiations between his father and the Dutch government on BBC television and radio. In addition, a Valencia-born inmate, to whom he had promised a job upon his eventual release, had translated every available Dutch report on the matter into Spanish for him. The information that his father had been unsuccessful in gaining his immediate freedom had been disappointing. Not that it would matter in the end. Juan knew that it wouldn't take long to be broken out of whichever Colombian jail he was sent to.

Dressed in a fresh set of prison clothes, the young Colombian was taken to his cell to collect personal effects: toiletries, a stack of letters and a few items he had made in the prison's manual art classes. To Juan, the wood carvings and leatherwork would be souvenirs of an unpleasant experience with a delicious, yet to be played out ending: the humiliation of his Dutch captors when he was finally freed.

Five minutes later, in the prison courtyard, shackles were applied to his arms and legs before he was loaded into an armoured van which, with a two police car escort, left for Schiphol airport. The restraints were not to prevent escape. The warden knew there was no danger of that. The young criminal would be foolish not to take full advantage of this pipeline to virtual freedom fully protected from his enemies by the Dutch government. The shackles were a symbol, a statement from the government of the Netherlands: Juan Vega was still a prisoner and would be treated as such as long as he was under Dutch control.

After a journey made slow by morning traffic, the convoy entered the airport through a security gate leaving behind a small media contingent that had followed from the prison and proceeded towards an isolated government Fokker 70. Waiting with the jet were a dozen commandos, members of the Special Support Unit, whose function would be to guard the prisoner while he was on the plane and, if necessary, defend the aircraft in the unlikely but conceivable event of a siege.

Officially, once outside the Netherlands, the commandos' franchise to interfere in any action involving Juan Vega stopped at the aircraft door. Unofficially, their commander had been told, by none other than the Minister of

Defence himself, to do whatever was necessary to protect Christina Jansen, all those aboard the aircraft, the paintings and the aircraft itself. The Minister had said that, if need be, the jurisdictional complexities could be sorted out later.

Otto Dolsch, State Secretary with the Ministry of Justice, arrived a few minutes later. Dolsch's assignment was to accept custody of Juan Vega from the prison warden and travel with him on the aircraft. He was to represent the government of the Netherlands in any country the aircraft visited and act on its behalf in the exchange for Christina Jansen and the paintings. Dolsch knew the true deal with Vega. His minister had given him a letter outlining the details, signed by the Prime Minister himself, with the instruction not to show it to anyone involved in the transfer until it became absolutely necessary. She had also made it very clear that when he was eventually contacted by Carlos Vega, he was to avoid confrontation and was to cooperate with any demand that did not endanger lives.

Two prison guards carried Juan up the steps into the cabin and removed the shackles. A corporal handcuffed Vega to a generously padded seat situated near the forward emergency exit and fastened his seatbelt while the warden and Dolsch took care of the paperwork to transfer custody.

At eight forty-five, the aircraft took off to the west. As they headed out over the North Sea, the captain announced that the flight to Bermuda, including a fuelling stop at Cork, Ireland, would take approximately seven hours. He added that a storm system was covering most of the north Atlantic and recommended that passengers keep their seat belts loosely fastened.

28

The noise and deceleration as the truck geared down woke Christina Jansen from her light and uncomfortable sleep. Her clammy skin immediately betrayed the burden of moisture in the air. Vega's convoy was now at sea level, heading east, parallel to the Caribbean coast. The border with Venezuela was just over two hundred kilometres ahead.

'Buenos dìas, señorita,' Vega said, rousing himself from a light slumber. It was five o'clock in the morning.

Christina moved closer to the air intake to catch some of its cooling breeze. 'Why are we stopping?' She hoped it was for another roadblock. As far as she was concerned, the more there were the better.

'We'll be getting out for a few minutes,' Vega replied, tucking in his shirt. He retrieved a plastic bottle from his bag and tossed it to her. 'For the mosquitoes.' After a patchy application to her bare skin, she handed the repellent back. Vega applied some to his arms and face.

The tanker followed the second escort car off the highway onto an overgrown private road. The derelict banana co-operative had been chosen from four possible stopping points scouted out by Rodrigo a month before the hijacking.

'Time to wake up, amigos,' Pedro announced over the intercom, in case they had not.

Vega reached for the button. 'Pedro, did anyone seem curious to see us leave the highway?'

'I don't think so, Carlos,' Pedro replied, then, after a short silence, 'We're pulling in behind the warehouse now.' They came to a stop a few seconds later. The engine was switched off.

Pedro came back on, his voice louder and clearer in the stillness, 'The men are checking around.'

'Josef, are you okay?' Vega asked. Josef had been driving the tanker since two o'clock, allowing Rodrigo to rest in the back of the second escort car.

'The coffee kept me awake, Carlos,' Josef replied. 'But Pedro, he slept like a baby.'

After a minute or two of silence there was a knock on the hatch below Christina's feet. It swung open.

Rodrigo appeared in the hatchway beaming a wide smile. 'Señor and señorita, welcome to Colombia's beautiful Caribbean coast. It is safe to come out.'

'Let's get some fresh air,' Vega said to Christina as he lowered himself to the ground.

Christina followed him out, the humid tropical air smothering her with its stagnant oppressiveness. She wondered how hot it was going to become inside the tank once the sun came up. It was horrible now. She was concerned about the paintings, the cases weren't designed to insulate against high temperature.

She stretched to regain the flexibility in her body, examining her moonlit surroundings as she did so. A thick growth of banana trees surrounded the entire location. She could see Vega's men stationed at both ends of the shed and one of the escort cars parked across the entrance to the property. Although she couldn't see any headlights, she could hear the cars and trucks speeding past on the other side of the shed. They sounded close.

'I need to go to the toilet,' she said to Pedro. He took her around the truck and left her behind a clump of banana trees. As bad as it was, it was a better option than the bucket in the tanker. Pedro stood nearby and relieved himself.

Christina overheard Vega farewelling some of the men as she walked with Pedro back to the truck. Pedro fetched his bag from the cabin and waited with her beside the tank.

A few minutes later, Vega appeared with Josef and Miguel both of whom were carrying a bag in one hand and a submachine gun in the other. 'We'll have some company from now on, señorita,' Vega said and told her to climb back into the tank. He and the other men followed.

As the five occupants were settling themselves on the pillows, Rodrigo popped up through the hatch. He handed two guns to Vega. 'From under the cabin seat.'

'Good, amigo,' Vega said, pleased Rodrigo had remembered. Guns in the cabin would be nothing but a liability at what was bound to be a heavily defended border. Vega lay them on the floor beside the hatch. 'Stay calm, Rodrigo.'

Rodrigo saluted and sank from view.

'It will be a little cramped in here for the rest of the journey, señorita,' Vega said as the hatch closed with a thump. 'But it's the best way for us to enter Venezuela . . .' He paused to kill a mosquito on his shirtsleeve. '. . . without being shot.'

With the headlights off and guided by two of the guards, Rodrigo manoeuvred the truck through the mist laden predawn air back towards the highway.

'So your other men are on their way home?' Christina asked Vega as the tanker got up to speed. She was after anything to help the police find them later.

'No, señorita,' Vega replied dismissively. 'After they've escorted us close to the border, they will disperse.'

'They'll need some good hiding places.'

'They will vanish, señorita, anywhere they choose in this beautiful country.'

'Is it beautiful?' she responded, giving up on her attempt at information gathering. 'I haven't seen much of it.'

'My apologies for not being a better host,' Vega replied with a shrug. 'I should have put a window in the tank to allow you to see the regions of Colombia as we pass through them.' He gestured to the padded wall and, in a put-on voice which she assumed served the purpose of entertaining his men, announced, 'We just passed through Santa Marta, birthplace of El Libertador, the great Simón Bolívar, who freed our country from Spanish imperialism. And to the right is the beautiful Sierra Nevada. Outside you would see some very high snow covered mountains coming all the way down to the coast.'

'Sounds lovely,' she replied, endeavouring to show no appreciation for the mildly amusing act.

'Señorita, you must visit Colombia sometime,' Pedro remarked innocently. 'It is a beautiful country, I think you would like it.'

'I'm sure I would,' she replied, picturing a return to give evidence at their trials.

After helping herself to some water, she opened her book and was soon asleep. The men continued talking amongst themselves until tiredness caught up with them too.

Shortly after eight o'clock, Rodrigo came on the intercom. 'We just passed through Maicao. The men are stopping to turn around. Twelve kilometres to the border.'

'Okay, Rodrigo,' Vega replied, the sound of his voice stirring the others from sleep. 'Keep me informed.'

Ten minutes later, Rodrigo was back on the intercom. 'We will be at the crossing in a couple of minutes.'

The truck geared down shortly after. 'There's a long line-up,' Rodrigo said as they came to a stop. 'Dios! I think they are expecting us. Mierda! The whole army is waiting.'

Then, after an hour creeping towards the checkpoint, another announcement from Rodrigo: 'Only three trucks in front of us now.'

'Gag her,' Vega said handing Josef the duct tape. 'Put it crossways, not over the damaged skin.' Her right upper lip had a thin scab, the result of the duct tape injury on Saturday.

'There's just one truck in front of us now,' Rodrigo said ten minutes later.

Vega turned off the fans and closed the vents. 'Keep very still and breathe shallow breaths.' The fabricator had told him that with the vents closed and five people in the tank there would be sufficient oxygen for only twenty minutes.

'It's his turn,' Rodrigo said. 'A customs inspector is checking his papers.' A pause. 'The driver is getting out. Some soldiers are opening the back.' Another pause. 'Two soldiers have gone in. They're having a good look. Moving boxes around.' Another pause. 'Here comes a soldier with a dog, and a customs inspector. Quiet.'

A faint voice. 'Buenos dìas, señor. Shut off the engine please.' The engine stopped. Pedro and Josef took hold of Christina's arms and legs to prevent her from making any sudden moves. Without the cover of the engine, the slightest movement or sound could give them away. 'Señor, can I see your passport and the papers for your cargo?'

'I am empty, señor. I just delivered a load of benzene in Medellín.'

'When did you leave Medellín?'

'At six o'clock last night.' Rodrigo had papers showing him leaving a chemical plant in the southern part of the city at that time.

'You drove all night?'

'No, of course not, señor. I rested in Ciénaga.'

'Did you notice anything strange happening on the highway during your journey?'

'Nothing at all. But I have heard that Carlos Vega escaped from Medellín. So tonight, I did not pick up any hitchhikers.'

The inspector made no response to the attempt at humour. 'I'll need to check your passport and papers in the office. The cabo and his men will inspect your truck. Please come down from the cabin.'

The occupants of the tank sat motionless, listening and wishing for air. There were bumping sounds through the intercom as items were moved around the cabin. Something metallic tapping along the sides of the tank, then underneath. Footsteps up the ladder and along the top. The inspection hatches being opened and closed. Then the footsteps back down followed by muffled conversation.

A dog barked. It seemed as though it was under them. A whistle. Then a shout. 'Sargento, over here!'

'A stupid dog,' Vega groaned through his teeth. He grasped one of the guns and, realising the futility of his action, released it.

As the barking continued, Vega searched his mind for a

possible slip-up. He looked into the sweat-framed eyes of his men, then up at the cardboard boxes on the shelves. Each kilogram of merchandise had been packed in two plastic zip-lock bags and then sealed with tape. Rodrigo had supervised the loading himself. He would not have tolerated any carelessness. He would have ensured that the boxes and the people who packed the cocaine and heroin didn't touch the outside of the truck at all. And he had confirmed that he'd pressure washed the tank and prime mover on the way to the warehouse. That should have removed any stray dust. There could be no trace of the merchandise on the outside, it was impossible. And the odour couldn't be leaking out: the vents and hatch had rubber seals. The merchandise was literally inside a tin can, as were they.

The barking ceased. There was the sound of soldiers running. Then orders, 'Lean up against the side! Don't move!' Then pleading. It was a woman's voice. Vega breathed again. The soldiers had found something in another vehicle. The noises outside lasted over five minutes.

The engine started and they moved forward. 'Mother of God,' Rodrigo said, the dryness in his voice coming through the wire. 'They found something in the car in the next lane. Marijuana, I think. Just kids.'

Vega spoke into the intercom. 'They picked a bad day to cross the border, amigo.'

'I've never seen so many guns in my life.'

'Bravo! Rodrigo,' Josef called out. Miguel followed suite.

Vega opened the vents and turned on the fans while Josef, unmindfully, removed the tape from Christina's mouth too quickly.

'Ouch!' She recoiled, clamping her hand over the burning skin.

'Sorry, señorita,' Josef said meekly.

Vega examined her face. 'It's not bleeding. You'll be fine.'

'Next time let me take it off,' Christina responded and checked her hand for blood. There was none.

'How is your cheek?' She was still wearing the dressing Avery had applied.

'Fine,' she replied, not wishing to discuss it.

Vega fell back against the side of the tank and breathed some of the rapidly improving air. 'We made it, compadres.'

Josef took this as a cue to pull out a small bottle of rum he had bought for the occasion. He handed it to Vega who offered it to Christina. When she declined, Vega took a swig himself and passed it to the others. The bottle went around twice before it was empty.

'How long to Maracaibo now?' Christina asked, her patience worn thin by the oppressive atmosphere.

'Señorita, you are always in such a hurry.' Vega, too, was irritated by the heat. 'We are trying to relax, to get some fresh air into our bodies.'

'I'm worried about the paintings, it's a sauna in here.'

'Maybe an hour, maybe an hour and a half.' Vega then spoke to Josef and Miguel in Spanish.

Christina could understand enough of what was being said to deduce the rest. Vega was suggesting they celebrate their success by opening one of the paintings.

'No,' she sighed. 'Leave the paintings.'

'Your Spanish is better than I thought, señorita,' Vega said.

'Just leave the paintings alone.'

'My men need to celebrate and we are out of rum.' He tapped his fingers against the shelves at the front. 'No harm will be done. This is the only chance they will have in their whole lives to admire a van Gogh and hear about it from the talented Doctor Jansen. Why not, eh señorita?' He winked at Pedro.

'It's too humid and my Spanish isn't good enough for Miguel to understand. So let's forget it, okay?' It seemed to her that the alcohol had given Vega's machismo a boost.

'We may be bound by language, but the paintings are not. Anyway, I can translate for Miguel.' Vega got to his knees and began to unfasten the straps holding the cases on the bottom shelf.

She held the straps, trying to stop him. 'Let's wait until we stop, then I'll show them as many as they want.'

'We may not have time.' Vega brushed her hands aside and selected the case he wanted, marked CYP. 'This one's a nice size for in here.' He pulled it out. '"Cypresses", is it not?'

'Okay, okay, give it to me.' She took the case from him and lay it on the floor. 'If I tell them about this one, promise me you'll leave the others alone?'

'Agreed, señorita,' Vega responded.

'This is going to be quick.' She retrieved the guide from her bag and found the appropriate page, page fifty-nine. The hellish atmosphere made even that task and the subsequent arithmetic a challenge. Painted in 1890, that's eighteen plus fifty-nine. She rolled seventy-seven. Then ninety minus fifty-nine, thirty-one. 7731. She opened it. 'I'm going to leave it in the case.'

'Very well,' Vega replied. The four men gathered around Vincent's "Cypresses": A scene shaped by the mistral, a cool dry wind which regularly blows across southern France for days on end, tormenting the spirits of many in its path. A row of tall cypresses, deep green and flaming in the wind, reaching for a sky of equally tormented clouds. Two women walk in the garden beneath the trees, their dresses, white and long; their faces, featureless. Across the field behind them, a small stone dwelling stands strong and steady in the turmoil.

'Don't dribble on it will you,' she said, realising they might. 'And don't let any sweat drip on it either.' All the faces were wet with perspiration. 'Take a good look.' She stopped herself from adding a barb about future incarceration. 'Vincent painted "Cypresses" while he was a patient in the asylum at Saint-Rémy in the south of France.' She paced her commentary to allow Vega to translate the highlights for Miguel. 'Vincent was fascinated by cypress trees. Entranced by them. He thought the cypress had the beauty and proportion of an Egyptian obelisk.'

'An obelisk is a tall monument, true señorita?' Vega interjected, for the sake of his less well informed companions.

'Yes, a column, with a pyramid on top. There's one in Paris, near the Louvre. Napoleon brought it from Egypt. Vincent would have seen it.' She continued, sweating less now that she was still, 'Vincent saw the cypresses as black flames burning from a troubled earth. See how the wind is shaping them, these ones too?' She pointed to some behind the stone house. 'See how tormented they look?' She grasped the top of the case. 'I'll put it away now.'

'Not so quickly.' Vega held the case open. 'Can't you see, my men are fascinated?'

The men, more interested in the play between their boss and his determined captive than the painting, smiled and nodded in agreement.

'You must satisfy their appetites, Christina. You must tell them a little more.'

'Whatever you say,' she said, knowing it quickest to agree. The less time the painting was exposed to the humidity, the better. 'Some people say Vincent liked the cypresses because their tormented shape reflected his own mood. He did several cypress paintings while he was in southern France. There's one, my favourite, with a road at night, and a carriage . . . in the Kröller-Müller museum near Otterlo.' She looked to him. 'Enough?'

'Thank you, señorita.' Vega closed the case.

The other men said their thanks and moved back to

their pillows while Vega strapped the case back in place. 'Your guide mentions a painting not in your collection, it has cypresses and very bright stars.'

'"Starry Night", it's mentioned in an excerpt from one of Vincent's letters. What about it?'

'I was interested to read of it.'

'You should look it up in a book sometime, it's worth seeing.'

'I could afford the original,' Vega joked before getting back on his intended track. 'Vincent was fascinated by peasants, sunflowers and cypress trees. Now I find he was also fascinated by the stars.'

'Where's this conversation leading?' she asked, wondering if there was more involved than an attempt to impress his men.

'Tell me about the starry painting.'

'Whatever you say.' She didn't mind, it filled time, and it was exactly the type of thing the psychiatrist on CNN had recommended. 'Vincent was fascinated by the night sky. He likened the bright stars with their dark background to the black dots of the cities and towns on a map of France. He said that if a person could take a train to one of the black dots on the map, perhaps they could travel to one of the stars too, by dying. He imagined death as a means of celestial transportation. Diseases like cancer were fast ways of getting to a star, just as a train was the fastest way of getting to a town on the map.'

'Perhaps Vincent found the idea a little too seductive,'

Vega said. 'He went to the stars very quickly. By jet, one could say.'

'You mean death by gunshot?'

'Yes. Did he say anything about dying of old age, as I hope both you and I shall?'

'He said it was like doing the journey on foot.'

Vega laughed. 'I must see this "Starry Night". Where is it?'

'Good luck! It's at the Museum of Modern Art in New York.'

'Have you seen it?'

'It wasn't there when I was in New York.'

'Perhaps we should stop off in New York señorita, so you can show me this painting.' He laughed.

29

The Netherlands government Fokker 70 with Juan Vega on board touched down at Bermuda's Kindley Field just before eleven o'clock on Tuesday morning and taxied to a secure parking bay in the airport's military sector.

The commander of the Bermuda Regiment was first aboard. After extending the compliments of the dependency's governor to Otto Dolsch, he went on to outline the various security and accommodation arrangements that had been made for the visit. Dolsch, impressed with the commander's preparation on all counts, expressed his approval and gratitude.

Juan Vega, displaying a conceited grin but saying nothing, was transported inside an armoured personnel carrier to the military base where he was locked under guard in the otherwise empty jail. Seeing his prisoner secure, Dolsch phoned The Hague to inform his minister of their arrival and to find out if there had been any further word from Colombia. There had not.

At one thirty, after a pleasant lunch in the officers' mess, Dolsch went to his room to rest. He hoped the wait for Carlos Vega's next direction would not be a long one.

Two and a half thousand kilometres to the south, Vega's tanker was nearing its destination, a warehouse in the large oil and industrial city of Maracaibo. Its five fatigued passengers sweltered inside the tank which was becoming hotter by the minute as the sun climbed higher in the hazy tropical sky.

'Here's the turn-off,' Rodrigo announced over the intercom as the truck decelerated.

Ten minutes later, after a series of turns, each one seemingly sharper than the one before it, they stopped.

'We're here, amigos,' Rodrigo said as the engine died. 'The door is closing behind us.'

Vega opened the hatch. Josef, armed with a submachine gun, got out first. Three taps on the side of the tank a short time later indicated that all was clear. Miguel exited next, followed by Pedro who had Christina lower herself into the hatchway where he blindfolded her before helping her into the open.

She savoured the wonderfully cool air listening all the while for information. Two voices without names greeted Vega, one outlined the arrangements for her confinement.

'She needs to wash,' Vega said.

'Certainly, Don Carlos,' one of the voices replied. 'Bring her this way.'

Pedro, carrying her overnight bag, guided Christina behind the man to a small bathroom at the back of the warehouse offices. After ensuring that there was no means of escape, he removed the blindfold and left her alone.

The room was basic, just a sink and toilet. There was a box of towels on the floor. It would do, she thought. At least it was clean. After all the sweating in the tank, she was desperate for a good wash and change of clothes.

'It's clear,' one of the Venezuelans shouted when Pedro reappeared.

An older man wearing a baseball cap and carrying dark glasses emerged from behind a rental truck. 'Welcome to Venezuela, Don Carlos.'

Vega grinned widely at his friend and embraced him. 'It's good to see you again, Bernardo.'

Since he planned on staying in the area long after Vega was gone, Bernardo Molina, the Medellín cartel's chief contact in Venezuela, had insisted upon precautions to prevent Christina Jansen from seeing anything of him, his men or the surroundings.

'I'm honoured by your trust, Don Carlos,' Bernardo said, his tone and body language humble. Over the years Bernardo had made many pilgrimages to Medellín to visit Carlos Vega. Today was the first time Vega had visited him.

'And I'm grateful for your help and hospitality, compadre.' Vega was back in his role as pope. The two men sat together on the tanker's front bumper. 'Have you noticed

341

anything unusual around here in the past two or three days?' Vega asked.

'Not around here, Don Carlos. But one of my men flew in from Caracas last night, he said there were many soldiers at the airports.'

'The whole army is looking for me, compadre.' Vega pulled a yet unused phone from his pocket. 'And the air traffic controllers?'

'In place. I saw the shift roster myself, there will be no problem.'

'Good,' Vega replied and punched in Rafael's number. 'Please excuse me, Bernardo.'

The answer was immediate. 'Buenas tardes.'

'Buenas tardes, señor,' Vega said into the phone. 'We're here, are you ready?'

'Si, señor. We visited the property yesterday, it looks good. Shall we meet there this afternoon?'

'Yes, at the time we arranged. It's thirteen minutes past twelve now.' Vega was confirming that he had changed to Venezuelan time, an hour ahead of Colombia.

'We will be on time.'

'And how is your friend?' Vega asked.

'He is well,' Rafael replied.

Vega terminated the call.

'Satisfied that Rafael had his part of the escape organised and that Jim Avery had done nothing to arouse suspicion, Vega went on to review the details of this afternoon's operation with Bernardo. The Venezuelan was sure there would be no problem. He had triple checked everything.

Two years ago, Bernardo Molina had been advanced a large loan by Vega to purchase a sugar cane plantation on the Gulf of Venezuela north of their present location. The property came with a luxurious house overlooking the gulf and, more significantly, a paved runway built by the previous owner, a wealthy businessman, to enable him to commute to his office in Caracas in his own plane.

In that time, the sugar cane had proven an excellent cover for the property's primary function as a ferry point for smuggling. Vega's planes had used the runway hundreds of times carrying drugs one way, and chemicals the other, across the Colombian-Venezuelan border. It had also been used as a launching point for drug flights to Florida, Mexico and several of the Caribbean islands. The fees for the use of the runway as well as Bernardo's brokerage for the Medellín cartel's Venezuelan deals had been deducted from the loan while Bernardo and his family lived off the income from the cane. Today's hundred thousand dollar payment would settle the outstanding balance and guarantee the future prosperity of the Molina family.

'My wife has prepared some lunch, Don Carlos,' Bernardo announced when one of his men appeared carrying a box.

'Excellent, compadre,' Vega said. 'We are all starving.' The combination of heat and tension during the journey had caused Vega and his companions to leave the bulk of the food in the tank untouched.

Bernardo's man took a cloth out, spread it on the concrete floor and arranged the contents of the box on top of it: a selection of breads, cold meats, cheese and fruit as well as juice and coffee. Vega had Miguel prepare two plates and take them to Christina and Pedro in the office.

As they ate, Vega went over what was required of the three men who would be returning to Colombia tonight. After seeing Vega off, Rodrigo was to drive the tanker to a chemical wholesaler in Maracaibo where the tanks would be filled with acetone and ether. The wholesaler would provide falsified papers to facilitate the cargo's entry into Colombia. Then, with Josef and Miguel inside the compartment, he would drive back across the border and deliver the chemicals to a storage site on the outskirts of Medellín. Once that was done, he would take the tanker back to the fabricator who, over the next few days, would alter its appearance, its registration and its history.

'By tomorrow night,' Vega said to his men, 'you will be in your new lives, respectable wealthy men.' The men grinned contentedly as they visualised their idle futures.

After lunch, Christina was blindfolded and escorted back into the tank. It had cooled off to quite a comfortable level and, with the hatch open, was reasonably airy. Still drained by the overnight journey, she soon fell asleep.

After a wash and change of clothes, Vega went back into the tank to get some rest himself. Josef stood guard outside.

Even in the domain of an ally, the Medellín chief could not allow himself to be vulnerable.

Jim Avery spent the morning and most of the afternoon watching television in the motel room he shared with Rafael not far from Maracaibo's airport. Aware that his every move was being watched, he had not made any effort to contact the DEA.

At four o'clock Avery put on the uniform he had carried from Medellín: black trousers, a white shirt with epaulets and three stripes and a generic aviation cap. Rafael dressed casually in slacks and a sports coat. Neither was yet aware of this afternoon's final destination. The Gulfstream II which would be used for the journey had a range of five thousand five hundred kilometres, about seven hours flying. Avery had worked out that the destination could be as far as Rio to the south, Cape Verde in Africa to the east or Canada to the north. He presumed it would be a place where Vega had contacts in the police and military: Mexico or an island in the Caribbean, perhaps. At this stage all he knew for sure was that he had to fill out a flight plan for Nassau in The Bahamas and then fly to a small strip fifty kilometres to the north of Maracaibo. He had driven there yesterday with Rafael to inspect the runway and meet the owner. The runway was one thousand one hundred metres long, two hundred and forty metres shorter than the FAA take off specification for a Gulfstream II with maximum weight. He presumed the weight this afternoon would be considerably below the limit.

At four twenty they took a taxi to the airport's general aviation office. Rafael watched carefully as Avery filled out the flight plan for Nassau and presented it to the young woman behind the counter.

'Please wait señor, I must notify customs and immigration of your departure.' She picked up the phone. 'They will want to see you.'

The prospect of an interview and a search worried neither of them. Their story was believable; their plane, perfectly clean.

Avery checked the weather report while they waited. It was expected to remain clear over the whole Caribbean for the next three days. The satellite photograph posted on the board showed a storm system over the North Atlantic. 'I hope our friend doesn't want to go to Iceland tonight,' he whispered to Rafael, pointing to the thick cloud over it.

'No,' Rafael replied with a thin smile. 'He has enough ice of his own.' They both laughed. It was Avery's first indication that his perpetually suspicious companion had a sense of humour.

A customs officer arrived a few minutes later and questioned Avery as he perused the flight plan. As rehearsed, Avery told how he was picking up two Venezuelan oil company executives and their wives who were holidaying in The Bahamas. Rafael was with the oil company and was coming along for the ride. They showed their identification. The passports Vega had provided were the best money could buy. Rafael was carrying a Venezuelan passport in the name of José Fernández, and Avery, a Canadian one in the name Martin Glenn.

'Now I must see the plane, Señor Glenn,' the customs officer requested, handing back the passports. The twin-engine Gulfstream II on the tarmac outside had been fuelled and ready to go since its arrival from Jamaica yesterday.

The customs officer collected a sniffer dog before accompanying Avery and Rafael to the plane. The subsequent search uncovered nothing suspicious at all.

At ten minutes past five, with the sun just touching the hills to the west, the Gulfstream rolled down the runway and began a slow ascent. Avery kept the aircraft just off the coast and levelled out at five thousand feet. Ten minutes later, sighting the flare at the end of the plantation runway, he turned off the navigation lights and headed towards it. On the second floor of the Maiquetía Air Traffic Control Centre, Caracas, the en route controller responsible for the airways north of Maracaibo turned a blind eye.

Vega, Bernardo and their men watched from the far end of the runway as the Gulfstream came in low over the water and touched down with blue smoke and a squeal. It came quickly towards them and turned around. The rental truck carrying Christina, the paintings and the cocaine and heroin was backed up to the fuselage as soon as the engines had whined down.

Christina, who had been handcuffed and blindfolded before leaving Maracaibo, was carried onto the plane first. Rafael belted her into her seat while Pedro closed the window shades around her. She would never be able to describe Bernardo, his men or any of the surroundings in Venezuela.

Josef retrieved a ladder from inside the truck, set it up beside the three metre high port engine and climbed up to it. Then, with two passes of black spray paint over a simple cardboard stencil, he changed the registration marking from C-GAFP to C-GAER. He moved the ladder to the starboard engine and repeated the procedure.

The cocaine and heroin was loaded into the baggage compartment at the rear of the cabin and the fifteen painting cases identified with yellow string were jammed into the spaces between the back seats. The other cases were left in the truck. Bernardo would store them in a secret bunker below his house until instructed what to do with them by Vega.

The loading complete, Vega farewelled first Bernardo and his men and then, with a greater show of emotion, Josef, Rodrigo and Miguel each of whom was handed an envelope containing a key to a safety deposit box in Medellín. The boxes contained their payments, a quarter of a million US dollars each.

Avery started the engines as soon as the truck was out of the way. Even with the windsock showing a good afternoon breeze off the water, he still felt uncomfortable with the take off parameters. He would have liked at least another hundred metres of runway.

Vega entered the cockpit and handed him an envelope. 'Our destination.' There was a set of coordinates printed on the outside. 'There are pictures inside, look at them later.'

Avery read the coordinates aloud as Vega strapped himself into the right-hand seat. 'Forty-five thirty-one north, seventy-three forty-five west. That's a long way.'

'It's a little runway not far out of Montreal.'

'Canada,' Avery responded in a surprised tone, imagining snow and ice.

'It's just under four thousand kilometres,' Vega said. 'Well within our range. It should take about four and a half hours.'

'You've done your homework,' Avery said and went on to finish his pre-flight check. 'Okay, we're ready to roll.' He spoke into the public address system. 'Seat belts everybody, life jackets are under your seats. You know what the yellow masks are for if they pop out.'

The aircraft vibrated as Avery applied power while keeping the brakes on. Then, his pulse quickening, he released the foot pedal. The aircraft bolted down the runway, the acceleration pushing all on board heavily into the backs of their seats. They lifted off with two hundred metres to spare.

'Well done, amigo,' Vega exhaled, easing his grip on the armrests.

'Now, let's get back on course,' Avery said, flicking up

the landing gear lever. He banked left and headed back towards the assigned airway. 'So what have you got planned for Nassau?' he asked warily. The only clue he had was the change to the registration. 'Your controller friends can cover a fifteen minute diversion, but I don't see how they can cover Montreal.'

'There'll be no problem, Jim,' Vega replied, gazing down at the scattered farmhouses below. 'I'll just do a little magic.'

Twelve minutes later, the Gulfstream crossed the South American coast following its assigned airway at its assigned flight level.

'ETA is four hours and forty minutes from take off,' Avery said a short time later, folding his calculator. 'Montreal is one hour behind Maracaibo so we'll get there at 21:30h local time.' He opened the envelope and examined the aerial photographs of the runway and its surroundings.

'It's 1200 metres long, 4000 feet,' Vega said. 'In good condition. Should be no problem.'

'What about an alternate?' Avery asked.

'This isn't an airline, amigo. We land there no matter what.'

'Even if I can't see the runway?' Avery made no attempt to hide his alarm. He knew that such a runway would have little in the way of landing aids. 'There's a storm up that way.'

'You're the best, Jim. I'm sure you can handle whatever we run into.'

Avery was not amused. He wasn't going to kill himself trying to land in a blizzard. There would be an alternate runway whether Vega liked it or not.

An hour later, a second Gulfstream II, registration C-GAER, took off from Norman Manley International Airport, Kingston, Jamaica, on a flight plan which had it going up the eastern United States to Montreal. On board were an American pilot and a Venezuelan man carrying identification in the names Martin Glenn and José Fernández respectively. The black wax on the last two letters of its registration gradually melted and streamed off as it climbed into the starry darkness.

The shell game was completed forty-five minutes later as the two aircraft almost simultaneously crossed the Tropic of Cancer. The plane now displaying the registration C-GAFP descended towards Nassau while Vega's plane went on towards the open Atlantic.

It was snowing in the north.

30

A dejected-looking Luis Martínez was perusing some recently arrived faxes when Nelson Schoute walked into his office. It was now over twenty-four hours since the La Playa fire and both men were coming to terms with the increasingly inescapable conclusion that Carlos Vega had slipped through the checkpoints and was now outside Colombia.

And there were the six bodies Martínez had discovered at Vega's house early this morning, victims, he presumed, of the three men videotaped carrying the live body, almost certainly Margarita Vega, to the helicopter. The ease with which the men had entered the compound and the time delay between their arrival and departure led Martínez to believe they were known at the house.

'What a disaster,' Martínez sighed, tossing the faxes on his desk. He was mentally and physically exhausted. 'I can't believe I lost both, Nelson. Vega and his wife.'

'You did your best, Luis, no one can argue with that.'

Nelson sat down across the desk to share the misery. 'Anything new on Vega's house?'

'Not a thing. All I can think is that some of Vega's men had a war of their own going on and it ended last night, or some of them are out to blackmail Vega now that he's vulnerable.'

'Time will tell.' Nelson had seen the bodies too. All but the one in the main bedroom had been shot twice in the head from close range. Whoever the assassins were, they were professionals. The retired Dutch policeman had only read about such things before.

'It's just so damn frustrating,' Martínez said, tugging loose his tie.

'It's not over yet,' Nelson remarked, introducing a much needed positive tone to the conversation. 'Vega still has a few hurdles to jump.'

'Not my hurdles, Nelson, he'll be out of my jurisdiction.'

'And out of his own too, don't forget.'

'You're an optimist, compadre.' Martínez gave a soft chuckle. 'And the farther he moves from Colombia, the less influence he has.'

'And the easier he will be to catch,' Nelson added with raised eyebrows.

'We must drink to that,' Martínez said, wishing the pain behind him. 'Look at these.' He passed over the faxes he'd been reading and got up from his chair. 'The customs people in Panama and Venezuela had a very productive day. We made them look very good.'

353

Martínez outlined the successes to Nelson as he went about preparing fresh coffee. Some of the cases were bizarre. Panamanian customs had arrested a man attempting to smuggle thirty-two rare and endangered birds into the country. The birds, destined for the US market, were squeezed into short lengths of plastic pipe packed inside cardboard boxes. Eight were dead when they were discovered. At the same crossing, three sedated baby howler monkeys had been discovered in the trunk of a woman's car. The Venezuelans had seized nine stolen American cars and a van full of banned automatic weapons headed for Caracas. Both countries reported intercepting small quantities of marijuana and cocaine but no large shipments had been discovered. Nelson wasn't surprised. He'd learned enough about the way things worked in this part of the world to realise that the major smugglers would have been warned of the authorities' plans before they were implemented.

'Their courts will be busy,' Nelson said as Martínez placed the coffees on the desk.

'Good business for the lawyers.' Martínez lifted a bottle of dark rum from a drawer and added a portion to each cup. 'To the success of our neighbours,' he said, handing one of the cups to Nelson.

'And to your fine work, Colonel, that will lead to their success. Salud!'

'Salud!'

The Medellín police's efforts of the previous twenty-four

hours had not been entirely fruitless. The laboratory Christina had described in her diary had been located and the cook and several assistants arrested. Despite being offered immunity from prosecution in exchange for information leading to Vega's arrest, the cook and his assistants had provided nothing of value other than the fact that one of Vega's men, already known to the police, had taken delivery of a large quantity of cocaine last Thursday.

Six sets of fingerprints discovered in Vega's apartments had been identified as belonging to men with existing drug related criminal records. Their photographs, fingerprints and former aliases had been circulated to police and military officials throughout Colombia, directly into neighbouring countries and elsewhere via the Interpol network.

'I just spoke with Otto Dolsch in Bermuda,' Nelson said. 'I told him what you said about the cocaine, the two hundred kilograms Vega's man picked up from the laboratory.'

'Vega would be foolish not to combine a big drop with the exchange. Easy money, not that he needs it.'

'And Dolsch says Kees Vermeer came up with the same list of destinations as you. Mexico, the United States, Canada, in that order.'

'A good detective.' Martínez had been made aware of Vermeer's outstanding career by Nelson. 'It must be somewhere not too far from Bermuda. Somewhere he has contacts and room to run. Mexico City, Miami or New York, I'd say. Toronto or Montreal at the outside.'

'Vega's brazen,' Nelson remarked reflectively. 'It's not hard to imagine him dropping Christina and the paintings in Times Square. Or even at the front gate of the White House.'

'I hadn't thought of Washington,' Martínez said across the top of his cup. 'Vega may have some very good friends there.' They both laughed.

'Dolsch says he'll be ready to take off forty minutes after Vega's call.'

'Has he been practising?'

'He's Dutch, Luis,' Nelson replied with a grin. 'He says he can deliver his prisoner anywhere between Florida and Nova Scotia within three hours of the call.'

'A fast man,' Martínez responded, shuffling through the papers on his desk. 'I got a call from the DEA in Washington.' He found the piece he was looking for. 'Nicholson. Special Agent Nicholson. Says he's been keeping his eye on Avery for the last month, wanted to know what we knew about him.'

'If he was watching Avery, how come he didn't stop the hijacking?'

'I asked him that. He didn't have an answer. I'm not too happy with the DEA at the moment, especially their man in Bogotá. I told Nicholson too. I still haven't got that photograph of Avery.'

'It's a bit late now,' Nelson said, equally unimpressed by the failure. 'How's the DEA for integrity?'

'Not bad, from what I've heard. Unfortunately, it has the

356

same problem as all law enforcement agencies in the United States . . . mountains of paperwork. Agents spend most of their time covering technicalities so their cases won't get thrown out of court.' Martínez enjoyed a sip of the fortified coffee, leant back and closed his eyes. He could feel his frustration and disappointment being replaced by sad relief. 'Avery's picture is probably lying on someone's desk waiting for the proper form to be signed.'

The weather system responsible for four days of intermittent snow throughout the northeastern United States and across central and maritime Canada was weakening. Inside a US Air Force operations room in the Pentagon Building in Arlington, Virginia, DEA Special Agent Steve Nicholson watched the blip identified as C-GAER on the situation display console as it crossed the line defining United States' air space south of Cape Fear, North Carolina. The US Air Force Airborne Warning and Control System aircraft sending the picture had been tracking the Gulfstream ever since it took off from Maracaibo. The suspicions of the AWACS on-board observers, initially aroused when the jet made the brief stop north of Maracaibo, had been confirmed by the shell game over the Caribbean. They had been stalking C-GAER ever since.

A second blip on the screen identified a US Air Force F-18 fighter under the control of the air force liaison officer sitting next to Nicholson. It had been trailing three miles behind the Gulfstream for the past thirty minutes.

An FBI Gulfstream IV jet with a twenty member assault team on board had already taken off from Dulles and was due to pull in behind the target aircraft over Virginia in twenty minutes time. The FBI pilot's mission was to land behind the suspect aircraft and taxi as close as possible to it. Then, according to a well rehearsed drill, the assault team was to storm the target aircraft, rescue the hostage and arrest everyone else.

Nicholson had spent the past hour making one phone call after another. Now, at last, everything was in place. DEA and US Customs Service personnel as well as additional FBI teams were waiting with helicopters at various stations along the Gulfstream's projected flight path. If necessary, they would provide delayed back up for the assault team. Or, if the FBI aircraft was unable to land and they were quick enough, take on the role of the main assault force.

The Royal Canadian Air Force, the Royal Canadian Mounted Police and Canada Customs were also on alert in case the suspect aircraft followed its flight plan across the border into Canada.

This was a rare moment of shared anticipation for the two men watching the AWACS display. The marriage between their parent organisations had been imposed by Congress in the late eighties in the hope of reducing the quantity of drugs entering the United States from South America. Since then, the air force had provided the DEA with tracking facilities on a regular basis and, when the situation dictated such action, fighters had intercepted suspected drug flights and forced them to land. The air force chiefs, having no desire to flirt with the corruption that had infected all the existing forces involved in the fight against drugs, had, from the beginning, insisted upon limits to air force involvement. Consequently, air force personnel were prohibited from any form of contact with suspected drug criminals other than over the radio during an intercept mission. And when contact was made, personnel were not permitted to use their own names or any name that could be used to identify them later. In addition, air force pilots were forbidden from landing behind suspected drug carrying aircraft. Their standing orders were to stay in the air and leave any arrests to the US Customs Service, the FBI, the DEA or the local police on the ground.

The sophisticated attempt at deception over the Caribbean convinced Nicholson that C-GAER was indeed Vega's plane. He expected it to be carrying Christina Jansen, at least fifteen of the van Gogh paintings and a shipment of drugs. But was Vega aboard? That was the question which interested him most. Since his presence was not essential at the exchange point, Vega could be anywhere. As he continued to follow C-GAER on the monitor, Nicholson got a rare and powerful instinctive feeling which strengthened with time. Carlos Vega was coming to collect his son himself.

Both men watched as the blip representing the FBI aircraft appeared on the monitor and curved towards C-GAER. Nicholson was delighted with the progress so far. He knew he had done his job well. And he had done it as he had been trained to do it. That meant placing as little trust as possible in any of the South American law enforcement agencies. The photograph of James B Avery which the Colombian police had requested was in a place where it could do his cause no harm, in a file folder back in his office. The premature arrest of a key player and informant would have interfered with what he hoped would be the DEA's greatest victory since its inception, the apprehension of Carlos Vega.

Christina Jansen, gazing out her port-side window at the lights of a city below, hadn't noticed Vega emerge from the cockpit. 'Norfolk, Virginia.' His voice startled her. 'In case you were wondering.'

'I was,' she replied a little breathlessly. 'Is our destination still a secret?'

'We're headed for a small airport near Montreal.' He chose his words carefully. It was more of a challenge to deceive than to lie. 'How is your French?'

'Better than my Spanish. How long will it take to get there?'

'An hour . . . maybe a little more.' Vega retrieved a vacuum flask from the picnic box Bernardo Molina's wife had prepared for the flight. 'Coffee?'

'Thanks.' The coffee presented the first tenable opportunity to visit the cockpit. She hadn't seen Jim Avery since he left the apartment on Sunday. 'Does Jim want some?'

'How thoughtful of you to ask,' Vega replied. He'd taken out three cups.

She cursed to herself for sounding too keen. 'I just want to make sure Mr Culture is alert for the landing.'

'I think you like Mr Culture,' Vega said while pouring the second cup. 'Am I right?'

'You must be joking,' she scoffed. 'I'm just worried about the paintings.'

Vega grinned. 'Don't worry, the landing will be as soft as snow.' He put another cup on her tray and filled it. 'Take it to Jim, I'll help Pedro and Rafael secure our cargo.'

'You should put some of the boxes out here and put the paintings in the back, so they can be horizontal.' She would have fought for that had she not been blindfolded when they were loaded. Then, pointing to two cases jammed between the seats across the aisle, 'The paintings can't be facing that way when we land, the surfaces will vibrate too much.'

'We must consider weight, señorita. The merchandise is heavier, Jim says that it must go in the back.' Vega agreed that the way the cases were packed was entirely unsuitable and had already planned to remedy the situation. If the landing was to be anything like he imagined, loose as they presently were, they could become dangerous projectiles. 'I'll see what I can do.'

'Okay,' Christina replied, her mind more on Avery and the DEA than the landing. She took the coffees into the cockpit.

'Thanks, honey,' Avery said as he reached back to take his cup. 'Nice to see you again.'

'So, Montreal?' She edged herself into the right-hand seat.

'That's what the man says. I hope you packed some winter clothes, it's snowing up there.'

'I packed for Rio, remember?'

'I remember.' He leaned across and examined the burn on her face. She'd removed the dressing in Maracaibo. 'It's looking good, how does it feel?'

'Much better.' She glanced back through the partially open doorway. Rafael and Josef were rearranging the cardboard boxes in the baggage section at the back. Vega was strapping the vertical painting cases to the seat supports. She told herself not to worry. So far all the take offs and landings with the paintings had been very smooth. Hopefully, this one would be too. 'Have you managed to contact your friend?'

'Didn't get a chance. Rafael watched me like a hawk the whole time. You may get a chance before I do.'

'How do I contact him?'

'Dial zero and ask the operator for the DEA, Washington DC headquarters. There's a toll-free number. When you get through ask for Special Agent Steve Nicholson. Can you remember that?'

'Yes,' she replied and repeated the information. 'Can't you use the radio?'

'Too risky. Never know who's listening. We're not the

362

only baddies in the air tonight.' He took a sip of coffee and relaxed back in the seat. 'I'll be glad as hell when all this is over.'

'Me too,' she replied, wedging herself into the corner so she faced him. 'Are you looking forward to your new life as a protected witness?'

'I suppose it's one way of staying out of trouble, living in a neighbourhood with a bunch of FBI types.'

'I imagine it is,' she responded. Vega was right. She did, in a sort of a fashion, like Jim Avery. Was it the Stockholm syndrome? No. Avery wasn't a threat to her, there was no need to identify with him. He was a captive too, by his own choice. Bad choice. Foolish man.

'I curse the day I got involved in all this,' he said, gazing into the blackness ahead.

'Why did you get involved? Pilots make good money don't they?'

'Greed, damn greed. It overcame my good sense.'

'How did you let that happen?' She checked behind. Vega and his men were still working on the cargo.

'It's not a pretty story. I should write a book about it when I'm in Boise, Idaho, or wherever else I end up.'

'Wherever you end up, it has to be better than the alternatives. Prison or the Colombian necktie you told me about.'

'True, quite true. You won't find me complaining.'

'Are you married?' She couldn't imagine a wife and children waiting for him at home.

'Used to be. My wife took off on me about four years back, with my daughter. I don't blame her. I was taking cocaine, or it was taking me is more the truth. Not even a jet pilot's salary can fund that little habit, and a family.'

'You flew while you were hooked on cocaine?' she asked in disbelief.

'You bet, and guess what?' He looked to her with wide open eyes. 'Nobody noticed. Cocaine's not as bad as you think, it just helped me function, gave me a boost. If it wasn't for the cost, it wouldn't have been a big problem. I didn't overdo it.'

'You've quit now?' she asked, earnestly hoping he had.

'Over a year ago. It wasn't hard. Easier than giving up cigarettes, according to a guy I know who quit both. Now I spend my money on other things.'

'Such as?'

'The usual, gambling and women. Don't know which one's worse.'

'Ever try to get back with your wife?'

'She found a replacement, an optometrist in Tampa. They're having a very boring life together.'

'There's something to be said for a boring life.' Christina sipped some more coffee. 'What about your daughter, how old is she?'

'Eleven this July and as cute as a button. I see her every now and then. Any more questions, Doctor?'

'Sorry, I didn't mean to pry.'

'You're forgiven. How come you're a single gal, anyway?

You aren't too hard on the eyes and seem to have a pretty nice personality. Haven't met any fellas rich enough or smart enough . . . or what?'

'Something like that. My mother tells me I'm too fussy.'

'Well, Christina, don't lower your standards, that's my advice. Not down to my level anyway.' His expression betrayed a hint of self doubt.

'Don't be so hard on yourself,' she replied quickly, sympathetically. It was the first time she'd glimpsed anything of the real Jim Avery. 'You're doing the right thing now, that's something in your favour.'

'Don't be under any illusions about James Avery,' he replied, his shell back in place. 'I wouldn't be helping the DEA if they hadn't busted me. But thanks for the compliment. You're a nice gal Christina Jansen, too bad you had to get caught up in all this.'

'It will be something to tell my grandchildren,' she shrugged.

'You'd better get started on some children first, or didn't they teach you that part in art school?'

She laughed. 'No, I had to learn that for myself. After hours.' She glanced down the cabin again. Vega seemed to have finished strapping the painting cases. He was talking to Rafael.

'I'm pleased the male of the species hasn't been totally deprived of your charms.'

'I was even engaged to be married once.'

'Is that so? Who was the fella?'

'A man from Copenhagen. He was a scientist with the European space agency in The Hague.'

'Great, a rocket scientist. You date rocket scientists.' He shook his head. 'You must find my attempts at conversation a little simple-minded. What happened, if you don't mind me asking?'

'He just wasn't right for me,' she said, a touch of regret creeping into her voice.'

'Was he into art?'

'More than you are, that's for sure.'

He laughed. 'Not my speciality, I must admit. But I did enjoy your talks more than I let on.'

'Christina,' Vega interrupted from behind. 'Please go back and check the paintings.'

'Okay,' she responded, a little startled, and got up from the seat. Then, to Avery, 'A soft landing, right?'

'Yes, señorita,' Vega said and eased her past. 'Jim is the best pilot on the coast.'

'Don't worry, honey,' Avery said as she left, 'I'll do my best not to bounce those pictures around.'

Vega took the right-hand seat and withdrew a small card from his pocket. 'Where are we?'

'About forty-five minutes out of Montreal. That's Atlantic City over there.' He pointed to an expanse of light to the right of the aircraft.

Vega checked the display on the aircraft's satellite-fed Global Positioning System. The latitude numbers were changing quickly and went through 40°N as he watched. The longitude was decreasing towards 74°W.

A short time later, high above New York City, they were slotted onto airway J37 leading to Montreal.

'We're not going to Montreal,' Vega announced matter-of-factly as they approached the edge of the city.

'What?' Avery's head shot around.

'We're landing at a strip, latitude forty-two seventeen.'

'Four two one seven,' Avery looked at the display and did the arithmetic. 'A bit over a degree . . . sixty nautical miles ahead.' He felt a sudden dryness in his throat. 'What's there?'

'Athens, New York.' Vega referred to the card in his hand. 'We'll begin the descent at forty-one forty exactly, that will give you enough space.'

'Is that the runway in the pictures?'

'Yes, it isn't as long as I told you, just 750 metres, 2500 feet. There's a large flat field at the end.'

'What!' He looked to Vega in disbelief. 'With ice and snow, you must be kidding me?'

'It will be lit up with portable lighting,' Vega continued, 'The snow was cleared late this afternoon but some may have fallen since then.'

'Forget it! It's too short. No way, Carlos. Point me some-where I can get this thing down safely.'

'You'll land where I tell you to land.' Vega kept his eyes on the GPS display. 'There's a one hundred thousand dollar bonus in it for you.'

'That won't do me much good in the cemetery, will it?'

Vega grabbed the PA microphone. 'Rafael, bring Christina.'

'Why are you getting her?' Avery asked, looking nervously into the darkness ahead. Vega made no response.

'What's going on?' Christina asked as Rafael pushed her inside the cockpit.

Vega pulled a knife from a scabbard on his leg and put it to Christina's abdomen. 'Land where you're told to land, Jim, or she gets hurt.'

'You're crazy, man,' Avery responded instinctively, immediately regretting his words.

Vega, his jaw clenched, brought the knife to Avery's throat.

'Leave him alone!' Christina shouted.

'You forget who you're talking to, Jim,' Vega murmured coldly, his eyes locked on the pilot. 'You've seen what happens to those who disobey me.'

'Okay. Sorry.' Avery held up his hands. 'I'll try, but I may have to go around a couple of times to get a feel for it.'

'You'll land first time, or Christina gets cut.'

'I'll do my best, but if I have to go round, I will.' He returned Vega's stare. 'Better she's cut than we're all dead, right Carlos?'

'Very well,' Vega replied after getting the measure of the pilot's resolve. He returned the knife to the scabbard.

'I'll need help,' Avery said, turning his attention to the controls.

'Just tell me what you want.' Vega's tone was suddenly businesslike. He turned to Rafael, 'Take her back.'

'Wait, both of you,' Avery said. 'When I say brace, get in the crash position. That's strapped in tight, pillow on your lap. Arms around your knees.' He demonstrated by wrapping his arms around his own knees. 'And no sharp objects in pockets, okay?'

'And give those instructions to Pedro,' Vega told Rafael who then took Christina back to the cabin.

'Forty-one thirty-five,' Vega read from the GPS display. 'Almost there.' Forty seconds later they passed through 41°40'N. 'Turn off the navigation lights.'

'Lights off,' Avery said as he complied with Vega's demand.

'Now bank left and drop like a rock. We're going straight up seventy-three fifty-one, four kilometres that way.' He pointed to port.

Avery banked the aircraft slightly to port and levelled out before moving the throttles to idle and extending the speed brakes. He then fastened his shoulder harnesses and suggested to Vega that he do likewise.

The rapid acceleration to a descent rate of 4500 feet per minute gave all on board the feeling they were indeed falling. Avery banked back to starboard along 73°51'W.

'I'll be busy looking for the runway,' Avery said. 'I want you to read out latitude and keep me on a due north track. When we're close to the ground you can tell me altitude and air speed too.' He pointed to the appropriate indicators.

'Sorry about before, Jim,' Vega said, thinking it wise to

make amends for his reckless loss of temper. He didn't want Avery thinking about anything other than his flying. 'I'll double the bonus, two hundred thousand.'

'Okay,' Avery replied with a glance to Vega. 'Sounds good. You can start reading latitude now.'

'We just passed through forty-one degrees, forty-two minutes.'

'Just the numbers.'

Vega continued to read out the latitude positions as they dropped quickly towards the moonlit, snow covered hills.

'Forty-one forty-nine,' he reported as they descended through 26 000 feet altitude. 'Move a little left.'

Avery caught sight of a small town some distance ahead.

'It's Catskill,' Vega said and looked up to see it. 'We're on course. The runway is seven kilometres north of the town.' Then, back to the instruments. 'Forty-one fifty-five.'

'Okay.' Avery glanced at the altimeter just as it passed through 19 900 feet. 'Give me altitude from now on.'

Vega reported constantly as they continued their fall in the cold, still air. 'Forty-two zero one, heading good, altitude one four zero hundred.'

'Looks like a frozen river down there to my left,' Avery reported at 10 000 feet.

'The Hudson,' Vega said. 'You cross it soon. Forty-two zero six, move a little left, altitude ninety-five hundred.'

The river closed in rapidly from the left as they approached the snow-brightened lights of Catskill.

'Forty-two zero eight, altitude six nine hundred.'

Avery eased back on the descent rate. 'We're over the river, Catskill is coming up on the left.'

'Forty-two one two, altitude thirty-eight hundred. Watch for train tracks north of the town.'

'Can't see any yet. What's my air speed?'

'Ah . . . one ninety.'

'Give me that from now on.'

Catskill shot past on the left. 'I can see the tracks,' Avery said. 'No runway though. Sure it's lit?'

'Yes, they've been listening to our radio. It's between the tracks and that highway.' Vega looked up in search of the highway.

'Eyes on the instruments,' Avery said. 'I can see it . . . the highway. No runway yet.'

'Forty-two one five, heading good, altitude fifteen hundred.'

'I see the lights,' Avery said and inhaled a deep breath. The dim runway lights alone in the darkness ahead ran to the right of their heading. He grabbed the PA microphone. 'Brace, brace, brace.' He banked the aircraft sharply to port. 'Just give me altitude and air speed now.'

'Okay. Nine hundred, one ninety.'

'Gear down. Thank God it's not windy.'

'Seven hundred, one seventy.'

'Bloody snow!' Avery banked the plane to starboard, lining it up with the runway.

'Four hundred, one sixty.'

'Lights on.'

'Three hundred, one sixty.'

'Shit!'

'Two hundred, one sixty.'

Avery slammed the plane onto the end of the runway and immediately engaged the reverse thrusters. The lights rushed past as they ploughed their way through the snow. He shut off the engines at the last lights. They slid on, through a fence, over a road and onto a field. There was a loud hard thud, a sideways spin just missing a tree. The nose dipped. The starboard wing hit a snow bank twisting them to a wrenching stop. 'Out, everybody!' Avery shouted into the PA. He was worried about a possible fuel leak from the damage.

'Not so quickly,' Vega countered and removed the revolver from his hip. 'We have to unload.'

Rafael already had the front door open when Vega and Avery emerged from the cockpit into the upwardly sloped cabin. He hadn't lowered the stairs, the collapsed nose wheel having rendered them unusable.

Rafael and Pedro jumped out and took cover behind the depressed nose. They waited, their guns at the ready, while a truck came across the frozen field towards them. Over a dozen men, many with long hair and beards, jumped out of the back of the truck and swarmed onto and around the plane.

Vega wasn't surprised to hear an aircraft circling overhead when he emerged. He wasn't worried either. He knew it couldn't land, the runway was now invisible.

Certain that C-GAER no longer posed any threat to national security, the F-18 pilot, his aircraft low on fuel, turned for home. Meanwhile, the FBI Gulfstream circled as on-board observers, handicapped by high speed and tree cover, attempted to watch and film the activity on the ground using infrared equipment. It had pulled out of the chase at 3000 feet, its pilot alerted to the inadequate runway length by an AWACS officer.

The FBI informed the Athens police of the crash landing but asked them to stay away until called upon. There would be no lambs to the slaughter.

Two helicopters carrying FBI, DEA and US Customs Service agents arrived from Albany approximately fifteen minutes after the crash landing. They found nothing but an empty aircraft, some chained tyre tracks in the snow, two enormously long sets of outdoor lights and a generator.

Vega's convoy had merged with the traffic on Interstate 87 heading south towards New York City.

31

The anonymous large truck with the cartel's customary forward and rear escort vehicles took the second Yonkers exit off Interstate 87. It was almost eleven o'clock on Tuesday night.

After undertaking a series of circuitous turns to allow the men in the rear vehicle to check there were no tails, the convoy turned into a snow covered alleyway. The lead and rear vehicles blocked the ends while the truck stopped part-way down in order to disgorge the thirteen unarmed members of the Vicars of Lucifer motorcycle gang who had been hired to set up the landing lights on the Athens runway and unload the cargo from the Gulfstream. The bikers, awe struck and intimidated by the man they knew by bloody reputation, farewelled Vega with respectful nods and salutes.

The Vicars of Lucifer had been an integral part of the Medellín cartel's operation in the northeastern United States for a number of years, its members providing the crucial buffer and delivery service between the expatriate Colombian and Mafia wholesalers and the street dealers. In return, they enjoyed the benefits of a reliable source of high quality drugs for their own use as well as considerable wealth and prestige.

The chief of the New York syndicate had chosen the motorcycle gang for tonight's operation because of their demonstrated reliability, efficiency and loyalty. He knew there would be no problems. The gang behaved more as a subcontractor than a group of employees. On the rare occasions in the past when individual bikers had breached trust, he had not needed to take any action. The Vicars of Lucifer had their own very effective ways of dealing with traitors.

The convoy returned to Interstate 87 and continued south through the Bronx and onto Interstate 95. As they had done for the entire journey, Vega, Pedro and Rafael sat against the front wall of the truck's box, cloaked in blankets, their submachine guns at the ready. Christina Jansen, blindfolded and her hands cuffed, sat propped up against the side next to Jim Avery. They, too, wore blankets provided by the New York host.

Vega hadn't shared tomorrow's plans with Pedro and Rafael, his secretiveness a well reinforced habit which he had no intention of breaking now. Not that betrayal was a concern, their futures being tied to his success. Once the operation was over, both would take on new identities and return to South America. Pedro would meet his family in

Buenos Aires and travel with them to the large wheat property he had recently purchased near Rosario. Rafael, a bachelor, would go to Santiago where he hoped to fulfil a long term ambition to own a nightclub. Money would be no object for either of them. Tomorrow, if all went according to Imthorn's plan, they would each receive one million US dollars for their part in the success.

As usual, Jim Avery was Vega's main concern: the most likely Judas. Avery had said very little since the landing in Athens. Shock, Vega surmised. It had been a terrifying experience, more so for the pilot than anyone else. Or it could be fear for his life now that they were safely on the ground. Vega had decided against telling Avery that he had a part in tomorrow's operation and therefore was still indispensable. It was better that he remain on edge.

Vega knew that the next fifteen hours would be critical. By mid-morning tomorrow, if all went well, he would be in a safe house in New Jersey ready to orchestrate the exchange of Christina and the paintings for his son. In three weeks, he and Juan would be smuggled across the Canadian border to Toronto where they would slip into the Venezuelan backgrounds and identities that had already been established for them there. Margarita would join them a week after that and, two years from now, they would quietly return to South America to the house that waited for them in the hills of Bolivia.

The convoy crossed the Bronx Whitestone Bridge and continued south exiting the highway into Queens. After several precautionary turns, they drove into a small warehouse just outside the perimeter of La Guardia Airport. As the truck slowed, Vega had everyone take cover behind boxes stacked across the middle for that purpose.

Vega, Pedro and Rafael pointed their guns towards the back as the door was opened. 'Buenas noches, Don Carlos.' A middle-aged Hispanic man wearing a wide grin appeared in the opening. He raised his hands when he saw the guns. 'Welcome to New York.'

'Buenas noches, amigo,' Vega said, consciously omitting the man's name from the greeting.

Rafael climbed out, followed by Pedro. After checking around outside, they called out to Vega that it was safe.

'It's wonderful to see you again, amigo,' Vega said, embracing the expatriate Colombian. As one of only three of Pablo Escobar's lieutenants still alive, Francisco Pino, also known as "the Bookkeeper", was considered a curiosity by many in the drug business. He owed his survival to some accounting problems in the New York operation which brought him north the day before Escobar was assassinated. Suddenly finding himself in no hurry to return to imprisonment or death at home, Pino accepted a job from the then head of the New York operation who, unfortunately for himself, made the twin mistakes of undervaluing his new employee's talent and underestimating his resourcefulness. Pino quickly discovered that the New York employees, many of whom were recent arrivals from Colombia, resented the low wages and arrogant treatment they received from the second generation American management. Capitalising on the discontent, he went about building support with his underlings and, two years after his arrival, spearheaded the overthrow of the three men above him. In order to imprint his style of leadership on those who had supported his coup, Pino disposed of the previous managers using one of the more terrifying of the cartel's techniques: one by one, alive and without parachutes, they were pushed out the door of a plane seven thousand feet above the Atlantic. Their bodies had never been found.

'I have some coffee and cakes in my office,' Pino said cheerfully. 'For you and your men.'

'We'll take care of the señorita first,' Vega said and ordered Pedro and Rafael to bring Christina off the truck, reminding them that her blindfold was to stay on. Pino, like Bernardo Molina in Maracaibo, had insisted that precautions be taken to prevent the hostage from seeing anything of him, his men or the surroundings.

Pino directed his men to show Pedro and Rafael to the room he had set up for Christina before leading Vega and Avery to the lunch room where a table was set with cups and a plate of cakes. 'Please sit down,' Pino said as shouting started outside. Vega, recognising one of the voices as Pedro's, grabbed for his weapon but found himself looking down the barrel of Pino's revolver before he had it off the table. 'Don't move, either of you,' Pino ordered as three of his men rushed into the room.

'What is this, Francisco?' Vega demanded, enraged by the turn of events. He glanced at Avery in search of signs of complicity but could see none.

'I'm sorry, Carlos, there have been some changes,' Pino replied. 'Let go of the gun.'

Vega complied and raised his hands. One of Pino's men removed the gun from the table while another took the revolver from Vega's hip.

'Cali?' Vega sneered as he delivered the rival city's name.

'Si,' Pino replied, the guilt he felt showing on his face. 'I had no choice, amigo.' Representatives of the Cali cartel had approached Pino just two hours ago and, after outlining their strategically timed plan, had given him a choice: support them and thrive or stay loyal to Vega and perish. Pino, convinced of their ability to succeed in their endeavour with or without him, had transferred his loyalty with all the zeal he could muster. Forcing Pino's support had been an important step for the men from Cali. Gaining Vega's was crucial.

'They have your wife,' Pino announced as his men pulled Vega and Avery to their feet.

'Where is she?' Vega's eyes burned into Pino's.

'You will see her soon.' One of Pino's men discovered the knife Vega had attached to his leg and held it up for his boss to see. 'A nasty little thing, Carlos.'

'I hope for your sake, Francisco, Margarita has not been hurt.' Vega was oblivious to the comment about the knife.

One of the men hustled Avery out of the room. Another handcuffed Vega while Pino pulled a phone from his pocket and punched a memory button. 'It's done,' was all he said and turned it off. He told his men to bring Vega into the warehouse.

They watched as the roller door was opened and a deep blue van with heavily tinted windows backed in. It came to a stop beside the group. The side door slid open. Margarita Vega, handcuffed and belted to her seat, her mouth gagged with tape, communicated her distress with her eyes. Two well dressed Hispanic men were in the back with her.

Vega thrust himself into the doorway. 'You scum!' He lunged towards the man closest to him but Pino's men pulled him back before he made contact. 'I'll kill you if you've touched her.'

'No one has touched her, Señor Vega,' the closest man said and then removed the tape from Margarita's mouth.

'Have they hurt you, Margarita?' Vega asked. As far as he could tell, she looked unharmed.

'I'm okay, Carlos.' She'd been raped back in Medellín by each of the three men who kidnapped her, one of whom she'd recognised as a recently hired bodyguard of her husband's. Their silence over her lover would last as long as her silence over the rapes, and vice versa. That was the deal they had struck with her. She willed each of them a horrible death.

'What happened?' Vega asked his wife, pulling towards her.

'Some pigs kidnapped me at the house yesterday morning.' Then, flinging her head in their direction, 'These two brought me here through Mexico, they haven't told me anything.'

'They're from Cali,' Vega said and was pulled back as the man who had spoken before got out of the van.

He came face to face with Vega. 'Señor Vega, I am authorised to act on behalf of my superior in Cali, Señor Díaz.'

'Who the hell are you?' Vega demanded, furious at the humiliation being forced on him.

'Call me Angel.'

'What's your name?'

'I won't tell you that señor. You know why.'

Vega did. Angel was protecting his family. 'Okay, Angel, why don't you tell me the deal.'

'Señor Díaz is aware that you are retiring from the business. He has no love for trouble and the bloodshed it brings, he prefers subtle way of accomplishing his . . .'

'Get to the point,' Vega interrupted. 'What does Señor Díaz want from me?' He already knew the answer: the Cali cartel wanted his blessing to take over Medellín. And he knew it would have to be now, while he still had influence with the laboratory owners and growers. What he didn't know, but wanted to know, was who in his organisation had betrayed him.

'We want you to tell the people in your city to support us,' Angel said, the words understating the sacrifice they implied.

'Medellín will never become a branch of Cali.' Vega ended the declaration by spitting in Angel's face. Pino's men jerked him back and waited for the signal to punish. 'Tell Señor Díaz that's what I think of his deal.'

'I will ignore that, señor,' Angel said, signalling for the guards to relax. He had been told to get Vega's consent without resorting to violence. He wiped his face with a handkerchief provided by Pino and continued, 'You seem to be having trouble coming to terms with your new circumstances, Señor Vega.' Angel's speech was pompous. 'Look around. You are no longer in control. Señor Díaz's offer is very generous. If I were you, I would want to hear it.'

'Go on.'

'If you agree to support our takeover, within three days, we will pay your suppliers in Medellín the agreed amounts for their portions of the shipment you brought with you. We will also pay you.' Angel's companion produced a large briefcase and placed it on the floor next to Vega.

'How much is in that?' Vega asked, knowing the case wasn't anywhere near large enough to hold his share.

'One million dollars. A deposit. In hundred and thousand dollar bills. Another four million will be deposited into an account that has been set up for you in the Cayman Islands.'

'That's quite a deal for you, isn't it?' The money on offer was a fraction of his true share. 'And if I don't support you?'

'We will take the merchandise and hold out paying your

suppliers until they beg us for the money. Of course you would get nothing.' He paused and looked Vega in the eye. 'And there is your wife, and your son.'

'What about them?'

'If you accept, Margarita will join you in New Jersey tomorrow. And Francisco will help you get your son.' He paused to allow the proposal to sink in. 'I don't think we need discuss what would happen if you refuse Señor Díaz's generous offer.'

'Generous! It's a gun at my head.' He glared at Angel, the loathing showing in his eyes. 'One day I'll hold one to yours.'

'You just have to say yes, Señor Vega.' Angel smiled. 'I think our offer is fair. You're leaving Medellín anyway.' Edging closer, he continued his pitch, 'We will move in immediately, there will be no bloodshed, no fight to see who will succeed you.' He stopped to close. 'You must give me your answer now.'

'What choice do I have?' Vega felt a numbness overtake his body as he delivered the bitter tasting words of surren- der. 'You win, Angel, tell your boss we have a deal.'

Angel smiled an exaggerated smile and patted Vega on the cheek. 'Very sensible, señor.' He withdrew an envelope from his coat pocket and asked Pino to release Vega from the handcuffs.

'A letter for your contacts in Medellín, Señor Vega.' Angel unfolded the letter and handed it and a pen to Vega.

Vega perused the letter. It was short and to the point,

confirming a truce between him and Díaz and recommending that the growers, laboratory owners and distributors presently loyal to him, transfer their loyalty to the Cali boss. It also outlined the payment plan, the element in the agreement of most immediate significance to the laboratory owners. They had employees, middlemen and growers to pay. Repercussions would be swift if there was a delay in the flow of money. Vega knew the agreement would cause offence to many of the people who had been loyal to him. But he had no choice, he had to sign it. Many of those same people may die if he didn't.

He signed the letter against a window and thrust it back at Angel who taunted him by blowing on its already dry ink.

'You may say goodbye to your wife, Señor Vega,' Angel said, returning the letter to his pocket. 'You will be reunited with her at the safe house tomorrow.'

Within a minute, the van was gone.

Vega picked up the briefcase and walked with Pino back to the office. Pino's men followed behind, ready to restrain the fallen drug lord if he moved against their boss.

'You're a thief as well as a traitor, Francisco,' Vega said to Pino with measures of both hostility and disappointment. The loss of money was not as big an issue for him as the betrayal and humiliation. Cali had stolen something far more precious than money, they had stolen his honour. And for that, he vowed, one day, Díaz, his minion and Pino would die.

'I'm sure you will survive, amigo,' Pino said, laying a hand on Vega's shoulder. 'I know you have many millions here in the United States already. And I have the bank drafts for tomorrow. They will be placed in the morning, as planned.' The money, already owed by Pino, was marked to be used by Vega to pay the three men with him.

Back at the table, Pino finished pouring the still-warm coffee.

'Francisco,' Vega said, reaching for one of the cakes. 'Suppose I was to split the merchandise with you?' He knew that a positive response was unlikely but thought it worth a try.

'Ah!' Pino smiled. 'Thank you my friend, but I must say no to your offer. You see, you are on your way out and Cali is on its way in. It would be bad business to cross them. And fatal too, I think.' He touched Vega's arm and then took a cake for himself. 'No hard feelings, Don Carlos. I will still help you get your son tomorrow.'

'With everything in Imthorn's plan?'

'Almost everything,' Pino replied, peeling the paper cup from his cake. 'The men from Cali have made a change in the plan.'

'And what is this change?' Vega grasped Pino's arm as he was about to bite into the cake.

'Instead of you going to New Jersey in the morning they want you to be there at the exchange.'

'What?' Vega said in disbelief. 'The streets will be full of police!'

'We will make you look like an American businessman, Carlos,' Pino said sympathetically. 'You will blend in with the crowds.'

'They want me dead, Francisco.' Bewildered, Vega collapsed back in his chair. 'But they don't have the courage to do it themselves. They have arranged things so I will be killed by the American police.'

'Not true, Carlos. My men are ready to help you, the plan is good, it will work.'

Vega cupped his hands over his face, thinking above the ringing in his head. For now, he must put aside the anger he felt towards Cali. He would accept the fear he felt about tomorrow. He would use all his wits and all his strength to grasp the freedom so close before him.

Pino pulled a bottle of rum and two glasses from a cupboard and poured them both liberal portions. Soon joined by Pedro, they talked until two o'clock in the morning mostly about the revised plans for tomorrow but also about happier times in the past.

32

A knock on the glass of the locked office door woke Vega from a cold and tortured sleep. The sleeping bag Pino had provided had not been warm enough and the rubber mattress was too thin to cushion properly against the vinyl-covered concrete floor. Watched by two of Pino's men, Vega looked in on Avery, Pedro and Rafael who'd spent an equally uncomfortable night in the room next to his.

After a brief conversation with his men, Vega revived himself under a hot shower, the guard outside the bathroom door a reminder of his diminished status.

A short time later, dressed in a suit he'd brought with him from Medellín, he submitted himself to Pino who fastidiously greyed his hair with a theatrical treatment. That done, he knocked on Christina's door and told her that she was to shower and then dress in the suit she'd brought with her.

At ten minutes to nine o'clock, Pino gave Vega a new phone and sent him for a drive with two of his men.

Five minutes later, as the car travelled along Flushing Bay, Vega entered the number of the phone Willem Imthorn had sent the Dutch Prime Minister.

'De Groot.' The answer was immediate.

'Good day, Prime Minister.'

'I'm listening, Mr Vega.'

'I would like you to have Juan flown to New York City.'

'You're there now?' de Groot asked.

'I'm in the area,' Vega replied, 'you know that.'

'I know about the crash landing last night. Was Doctor Jansen hurt?'

'No one got even a scratch, Prime Minister.'

'I hope that's the truth, Mr Vega. Hold on, I have the travel time to New York.' There was a short pause while de Groot found the appropriate entry in a table of flying times prepared by an air force officer for this conversation. He added the forty minutes Dolsch needed to get ready. 'Your son will be there in two and a half hours. And Mr Vega, from now on, you must deal with my government's representative travelling with the prisoner. I'll give you his name and number.'

'Go ahead,' Vega replied. He was prepared with a pen and notebook.

'He's the State Secretary to the Minister of Justice, Otto Dolsch.' De Groot spelled the name and then gave the phone number that would work anywhere in North America. 'Mr Dolsch has the authority to act on my government's behalf.'

'Very sensible, Prime Minister.' Vega had expected some such arrangement for the exchange.

'Is there anything else, Mr Vega?'

'No, Prime Minister,' Vega replied. 'It's been a pleasure dealing with you, goodbye.'

De Groot hung up without replying and pressed the button on his own phone which put him in contact with Otto Dolsch in Bermuda. After a brief conversation with the State Secretary, he pressed another button which put him straight through to the White House.

The President's private secretary interrupted a meeting her boss was having with his Chief of Staff. It was the third time in as many days de Groot had spoken with the President on this matter. He'd also spoken with the leaders of the other countries it was thought Vega may choose: Canada and Mexico.

That brief conversation over, De Groot asked his secretary to have the Minister of Justice, Kees Vermeer and Albert Voss come to his office as quickly as possible. He also asked her to reschedule the remainder of his afternoon appointments. He needed to be available in case Otto Dolsch ran into trouble.

The Dutch government Fokker lifted off from Kindley Field at 10:37 a.m., thirty-eight minutes after Dolsch received de Groot's call. Before leaving, Dolsch had contacted the Dutch consul in New York and advised her of their arrival details. She, in turn, had relayed the information to the head of the FBI in New York who passed it on to his counterparts in the New York Police Department and local DEA. At a higher level, the Washington chiefs of the FBI and DEA and the mayor of New York had been contacted by the President who asked that they do all in their power to bring the case to a happy conclusion.

DEA Special Agent Nicholson had moved as soon as he'd received the news. He was airborne en route to New York.

33

The McDonald's Egg McMuffin she held in her hand reminded Christina Jansen of Los Angeles, the only place she'd had one before. 'Honey, in this country, even the hoods send out for food,' Jim Avery quipped as he sat down next to her on a sleeping bag spread on the floor. It was nine forty-five. Christina had showered and dressed in her light grey suit, as specified by Vega.

Avery held back from biting into his sandwich until he'd revealed what he knew of the events of last night.

'That's bad for Vega, maybe bad for the paintings and me too,' Christina said, disturbed by the news. She'd heard nothing from outside since the shouting immediately after she was locked in the room and the blindfold applied during two escorted trips to the bathroom had prevented her from seeing Vega under guard. 'What's going to happen now?'

'No idea, but something's happening, the boss sent Vega out this morning with a couple of his men.' The American was anxious. He needed to do something very soon to raise his value in the eyes of the DEA. 'Do you remember the name of the man in Washington?' he whispered, conscious of the presence of a guard outside the half-open door.

'Nicholson, Steve Nicholson,' she whispered in reply.

'I'll phone him first chance I get,' Avery said. 'If nothing else, I can tell him where Vega left the paintings in Venezuela.'

'Good,' she replied with a nod. 'Do you know what's happened to the paintings here?'

'Nope, haven't seen them. But take it from me, no one in New York is stupid enough to ruin a bunch of van Goghs. They're worth too much money.'

'I hope you're right.' She lifted the lid off the coffee that accompanied her sandwich and added the small container of cream. 'Vega hinted we were coming to New York,' she said after taking a sip of the coffee. 'When we were in the tanker, he joked with me about coming to see "Starry Night".'

'A starry night?' Avery asked, perplexed.

'No, "Starry Night". One of Vincent's paintings . . . here in New York.'

The door swung open. It was Vega and Rafael. Rafael held a black woollen coat in one hand and a pair of leather boots in the other. 'For you, señorita,' Vega said as Rafael handed them to her. 'They should fit.' He left once he saw they did.

Rafael then had Christina get her make-up from her bag

and, after blindfolding her, led her along the hallway into the bathroom. He left her with the instruction that she had five minutes to disguise the burn on her cheek.

Several minutes later, after checking her work, Rafael led her, blindfolded again, to a white van with tinted windows parked in the warehouse.

At ten o'clock, with Avery at the wheel and Vega sitting behind him studying a New York street map, the van pulled out of the building. Rafael, Pedro and Christina sat in the back with the cases containing the van Goghs. Pino, recognising the dangers posed to Vega because of the money and art he was carrying, had, just before closing the sliding door, returned Vega's revolver, emptied, along with an envelope containing three rounds. He'd added a reluctant warning that if any of its doors or windows opened on the way out, his men would fill the van with lead.

Vega directed Avery south along 94th Street and onto Northern Boulevard. The day was clear, the sky a rare blue. White columns of freezing steam billowed from chimneys and heating systems as far as the eye could see.

Once on the Queensboro Bridge, Vega folded the map and took in the looming skyline ahead. 'I recognise the view,' he said after a while; then, pointing to the south, 'The World Trade buildings were over there somewhere, right?'

'They were,' Avery replied soberly. 'I still have trouble believing what happened that day.'

Vega was pleased to have the American at the wheel. Although Avery wasn't familiar with New York, he was a proficient driver used to United States' driving regulations and customs. Driving here was not a task he would have given to either Pedro or Rafael. Their Medellín-bred chaotic and emotion charged technique would have drawn attention even in this aggressive city, and the last thing Vega wanted this morning was attention.

He went back and removed Christina's blindfold. 'Señorita,' he said, gesturing ahead, 'Manhattan.'

The thick cluster of monumental structures both impressed and intimidated her. She hoped they represented her freedom.

They exited the bridge onto 63rd Street. 'Christina, I want you to have a look at this,' Vega said, opening a cardboard box that was wedged in the midst of the paintings. She leaned over the back of her seat to see. The box contained a large plastic bottle of gasoline and a detonator attached to a phone which was switched off. 'If I press this memory button,' he said, demonstrating with his phone without actually pressing anything, 'a call is made to this one which sets off the bomb. There's enough fuel to destroy the van and everything in it. And there's a bomb just like this one with the other paintings in Venezuela, that's what this one is for.' He pointed to the neighbouring button. 'Don't make me use them.'

'I won't. Just leave the phone off.'

'For now,' Vega said, closing the box. Then, grasping Rafael by the shoulder, he reminded him to turn the phone on before leaving the van.

As they continued along 63rd, Vega removed two spectacle cases from his coat pocket and handed one to Christina. 'Put them on.' She did. Both pairs had executive type frames and plane lenses. 'There are some gloves in your coat pocket,' he added, pulling on his own. 'You'll need them.'

He directed Avery into the right-hand lane as they approached the turn onto Fifth Avenue. Then, a right off Fifth at Grand Army Plaza put them onto Central Park South. They were stopped at the end of the block by the traffic lights at Avenue of the Americas. 'Let's go,' Vega said after drawing a deep breath and slid open the side door. He and Pedro ushered Christina out of the van and then in front of it across the street. Had things gone strictly according to Willem Imthorn's plan, Vega would now be in the New Jersey safe house and two of Pino's people would be escorting Christina.

They headed back along Central Park South towards the grand marble building occupying the eastern end of the block. Vega, more exposed than he had been in years, yet feeling strangely free in the anonymous environment, carried the briefcase containing the money from Cali. Pedro, carrying a smaller case, walked behind the businesslike pair.

The coldness was metallic. Their faces parted clouds of their own condensed breath as they walked along.

Vega directed Christina through The Plaza hotel's front door and across the grand lobby to the elevators. He inserted the security card provided by Pino as soon as Pedro was inside and pressed 6. Emerging into an empty hallway, Vega led the way to room 617 and knocked twice on the door.

The Hispanic man who answered held a magazine to his face. 'The duplicates work,' he said as he handed Vega some keys and a piece of paper. He left.

Vega entered the spacious suite and walked straight to the window. Pedro followed Christina inside and locked the door behind him.

'Couldn't be better,' Vega remarked, looking across to the park. He removed the loaded revolver from his coat pocket and stuffed it in his belt before taking the coat off and throwing it on the floral quilted bed. He then retrieved a pair of binoculars from the case Pedro had carried and, standing away from the window, looked along the street to the park entrance opposite Avenue of the Americas. 'Perfect,' he remarked and then turned his attention to some cross country skiers taking advantage of the recent snow. 'Just like in the movies,' he said and passed the binoculars to Pedro directing him to take a good look at the park entrance that was destined to play an important part in the day's activities.

Pedro met Rafael and Avery in the lobby at eleven twenty and brought them to the room. 'Did you turn on the phone?' Vega asked Rafael.

'It's on,' Rafael replied and handed Vega the van's keys and parking stub.

Vega then directed Pedro to shut Christina in the bathroom. 'It will be for just a few minutes,' he said and turned on the television so she would not overhear the instructions for the last stage of the operation.

Vega finished the briefing by arranging the six keys Pino's man had given him into pairs on the table. He wrote the letters P, R and J on cardboard tags attached to the originals. 'I'll tell you where the lockers are when I phone later,' he said and handed each man the appropriate duplicate.

That done, he stood and put the three original keys into a trouser pocket. 'It's time for me to go.' He embraced Rafael first: a stoic farewell followed by a request for him to retrieve Christina from the bathroom. Pedro's was more emotional with tears welling in both men's eyes when the break was finally made. Avery feigned sincerity but felt nothing but relief when Vega embraced him for the first ever, and, he trusted, last time.

'Say goodbye to my men, señorita,' Vega said as Christina entered. 'You won't be seeing them again.'

She responded with a single undirected 'Goodbye.'

Pedro and Rafael farewelled her with grins and good wishes. Avery helped her with her coat and then, with Vega beside him, squeezed her tight. 'Good luck, honey, it's been great knowing ya.'

After putting on his coat, Vega retrieved two phones from the smaller of the two cases. He handed one to Pedro and put the other in his left pocket. The phone already in his right pocket was set up for the three Ds: Dolsch, de

Groot, detonator. All calls on it would be monitored. The second phone would be anonymous.

Picking up the case with the money in it, Vega led Christina to the door. He turned just before he vanished and saluted. 'Adios, amigos.'

Christina glanced back to Avery as she followed Vega out. She'd hoped for a chance to find out from him where the van was parked but Vega had been too careful. She prayed that somehow he would get hold of Nicholson.

They shared the elevator to the lobby with two Asian businessmen who acknowledged them with polite bows and smiles. Vega responded in kind. Christina, restricting herself to a smile, wished that, tonight, they would be phoning their families to tell of their elevator ride with the captured drug baron and his freed hostage.

Vega led Christina by the arm through the hotel's eastern door and then right, past the Pulitzer Memorial Fountain, dormant because of the freezing weather.

They joined the thin pedestrian traffic along Fifth Avenue, turned right at 51st Street then into Rockefeller Plaza, stopping, as Vega had planned, above the ice skating rink. He took the phone from his right pocket and pressed the second memory button.

Dolsch, aboard the recently arrived Fokker at John F Kennedy International Airport, answered immediately. 'Mr Vega?' The FBI had wired him with an earpiece and microphone and fitted a tap to his phone.

'Señor Dolsch, I presume you have landed?'

'Yes, Mr Vega.'

'I want you to bring my son to Central Park West, near Columbus Circle. Park there and wait for my next call. Understand?'

'Yes, what will . . .'

Vega turned off the phone. He just wanted to hear "yes". The authorities would be given as little time as possible to ascertain his location.

'Sir, ma'am, good morning.' Vega lurched around to the voice. The exuberant panhandler had caught him by surprise. 'A fine cold day ain't it, sir, ma'am? I wonder if you could spare some change?'

Vega found a dollar bill and stuffed it in the otherwise empty Burger King paper cup, staring warily at the tall African-American as he did so.

'Why thank you sir, you're a real gentleman,' the man said, and tipped his cap. 'Ma'am, sir, you be sure and have a nice day.'

'He won't be spending it on a newspaper,' Vega murmured as he watched the man shuffle towards his next mark.

'Probably not,' she answered, thinking how well the busy impersonal city served Vega's purpose.

Not in any particular hurry, Vega took a few minutes to watch the skaters before leading Christina back to Fifth Avenue. They continued south to East 42nd Street and climbed the grand stairs into the New York Public Library. Vega used the sketch provided by Pino's man at the hotel to locate the three engaged but unoccupied lockers. He looked around as he opened the first, Pedro's. There were five or six people at lockers around them, all seemingly intent on their own business. He removed three envelopes from his pocket. Each contained a bank draft made out to a false identity already established for each of the men. Pedro's and Rafael's drafts were both for one million dollars. Avery's was for two.

After placing the envelopes, he took a plastic bag from his briefcase and added it to Avery's. The bag contained two hundred thousand dollars, the money he'd promised during the descent towards Athens. Now as always, in dealings with his underlings, Vega would demonstrate that he was a man of his word.

Back on Fifth Avenue, he spotted the coffee shop from where he was scheduled to make his next call. He checked his watch. According to Pino's schedule, Dolsch would still be on his way from the airport. He took Christina inside and sat her at a corner table while he ordered two of today's special from the counter.

Christina retrieved a newspaper from a rack on the wall next to her. The story headlined "VAN GOGH DRAMA COMES TO NY" took up a quarter of the front page. A picture of the damaged Gulfstream along with a photograph of her and a sketch of Vega accompanied the text. 'Front page of "The New York Times",' she whispered when Vega arrived with the coffees. 'Your mother would be proud.' She passed him the paper.

'It won't be flying again for a while,' he commented as he examined the photograph of the floodlit plane. The picture revealed extensive damage to the right wing, more than he'd been aware of last night. 'We were lucky it didn't catch fire,' he said and went on to peruse the text. 'It may help identify someone else, but not me,' he remarked smugly after convincing himself that the sketch above his name posed no threat. Christina's photograph was the same one that had appeared in the Medellín newspaper, taken from her identity card at the Van Gogh Museum. Her shorter, darker hair and the glasses had rendered its publication ineffectual.

At twelve thirty, just as the coffee shop's lunch crowd was starting to build, Vega phoned Dolsch. He faced the wall to speak. 'Are you in position, Señor Dolsch?'

'Yes, Mr Vega, I'm waiting with your son,' Dolsch replied from the back of an unmarked police van parked on Central Park West, Juan Vega sitting opposite him.

'I want you to walk with Juan along Central Park South to the Avenue of the Americas park entrance. There you will find a statue of a great man on a horse. That is where my son will be freed. He is not to be restrained, he must be free to walk.'

'Okay, Mr Vega, to the park entrance at Avenue of the Americas, near a statue of a man on a horse,' Dolsch replied.

'Do as I've said Señor Dolsch, and very soon I will tell you where Doctor Jansen and the paintings are.' He turned off the phone.

'Okay, señorita, let's go.' He swallowed the last of his New Guinea Gold and got up.

They returned to the now busier sidewalk and continued along Fifth Avenue to 53rd Street where another extroverted panhandler benefited from Vega's generosity.

Vega spotted what he was looking for from the corner. 'That's where we're going.' He pointed to a glass building halfway down the block.

'MoMA,' Christina murmured in disbelief as the WALK light came on. Vega was taking her to the Museum of Modern Art, home to Vincent's "Starry Night".

Vega stopped outside the museum entrance. 'Remember the bombs.' He lifted the relevant phone from his pocket. 'It will take one second.'

'Just leave it off.' She tugged his arm from the pocket. 'I'm not going to do anything.' They went inside.

Vega paid the entrance fees and handed Christina the brochure that came with the tickets. 'You find where "Starry Night" is,' he said and discreetly put his revolver in the briefcase before locking it and depositing it at the check room.

Then, with her leading the way, they walked through the security check and up the escalator past a glass-walled courtyard to the second floor, then on into the Post-Impressionism galleries.

Cezanne's "Turning Road" which she had seen on her visit to MoMA four years ago, Picasso's "Les Demoiselles d'Avignon", then "Starry Night". Christina stopped, mesmerised despite the context. Another visual escape. Eleven radiant stars: yellow, white, green and blue fuel a deep blue and violet sky. A haloed crescent moon shines on the hills and village below, while in the foreground, Vincent's cypresses flame wildly skywards.

'I can't believe this,' she murmured.

'I planned on having you left in a church,' Vega said. 'But this was a better idea, more poetic.'

A group moved into the gallery, a guide directing them. Vega pulled Christina back as they huddled towards the van Gogh.

'Vincent painted "Starry Night" in 1889 while staying at the asylum in Saint-Rémy,' the elderly female guide began in a soft and confident tone. 'It wasn't easy for him. He was a great advocate of painting on the spot, even at night. But in this case he wasn't able to do that. He was forced to paint in a studio he'd been allowed to set up in the asylum, without the view. So Vincent composed a view. He included the cypresses from a painting he had drying in the studio. The mountains came from a daytime landscape he'd done outside. And he included things from memory. The village isn't pure Saint-Rémy. The church spire is more Dutch than French, like ones he did early in his artistic career in Holland. So "Starry Night" is a mixture of north and south, Vincent's past and present.'

'The sky is bizarre,' one of the tourists said, his strong emphasis on the last word drawing a chuckle from the group.

'It is,' the guide replied without hesitation. 'And Vincent's letters don't reveal the thinking behind the sky. The inspiration may have come from Joseph's dream in Genesis, of eleven stars and the sun and moon worshiping him. The brilliance is certainly bizarre. Of course, in those days there weren't many lights to dull the night sky so Vincent would have seen a sky full of stars . . . some very bright.'

'Does it meet your expectation?' Vega whispered as the group moved on.

'It does,' she replied, her eyes fixed on the work.

Vega checked his watch. 'Señorita, do you remember what you told me about travelling to stars?'

'You mean Vincent's idea that death may be a way of doing that? Celestial transportation.'

'He said a disease will get you there quickly, like a train ride to the village. And dying of old age is the slowest way to go, like walking.'

'You remember it well,' she responded, praying that this was a prelude to a goodbye.

'May you walk to your star, señorita,' Vega said and took hold of her hand. 'This is where I leave you. Stay in this room. The police will arrive in less than half an hour.' He raised her hand and kissed it. 'Good luck, Doctor Jansen.'

'Bye,' she mouthed. She felt a strange sympathy for Vega as she watched him leave. Perhaps she didn't hate him as much as she should.

Was it really over? She waited and watched, half expecting Vega to reappear. The gallery entrance remained clear, non-threatening people were walking past. Tourists. She was alone again. He was really gone. She felt her prison walls collapse around her. Freedom! She closed her eyes and breathed deeply, certain, that from now on, whenever she saw a reproduction of "Starry Night" she would think of this moment of liberation.

Now what to do? she thought. She examined her options. She could phone Nicholson, but that may put the paintings at risk. Better to do what Vega said. Avery would contact Nicholson at some point, to save his own skin. And he knew where the van was, she didn't.

She sat down on a bench in the middle of the room and gazed towards Vincent's turbulent sky, waiting.

After retrieving his briefcase and returning the revolver to his coat pocket, Vega left the museum and walked back towards Fifth Avenue. He stopped near the corner and pressed the first memory button on the second phone. 'Are they there?' he asked Pedro.

'Yes, they've been waiting about ten minutes.' Pedro was watching Dolsch and Juan Vega through the binoculars.

'Okay, you men are on your own. The lockers are in the New York Public Library on the corner of Fifth Avenue and East 42nd Street. It will take you about ten minutes to get there, if you hurry. I'll phone Dolsch in fifteen. Fifth Avenue and East 42nd Street. Good luck. And watch Jim.'

He crossed Fifth Avenue, followed it south to Saint Patrick's Cathedral and went inside.

As anticipated, there was a Mass in progress. The priest's voice was a whisper in the cavernous building, a calming monotone above the ever present ringing. He walked down the left aisle past some people waiting at the confessionals and knelt in a pew near the side entrance.

Three minutes after Vega's call, Pedro, Rafael and Avery exited the hotel onto Fifth Avenue. Pedro joined the lunchtime flow past the Pulitzer Fountain with Rafael close to Avery behind. Three-quarters of the way across 57th Street, Avery made his move. He took off west between two lanes of stationary traffic, mostly taxis, then down the middle of the road. He glanced back. The lights were still red behind Rafael and Pedro in pursuit. Hard left into the front of a van edging forward then on along the gutter. Up onto the sidewalk. He looked back along the street. Red turned to green. Rafael was gaining. Another three car lengths before glancing back a third time. It had to be now. Right between two taxis. The car on the inside lane braked too fast. A crash, blaring horns and swearing. He sprinted across the street just ahead of the accelerating westbound flow. Rafael, stalled in the middle, shook his fist as the American climbed aboard a taxi.

'Where to, señores?' a Hispanic taxi driver asked the Colombians less than a minute later.

Out of breath, Pedro looked at his watch before replying. 'The New York Public Library.'

Avery left his taxi at the Central Park South entrance of The Plaza and followed the signs to pay phones near the shops at the back. He made a mistake with Nicholson's number the first time but got it right the second. There was a message as the call was diverted. Then Nicholson's unfamiliar voice. 'DEA, Nicholson.' Nicholson was just around the corner on Avenue of the Americas, inside the New York Police Department's mobile command post. He was the only DEA agent in the unmarked trailer otherwise occupied by members of both the NYPD and FBI, all of whom were busy either commanding agents in the field or operating various pieces of surveillance and communications equipment.

'It's Avery, I'm in New York.'

'Where's Vega?' Nicholson had listened to Vega's calls to Dolsch.

'With Christina, somewhere not far from Central Park.'

'Anything more specific?'

'No, but I have three things for you. You need to move fast on all of them.'

'Tell me,' Nicholson replied.

Avery described the van and its location and told him about the bomb and how it could be detonated. He also gave the coordinates of the sugar cane plantation in Venezuela. Then he betrayed Pedro and Rafael. He knew it was more than enough to ensure a jail-free future.

'We'll get right on that,' Nicholson said. 'Where are you now?'

'The Plaza hotel lobby.'

'Stay there, I'll send someone to get you.'

Avery hung up the handpiece and took a deep breath. He was on a high, better than he'd ever got from cocaine. His mind went to Christina, she could be in trouble if Vega somehow found out that the paintings in the van had been recovered. Then he remembered Vega's clue. He hurried back to the front desk. 'The van Gogh painting, "Starry Night", where can I see it?'

The young attendant proceeded to key an inquiry into her computer. It took only a few seconds. 'It's in the Museum of Modern Art on West Fifty-third, sir. Just a short walk down Fifth Avenue, turn right on Fifty-third.'

Avery ran and, despite mixed luck with crossing lights, got to the museum in just a few minutes. Gasping for breath, he paid the entrance fee and asked for directions.

A minute later he was on the bench in font of Vincent's swirling sky with Christina. 'Where's Vega?'

'Gone,' she said, her eyes wide in amazement. 'Don't know where.'

'I talked to Nicholson. He'll get the paintings, the ones in Venezuela too. And Pedro and Rafael at the library.'

'Great!' Christina breathed a sigh of relief.

'Let's find out what's happened to Vega.' Avery took her by the arm and led her back towards the escalators. 'He's got his son waiting with some big shot from Holland across from the hotel.' Avery spotted a pay phone near the check room.

A short distance to the south, the lunchtime Mass in Saint Patrick's Cathedral had just ended and the two hundred strong congregation of mostly city workers was leaving. Vega pressed the memory button for Dolsch.

Dolsch's position was being covered by three FBI snipers, two inside buildings opposite the park entrance and one in a large fir tree just inside the park. There were over twenty FBI and NYPD plain-clothed officers on foot in his immediate area. The surrounding streets and other park entrances were being covered by marked and unmarked NYPD cruisers. Additional units stood ready to block all Manhattan's bridges and tunnels and two police helicopters were on stand-by at the north end of the park.

'Señor Dolsch, the paintings are in a white Plymouth van parked in stall 215 in the Mobil parking garage on Central Park West near Sixty-fifth. I'm in control of a bomb in the van and another with the second set of paintings. I will detonate both if anyone tries to interfere. Do you understand?'

'Yes,' Dolsch replied, already aware that the paintings on Central Park West had been found and the bomb with them, neutralised. An FBI agent in the command post had relayed the information via his earpiece a few seconds before Vega's call. 'And Doctor Jansen?'

'When Juan and I are ready to leave, señor. Is Juan free to walk?'

'He's free,' Dolsch replied.

'Stay where you are Mr Dolsch.' Vega terminated the call.

Access to Central Park South was now closed between Fifth and Seventh Avenues and plain-clothed police officers and FBI agents were busy directing pedestrians out of the area or into the surrounding buildings.

Vega took the phone from his left pocket and pressed the second memory button. Pino's man answered. 'Go now,' Vega said and turned it off. Blessing himself with holy water on the way out of the church, he headed back along Fifth Avenue towards Central Park.

'I've got Christina Jansen,' Avery announced the instant Nicholson answered. 'Vega left the MoMA gallery twenty minutes ago.'

'Where are you?'

'On my way back to the hotel.'

'I'll meet you there, in the lobby,' Nicholson said. 'We got the paintings in the van.'

Vega was seized by anger when he saw them on the other side of the street while he was waiting for the lights on 56th. He summed up the situation in an instant and reacted automatically to institute the one course of action Avery's treachery had left him. He hurriedly jaywalked through the traffic across Fifth Avenue and caught up with them crossing 58th Street towards the hotel. 'The price of betrayal, compadre,' Vega said from behind, pulling the revolver from his coat. Avery pivoted and lunged towards the rising gun, his mind slowing time as he watched Vega's finger move the trigger back. Screaming his name, Christina clasped Avery's arm as the impact threw him backwards onto the road. People ducked and scattered. Vega reached around Christina's waist, locked her against him with the briefcase and pulled her away from Avery's squirming body. 'Cooperate, or you'll be next.' He pressed the gun to her neck. 'Take the case and hold it in front of you.' She grabbed hold of the briefcase with trembling hands. 'Now walk towards the park.' Vega, his head ringing wildly, took the phone from his right pocket and pressed the button for Dolsch. He spoke quickly. 'Change of plans. I'm holding a gun at Christina Jansen's head. Anyone comes near me, I shoot, okay?'

'Okay, Mr Vega,' Dolsch replied. His FBI contact had just informed him of a shooting near the Pulitzer Fountain. 'Please don't do anything foolish.'

'Have Juan ready to leave you,' Vega said, pushing Christina ahead of him.

'Yes, Mr Vega,' Dolsch responded.

Upon seeing the police cars at the intersection ahead, Vega pushed Christina up the hotel's eastern stairs. The wide eyed doorman held the door open and yelled for people to stand back. To screams and fleeing bodies, Vega pushed her on through the lobby and then outside onto an almost deserted Central Park South.

Dolsch's FBI contact announced that there was a heli-copter coming towards the park from the north.

'For anyone listening to this,' Vega said as he pushed Christina towards Avenue of the Americas, 'I have men in the helicopter armed with machine guns. Any interference and they open fire.'

'There won't be any interference, Mr Vega,' Dolsch replied. He could hear a helicopter approaching.

Arriving on Avenue of the Americas opposite the statue of Simón Bolívar, Vega positioned himself against a wall and held Christina in front of him. The only people on the street now were plain-clothed police and FBI agents. 'Señor Dolsch, hand the phone to Juan.' Vega watched as Dolsch complied. 'Buenas tardes, my son,' he said, smiling over Christina's shoulder at his son across the street. 'It's wonderful to see you.' His immediate impression was how well his son looked. Clearly the Dutch prison was a far more humane place than its Colombian counterparts. The repetitive thudding of the helicopter was now echoing off the buildings around them.

'Father, hello,' Juan said with a small wave of his hand. 'Get me away from this pig.' Vega saw his son spit on Dolsch.

An old Huey, its military insignia painted over with black paint, emerged through the bare trees just to the east. A wild storm of ice particles, grit and paper accompanied its descent onto the road. Two men, manning M-60s, lay behind sandbags in the doorways on either side of its deck.

'Go Juan! Hurry!' Vega shouted into the phone and tossed it away. Juan held his head down as he sprinted towards the door on his side while Vega pushed Christina ahead of him across the street.

Stationed at one of the third floor windows in the apartment building across from the park entrance, the lead marksman gave his number two, stationed in the adjacent building, and his number three, in a tree in the park, the command to fire. The subsequent events took only ten rapid heartbeats. The targets manning the machine guns jerked as their lives ended simultaneously, both with clean shots to the head.

'No!' Vega screamed as he saw his son die while reaching for a gun on the helicopter deck.

Christina, running towards the sidewalk, turned to see Vega, his eyes empty on her, drop his gun and raise his hands. It was over.

A group of plain-clothed police converged on Christina and bundled her into a car. At her frantic insistence, they took her around the corner to the Pulitzer Fountain where Avery, strapped onto a stretcher and surrounded by police, was about to be loaded into an ambulance.

'Is he okay?' she pleaded with the paramedic who was adjusting a drip apparatus mounted on the side of the stretcher.

'Hi, honey.' Avery lifted his head. He was very pale. 'Winged me.' The paramedic told her that the bullet had passed through his shoulder.

'Thank goodness you're okay.' She lay her hand softly on his forehead. 'Juan Vega's dead.'

'I know,' he said. 'Nicholson told me.' He lifted his head towards the man standing at the bottom of the stretcher.

'Good to see you're okay, ma'am,' Nicholson said before introducing himself and then, 'I've got to get this man out of here.'

'One second.' She kissed Avery on the forehead. 'Thanks, Jim Avery . . . from Vincent and me.'

'Bye honey,' he replied with a tired grin.

Nicholson followed the stretcher into the ambulance which moved off the instant the doors were closed.

34

Christina Jansen, reclining on her own familiar couch, her phone off the hook and a glass of Bordeaux by her side, savoured the calm of her own apartment. It was over twenty-four hours since the shootings in New York.

Christina had arrived back in Amsterdam aboard the Dutch VIP jet early in the afternoon and had been busy ever since. Her first duty had been to accompany the paintings to the Van Gogh Museum where she had supervised their unpacking and inspection. After that, a government doctor had visited the museum and given her a thorough physical examination which, apart from the obvious burn to her face, highlighted nothing of concern. The check-up was followed by an hour-long preliminary debriefing session with Chief Inspector Kees Vermeer of the Dutch police. Then two shorter meetings: the first with the director of the Vincent van Gogh Foundation who had hugged her, thanked her, congratulated her and welcomed her back. The other with a psychologist assigned by the

Ministry of Justice to provide her with some post-trauma counselling.

The meeting with Albert Voss had been interrupted twice. First by a phone call from the Prime Minister who, on behalf of the people of the Netherlands, had welcomed her back and praised her for her courage during the ordeal. He finished by inviting her to join him and the other people involved in the case for lunch next week. A short time later, amidst much excitement from the staff members who saw the envelope, a letter arrived from the Paleis Noordeinde requesting Christina's presence for an audience with Queen Beatrix next Tuesday afternoon. And there was another invitation too, from her aunt and uncle, Marieke's parents, to visit them for dinner when things calmed down.

Her last official task for the day had been at the request of the foundation director, to answer a few questions from a group of journalists who had been waiting outside the museum all afternoon.

The informal press conference had been followed by dinner with her much relieved parents and brother. Her father had just dropped her back home in time for the evening television news.

She turned up the volume as soon as the "NOS Journaal" logo appeared. The anchor led straight into the story with a summary of yesterday's events in New York over video images of the covered bodies and the Huey helicopter on a desolate looking Central Park South; Vega being bundled into a police wagon; NYPD mug shots of

Pedro and Rafael; the paintings being delivered to the Dutch VIP jet at John F Kennedy; and the jet's arrival at Schiphol this afternoon. Christina appeared next with the director, Albert Voss, standing behind her.

'How are you feeling, Doctor Jansen?' was the first question that came from the huddle of reporters she'd faced three hours ago.

'I'll be fine after I get some rest,' she responded with a nervous smile. She had felt a little overwhelmed by the attention.

'Have you heard anything on the condition of the American pilot?' another reporter asked. The journalists thought it curious that the FBI had not issued a press release on the matter.

'I haven't,' she replied. She would phone Nicholson tomorrow and endeavour to find out. 'I hope he's okay.'

'Doctor Jansen, did you feel sorry for Carlos Vega when his son was shot dead in front of him?' She remembered the ugly looks some of the journalists gave the woman who asked this question. She'd answered it anyway.

'I did,' she said, grimacing. 'He is a criminal, I know, but I feel sorry that he lost his son.'

Annoyed by the lack of sensitivity shown by the last questioner, Voss intervened. 'Doctor Jansen is very tired. Just one more question.'

'Christina, what is the condition of the paintings?' a television journalist called out.

'All of them have superficial damage from the crash

landing in New York.' She'd spent the latter part of yesterday afternoon with the curatorial staff of the Museum of Modern Art in New York describing and photographing the damage. An FBI photographer had also taken a record of the damage for his agency's files. 'I've been told by the experts that, except for "Reaper" and the self-portrait, they're all easily repairable.' The conference ended there.

After explaining, with graphics, how the US Air Force AWACS had watched Vega's escape from South America, the anchor interviewed Nelson Schoute, now in Maracaibo.

Nelson spoke enthusiastically, outlining how the Venezuelan police and army as well as the American DEA had raided Bernardo Molina's sugar cane plantation while the drama in New York was unfolding. He revealed that the van Goghs left by Vega in Molina's care had been recovered unharmed along with large quantities of cocaine and lesser amounts of heroin. There had been no bomb with the paintings, Vega had bluffed on that.

Christina was looking forward to seeing Nelson tomorrow afternoon. The VIP aircraft that had brought her from New York was presently on its way to Venezuela to collect him and the remaining paintings.

The anchor then introduced a reporter in Medellín who revealed how information provided by Molina and his men had led to the arrest of seven of Vega's men and the recovery of the tanker truck used in the smuggling operation. The report included images of the truck, inside and out. It all seemed very strange to Christina. So close in time, yet somehow very distant.

The US Federal Attorney General appeared next and explained that Carlos Vega was in custody and would be facing charges relating to his involvement in the trade of illegal substances. She added that should he be found guilty, he would serve his sentence in a US federal penitentiary.

Finally, over images of Margarita Vega being escorted by police into a terminal at John F Kennedy airport, the anchor announced that, since her release by her kidnappers yesterday afternoon at Grand Central Terminal, she'd been questioned extensively by agents of the FBI and DEA none of whom had found reason to detain her. She was being allowed to return to Colombia with the body of her stepson.

Jim Avery's name was not mentioned at all. It never would be.

Christina dropped the volume using the remote control, pulled the quilt to her chin and closed her heavy eyes.

Sixty kilometres to the southwest, in the company of a now half-empty celebratory bottle of cognac, Willem Imthorn, his corpulent body deep in a large leather chair, peered into the crystal snifter he cradled against his chest and reflected on his success.

The deviation from his plan had, at first, disappointed him. Had Vega gone to New Jersey the morning of the exchange, he would be free and his son, alive, Imthorn was sure of that. But as Francisco Pino had explained on the phone, it was all for the best: an angry man in an American prison would cause far fewer problems in their future dealings with Cali than the same man in hiding.

As he reached for some cheese, Imthorn glimpsed the memento on his coffee table: the postcard Vega had returned five months ago to acknowledge acceptance of the plan. The card, which Imthorn himself had purchased at the gift shop in the Van Gogh Museum, was of Vincent's "The Sower". He pushed the wedge of Brie into his mouth, gazing at the picture as he chewed. Vincent's peasant spreading seed before a halo-like setting sun: simple, dignified, devoted to his task. In Imthorn's view, a lower form of life. 'Thank you, señor,' he snorted, remembering how eagerly Vega had taken the bait. 'I could not have done it without you.'

The drunken raucous laugh that followed was truncated by a rasping cough, then, after regaining his breath, Imthorn turned the card over and re-read Vega's short note: "Amigo, it is the work of a genius." It was signed "Peter", a favoured code name of Vega's, the name of the first pope. Vega had been right in his assessment, more so than he ever knew. Relishing his conquest, the Dutchman downed the remaining cognac in one fast gulp.

Acknowledgments

Thanks to Bernadette for your artistic enlightenment; Bob for sharing your knowledge of aviation; Feé and Marcel for your guidance on things Dutch; Wendy for your research in New York; José for your translations to Spanish; Barbara, George, Geraldine, Glenn, Hugh, Kathryn, Keith, Liane, Marion, Michelle, Rosalyn and Steve for your encouragement and insightful suggestions on story, structure and style; Avis, Dale, Elnora and Kate for your moral and practical support; Wilfred Arnold whose book *Vincent van Gogh, Chemicals, Crises and Creativity* published by Birkhäuser outlines the AIP hypothesis referred to in Chapter 14.